THE WORLD

Neil Bissoondath was born in Trinidad and lives in Quebec. He
is the author of several award-winning works of fiction, including *On the Eve of Uncertain Tomorrows*, *A Casual Brutality*
and *Digging Up the Mountains*.

Neil Bissoondath

THE WORLDS
WITHIN HER

V

VINTAGE

Published by Vintage 2001

2 4 6 8 10 9 7 5 3 1

First published in Great Britain in 2000 by
William Heinemann

Vintage
Random House, 20 Vauxhall Bridge Road,
London SW1V 2SA

Random House Australia (Pty) Limited
20 Alfred Street, Milsons Point, Sydney
New South Wales 2061, Australia

Random House New Zealand Limited
18 Poland Road, Glenfield,
Auckland 10, New Zealand

Random House (Pty) Limited
Endulini, 5A Jubilee Road, Parktown 2193,
South Africa

The Random House Group Limited Reg. No. 954009
www.randomhouse.co.uk

A CIP catalogue record for this book
is available from the British Library

ISBN 0 09 928385 9

Papers used by Random House are natural, recyclable
products made from wood grown in sustainable forests.
The manufacturing processes conform to the environ-
mental regulations of the country of origin

Printed and bound in Great Britain by
Cox & Wyman Limited, Reading, Berkshire

for
Anne
and
Élyssa
who make it all worthwhile

The author wishes to thank Anne Holloway for the brilliance of her editing and Doris Cowan for copy-editing par excellence. From both, I have learnt a great deal.

The author also wishes to thank the team of CBC TV Montreal's *Newswatch* for their generosity in showing me how things work.

Serafino shows me the little blue shack where Che supposedly lived. There was a photo of him on the wall inside for many years, but they had to take it down in the 1970s. Yes, I say sympathetically, it wasn't safe to keep a photo of Che during those reactionary times. "No," Serafino says, "they had to paint the place."

PATRICK SYMES
"Ten Thousand Revolutions"
Harper's, June 1997

Prologue

[1]

Some silences vibrate with a voiceless chaos, felt but unheard.

It is into such a silence that Jim says, "You can still change your mind, Yas."

And it is because of that silence that she replies, "You won't forget to water the plants?"

"Yas—"

"You worry too much. It's only three days, not much can happen. My father's relatives'll take care of me."

"Just the same, I wish you weren't staying alone, in a hotel. If your mother's family were still there…"

"What difference would that make?" Yasmin turns away from his quiet fervour, her hands tucking with fruitless busyness into the suitcase. She is, at this moment, unwilling to engage the old discussion: his accusation that choice is, for her, the possibility of redemption; her accusation that choice is, for him, the avoidance of possibility. A discussion that has failed to find resolution through fifteen years of marriage.

She is forty, Jim seven years older. And yet his fears make him wish for the impossible. Yasmin's grandparents are long gone, and her mother's only brother, Yasmin's uncle Sonny, lives in Belleville, where he taught school for many years before sliding into a lonely Alzheimer's twilight. There are cousins perhaps, but too distant in blood and time to be sought out. Her mother never spoke of them, and so Yasmin has no memory—has been given no sense—of having known them. She is unlikely even to recognize their names. And a knowledge of common maternal blood is insufficient.

Jim says, "I could still come with you, you know. It wouldn't be too difficult to rearrange things—"

She busies herself at the closet, shuffling through clothes, rejecting, selecting. "I haven't changed my mind." She tosses a pair of slacks onto the bed.

He picks up the slacks, folds them neatly into the suitcase. "But why do you have to go alone? I still don't—"

"Neither do I, Jim. I just know I have to." She sees his hands clench. "It doesn't have anything to do with you, I swear. Really."

"Really?" he echoes. His tone is sceptical, but after a moment his fists unfold, and she watches his palm reach into the suitcase to smooth out the slacks: hands that have not lost their gentleness but have, even so, grown subtly inadequate over the years.

He forces a smile through his melancholy, offers a decisive nod of the head. "Okay," he says. "Just don't forget to call. I want to know you're okay."

When the packing is done, she sits, weary, on the edge of the bed as Jim locks and belts the suitcase. Checking the name-tag, he hefts it into the living room. She follows his stockinged feet as they flop silently across the carpet.

And she wonders with a start when it was, and why, that this peculiarity of his walk—the large feet turned outwards, once endearing, long unremarked, now seen afresh—

became disagreeable to her. She has not misled him in insisting that her going alone has nothing to do with him, but now, as she feels herself grow queasy with tension, she is no longer sure.

Jim says, "You all right?"

Yasmin nods. "The aspirins are helping."

"You have your ticket and passport?"

"It's a little late to ask, isn't it?"

"We're early. There's time."

Yasmin reaches into her purse for her sunglasses. It is a bright, lucid morning, traffic heavy but flowing.

Jim says, "Your father must've been a strange man."

"Why would you say that?"

"Your mom must've mentioned him once or twice, no more. And you've never really talked about him."

"There's not much to talk about. I know it must seem strange, Jim, but I've never been all that curious about him. If I had any memory of him, it might've been different, maybe I'd have wanted to know more, about him and the island. But you can't miss someone you don't remember knowing. And I had mom, you see. She was enough."

"But she must have told you *something* about your father."

Beside the highway, in the railway marshalling yard, a locomotive tugs at its sluggish tail of metal containers.

"Oh, sure. He was a politician. A hard worker for his people. He might have ended up prime minister if he hadn't been shot."

Quickly, the train is gone, left behind.

"But didn't she ever talk about the man? Did he read books or play cards? What'd he do in his downtime?"

"She didn't tell many stories about him. They seem to have had pretty separate lives. As far as she was concerned, he played politics all the time."

"Do you think they were happy together?"

"I think my mom admired him."

"But were they happy?"

"The way she spoke about him, yes, I'd say so. She once said he was extremely devoted."

"To her?"

"She didn't say." Yasmin looks away. On the other side of the highway, the rush hour proceeds lugubriously towards downtown. "She never really wanted to talk about him, I don't think. And you know my mom—she's good at keeping her mouth shut when she wants to."

"Was, you mean," Jim says gently.

"Yes. Was."

"Are you nervous?"

"A bit apprehensive. Yes."

An ambulance flashes by, cars ahead weaving out of the way. Jim concentrates on his driving.

When the flow settles down, Yasmin says, "I know it's what mom would've wanted."

"But does it really matter?"

"Doesn't matter if it matters or not. It just feels like the right thing to do."

"For her or for you?"

A sliver of pain knits a passage across her eyebrows, and she turns away from the cars halted now on the other side of the highway, sunlight glinting off their glass and chrome.

She says, "There was a movie on TV many years ago, I've forgotten the title. About a white woman who'd married a Japanese-American man just before Pearl Harbor. He was interned, I think, and he ended up dying, I don't remember how. But the last scene, it was very quiet, very moving. The woman was washing her husband's body, gently, in total silence. Tears running down her cheeks." Her voice trembles and she pauses to swallow the tightness away.

On the railway tracks, a commuter train buzzes by. She glimpses heads in the windows, people heading from the suburbs to downtown office towers. And she senses a growing disconnection from them, as if she were already being lifted out of the context they share. But she feels no sense of liberation.

"It wasn't her immediate tragedy, it wasn't what had happened, wasn't the loss of someone she loved that was so moving. Or maybe it was all of that. Mostly it was the derailment of possibility. The life they should have lived. Together."

"You can't guess at what might have been, Yas. Might-have-beens don't get you anywhere. They're useless."

"It's not what might have been, that's not the point."

"So what is the point?"

"When I find out I'll let you know."

[2]

Is the tea too strong, Mrs. Livingston? Shall I brew another pot? Are you sure? Well, if you're sure. Here's your lemon wedge, I don't know how you stand it. Upbringing explains a lot, I suppose. Sugar and milk. I don't think I could bear the taste of tea any other way. Ahh, that's good.

Now, to get back to your question—why don't I call you Dorothy? As you say, we are neighbours. We have known one another for some years, and we are both of an age that prompts either politeness or impatience. But, as I say, upbringing explains a lot. Do you know, Mrs. Livingston, that not once did I call my husband by his first name? Others called him Vern or Vernon. Those were the ones who didn't know him very well. People in the diplomatic corps or the cabinet. Those who knew him less called him Mr. Ramessar. But those who knew him best called him Ram. For me, he was Mister Ramessar before we were married. He became nameless for a while after our marriage, and finally he became, for me too, just Ram. Never, ever, Vernon. You know, after a while, Vernon hardly seemed to be his name. It didn't suit him.

Now, why don't I call you Dorothy? Well, my dear, as with Ram, you do not strike me as a Dorothy. Blame it on *The Wizard of Oz*. Dorothys live in places called Kansas, and they get swept up by things called twisters. They are tossed hither and yon—why do you laugh? 'Hither and yon' may no longer be part of the vernacular but the phrase still serves admirably. Now Dorothys—Dorothys have their lives turned upside down by these twisters. They find themselves in situations that make no sense in *your* world. They meet, and must accept, tin men and cowardly lions. They encounter beings both good and evil, and sometimes they triumph, sometimes not. And sometimes, when the twister has returned them to their world, they have no idea which way things have gone. My dear Mrs. Livingston, if I do not call you Dorothy, it is because you are less a Dorothy than I. Do you see what I mean? Yes, of course you do.

You must not hold it against me, my calling you "Mrs.

Livingston". You must know that even my son-in-law James remains Mr. Summerhayes to me. And I do have great affection for him. He's a good man. Yasmin is Yasmin. She has been Yasmin from the moment of her birth. But she is the only one.

Now then, another cup perhaps?

[3]

The instructions themselves do not interest her. She has already heard them in English, in French, countless times over the years. Her luggage is safely stowed under the seat in front of her; she knows how to buckle her seat belt, how the oxygen mask will tumble, how to brace herself in case of emergency—not that it would help much, she always thinks.

She averts her eyes from the flight attendant's vaguely embarrassing pantomime, but she finds herself listening to the piped-in speech, to its cadences leavened by the rhythms of elsewhere. She hears, not for the first time but with a new clarity, aspects of her mother's speech patterns heightened, a syllable elongated here, a conjunction attenuated there.

Only as the aircraft gathers speed, only as its nose lifts from the tarmac like an animal alerted does it occur to her that she has hardly thought of Jim since the hug, the kiss, the enforced smiles two hours ago.

When the aircraft levels off above the clouds, when bolts of sunlight file unfiltered down the cabin, the pages of a childhood book of Greek myths come to her and she thinks of Icarus, condemned for the arrogance of overweening ambition when his only fault had been inadequate preparation. The pages turn in her mind to sky and sun and sea below, and Icarus, youthful and brown-limbed, looking back aghast at feathers falling away from the wax melting on his arms.

[4]

Friends, Mrs. Livingston? But you *are* my friend, I like to think. I suppose it all comes down to the meaning of the word, if you see what I mean. There are people who have countless friends, people who collect friends the way some people collect matchboxes, with a glorious indiscriminateness. They count as friends people they do business with, people with whom they regularly chat about the weather... It may have something to do with the debasement of language, don't you think? The word "acquaintance" is such a good one, precise in its way.

To me, friends are people who come back, despite everything. Do you see what I mean? That brooch you are wearing, for instance. A gift from your son, if I'm not mistaken? Last Christmas, no, two Christmases ago. Well, that brooch, my dear Mrs. Livingston, of which you are evidently so fond, you wear it so often, is one of the most hideous pieces of jewellery I have ever seen. It is simply dreadful. It looks like a squashed cockroach. It sits like a stain on your chest.

Oh, dear, have I offended you? Such was not my intention. Or maybe it was, to be perfectly honest. But it was not gratuitous. I am making a point. My judgement of your brooch is not a judgement of you. It is a judgement of the brooch, and of your son's taste in jewellery. But my point is—would you hold this against me? Would you allow that ugly thing to get in the way of our friendship?

There! I thought not. You will come back, won't you? Despite my opinion of your brooch. My comment is not something an acquaintance could get away with, though. Your brooch, and its emotional weight, are worth more to you than mere acquaintanceship. And our friendship is worth more to you than your brooch. Or so I hope. You see what I mean. Yes, of course you do.

A friend, in my opinion, Mrs. Livingston, is someone who will bury you not out of obligation but out of a profound sense of comradeship. You see, it is not always easy being a friend.

Now, do be a dear and put that horrid thing into your purse...

Thank you ever so much. Now then, shall we have a cuppa?

[5]

Drinks are served, and soon the volume of conversation in the cabin rises, acquires the intensity of a party losing its inhibitions.

Yasmin, unable to concentrate, closes her book, a plump paperback tour through the crumbled remains of empire in contemporary Eastern Europe. The headache she thought appeased reasserts itself and she regrets having had just a coffee. Everyone else seems to be holding wine, beer, whisky, rum-and-Cokes: tourists assuming their new care-free personae.

She wonders briefly at her choice of book, the topic on the face of it so remote from the place she has left and from the place to which she is going; and she wonders whether this might be the reason the book attracted her, for its very distance from the worlds that are hers: a sign, possibly, of her fear.

But then she grows irritated with herself. Couldn't it be much simpler than that? It was Charlotte who once said that life is not a novel, that it is full of the meaningful *and* the meaningless; Charlotte who pointed out that we underestimate the pleasure we get from the empty and the insignificant.

And so Yasmin reminds herself of why she's bought the book: because a colleague in the newsroom recommended it; because she is curious both personally and professionally; because she likes to read about her world and about worlds different from her own; because it was there, in the book-store at the airport, with a cover that caught her eye. All reasons so prosaic, so pedestrian, she tells herself, that they can have nothing to do with fear. It is, she realizes, one of the faults of her profession: seeking out patterns, links, events that will form a chain. And when none is discovered, the instinct is to impose one. This book, her worlds, her fears: this seeking after significance is not self-awareness; it is, she suspects, its very opposite.

She signals to a passing attendant and asks for a vodka and orange juice.

"Yeah, sure, honey," the attendant replies, offering her seat companion another beer.

The man, red-eyed, holds up his empty can in a large, work-scarred hand, the muscles of his forearm rolling and tightening under his dark skin. Unexpectedly he catches Yasmin's glance, returns her smile with a shy resignation. She sees that he is working at containing a submerged skittishness.

The drink, when it comes, contains much vodka and little orange juice, the ice cubes floating around hollow and fragile. Through the window, a few high clouds scud by, suffused with sunlight...

White on blue, up and down, spinning around and around and around faster and faster...

White on blue, glimpses of green, white on blue, up and down faster and faster white white white—

Hold on tight!

Faster and faster, green white blue

Don't let go! Don't—

A cascade of green brown blue white...

Umph!

Green. And brown. And white on blue.

And darkness crowding in at the edges.

A gathering up in hands.

The shadow of a face against the blue.

"Hi! How ya doin'?"

The voice brings her back to the rumble of the aircraft, to the cabin restless with laughter and conversation. Her eyes flutter open to a young woman standing in the aisle, a drink in her hand. She is leaning in over Yasmin's seat companion and seems determined, despite his reserve, to engage him in conversation.

"Fine," he mumbles.

"You on your way home?"

"Yes."

"Were you here on vacation?"

"I was workin' in Niagara, pickin' fruit. Temporary work permit."

"Yeah? That's great."

"Not really. Fall off a ladder, hurt my back. So is back home for me."

"Gee, that's too bad. Hope you get better soon."

"T'anks."

The woman's gaze shifts to Yasmin. "You on your way home too?"

"No."

The woman's eyes narrow in curiosity. "Have we met somewhere? You're familiar somehow."

"I don't think so."

"I know I've seen you somewhere. You work downtown?"

"Around there."

"Probably seen you buyin' lunch or something. So... you on vacation?"

"No, I'm taking my mother back to her home."

"That's great!" Her head swivels around. "Where's she sitting?"

"Actually, she's in my suitcase."

The woman freezes, cocks her head in puzzlement.

"Oh, don't worry," Yasmin says, enjoying the cruelty of the moment. "She's dead. We had her cremated."

The woman's face distorts in dismay. She turns abruptly and begins pushing her way up the crowded aisle back to her seat, her vacation off to a bad start.

Yasmin immediately regrets the callousness, regrets the pleasure it has given her. Jim would be appalled.

But her seat companion is grinning. He says, "You really livin' up here?"

Yasmin nods.

"Serve her right then, if you follow my meanin'."

Yasmin smiles and the man, with nothing more to say, settles back into his seat and shuts his eyes.

Yasmin takes a sip of her drink and returns her gaze to the sky, the clouds and the consequences of reaching too far into the unknown.

Returns to Icarus.

One

[1]

Darkness comes quickly, reminding her of what her mother once said: in the tropics dusk is a state of mind.

The brightness through which the plane descended —the dense, late-afternoon rays affording glimpses of mottled greenery rising from concentric shades of liquefied blue—has vanished by the time she clears immigration and customs, and emerges to night and lights and the competitive shouts of taxi drivers. Her arm is grasped, she feels herself led.

She is in the back seat of a car, bare arms sticky against the vinyl seat, night hurtling by beyond the rolled-up window, the driver's breathing labouring rhythmically against the raucous gear-shift.

Impossibly small: her exact impression of the island when first seen on a map.

The summer she was ten she drove east with Charlotte's family in a Volkswagen van, she and Charlotte following their progress in an old school atlas. Montreal, Quebec City, Edmunston, Fredericton, Moncton—a day and a night per city—and up into Cape Breton, their destination.

Yasmin remembers the surreptitiousness with which, as

they drove out of New Brunswick into Nova Scotia, she let her gaze wander south on the map, down past New York, Philadelphia, Washington, Richmond, Savannah and Miami; past Havana and Port-au-Prince, Santo Domingo and San Juan; and farther south still, following the concave sweep of islands. When she came to it, she saw that the island was almost obliterated by its own name.

Charlotte said, "Wha'cha looking at?"

Yasmin's fingertip pressed at the tiny island, hiding it. "That's where I was born," she said.

Charlotte moved her finger away and stared intently at the pinprick of green on the blue sea. "Gee," she said, "I don't think of you as a foreigner."

And Yasmin thought: Is that what I am?

Three years later, perhaps four, Mrs. Livingston lent her an issue of *National Geographic*. She tapped a finger at the contents listed on the cover. *Volcanoes of the Caribbean*.

The article devoted two pages to a long-dormant cone in the island of her birth. The text confined itself to a geologic history of the volcano whose last eruption would have been witnessed, if it all, by the Arawak Indians who did not long survive Columbus's arrival approximately a century and a half later.

Of greater interest to Yasmin were the accompanying photographs. An aerial shot of the cone—deeply forested with a small turquoise lake in the centre. A rectangle of townscape—red-roofed buildings, ringed with balconies of filigreed metal, sandwiched between blue water and blue sky. The town's red roofs spread from a narrow coastal plain into the foothills of the mountain range within which the volcano slept. A rectangle of beach, water and horizon—foreground of rock and mossy earth crowned by foaming surf and framed on either side by two palm trees and, above, by the hammock strung between them tossed heavenward by a mighty wind.

This was how the island remained with her for decades. Impossibly small, swathed in primary colours, with a molten heart forever stilled.

With a single motion, the taxi driver swings her suitcase out and shuts the trunk.

It is this slamming of the trunk—a resounding thud in the still evening—that causes her to notice the silence. The island's reputation for bacchanalia has prepared her for noise, a continuous pandemonium. The silence unsettles her. She follows the driver up the stairs and into the hotel as if seeking cover.

"Jim. Hi, it's me. I'm here."

Through the small window above the night table she sees the light of a street lamp, vague suggestions of street and sidewalk down below.

"Jim?"

She brushes at the window panes with her fingertips, seeking to wipe the dust away. But they are clean. The view is what it is. She sees that the panes are old and cloudy, the light flooding not through the glass but into it, making it almost opaque.

"Are you less worried now? Good. I told you, there's no need to worry."

The window, it occurs to her, is like a carnival trick: it promises a view illuminated by the street lamp beyond, and yet it is the glass and the light together that defeat that promise. A little laugh escapes her.

"Nothing. I'm just tired."

She turns away from the window and its sightless view, to the small air conditioner that sits in a cavity beside it. It is on, but its effect is minimal.

"No, I wanted to call you first. I'm tired, I'll call her tomorrow."

Idly, she presses the off button and the unremarked hum coughs to a stop. It is like breath held—a new silence vibrating in its wake.

Her chest tightens, and she sees her finger dart to turn it back on. The air conditioner wheezes, rattles, settles back into its hum.

"Small. Plants, whitewashed walls, wainscoted of all things. Kind of Somerset-Maugham-ish. Know what I mean? And there's an armed guard downstairs in the lobby."

She sits on the edge of the bed, realizes she feels better, safer, for speaking with Jim.

"Oh, yes, I almost forgot. Well, good luck. Hope they sign on the dotted line."

Even though he is thousands of miles away, he knows where she is, and this makes her feel somehow anchored. It soothes her fear of disappearing.

"Of course, I will. Yeah, me too. Bye."

She hangs up, slips her shoes off, pushes them away. Places her bare feet squarely on the parquet floor: feels the cool of the lacquer, the hardness of the wood. Feels, after a moment, the tickle of its smoothness.

She sits like this for a while, looking around at the uneasy intimacy of the small room: at the whitewashed walls finely etched by hairline cracks; at the heavy door, which she has double-bolted and chained at the insistence of the hand-written sign taped above the light switch; at the bathroom of surprisingly generous proportions, white tiles startling in the brightness of the ceiling light.

And then her feet feel a vibration through the floor, the waves of a distant movement, the way the rumble of a subway train underground can be felt on the surface. But there is no subway here.

She quickly turns off the air conditioner, listens. And she hears in the distance the asthmatic gasp of the ancient elevator. When it stops, so too does the vibration.

A latch on the top of the window frame catches her eye. She turns it, tugs, but the window remains secure. Then she sees that it has been nailed fast, limiting the room's perspective to itself.

After a few minutes, she thinks: Explanation is not always a comfort.

With her toes, she reaches for her shoes.

[2]

Passion? Such words you use, my dear Mrs. Livingston! For tea? I like tea, I enjoy tea. It calms me. But I would not say I have a passion for it. Passion! It seems such a naked word. Tea has just been part of my life for so long. I came late to it, you know. After my marriage...

Love, Mrs. Livingston? I wouldn't have believed it: after all these years, you still have the capacity to surprise me. I have never once thought of you as a sentimentalist. And now you bring up this subject. Passion. Love. How very... Harlequin of you.

Of course not, Mrs. Livingston. Love had very little to

do with my marriage. Oh, there was affection, certainly. After some time. He was persistent in his courtship, even though his mother believed he could do better. But my husband took a longer-term view of his needs.

He was of a family that had prospered. Large land holdings. Cocoa. But money could not buy the kind of social standing that counted, you had to be born to it. By marrying me, though, my husband was marrying my family and the entire past that was ours. And, certainly at the time, this connection was essential to electoral success. You see, even then, as a very young man, he harboured political ambitions. He knew that empire was crumbling. And he knew that this crumbling would create new opportunities, new powers to be claimed. But people do not follow those who are like themselves, they follow their betters. What is the point otherwise? That was the genius of the Perón woman in Argentina—to see that, and to play to it. To make the ordinary people believe that, through her, they too could sparkle in the lights. My husband needed the social respectability my family could offer—and, to be frank, my family needed the financial security he could offer. We had pretensions, intellectual pretensions, we could hardly afford. We believed our caste made us special. But how to pay for it—that was the problem.

His mother, my dear? Ah, yes. That charming lady. A suitable subject for the *Reader's Digest* feature—what was it? 'My most unforgettable character'? Oh, I suppose I'm being unfair. Like every mother she wanted the best for her son, and I was not her idea of the best. I was a little too educated, I suppose—by nuns, at that. And although I had spent my early years in the countryside, I came from the town, while the Ramessars were still, you know, country people to all intents and purposes. We were non-practising Hindus, while they had converted to Presbyterianism. My mother-in-law could give her children Christian names but she could not rid herself of the guilt of having forsaken her religion. And so I suppose in many ways I was a threat to her. At many levels, if you see what I mean.

But, as I have said, he was a persistent suitor. And an accomplished liar. Traits that were to serve him well later on in his career. In order to see me, he pretended to develop a great interest in sport. Every Sunday he would tell his mother that he and his friend Dilip were off to see the football at the stadium in town. Dilip's job was to bring along a box of chocolates and a bouquet of flowers, and to go to the game so that he could provide a full report later. If there were no game, they would invent one. And since his mother knew nothing of sport, her questions were easily answered.

Disturb me? His lying? No, later perhaps, a little. But at the time I was flattered. A man who wanted me enough to plan his lies. Yes, I was flattered, Mrs. Livingston, I felt coveted. I was seventeen when he courted me, eighteen when we married. Of course I was flattered. I was *seventeen*.

It was all a game to me then. His lies to his mother, our Sunday afternoons together. Oh, we did nothing grand. We sat, we walked, we talked. We strolled in the botanical gardens. He never actually took me out, you know. To the cinema, yes, the four-thirty showings. I can hear him still, asking if I was interested in the four-thirty. But never dancing or dining. Couldn't, you see. He had to be back home in the early evening, at a reasonable hour, or his mother would have grown suspicious.

Seventeen, dear God! What an age!

And so, after about a year, he asked me to marry him. I said yes. And he told his mother it was the way it would be. We both knew—we all knew—it was for the best. We all had a great deal to gain.

Oh, yes, my dear, I know. I make it all sound so cold-blooded, don't I? But it wasn't. The emotion, you see, was—how shall I put it?—displaced. It was not the narrow and utterly selfish emotion of the love of a man and woman for one another. It was an emotion that was a great deal less personal, but no less important for that.

Circumstances, as you are well aware, are everything. They create opportunity and responsibility. Ours was not a time that permitted great indulgence in the personal. We were being pushed by entire worlds. The worlds of family and community. The world of history, the enveloping memory of the immemorial poverty out of which we had risen. The emotion of the moment was bound up with all of this, and the question of whether he made my heart flutter and my pulse quicken was, well, mostly immaterial.

So we married...

Dear God, no, my dear! It most certainly was not the happiest day of my life. I had many happier days before and have had many happier since. Look here, I do not mean to be contrarian, but I do believe that any woman who makes of her wedding day the happiest day of her life—who measures all the events of her life against the day of her marriage—is, well, a sad creature. We do not assume—or expect—that a man's wedding day will be the happiest day of his life, do we?

Oh dear, I've offended you once more, haven't I? But you must understand, my dear, I have little religious feeling, and as for passion... As I have said, I was fond of him.

And it was all a little complicated, you know. The ceremonies of one religion and the other. The finery. All this theatre to satisfy other people. A cousin kept asking me if I felt like crying. I don't think she ever really forgave me for my dry eyes. What remains most vividly with me is the difficulty I had filling my lungs with sufficient oxygen.

[3]

"You goin' out, ma'am?"

The anxiety in the desk clerk's voice brings Yasmin to a halt. "Just going for a little walk. I need to get some air."

The clerk—Jennifer, according to her badge—picks up a pencil and twirls it between her fingers. Yasmin recognizes the gesture: a smoker might have reached for a cigarette. "Pardon my askin', ma'am, but—somebody meetin' you?"

"No, is there a problem?"

From behind her, the security guard—a young man dressed in grey, a revolver strapped to his waist and a small submachine gun hanging from his shoulder—says, "Is not a very good idea, ma'am, it getting dark."

"You're saying it's not safe?"

Jennifer says, "Is better not to take a chance, you never know."

The guard says, "Things not really back to normal yet, ma'am."

Jennifer nods reflectively. "An' even then," she says. "Normal…"

"You know, ma'am, maybe you heard about the little trouble we had here some time ago?"

Yasmin nods. "More than heard about it. I introduced—
That is, I saw the BBC reports on the news at home."

"So you know…"

"It must have been a terribly difficult time for you."

Jennifer's eyes shift uneasily. Then she says, "Well,
ma'am, nobody used the word war, but is what it was. A little war, no holds barred."

"I wasn' supposed to come to work that evening, ma'am,
but the girl working the desk take sick and call me up to
replace her. I had some studying to do—I taking a secretar-
ial course, nuh, computers and everything—but I figure I
could bring my books, it usually pretty quiet around here in
the evenings, so I say, Sure, girl, no problem. My brother
give me a ride over. It was jus' beginning to get dark when I
get here…"

They had emerged from the brief dusk, heads encased
in knitted caps, some in jeans and running shoes, others—
those in charge—more elaborately outfitted in flowing
gowns, white, sky-blue, the dun of desert sands. They had
brandished rifles and revolvers and submachine guns. They
were said to be well-provisioned in ammunition and sticks
of dynamite. They moved with quick efficiency, spreading
by the carload through the city, heading for the police outposts, startling the small garrisons and easily overwhelming them.

"Is the most frightening sound I ever hear, ma'am, coming from everywhere, as if a ton o' iron was falling from
Heaven itself. I freeze right there, jus' outside the door for I
ain't know how long before the girl I was coming to replace
pull me inside."

The insurgents had believed that confusion would carry

the day. They had convinced themselves that public joy would greet them. But the army, so long viewed with derision, had proved disciplined, and the people so long thought to be malleable showed that fear was more persuasive than discontent. The disturbances that did arise were contained with more loss of property—what could not be stolen was destroyed—than of life.

Within hours the police outposts had been surrounded, one group isolated from the other. The largest—a dozen men who had taken a dozen cabinet members hostage—found themselves besieged in a meeting room of the parliamentary building. The ministers were tied to their chairs and dynamite strapped to their chests.

Then they waited.

"It go on for days, ma'am, the whole island shut down. From time to time, night and day, you hearing gunshots, sometimes jus' one or two, sometimes so much at firs' you think is an explosion but after it go on for two-three minutes... I spend the whole time here, ma'am, in the hotel. We push some furniture up agains' the doors, jus' in case, nuh. The telephone was still working so I manage to talk with the family to make sure everything okay, but nobody knew what was going on. Everybody was saying *coup, coup,* but who, why, where, nobody could say."

One by one the police outposts were retaken by soldiers wearing ski-masks. A few prisoners were taken, many others were shot. Two of the outposts exploded in flames, the fire spreading quickly to adjacent buildings.

Around the parliament building they continued to wait.

"And then early one morning we hear a boom. Then nothing. Then a lot o' wild shooting. Then it was over. We watch it on TV. Fellas coming out with their hands up, soldiers aiming at their head, pushing them rough-rough to the ground.

"I give it a couple of hours before heading home. You know, ma'am, when I step out the door, everything felt different. Even the air felt kind o' dead. It was like the whole world had changed. I mean, here, at home, we had people countin' bodies."

Yasmin feels the evening darkness weighing on the town, feels it tightening around the hotel, feels the hotel tightening around her.

Jennifer says, "Is like everybody just waitin'."

"What for?" Yasmin asks.

Jennifer shakes her head. "Just waitin'."

The guard, gesturing towards a glassed door beyond the desk, says, "Maybe a drink is a better idea than a walk, ma'am."

Yasmin considers the suggestion. She imagines pushing that door open to ferns and Tiffany lampshades, to a worldly and timeless elegance of long evening dresses and white jackets, as in countless old black-and-white movies. Claudette Colbert would be nursing some exotic drink at the bar. Over in the corner, Leslie Howard would be picking out a melancholy melody on a grand piano. Yasmin says, "Is there a piano in there?"

"Yes, ma'am," Jennifer replies. "There's a piano."

"Is there a piano player?"

Jennifer smiles sadly and opens her palms in regret.

The room has grown warm. She kicks off her shoes and stretches out on the bed. For the first time she regrets Jim's absence. She closes her eyes, listens to the air squeezing through the air conditioner, squeezing into her lungs, and waits for the regret to pass.

Regret begets, regret.

She regrets that her memories come in bits and pieces— sound bites of the mind. What she wants, what she yearns for, is memories that unroll like film: a long and seamless evocation of mood and nuance.

Her daughter is sitting on the carpet in front of the door. She is struggling with the straps of her new shoes; they are stiff and will not slip easily into the buckle.

Jim, briefcase in hand, waits impatiently beside her, car keys already jingling in his hand.

When her daughter sighs and begins again, a shadow crosses Jim's face. Yasmin is about to rein in his impatience when, inexplicably, his features soften. He puts down the briefcase and crouches, his hand lighting on the curve of her daughter's back.

Their daughter's back.

As the unskilled fingers slip the strap into the silver buckle, as they tighten and secure it, Jim gently runs his thumb down her backbone: a long and languorous caress. He is as if in awe: of the shape, of the solidity, of the very reality of the child. He has, Yasmin sees, stopped the world.

His love, she thinks, rarely glitters. Rather, it glimmers in subdued constancy; and only occasionally—as at that moment years ago; as at that other moment years before that when he first held their newborn daughter—does it sparkle.

This waiting for the regret to pass: it is, she thinks, the only wisdom she has acquired in her fifteen years with Jim.

[4]

The only trick, my dear, is patience. The preparation is really quite simple. You see this little implement?

Yes, you're right. It does rather look like a miniature milk pail with handle and spout, doesn't it.

I bought it specially, you know. It's used for making both Turkish coffee and Moroccan mint tea. So, at least, I was told by the man in the shop. You put the mint leaves in with the water and you let it boil for five minutes, until it grows thick and fragrant. Then you add mounds of sugar and sip it piping hot.

Exotic, my dear? I suppose so, but that is no reason to fear it, is it now? I don't mean to compare myself to tea, but I know what it is to be exotic, my dear, to be seen as being so different you are disliked for it... But I've told you the story about my husband in the London hotel, haven't I?

It was soon after my husband's posting to London. Springtime, I think. I remember it was wet and cold, humid —but not the unpleasant, piercing humidity of fall and winter. No, there was a weak sunshine, with the promise of much more to come, and the sense of a great drying up, of grass turning green and hints of indiscreet colour. So it must have been spring—but the season actually is beside the point. This could have happened in any season...

What's the matter, my dear? Don't you fancy the tea?

So what's the meaning of that face then? Sweet? Of course it's sweet. It's supposed to be sweet. Just sip at it, dear. Gently does it.

In any case, we were walking around, exploring the city, acquainting ourselves with it. We weren't far from Buckingham Palace, as I recall, but I may be mistaken. There was a large park—

Hyde Park? Who knows? Possibly. There are other parks in London, you know.

My husband experienced a sudden and rather urgent need to visit a washroom. We spotted a row of hotels on the far side of the park and headed quickly towards them. He chose the closest and we went in.

The lobby was not large but it was grand in a sombre, conspiratorial sort of way. All dark, polished wood and heavy drapery that absorbed the light from the chandeliers. There was a clutch of American tourists at the desk, so he turned to the doorman who was standing in his uniform— a cherry-red affair, with brass buttons and gold tassels— rather grandly surveying the scene. My husband asked if he would be so good as to point out the nearest washroom. The doorman cocked a cold eye at him, surveyed him with obvious contempt from head to foot—and said nothing.

My husband repeated his request—positively offending the man. I thought he was about to spit! Look, my husband said, either you show me where the washroom is or you and I are both going to be very embarrassed in a moment.

The doorman froze, just long enough, I imagine, for him to decide that this savage was indeed capable of, well, you know, embarrassing them both. Then he flicked his gloved hand in the direction of an unmarked door beside the main desk.

Afterwards my husband made a point of thanking him as we left—but he was seething inside that the English, as he saw it, were the kind of people to make a man beg even to have a pee in private. He tended to elevate an individual's bad manners to a judgement on the society as a whole, you see. Of course he didn't forgive the man, either. He understood that the fellow was simply performing his duties, but he felt he was doing so at the expense of his own humanity. He always insisted, my husband, on the superiority of individual conscience over group or professional demands. He felt the hotel doorman had sold his conscience, and so his dignity, to a place where he himself would be welcome only as hired help. He was the living embodiment of a lackey— and lackeys earned nothing but contempt from my husband —unless they happened to be *his* lackeys.

So you see what I mean about being exotic, my dear. It means you are never at the centre of things, and the centre was where my husband always wanted to be. He used everything, even our wedding, to get there.

But more about that in a moment. First, shall we indulge in another drop or two?

[5]

It had been warm, too, and moist, that day in the wine bar. Yasmin had paused, uncertain, on its aluminum threshold. But Charlotte was already inside scouting out a table.

They were both single, still close friends despite the many years they had known each other. Yasmin no longer counted the number of times she had found herself enlisted by Charlotte in activities calculated to benefit her mind, body or soul—in yoga sessions, ceramics classes, art appreciation seminars, badminton lessons, kite-flying, egg painting. No enthusiasm, though, ever lasted beyond the next man, and few men lasted beyond the lure of an enthusiasm. Charlotte, in a rare moment of insight, had once said of herself that she feared being the kind of person who enjoyed falling in love but detested being in love.

Yasmin had always been struck by their differing reactions to physical attractiveness. Beauty disarmed Charlotte; it made her helpless. But beauty, by its very nature, suggested to Yasmin the untrustworthy; it put her on her guard.

There was Garth, for instance, a researcher at the station. Tall, confident, athletic Garth. He had appealed to Charlotte, the ease with which he carried himself, the width of his shoulders, the narrowness of his hips. Gorgeous Garth, Yasmin had called him, and Charlotte, in the grip of her infatuation, had misconstrued the sarcasm as admiration. "He's not your type," she had retorted. That Garth knew himself to be attractive was, in Charlotte's view, no hindrance. Charlotte's attractiveness was no secret to herself either.

Then one afternoon Garth, spotting a photograph of a bikinied woman on the fashion reporter's desk, had called out, "Hey, who's the babe in the 'kini?" He seized the photograph and examined it with an adolescent avidity.

"Christ!" Charlotte said afterwards. "I thought he was going to jerk off right there."

"Thought or hoped?" Yasmin said.

Charlotte shook her head, as if to free it of shattered illusions. "Yet another one," she said, "who seems like a normal human being until he's caught off guard."

It was a day or two later that Yasmin found on her desk a flyer advertising the wine-tasting evening at the local wine bar.

From the street its location, in the basement of an office building, had not been promising. And from the threshold where she stood, Yasmin thought the interior offered little hope of improvement. It was dimly lit, probably to enhance its approximation of old-world intimacy: wall-panelling of weathered planks, wooden beams which, she was sure, would ring hollow when tapped.

She saw with relief that every table was taken and had begun to hope they would have to return another day when Charlotte, with the boldness that made her good at her job, approached a man sitting alone at a table in a corner. She beckoned Yasmin over.

The man introduced himself as Jim Summerhayes. He was an architect. He was here, he said, because he liked to expand his horizons.

Yasmin thought: Great, another winner…

His gourmet-cooking course had ended the week before, and learning more about wines seemed the next logical step.

Charlotte nodded eagerly. "Absolutely."

Yasmin said, "You must have a lot of time on your hands. You unemployed or just no good at what you do?"

Charlotte said, "Yas!"

Jim looked thoughtfully at her. Then he laughed. "Neither of the above."

Yasmin guessed him to be in his early thirties. An ordinary, intelligent face, angular. He was casually dressed, in a tan turtleneck and tweed jacket. His palms were broad, with long slender fingers and neatly trimmed nails. He wore no wedding band, but that meant nothing.

The wine tasting continued. After each sampling the expert on hand gave his impressions, reading the effects of the wine on his tongue. His vocabulary was so esoteric that by the third glass Charlotte and Yasmin both stopped scribbling notes on the forms they'd been given. Jim, though, was assiduous in filling out his, intense in the way of university students who noted down the lecturer's every tic and cough.

"Nutty?" Charlotte repeated as the expert intoned his judgment. "Him or the wine?"

Jim smiled, whether from politeness or genuine amusement Yasmin could not say. But he continued to scribble, paying close attention to the expert's opinion.

Yasmin, nibbling on dry bread, settled back to enjoy the glow of the wine. On a poster pinned to the wall behind Jim a red and yellow ribbon swirled into the shape of a bottle. Sipping at her fifth or sixth glass, the wines all tasting the same now, Yasmin found herself enjoying its movement, the touch of gaiety it lent to the sedate atmosphere.

Beside her, Charlotte sighed unhappily and Yasmin knew she would not soon wish to return to the bar. Its earnestness discouraged the mingling and easy conversation that led to the discovery or invention of mutual interests, to the exchange of phone numbers.

Yasmin's gaze fell from the poster to Jim's hands, the left lying palm down on the table, the right holding the glass to his lips. Tenacious hands, she thought, but composed. The hands of a man at ease with himself. She wondered what it would feel like to touch them, what it would feel like to be touched by them. She had once seen Charlotte take the hand of an attractive stranger and, under the pretext of reading his palm, arouse his interest with the caress of her fingertips. Yasmin was not timid, but she did not share Charlotte's impetuousness.

Jim slowly placed the glass on the table, his eyes following it as if in silent interrogation. He made a note on his form, put down the pencil and reached for a heel of bread.

He said, "Did you know that the Russians claim that if you just sniff at some bread or a pickle you won't get drunk? On vodka, of course."

Charlotte said, "I've heard that."

Yasmin said, "Think it works with wine?"

He held the bread up to her. "Here. Try."

When they left not long after, Charlotte said, "I saw that. Daring."

"What?"

"You know what. He'll call you for sure now."

"I don't know what—" But her face was burning hot.

"Did you see the look on his face?"

No, she hadn't. She hadn't seen anything but the spongy whiteness of the bread, had sensed with a dizzying keenness the swirl of red and yellow ribbon on the wall above.

"Bet you anything he's heading home to a wet dream."

"Charlotte!"

"Give it up, Yas. No man's going to forget a woman who licked his finger the way you did."

"It was an accident. The wine. I—"

But Charlotte had no interest in explanations. She hailed a passing taxi.

On the way home to the apartment they shared, Charlotte teased Yasmin by licking at her own index finger and making faces of ecstasy.

Yasmin ignored her. The smoothness of his nail was imprinted on her tongue. As the taxi pulled up to the apartment building, an icy shiver radiated down her spine. For the first time in her life, she had done the unthinkable.

[6]

Here we go. There's nothing like the odour of a fresh brew, is there, my dear?

Now, where was I? Ah, yes, my wedding. Tell me, Mrs. Livingston, do you know what privilege is?

Having the supermarket deliver your groceries for free? Well, yes, I suppose. But, my dear, you are aware that privilege has a less pleasant side, are you not? In my part of the world—or at least that part of the world that used to be mine—it was a deadly serious game of exclusion. Privilege, you see, manifested itself through the colour of one's skin.

I won't bore you with the countless ways in which skin from light to white eased lives, both social and professional. Suffice it to say that entire careers were built on that one qualification, just as entire lives were derailed because of it. My husband used the occasion of our wedding to begin the process of lifting this prejudice from the shoulders of our people.

Keep in mind there are two ways to look at this story. His supporters saw it as proof of his commitment, his detractors as proof of his opportunism—

How did I see it? Let me tell you the story first, my dear. Now, where shall I begin? With another sip of tea, I should think. It is rather dry in here, isn't it? Oh, that's good. Now then...

At the time of our marriage, you see, my husband had begun to acquire a small reputation as a leader in some quarters, as a troublemaker in others. He needed—

No, let me put it less indelicately. Politics is drama, and drama needs event. My husband knew he would benefit greatly from an event that would earn him the right enemies, and it so happened that our wedding presented him with just such an opportunity.

We had a club in the island, you see. Its name alone—"The Majesty"—bespoke glamour. It was a large lounge, really, in a hotel in the town—the island's first hotel, if I'm not mistaken. There was a tennis court out back, I seem to remember, and a swimming pool—and members were allowed to run up tabs, which seemed a particularly stylish thing to do. When I imagined the goings-on at the Majesty, I always pictured the women in evening dresses, the men in dinner jackets—and the entire scene in black and white. It was the vision that had been given to me, you see, by the movies, and I could not—indeed, it never occurred to me to —make the leap to colour. And it was only much later that I realized this. To me at the time, it was quite normal. Elegance came in black and white—which is an irony much too simplistic for words...

The one time the queen visited our island, she was conveyed from the royal yacht *Britannia* directly to the Majesty for a reception. You see the kind of cachet this place had.

Now, the only problem with the Majesty was that it was exclusive to the whites of the island. Understand: this was not a rule, it was not written anywhere; it was more of an understanding, a social convention, and so all the more powerful. Once, on New Year's Eve, which we called Old Year's, my husband and some of his friends, having already imbibed a fair amount, were turned away, a sting that never stopped smarting—and which later led to accusations against him of personal vendetta. Some pointed to the personal slight as proof that he was not principled.

But things change. This was a time when a lot of our young fellows were going off to England to become doctors or lawyers, and quite a few of them returned to the island with white wives. It was said—and whether this was true or not I cannot say—but it was said that the club was considering allowing in the wives but not the husbands, so that —had they not still been in England at the time—Celia, for instance, could become a member but my brother-in-law Cyril could not. He would be allowed to drive her there and then pick her up, of course. But if he wished to wait for her, he would have to sit in the car or while away the time in the botanical gardens across the street.

And so my husband got it into his head that our wedding reception would be held there, at the Majesty. He submitted a request for rental of the premises—and received a reply stating that the premises were not available on the requested day. He changed the day, and still the premises were booked. This was the usual tactic.

Now, by this time journalists had begun attaching themselves to my husband, so he had one of them call up an officer of the club. The newspaper, the hack claimed, was looking into reports that Mr. Vernon Ramessar, an up-and-coming political leader in the East Indian community, was being refused rental of the club's premises for his wedding reception, a notable event in the community. Was there any truth to this?

The club's members were not unmindful of the growing resentment against them; they were not unaware that profound forces were at work outside the confines of the Majesty. The club officer pleaded simple scheduling conflicts—but he assured the hack they were working on a solution. By the following day it was all arranged. The club asked only that there be no goat-slaughter on the premises, no outdoor cooking fires, and that noise be kept to a reasonable level.

It was something, I tell you, Mrs. Livingston. We were drummed into the Majesty in full regalia, me in my sari, my husband in turban, kurta and dhoti, heads held high. You could practically hear the sound of privilege crashing down. Even the kitchen and dining-room staff stood and applauded. You cannot possibly imagine what it was like, my dear. The discrimination—

Ahh, yes, of course. How insensitive of me. Your name tends to suggest a different history. One does forget, you know, that you acquired it from your husband. Italian immigrants after the war. You were still the enemy, weren't you…

But listen to us, trading old humiliations—let us not forget the triumphs, too! Do you know, my dear, what I consider to be the greatest triumph of all? That we've survived, Mrs. Livingston. We've survived, and we're here to savour it.

The next day there were photographs in the newspapers, and lengthy stories turned out by the hacks. But the real story, as everyone well understood, was that the Majesty Club could not go back to its old ways. We celebrated Old Year's that year at the Majesty, and we were far from alone…

There's a touch left, my dear. Would you…? No? Then I think I shall…

Yes, yes, I know. All this sugar. But I am treating myself just for today. I shall return to my sensible ways tomorrow, don't you worry.

So to get back to your question, how did I see it? My dear Mrs. Livingston, I saw it as the action of the man I had agreed to marry. I didn't judge it. I admired his courage—but I did think, I confess, that he might have chosen a more appropriate occasion…

Regret? No, I don't think so. I entered this marriage

with full knowledge of his ambition, but I was only just beginning to learn just how deep that ambition went.

But this explains, Mrs. Livingston, why I know what humiliation feels like, and far worse. It is, my dear, why the colour of my skin is precious to me, even though it does not define me. You see, on our wedding day my husband reclaimed the dignity that had so long been denied us, and dignity opens up the world. After that day, how could I be ashamed—of anything?

Precious, precarious world, isn't it?

[7]

After breakfast in the lounge—dark panelling and wicker greedily absorbing the sunshine from the steel-barred windows—Yasmin smiles at the new desk-clerk, nods at the new guard, and steps outside. She expects to be called back, cautioned. But daylight changes everything: they barely acknowledge her.

The morning air is cooler than she expects, the sun bright and splintery and gentle on the skin. Across the street, swallowed by the darkness of the evening before, effaced in the diminished view through her window, is a large park: trees and lawns and paths, beds of tended flowers, sprays of shrubbery. Tacked to the tree trunks and rising above the flowers are the rectangular plates of botanical identification.

She feels herself lighten, feels a smile come to her lips.

Farther down the street, she sees a sight a TV story producer would film for 'local colour.' A discouraged horse harnessed to a wooden cart, the tray heavy with a mound of fresh coconuts. A man in ragged shorts and a hat leans against the tray sipping from a metal cup. He is shirtless, so thin that his chest appears concave. A producer would get him to wield his machete, to open up a nut: *local enterprise in the dying economy*.

She thinks of Martinique, with Jim, two weeks in February a few years ago. A bus tour through the misty mountains of tropical rain forest, through the remnants of St. Pierre ruined at the turn of the century by volcanic eruption, past endless banana plantations. She remembers the tall coconut palms, with their clusters of green nuts high above. The woman in the seat ahead had pointed to them, asked her husband what they were. He didn't know.

"Coconuts," Yasmin had offered.

"Coconuts?" The woman was doubtful.

"Fresh coconuts. That's how they grow."

"You sure?"—the doubt in her voice hardening—"The only coconuts I've ever seen are brown."

Yasmin had fallen silent at that. She saw the woman— wisps of grey revealed at the nape of her neck by the severe upsweep of too-brown hair—bridling at the possibility that the coconut could be other than she knew it to be. Like the many who tuned in to the newscast not to learn of the world but to confirm their views of it.

"Coconuts." Jim, sitting beside her, had squeezed her hand. "Sure couldn't tell just by looking at them."

"Helps to ask," she replied. "Usually."

"Penny Pradesh, please."

"Who callin', please."

"My name is Yasmin."

"Jus' a moment, please."

Penny Pradesh is her aunt, her father's sister. They have spoken only once before, when Yasmin called to give her aunt the news of her mother's death, and to ask her help in its aftermath. *Call Penny, if there's anything...*, her mother had said more than once. *Call Penny...* She had shown her where, in the little phonebook, she could find Penny's number, one of the few written in ink. And Yasmin has always known the sole circumstance in which she would call Penny.

Through the phone, she hears a distant shuffling, the sounds of Penny approaching.

Penny. Her aunt. Her father's sister.

Yasmin has no belief in the romance of family ties. There is to her no point in comparing the thickness of blood and water: with time, with distance, with no network of shared experience, blood might as well be water. Yasmin knows Charlotte's life to be more precious to her than Penny's.

"Hello. Yasmin?" Penny has a rich, warm voice. A voice of a timbre that would do well on radio.

"I'm here," Yasmin says. "At the hotel."

"And Shakti?"

"It went well."

There is a silence, and Yasmin wonders if Penny is struggling with the same image that comes to her: of flames licking at her mother's face, enveloping her body.

"I coming pick you up," Penny says. "Twenty minutes."

[8]

You often speak, my dear, of the first apartment you lived in with your husband. You have spoken of it as such a glorious time. You were happy, weren't you? I was not so lucky, you know. This living on your own as a newly-wed couple—it simply wasn't done where I come from.

Instead, I moved into his family's house, to his room really. He made space for my clothes in his wardrobe and then, well, he was gone much of the time. He was a surveyor by profession, you see, in government employ, and his duties took him all over the island. He would leave home early and return late. This was how he actually began his political career, you see, by travelling around, meeting people. Surveying the populace as much as he surveyed the land.

My life sounds lonely to you? Does it really? I see what you mean. I suppose there were moments, yes. But I managed to keep busy, you know. I spent my days at the house, working at my own duties, which were essentially to help the maid. Yes, my dear Mrs. Livingston, believe it or not, to help the maid. She was a young woman of approximately my own age. Amina. A mouse of a girl with little education, but certainly pleasant in every way. And embarrassed, I think, by having to share her work with me. But we managed, and grew as fond of one another as our stations would permit. She called me "mistress," you see. I was the one to sweep the floors, but she was the one to wash them. We both knew that my duties were really like a game for my mother-in-law's benefit. And that one day, in one way or another, the game would end for me—

A spill? Where? That? Oh, don't bother your head, my dear, it's only a few drops of tea. We'll tend to it later. We are in no hurry, are we? At our age, time does not seem long, but it certainly does seem to sprawl, if you know what I mean. All this free time...I've always enjoyed companion-ship in my free time, you know.

Like those free afternoons once my chores were done. I would spend them with my sister-in-law, Penny. She was the youngest in the family, a bit younger than I, my husband being the eldest followed by his brother, Cyril, who was away in England at the time reading for a law degree. Their father—the man who had started it all, who had bought the land and built the house—had died accidentally some years before. He had just boarded an inter-island schooner for a visit to Trinidad, where he had relatives, when he realized he had forgotten his bag of religious implements on the dock. He was a pundit, you see, a holy man. He called out for it as the schooner was casting off and someone—the story never made it clear who precisely—flung it up towards him. The old man reached out for it desperately, missed it by a good foot or two and lost his balance. It was said that he and the bag hit the water at exactly the same moment, though which sank faster no one could say with any accuracy.

Mrs. Livingston! Well I never! Laughing! Don't you realize this is a sad story? Well, I can't say I blame you. It took me some time to realize it too. Whenever they trotted the story out, they mistook the water in my eyes for tears of sadness. They had sanctified the old man and his death, you see. But should I feel guilty that the image of this man in turban, kurta and dhoti plunging after his bag has always given me an acute case of the giggles?

In any case, Penny and I would while away the afternoons. Walking in the fields, or rocking the time away in hammocks strung up between the pillars that supported the house. It sat on a hill, and afforded a truly spectacular view of the bay. Often you would see ships heading into port from the open sea, and sometimes you could see storms blowing in. My husband claimed that, as a boy during the

war, he once watched a cargo ship go down after being tor-
pedoed. Penny and I were comfortable there, under the
house. It was shaded and cool and the floor of poured concrete tickled the soles of the feet in the most pleasant way...

My dear, will you please leave that spill alone! I've told
you, it can wait. I do declare, sometimes it is like speaking to
the Berlin Wall! Thank you...

One day, about a year later, I imagine, my husband
received a letter from his brother announcing his imminent
return from London. The letter said only that he was not
well; that the doctors had prescribed a lengthy period of
rest; that he had no choice but to postpone his final year of
study until he was recovered. He and his wife—an English-
woman no one in the family had yet met—had already
booked passage and would be arriving in a few weeks...

Oxford or Cambridge? I couldn't really say, my dear. It
was a British university, that's all I remember. In any case, it
hardly matters, does it now?

My husband's first thought, as a practical man, was
that there was not enough space in the house. Cyril and
Celia could have Amina's room—but where would we put
Amina? In no time at all, he had that wonderful open space
bricked in and divided up into storage and wash areas, and a
bedroom for Amina. Oh, it was a loss but it couldn't be
avoided. That's how I viewed it at the time. But you know,
Mrs. Livingston, I resent it still today. The attitude, I mean.
Practicality above all else. It makes for efficient ugliness.

The night before they arrived we were all up late,
watching for their ship. And we saw it gliding in through the
darkness just after midnight. My husband said, "That's
them." My mother-in-law sighed. I couldn't read my husband's feelings just then. He wasn't happy or sad or angry

or apprehensive, or maybe he was all of those things. But there was a quality to the night—the silence, the stars, the lights of the ship—that made me, maybe all of us, uneasy. Then he took me by the arm—something he rarely did, this easy touching—and led Penny and me back inside. He said the ship would be hours docking, and it would be mid-morning before they disembarked. I remember sensing, at that moment, that he was almost turning his back on the night.

The next morning we met them at the docks. Cyril was very different from my husband, his physical opposite. More like their mother. He was short and round and his hair was already thinning. He wore thick eyeglasses. His right eye was hidden behind a large bandage—

I'm coming to that, my dear. A little patience.

Celia was a little taller, thinner. She was already tanned, and had hair so fine—rather like yours, I should think—that I'm sure I wasn't the only one to wonder how much hairspray she needed to give it shape. She greeted us with a smile that was so earnest it seemed forced. A smile that revealed how uneasy she was. I felt for her, and I wondered how we looked to her eyes. Oh, we had all seen white peo-ple before, but what made her seem alien was that she was a member of the family. And it occurred to me that we must have looked even more alien to her. Her smile was one of hysteria. We shook hands when my husband introduced us, and she held my hand a touch longer than she'd held the others, as if taking a little refuge. I felt then that she recog-nized me—a sister-in-law married into the family—as a fel-low alien...

Oh, if you must! There's a rag in the kitchen. At the sink. No, not that one, the blue one. There, are you happy now?

[9]

Yasmin, buckling her seat belt, says, "What should I call you?"

"Penny will do. Nothing else really fits, eh?"

She puts the car into gear and pulls out quickly. They turn a corner, then another.

Penny says, "You probably don't remember much—"

"Nothing. Not really."

"Well, you were so young. Three? Four?"

"Four." Yasmin gazes through the tinted window: at the sidewalk, at houses—cream, white: strangely colourless—cool and inaccessible behind fences and shrubbery. And she, neither resident nor tourist, aid worker nor investor, senses herself distanced from it all. She thinks of the woman on the aircraft, and she wonders whether her cruelty had issued from her own indefinability, from an unsuspected envy. But she does not wish for greater involvement with, or even greater knowledge of, the world she sees through the window. She is here, she tells herself, to fulfil an obligation. And then to leave.

So she turns away from that world and, with her eyes alone, looks at Penny. At her silver hair swept tight on her scalp and knotted into a bun at the back. At the face burnt a rich brown: the nose flat, the lips dark and finely shaped. A face, like her mother's, without wrinkles, unblemished by the years. She does not—as her mother would say—look like a Penny.

She turns suddenly towards Yasmin, catches her gaze. Holds it for a moment, and smiles. Then her eyes fall to the purse on Yasmin's lap. "You didn't bring her," she says.

"I'm not ready," Yasmin replies. *Bring her. Bring it.* She is surprised at the depth of her unease.

Eyes on the road, Penny nods.

Yasmin is grateful for that, senses—hopes—that perhaps the warmth of the voice...

And then, with the turning of a corner, they are in traffic. The sidewalks are wider now, crowded with people and
ramshackle booths festooned with colourful bric-à-brac.
Almost hidden behind them, small stores huddle in the
shadows, reminding her of the houses a street or two ago,
inaccessible behind their walls and their shrubbery. A
bustling street, but not lively. Fidgety, rather, Yasmin
decides. Fretful.

"You feel it?" Penny says.

"What?"

"The frenzy."

"They told me at the hotel things aren't back to normal
yet."

"Yet!" Penny laughs, a cascade of throaty merriment.
"Well, is good to know we still have some optimists in this
place."

Farther down the street, the backdrop of stores falls
away to a sudden vision of apocalypse: to the broken husks
of buildings, to wood turned charcoal, to walls blackened by
fire, beams warped by heat. Block after block of the devasta-
tion she remembers introducing on the evening news.

Penny says, "They went after the big stores, but of
course it just spread all over the place. We could a' lose the
whole town. As soon as they surrendered, the fire brigade
moved in."

Yasmin says nothing. There is nothing to say.

The street ends abruptly, branching to either side at a
high stone wall. Just above it, Yasmin sees the sea—a brack-
ish blue sprinkled with small boats—and a hazy horizon.

Penny turns right, driving swiftly along the sea road. "How your husband doing?" she asks.

"He's fine. He wanted to come, but…"

"Is not really his place, eh?"

On the left, Yasmin sees the city docks: large rusted sheds, the funnels of cargo ships. At the main gates, there are sandbags, and soldiers in helmets. She says, "He and Mom were close."

"I know."

"Maybe he should have come."

"Don't think I'm pryin', but everything all right with you and Mr. Summerhayes?"

"His name is Jim."

Penny laughs. "Shakti trained me."

Yasmin wonders how often her mother and Penny spoke. She wonders how much her mother said, and how much Penny may have embroidered from what she said. She realizes that she does not, that she cannot, trust Penny. After a moment she says, "Everything's fine."

[10]

He owned a cat, a bony, manic creature that would not let itself be stroked. It seemed an odd animal for him to have. When he'd mentioned he had a pet, she'd imagined a dog, a golden retriever, a Labrador, something large and gentle. But Anubis slunk around the apartment, scurrying across open spaces, hugging the walls with the stealth of a shoplifter. Small and lean in the way of the chronically agitated, she inserted herself into impossible nests from which she would emerge defensive and aggrieved.

The first time Yasmin sat on the sofa, Anubis announced her presence among the cushions with a yowling exit. The slash of protesting shadow left Yasmin unnerved for several minutes, as the cat, heaving with fright, glared at her from Jim's shoulder.

When he saw that Yasmin and Anubis would not be easily reconciled—he had held the cat out to her, its body limp, its eyes malicious; it had growled and spat at her—he said he would exile it to the bedroom. He spoke with dispassion, but Yasmin did not miss the regret—or was it a suppressed dismay?—that wove its way through his words. His consideration for the animal left her perturbed, yet there was something indefinably reassuring about it. She was glad to have Anubis gone.

His apartment was large, conventional in design, with picture windows opening the living room to a spacious balcony, sky and wooded hills. A discreet glimpse of the expressway that wound downtown reminded her of the night she and Charlotte had ridden it through a raging midnight storm, the speed dangerous, the music deafening. It had been an exhilarating ride, but Yasmin had found herself breathless with fright at the end. His furniture too was conventional, classic, of an unmemorable timelessness. The walls were hung with framed photographs, his successes. He had spoken of his photography, his interest in playing with light, seizing its elements: the moment, he had said, when everything was contrasted, highlighted, clarified. His camera accompanied him on trips to aid not memory but rather exploration—not of people, he had said, but of landscape: to help him see the obvious. And as she scanned the walls, few faces looked back at her. Those that did were snapshots clustered in frames beside the front door, as if they had been ushered in without quite being welcomed. Age and resemblance told her they were of relatives, parents and grandparents, smiles fixed, attitudes posed. Well-to-do people, she decided, respected in their communities, satisfied with their lives. But that was the lie of shapshots, as Jim had said: regrets and dissatisfactions momentarily displaced for the camera.

She moved on. To a wooden frame within which a drainpipe the shade of pewter emerged from a flowerbox swollen with colour, ran down a lemon wall to the sidewalk, and finally disgorged onto wet cobblestones what looked like gushing water flash-frozen to ice. Beside it, in a brass frame, two walls of unfinished concrete met in the middle, each centred by a clear-glass window, one reflecting rugged, snow-topped mountains, the other a field of thick vegetation. Clever photographs, she thought, well composed, and suggestive of more than the simple pleasure offered the eye.

The next photograph, though, immediately unsettled her. It was, in its details, not an extraordinary composition, merely a rectangle divided into two triangles. The first, forming the base, was of a hill sloping from the upper right corner precipitously down to the lower left; its short grass was bathed in a thick golden wash, as if from the furnace of a setting sun. Filling the space above it, looming impenetrable above its brilliance, the other triangle suggested the darkest of nights, a sky of storm cloud. There seemed a permanence to the darkness, as if the stars would never return, and a desperation to the light, as if it knew itself to be on the edge of extinction. Yasmin hugged herself. It was, in the quiet intensity of its contrasts, a terrifying photograph.

Jim emerged from the bedroom rubbing his eyes. He had changed into jeans and an untucked shirt. "She's calmed down."

"Oh, she has, has she." Her tone was flattened by sarcasm. She swallowed, and drew his attention to the photogaph.

"Switzerland, about three years ago. Three days of business and two days of hiking. I took exactly five photos. The other four didn't work."

The pride in his voice prevented her from confessing her discomfort—that would probably have pained him—and it yet insisted that she show further interest. She asked about the technical challenge: Surely he had used a filter to achieve the richness of colour?

"No, never."

She bit her lower lip, hard. He had told her this before—natural light was a point of honour with him—and somehow she had forgotten. He disdained lamps and flashes and filters of any kind. They effected frauds, he'd insisted, were a manipulation of the light rather than an engagement with it.

"Remarkable," she said into the ensuing silence, and the emptiness of the remark was apparent to her. She possessed the vocabulary—she could hold her own with the art crowd, with academics, saying much and meaning little—but the anxiety of the moment would not let the words come.

"Know what I like best about this photo?" Jim said. "It can't ever be duplicated. The right time of year, the right time of day, to the second. The right weather conditions. You can't plan something like this. You simply have to find yourself there. The right place at the right time." He let his gaze linger on it. Then he added, "The story of my life."

The words hung long between them.

Finally Jim laughed, embarrassed, and the sound of his laughter prompted a mewl of protest from Anubis.

Yet he did not hesitate as he leaned forward to kiss her, a brief brush of lips that quickly gave way, for them both, to a welcoming of passion.

[11]

Have you ever greeted someone at the docks, Mrs. Livingston? You haven't? It's terribly exciting, you know. There's a sense of occasion, of—strangely enough—accomplishment. Something to do with the distance travelled and the time required. Nothing like airports, with their air of imprisonment.

But the atmosphere was dampened somewhat that morning, for it was as we stood there on the docks, watching cranes heave nets of luggage and cargo from the ship, that Cyril told us what had happened in London. About the quiet dinner in the neighbourhood restaurant, the walk back to their flat through the dark, wet streets; the men—three, four, he wasn't sure—materializing out of an alley; the growls of *Black bastard!* and the blows that followed: fists, boots. Celia managed to run for help but by the time she got back with a constable, two minutes, no more than three, the damage had been done. They had broken no bones, but they had smashed the right lens of his glasses. They had damaged the eye, though not irretrievably. Sight would return, but impaired. It could have been worse, Cyril kept repeating, it could have been worse: as if trying to convince himself. But we saw in days to come that the attack had shattered more than his lens; it had shattered his illusions of London, of England and of all that these meant; it had enervated him, and turned him bitter. He still spoke of resuming his studies one day, but it sounded more like a hope than a plan.

Back at the house, my husband and Cyril supervised the hauling of their travel chest up the stairs. It was large, blue metal with leather straps and locks of polished brass, and heavy with clothes, books and knick-knacks—so Celia explained to my mother-in-law, Penny and me, but mostly to me, it seemed, as we sat in the porch waiting for Amina to serve refreshments. They had brought only light clothes, Cyril's lawbooks so he could keep up, and a few things to remind them of England: photographs, prints of the countryside and such.

Presently Amina arrived with a platter of glasses filled with soft drinks and ice. Conversation, of course, had not been easy. Question and answer, everybody terribly polite. And that is probably why I remember the tinkle of the ice in the glasses. It seemed awfully loud in the awkward silence. My mother-in-law motioned Amina towards Celia. Celia sat up, hesitated. And then, with that painful, apologetic, ornately wheedling manner of the British, which they have passed on to you Canadians, she asked if she could possibly, if it wasn't too much trouble, have some tea.

My mother-in-law turned to me and said, "Shakti?" She was not offering me tea, she was ordering me to make it. I was glad to have something to do, but as I stood to go to the kitchen, Celia said, "May I give you a hand?" She didn't wait for an answer.

In the kitchen, I put a pot of water to boil on the gas

range, then measured the tea leaves. Celia looked on without saying anything, but as I was about to pour the leaves into the water, she stopped me and asked if we had a teapot. She explained that she preferred her tea steeped rather than boiled. I fetched the teapot from the cupboard and watched as she prepared her tea. I offered sugar and milk, but she took neither. Not good for the figure, she explained. The figure, Mrs. Livingston! Imagine! This was not something we worried about. I was, I admit, dazzled. And when she said, "Would you join me in a cuppa?" I heard myself saying, "Yes, please. A *cuppa*." The word feeling wonderfully strange on my lips. And to hear my own voice… It sounded wonderfully strange to my ears too. I put sugar and milk into mine after the first sip, though.

Celia and I regularly took tea together after that, sitting in the porch and watching the sea, watching the ships come and go. It was not that I developed a passion for tea. No, rather, I had a passion for the style of the thing: the preparation of the teapot and the cups, the settling into the chairs in the porch at mid-morning. It was new, it was alien, and Celia had made me part of it. We didn't speak much, but we didn't need to. The fellowship we found in each other didn't require words. It was as if each of us was reassured by the mere presence of the other alien in the house.

Penny joined us occasionally but she wasn't much of a tea drinker. She and I still spent our afternoons together while Celia read or napped. As for my mother-in-law, she stayed away for the most part. She never knew what to say to her new daughter-in-law beyond offering sweets and asking after her health.

So you see, my dear Mrs. Livingston, I began drinking tea the way some people begin smoking cigarettes: for the style.

To be able to say to Celia, Feel like a cuppa? Or to myself: I feel like a cuppa. It was like offering myself a little luxury. And I've been offering myself that little luxury ever since.

[1 2]

They leave the city behind, climbing into gentle foothills, the land falling away from the edge of the road now to the sea bluer and more placid from here. In the distance, almost more cleanly etched at the horizon, she sees a cruise ship gleaming white and, far behind it, an oil tanker as low and fat and dark as a slug.

Penny says, "You seem...upset?"

"Why?

"You're not saying much."

"I haven't got anything to say." Yasmin feels herself bridling, as she often does at the suggestion—always vaguely insulting, intimating inadequacy—that she *should* have something to say.

"He was like that too, you know," Penny says. "Always keeping his own counsel."

"Funny, isn't it?" Yasmin blunts, with effort, the edge in her voice. "There was a time when we thought discretion was a good quality. Today it's a sign of emotional repression. I'm not sure that's progress. There's a lot to be said for the unsaid."

Penny considers this for a moment, then says, "You look like him too, you know."

"People always say I look like my mom." She is, once more, vaguely offended.

Penny does not notice, or pays no attention. "I knew them both. You look like him."

Yasmin has never heard this before, and she sits back in the seat wondering what it means, if anything. Wondering why it should disconcert her so.

Penny says, "I not doing too well, am I?"

"Let's just drop it."

"You do like the unsaid, eh? Strange for a journalist."

"I'm not a journalist."

Small houses of greyed wood hug the roadside. An occasional sign advertises Coca-Cola or Pepsi.

"Shakti said—"

"Proud mothers don't always get things right. Journalist is Mom's word for what I do."

In certain lights—harsh light subtly diffused, like the dusk that reigns beneath the anchor desk—her skin assumes hues of grey. She has had moments, waiting for the seconds to tick by, waiting for technicalities to be sorted out, that were not good: hand resting on hand in that false dusk, flesh as if unnourished by blood, tremors known only to herself.

They are not morbid moments, but they are sad ones. Sad for all the *necessary* things left unsaid, all the *necessary* things left undone.

Every life, she has often thought, is incomplete.

Yasmin has a certain reputation as a media personality. She is the regular replacement for the anchor on the local newscasts, but has never been asked to fill in for the national anchor. She has at times been allowed to interview municipal politicians and minor celebrities, but she will never be asked to conduct the year-end interview with the prime minister.

She is instead frequently invited to host public appear-
ances by soap-opera actors at shopping malls. She is not
familiar with these people or with their shows, but she
will sometimes accept. The money is good, her role small
enough that it will do no damage to her serious work; and as
an organizer once made clear, she brings to such occasions
the maturity of her forty-odd years, a glamour that does not
detract from that of the stars, and sufficient legitimacy to
impart a certain newsworthiness. Hers is a familiar face; she
is recognized in the streets and in stores. At the supermarket
she has become known, to her amusement, as the TV lady
who tips the bagboys well. Receptionists and cashiers tend
to be friendly.

The job is not difficult. It entails timing, some simple
acting, basic literacy. She is good at it, is at the age where
experience has honed her abilities, but she's not yet deemed
to be due for "face work." She holds that day off by anticipating the betrayal of the harsh studio lights, by conniving
with June the cosmetician to camouflage the blemishes that
cause anxiety in executive offices.

But Yasmin is lucky. She has been told that her face is
trustworthy, that she projects sincerity. She is good at the
theatre, at the trickery of adapting tone and features from
news story to news story. Good at projecting compassion
one moment, gravity the next, then amusement, disapproval, regret, all muted by an illusory impartiality. Her rule
is simple: I am moved because I am human, but only briefly,
because I am professional. She disarms viewers, Jim says,
offering them the comforts of a benign seduction.

Penny says, "Shakti was proud, you know."

"I know. She had this thing about her dignity."

"No," Penny says, changing gears. "Of you, I mean. She tell me once, Yasmin is not the kind to sit back and do nothing. She going to make her way in this world. She was very proud o' that. I think she was seein' your father in you, and it was a relief to her."

[1 3]

You are perspiring, my dear. Are you hot? It is rather stuffy in here, isn't it. I'll open a window. Or perhaps it's the tea? Just lie back, my dear. Lie back and do nothing.

What? *Like you lazy Caribbean people*! You are teasing me, aren't you? Of course you are, I knew that. Still, my dear, let me set you right on that score. Like everybody else in this world, we had times of lying back and doing nothing—

No, my dear, not under a palm tree, or a coconut tree as we called it. I never was one for lying about watching the waves roll in or building sandcastles. Like cooking—I've never seen the pleasure. The beach, all that fine sand—it got into uncomfortable places, if you see what I mean.

Mine was the minority view, though. The others were more enthusiastic. The men often enjoyed a game of cricket on the beach, or cards and whisky in the porch of the house. As for Celia, she spent hours lying on the sand willing her skin to brownness—a most bizarre ritual that, Mrs. Livingston! Often she would pose for Cyril's camera. She wore a bikini, you see, modest by today's standards but back then, especially in our island, most daring. I have this mental picture, and the actual pictures must exist somewhere, of her on the stump of a coconut tree, sitting back on her folded legs, hands on her hips, thrusting her smile and her breasts towards the camera lens—a kind of Rita Hayworth glamour. She also had a habit of swimming out beyond the breakers. She was proud of her swimming, you see, she had powerful arms.

I will admit that I did rather enjoy the salt water. I enjoyed taking a dip. But I was never one to romanticize. After all, even the sea—that beautiful Caribbean the tourist people would have us revere—even that sea holds its hazards. Sharks, barracuda. Jellyfish floating about with their tentacles doing nasty things to people's skin. And once—once, Mrs. Livingston—I saw what that sea could do to the unwary, or the unlucky. A drowning victim had drifted onto the shore. The body was not—How shall I put this? Not complete. Fish had feasted on him, you see—

My dear, are you in need of something? A cold compress perhaps? You are so wet. Is it the story? I do apologize. I shall spare you the details. It is rather gruesome, I admit.

We were all affected except my husband. He did not hide his fascination. He even crouched down for a closer look. This was the kind of man he was, you see. He could dissimulate when he needed to, but he didn't believe in blinking.

I was chilled to the bone, as they say. Cyril took my arm and said he was going to be sick. We headed back to the house together. My mother-in-law, a woman susceptible to distress, took to her bed. Celia busied herself preparing a pot of tea. She looked whiter than usual, especially in the lips and around the mouth—rather like you now, my dear. She offered some tea to Cyril and me, and we sat together sipping, talking little. And it was the tea that banished the chill from my flesh. Not that it made everything all right, never since then have I been able to eat fish. But it revived my centre, if you know what I mean. It even put some colour back into Celia's cheeks.

I see from your face, my dear, that this is not what you had in mind when you brought up this question of lazing about. But this is what you get for making such cracks. Now then, shall I continue in a more pleasant vein?

On the whole, such long and lazy days of doing nothing as we had took place not at the beach but in the middle of the city, on a hard metal chair in a covered pavilion over-looking the island's premier cricket field.

Yes, my dear, I said cricket...

No, it's not in the least like baseball. Oh, I do get tired of saying that! The similarities are superficial. That's like saying the moon's like the sun because they both shine in the sky. Or a bird's like an airplane because they both fly. You hit a ball with a bat and you score runs. That's about it. Any resemblance to any other sport, living or dead, is purely... ignorant.

Now, where was I? Ah, yes. Long and lazy days watching cricket. Friends and family around. Celia, and some-times Penny. Do you know—following my marriage, it was at cricket that I most saw my family? My parents were modern-minded, but still my marriage meant that I was no longer quite theirs. Not that I had become a stranger. More like a good acquaintance who now belonged to another family. A certain distance grew up between us—a distance that solidified, following the death of my parents. I have not known most of my family for decades.

My father was often there, drinking rum from teacups with his cronies, except when my mother was around. She only came occasionally, and just for the morning session. She didn't care for cricket. I think she came just to bring lunch. She'd arrive with two bags heavy with food. Dhalpuris, chicken and aloo roti—a kind of sandwich, my dear, stuffed with chicken and potatoes—tins of sweets. Funny thing about lunch. Celia and I always took white-bread sandwiches. Egg. Tuna. It would never have occurred to us to ask Amina to pack the food we usually ate at home. As soon as lunch was over, my mother would return to see to her household duties.

The one who was always there, though, was my brother, Sonny. He lives in Belleville now, and has trouble with his memory. Back then, he was quite the dashing figure. Always careful of his clothes, stylish. He dreamed of being an historian, of rescuing the lost stories of our people. And this created a certain bond between him and my husband. My brother wanted to secure the past, and my husband wanted to secure the future. So there was a kind of continuum between them. I'm not sure which of them had the harder time of it.

My brother earned his living as a high school teacher. He thought he could pursue his historical writing on his own, but he learned soon enough that there was no scope for the writing of history in our little society. So he became a reader of it, and fell into what I've always felt was a lifelong confusion. He developed an enduring passion for the Second World War. I cannot say for certain what fired his imagination but I suspect it had something to do with distance and exoticism. I think he came to believe—or perhaps convinced himself—that our history did not matter, that the war was grand and important and easy to lose yourself in.

Today my brother no longer recognizes me but back

then he would sit with Celia and Penny and me and follow the match with greater intensity than the rest of us put together.

My husband? Oh, no, he had no time for attending cricket matches. He was much too busy.

Oh, dear, my throat is going all dry on me. Pehaps, for a bit of a change, a nice glass of iced water?

Are you sure, my dear? Are you sure you haven't—

All right, if you insist. Oh, dear, it's gone cold, I'm afraid. But if you're sure a fresh cuppa will put some colour back into your cheeks, I shall prepare us another pot. Won't be long.

[14]

A little farther on, after a lengthy bend that unscrolls an infinity of sea and sky, the wooden shacks and shops give way to grassy fields and, suddenly, to a modern suburb of recent construction. Each house stands well back from its fence. Each is skirted by generous stretches of land, some with lawns freshly planted, others still chaotic with building equipment and rubble.

Penny says, "All this land use to belong to your grandfather. Use to be a cocoa estate. We had to sell it off over the years. A parcel here, a parcel there. Now one man owns it all, except for the piece we keep. He sells the plots and builds the houses. It worth more now with houses on it than it was ever worth with jus' cocoa trees."

Yasmin notices how she drives: with intensity; fingers fastened around the steering wheel as if fearful it will spin out of control without warning.

Presently they leave the construction behind. The road narrows, vegetation returns to the verge. On one side the land falling off to water; on the other undulating gently upwards in fields that end, farther back, at forest.

After another lengthy bend in the road, Yasmin sees a large two-storey house of concrete and brick, painted green and trimmed in white, sitting midway up the rise in the land. The house commands a view of an extensive lawn, and of the road and the sea and the horizon. To either side of it are trees, behind it the wild vegetation of the fields. The limits of the property are clearly marked by a chain-link fence. A gravel driveway leads from a gate in the fence to the house.

Penny slows the car as they approach the house, turns into the driveway, stops at the gate: it is locked in the middle, heavily chained at both top and base. Yasmin sees that braided through the uppermost squares of both fence and gate are several strands of barbed wire. She sees, too, that the lower floor of the house is without windows, and that its single door sits in the wall with the flush solidity of fortification. A stairway, clinging to the side of the house, leads from the ground to the second floor.

Penny sounds the horn twice and presently a shirtless young man—he is sixteen or seventeen, Yasmin surmises—trots around from behind the house. He hurries down the driveway, his brown skin glistening with perspiration, the muscles of his chest and arms taut and, even from a distance, scrawled with swollen veins. As he undoes the locks and unwinds the chains, Penny says, "That's Ash. He lives with us. His parents are cousins of ours. Distant—but family is family, eh? They take off for South America with a circus six, seven years ago. They wanted to take Ash with them, but I convince them he was too young, so they leave him here with me. Last we hear, about three years ago, they digging for gold in the Amazon."

Yasmin stares at the young man through the windshield. She wonders if this is what amnesia feels like—an unknown face, the knowledge of shared blood—and after a moment says the only words that come to her: "I see."

The gravel crunches lightly under the tires as the car proceeds up the driveway towards a spacious two-car garage beside the house. It is of wood, painted green like the house, but in a state of disrepair, large doors hanging open on broken hinges. One side is taken up with an old American car that sits on blocks, rear lights broken, chrome bumper detached at one end and resting on the ground.

Penny says, "Looks like we interrupted his workout. Weight-liftin'. Mr. America stuff, nuh." She pulls carefully into the garage, crowded with bags and boxes and dismounted bicycles. Puts the car into park, pulls up the hand brake, turns off the ignition and says, "Home."

Yasmin glances at her. Who, she wonders, is Penny talking to?

When they get to the top of the stairs, Yasmin is surprised to hear a voice say, "Hello, hello." It is a man's voice, musical and merry. "Welcome, welcome. I'm Cyril."

Cyril. Her father's younger brother. Yasmin smiles, extends a hand—and sees immediately that her action relieves him of the burden of how to greet her. He is a short man, and short of hair, with the neatness that so often seems innate to the balding. Even his belly, rotund and solid, hangs over the top of his belt with a certain precision, a belly indicative not of gluttony but of a measured satisfaction. The grasp of his hand is warm, and she sees, as he lets his gaze linger on hers, that he has invested her visit with hopes that Penny has not.

Penny says, "Cyril, keep Yasmin company while I help Amie in the kitchen." And turning to Yasmin she adds, "Something cold to drink? Or maybe some tea?"

Yasmin asks for coffee and Penny, after the briefest of pauses, says, "Instant or perked?"

"Perked, please."

Cyril, with some haste, says he too will have coffee.

Penny taps her chest and says his name as if in warning.

Cyril is adamant. "Is a special occasion," he says.

After Penny slides through the lace curtains hanging at the door, Cyril says, "You'd think is *her* heart that block up."

Yasmin chooses to ignore the invitation to inquire about his health problems. Instead she steps closer to the waist-high wall enclosing the porch and gazes out at a small boat cutting slowly through the water towards the horizon.

Cyril shuffles over beside her and she gets a whiff of baby powder. He says, "Your father was a romantic, you know. Ram use to stand here, on the balcony, with his hands just so"—he flattens his palms on the smooth top of the wall—"an' just look out, for hours on end. Dreamin' his big dreams."

And the view from here, Yasmin thinks, is one made for big dreams. It is a view that not only offers the spectacular but, because of the extra elevation of the house, dominates it.

"They say that from here you could o' watch the whole history of the island," Cyril continues. "Five hundred years ago you would o' seen Columbus sail across the bay. Then the Spanish treasure galleons goin' to and from South America. The raiders of one kind or another. French, Dutch, English. The traders. And the slaveships. For a very long time, the slaveships. And when the slavers stopped comin', other ships came, first with the Chinese and when they didn't work out, with our people."

Yasmin thinks: Our people?

[15]

When Yasmin mentioned with calculated nonchalance that she had met a nice man, her mother was not fooled, asking immediately, "Is it serious?"

Yasmin laughed. "You make it sound as if I have a disease, Mom."

"It's not serious, then," her mother said, sounding vaguely disappointed.

"Yes," Yasmin said after a moment, speaking as much to herself as to her mother. "I think it might be."

"Then you must ask him to tea next Sunday," her mother said.

Yasmin told Jim he should bring nothing. He insisted on stopping to buy a bouquet of flowers. She told him to keep it modest. He returned to the car with a cone of lilies several feet tall.

"I don't think she's got a vase that'll hold those," Yasmin said.

"She'll think of something."

"You aren't nervous, are you?"

"I'm meeting your mother," he said. "What d'you think?"

"She's going to love you."

When they entered the apartment, Yasmin saw that

her mother had been to the hairdresser. Her silvered hair, always well-tended, was tied back into its bun with a professional neatness. And she had been to the Indian shops. On the coffee table, several plates displayed the sweets now offered only to guests, her own health dictating abstinence.

"Mom, I'd like you to meet Jim."

They shook hands.

"Mister—?"

"Summerhayes," Jim said, cradling the flowers in his left arm. "But please call me Jim." He offered the flowers to her.

"For me? How kind. Yasmin, would you show Mr. Summerhayes to the living room?"

Yasmin said, "You don't have to be so formal, Mom." But her mother had already taken the flowers into the tiny kitchen.

"Can I give you a hand with those?" Jim called.

"No, thank you, Mr. Summerhayes, I'll manage. They're lovely. It's just that they're so…large."

Jim, feeling slightly swatted, turned to Yasmin for support, but she simply took his arm and led him into the living room. There, she patted his chest like an indulgent parent and turned her attention to the plates of sweets.

Jim, anxious, wandered over to the window. A northerly view: trees, roofs of houses. Directly below, some distance down, the grey stone buildings of educational privilege sitting adamant in the sunlight, girdled by an intimidating moat of lawn and sports fields, a paradigm of the old world transported to the new. In a field to the right, men in white were arrayed around a cricket pitch.

"Mr. Summerhayes," her mother called from the kitchen, "where are your people from?"

"My people?" he said, unsure of what she was asking.

"Yes. Your family."

"Montreal, mostly."

"And before that?"

"England. Wales."

"Your parents?"

"Grandparents."

He waited for further questions, but none came. On the windowsill was a pair of binoculars. He picked them up, glanced over at Yasmin in puzzlement.

"For the cricket," she said.

He trained the binoculars on the field below, adjusting the focus until the players, all black, came into sharp view: the bowler running up to the wicket, the ball leaving his hand, the batsman offering a defensive shot. The colours—white on green, the red ball rolling harmlessly back along the tan pitch—were vibrant through the lenses.

"You know cricket, Mr. Summerhayes?" She had placed the flowers, shorter by a foot, in two brass vases.

"I used to play when I was a boy. My grandfather taught me."

"Silly mid-on, silly mid-off and all of that?"

"I was the wicket-keeper."

"Ah," she said, taking one vase to the coffee table. "The anchor."

"Like the catcher in baseball," Jim said, fetching the other vase from the kitchen.

"Yes. I suppose." She glanced around the apartment. "On the credenza, Mr. Summerhayes, if you don't mind. Gently."

"Are you a baseball fan, too?" Jim eased the vase onto the polished wood, beside the silver-framed graduation photograph of Yasmin.

Her mother sighed, moved over to the window. "The Americans," she said, "have a way of simplifying things. They've changed a game for gentlemen into a pastime for boys. Is it your opinion that baseball, like cricket, shapes character, Mr. Summerhayes?"

"Baseball's more complex than it looks," Jim said. "That's one of its beauties. In fact, I've always thought that cricket was deceptively complex and baseball deceptively simple." He joined her at the window, his gaze following hers down to the figures in white. A batsman was making his way off the field while another strode on to replace him. Two players and an umpire were tending to the broken stumps.

"Does the name Sir Learie Constantine mean anything to you, Mr. Summerhayes? He was a wonderful West Indian cricketer, a man of superb talents. He once ran at full speed to the edge of the field to make a catch. He caught the ball behind his back, with one hand. Behind his back with one hand, Mr. Summerhayes! There was once hope for a people who could produce a man like that."

"I saw Sir Garfield Sobers once," Jim said. "He was pointed out to me in a nightclub in the Barbados—"

"Just 'Barbados,' Mr. Summerhayes. It's a single island."

Jim, Yasmin saw, remained unperturbed. "He seemed quite the local hero," he continued. "Everyone treated him with great deference."

"Not just a *local* hero, Mr. Summerhayes. And perhaps not deference but respect. He remains, I believe, although I may be mistaken, the only man to have hit six sixes off six balls. A wonderful achievement, even though it was only in a county game in England and not a test match. Has anyone ever come close to such a feat in your baseball, Mr. Summerhayes? Six home runs off six pitches?"

Jim smiled. He said, "Sobers played for Nottingham-shire, I believe?"

"Notts? Yes, perhaps. I honestly don't remember."

But Yasmin, nibbling at a piece of *kurma*—fingers of dough fried crunchy and caked in sugar—did not miss the note of surprise in her mother's voice. She had never known her mother to be easily impressed.

"All these men," her mother continued, "titled for their sporting prowess. Bradman. Sir Stanley Matthews, the foot-ball player. They were heroes to us, you know. Our children learnt about them in schoolbooks. Do they still knight sportsmen, Mr. Summerhayes? I'm quite out of touch now, it's been so long."

Jim didn't know. Canadians, no longer permitting the use of foreign honorifics, paid scant attention to news of the freshly anointed.

"Highly unlikely these days, I would think," her mother said. "Sportsmen have become such hooligans. The very idea of sportsmanship has been lost, don't you agree?"

Jim nodded, but Yasmin saw that her mother took little notice.

"My husband didn't like them, you know, men like Constantine and Sobers."

Yasmin's eyes fluttered up from the plates of sweets. She recognized the ever-so-slight shift in her mother's voice, as small talk was left behind.

"He couldn't help admiring their talents but he regret-ted their race. He felt that his people, our people, were hard done by. He felt that the Indian cricketers of the West Indies never got their due. This was how my husband saw things, Mr. Summerhayes. Through a racial prism. He didn't even like the name I chose for our daughter. Yasmin. It's a Muslim name, you see, and we are, traditionally at least, Hindus. But I liked the name. And he never objected to other family members being named Robert or David or Elizabeth. I always felt it held him back, this racial allegiance, although he saw it as inescapable. He was in political life, you see, and circumstances, I suppose…" Her mother's voice trailed off. She raised the binoculars to her eyes. After a moment, "Were you an aggressive batsman, Mr. Summerhayes?"

"Depended on the day," Jim said, his discretion allowing her to set the agenda. "And on the bowler, of course."

Yasmin reached for a nut of *kurma*, crunched it, licked the sugar residue from her fingertips. The light from the window was encroaching on Jim and her mother, the brightness softening their contours, making their edges grow indistinct. Listening to their exchange of unfamiliar jargon, watching them lose their tensions in the light at the window, Yasmin had the sense that she was seeing the convergence of her past and her future, neither whole, each shapeless, both unseizable.

"By the way, Mr. Summerhayes," she heard her mother say slyly, "what in the world were you doing in a nightclub in Barbados?"

Jim was taken aback for a moment. And then, with a smile, he said, "Recovering from the sun."

In the elevator on the way down, Jim said, "I've never seen anyone eat toast with a knife and fork before."

Yasmin thought of her mother's manner of eating the single slice of toast she had permitted herself at tea: the careful slicing of the toast into nine equal squares; the delicate spearing of each piece; its almost thoughtful consumption. "Do you find it weird?" she said.

"Say, eccentric."

"Eccentric…" Yasmin repeated the word to herself, weighing its implications. Her mother had always eaten toast that way, and the habit had never struck Yasmin as extraordinary.

Jim said, "Don't misunderstand me, Yas. I like her—"

"She likes you, too, I can tell."

"It's just that she isn't what I expected."

"You expected a woman in a veil and sari, I suppose. Serving you hand and foot."

He laughed sheepishly. "Hardly."

She took his hand. "Don't underestimate my mom. When I was young she wouldn't let me eat an ice-cream cone in the street. Once she said, 'I approve of masturbation, Yasmin'—Can you imagine?—'but I wouldn't recommend its practice in public either.'"

"She seems very…British," he said.

"Early in his career my father spent time in London, some kind of attaché at the High Commission or whatever it was called back then. He hated it, she loved it. He became an anglophobe, she became an anglophile. She watches *Masterpiece Theatre* religiously."

"That explains the tea," he said. "But why'd she come here after your father died? Why not England?"

"They wouldn't have her. My father's reputation. Guess they didn't appreciate his calling them monsters."

"Did he mean it?"

"I suppose. As much as any politician means anything."

"How old were you? You remember anything about London?"

"Oh, I was born later. From what I gather, my father wasn't in any hurry to have kids. He had too much to do. For his people."

"His people?"

At that moment the elevator doors opened. Yasmin hurried out. By the time they got to the car, she had changed the subject.

[16]

The ground is hard and uneven, less lawn than mere land, cleared of wild grass. The upward grade is subtle, perceived in the distance ahead but only felt more immediately.

Cyril says, "For a long time people aroun' here call me the Manager. People still call me Manager, but is not a title any more. Is just a name." His is a gentle voice, and although he has spoken wistfully, as of something lost, his tone betrays no pain, no plea for consolation.

"What would you like me to call you?" Yasmin says.

He thinks for a moment. "You ask Penny the same question?"

She nods.

"And she say?"

"Penny."

"Well, it'd be nice if you call me uncle, but I guess Cyril is probably the best idea. Or Manager."

"I prefer Cyril."

"Cyril, then." He smiles shyly at her and runs his hand —a small, soft hand—along his bare pate, as if brushing flat his extinct hair. His eyes squint behind the thick lenses of his glasses, the right eyeball dancing briefly off-centre.

Yasmin returns the smile but looks away from the unsettling eyeball: to the back of the house and its large second-floor balcony supported by two concrete pillars; to the roof of galvanized iron red with rust; to the iron pole rusted bronze that rises from one corner of the roof in support of a television antenna. To the land sloping away to the fence—the only thing with the gleam of newness—and beyond it the sudden ending of the land at water.

Yasmin says, "What are you manager of?"

"Was. The estate, when there was one. And Ram's campaigns."

"And now?"

"Oh, I try to keep things together, make sure they don't fall apart too much." He pauses, as if in thought. "Is not too much, really. You play the hand you're dealt. You know."

Yasmin lets her gaze wander across the bay. "It's a lovely view."

"It is?" He laughs quietly, as if in embarrassment. "Guess when you see something every day you stop seeing it for what it is." His gaze follows Yasmin's, and after a moment he says, "Yes, is a lovely view. Shakti always liked it. Is too bad she never see it again. I was in two minds, you know, about you two leaving, back then."

"Mom always said she chose to leave because it would have been dangerous for us to stay."

"Some people thought so."

"You didn't?"

"Was hard to tell. Maybe yes, maybe no. So I opt for prudence, nuh. The Canadians were very accommodating. More than the British. Hardly surprising. Things moved fast."

"I've always wondered why my mom didn't seem to have much in the way of mementoes. Photos, stuff like that."

"I think she jus' took a couple o' little things with her. Couldn' tell you what, though. After all, as you well know, it wasn' suppose to be forever."

"What do you mean?"

"She didn' tell you? You were suppose to stay in Canada for a few months, till things settled down, nuh. Then come back quietly. But when it was time, Shakti said she wasn' ready, she needed a little more time, and a little more time. Always a little more time. And is only now she come back, with you." He glances at her—in disbelief, in discomfort. "She never tell you any o' this?"

Yasmin shakes her head. "Not a word." And the implication of possibility not chosen causes her heart to race in bewilderment.

After a moment, he takes her by the arm, a touch as light as air. "Come, chil'," he says. "Let's go inside. Penny must be ready."

And it is only because of the gentleness of his manner that Yasmin allows herself to be led.

Penny is sitting in the porch when they return. She gestures Yasmin to an easy chair. "You enjoy your little walk?'

"It's a lovely place. So peaceful."

On a round brass table, in the centre, is a silver platter heaped with Indian sweets both familiar and unfamiliar. Yasmin recognizes the *kurma*, the golden *jilebi* —which she has always thought of as honey-drenched pretzels—and the white rectangles of *laddoo*. But she doesn't know the large yellow balls, or the smaller fried ones.

Cyril, lowering himself into another easy chair, says, "She like the view, too."

"Of course she like the view. What it have not to like?"

"I jus' mean—"

Penny turns towards the door. "They're here, Amie," she calls. "You can bring the drinks now."

Presently, the curtains at the door waft open and a short, elderly woman comes out with a platter on which are a coffee mug and two glasses of orange juice. She approaches Yasmin, holds the platter out. Yasmin helps herself to the coffee, whispers her thanks. Amie—in her sixties, and skeletal, with a face so pared it reveals the intimate contours of her skull—keeps her eyes lowered.

Next she serves Penny, who wordlessly takes her orange juice.

When she comes to Cyril, he shakes his head. "Amie," he says, "is coffee I wanted."

"But m'um say—"

"I ain't care what m'um say, I—"

"Thank you, Amie," Penny says firmly.

Amie quickly withdraws into the house.

Cyril says, "Now look here, Penny—"

"Yasmin, dear," Penny says, gesturing at the plate of sweets. "Help yourself."

Cyril's jaws clench, his chest heaves to the rhythm of his breathing now audible. He clenches the glass in his hand until it trembles. But he says nothing.

Yasmin, embarrassed at the spectacle of Cyril's anger so easily routed, looks for a way to busy herself. But what is she to do? She feels inept, graceless. Finally, she reaches for a piece of *kurma* and, nibbling at it, remarks on its freshness. Immediately, she sees Penny's disappointment, realizes she has deprived her of a little victory.

Penny says, "You know kurma?"

At the question, Cyril laughs out loud, and he takes a gulp of juice with a sudden and obvious relish.

Ignoring him, Penny says, "Well, wonders never cease."

Yasmin hears *wandas nevacease*: for a brief moment she is distracted by the distorting effect Penny's accent has on her words.

"I mean, Shakti wasn' really one for cookin'."

"Oh, she didn't make them, she bought them. And all kinds of other stuff, too."

"You eat spicy?"

"Depends on what you mean by spicy."

"You know how your gran'mother use to eat? With her hands, of course, always with her hands—and not because she didn't know how to use knife and fork, min' you. But that was a lady who liked spicy. Always had next to her plate a bunch of what we call bird peppers—small-small and hot-hot—or a pepper as big as your finger—"

"Like a big chili, nuh," Cyril adds.

"And she'd put some food in her mouth and toss in a bird pepper or take a bite out of the big one. I mean, she use to eat peppers the way people eat—" her hands dance in front of her, as if waiting for the simile to alight on her palms "—peanuts."

"Taste the mango chutney," Cyril says, pointing to a bowl sitting beside the fried balls. "Jus' dip a pulowri in."

Yasmin complies. The fried balls—the pulowri—are greasy to the touch, and the chutney, when she tastes it, has less bite than the one her mother used to buy. But she plays along—"Oh, that *is* hot."—for the sake of the family legend.

Penny smiles.

Cyril says, "And that was nothing for Ma. Nothing!" *Nutten'*. "She was one tough old lady."

Penny, seeing Yasmin's greasy fingertips, calls to Amie to bring some napkins.

Cyril, with merriment, suggests a fingerbowl instead.

His comment elicits a laugh from Penny. "Shakti ever tell you the fingerbowl story?"

Yasmin shakes her head, waits for the story.

"When Vern was with the delegation in London—You know he was a member of the team negotiating independence, eh?—the Queen had a big dinner for some Commonwealth bigwig. When the dinner finish, they brought out the fingerbowls and Vern watch in amazement as Mr. Bigwig—who was sittin' right next to the Queen, mind you—pick up his bowl and sip the water. Everybody went quiet-quiet."

The curtains part as Amie—so slight as to be almost insubstantial—returns with paper napkins, and then glides back inside without so much as a whisper.

"And then, to help him out, nuh, Vern pick up his own bowl and take a sip. And right away Her Majesty pick up her bowl and take a sip herself, imagine. Everybody breathe a sigh of relief, everybody take a sip from their fingerbowls, and everything was fine. Vern always say that is the day he learn what a real lady is, because she could o' leave the two o' them hanging there like two fools." Penny sits back straight in her chair, nods primly.

Yasmin, without thinking, says, "I've heard that story before."

"Really."

"Only it wasn't about my father or the Queen of England. It was about some African head of state visiting the Netherlands. And the queen was Juliana. Same fingerbowl, though." Hardly are the words out of her mouth than she realizes they are unwelcome. She forces a laugh, to make light of it. "Do you think maybe royals all over the world retell the same stories about how wonderful they are?"

Penny, back stiffening further, says, "Yes, well...Vern was there, you know. He saw it."

Did he tell you the story himself? Yasmin wants to ask. Did anyone else see it happen? And how do you explain Queen Juliana... But the story, she realizes, is not about the Queen. It is about her father, about solidarity, about subtle shifts in allegiance. The story, true or not, is their offering to her, an offering she has managed to soil. She feels their annoyance, their embarrassment, regrets her own thought-lessness. She realizes too, though, that anything she says to make amends will sound patronizing, so she says nothing.

Cyril sits up in his chair with summoned alacrity. "Tea was Shakti's drink, not so?" he says.

Yasmin, uneasy, nods: she is fearful now of despoiling the sacred.

"Did you know is my Celia that taught her to like tea?"

"No, I didn't." She is neither hungry nor particularly taken with the pulowri, yet she reaches for another: her own offering to Penny.

Cyril says, "Ey, take it easy, girl. Don't eat too much now, it still have lunch to come."

"Lunch," Yasmin says without enthusiasm. She is look-ing forward to returning to the hotel, to sequestering her-self in the silence of the room. "But I wasn't planning—"

Cyril will not hear of it. "Nonsense. Of course you staying for lunch." He turns towards his sister. "Not so, Penny?"

Penny gives a wan smile. "What Manager wants," she says, "Manager does get."

[17]

Tea? Really? But the box says it contains flowers. I enjoy flowers in a garden or a vase, my dear—but in my teacup?

Healthy? Oh, I see. You're still worried about the Moroccan tea and all that sugar, aren't you. Well, I thank you, my dear, for your concern, but it truly isn't necessary...

But listen to me, will you? I must sound terribly ungrateful. Lack of practice, I imagine. So thank you for this rather unusual gift. Drinking flower-tea is not so bizarre, when you think about it. The human palate is a rather flexible organ, after all. Why should we count fish eggs a delicacy but look aghast at those who relish chicken feet? My mother-in-law, you know, had a particular taste for fried goat's blood heavily spiced, accompanied by whole hot peppers.

Tell me, my dear Mrs. Livingston, have you ever seen a battleaxe, at the museum perhaps? A curious implement, don't you think? Honed and hardened, sharp-edged, designed for ease of use yet, if handled carelessly, capable of severing a member of the one wielding it. A kind of forbidding beauty, masculine, if you will. Battleaxe. It was with that term that people referred to my mother-in-law, you know, in whispers only, of course. It was meant to demean, but it was an appropriate term for her, peril and beauty finely balanced.

She was not a tall woman—she was several inches shorter than I, and I, as you yourself have delighted in pointing out, have the physical stature of a turkey in a roomful of ostriches —but she appeared tall because she wore her authority well. She draped herself in it, if you see what I mean. It was part of her finery, like the gold jewellery she wore.

She had the most extraordinary face. Like many women of her generation who grew from childhood poverty to the kind of ease that passed for wealth in those days, she acquired few wrinkles, so that her face reflected a kind of serenity, except when she was angry or upset—and then all you saw were two lines emerging to bracket her lips.

Funny thing—it was delightful watching her eat. She was quite at ease with cutlery, but usually insisted on using her fingers in the traditional Indian manner, gathering the food into a shred of roti...

A kind of bread, my dear...

Like this, you see, with little swirls and circles. She would scoop up a small amount of rice and curried vegetables and eat it with the deliberation of ritual. Then she would select a fresh hot-pepper from a saucer beside her and take a bite out of it—and that, believe you me, was always a remarkable sight. Understand what I'm saying, now. A whiff of these peppers was enough to bring tears to your eyes. A pinch seemed to sear the skin from your tongue. But she ate them as if they were dill pickles. It wasn't so much that she took an evident pleasure in every mouthful. No. It was more that she seemed to take no mouthful for granted. And, you know, she did at times appear to be praying or meditating or, at the very least, lost in deep thought.

She brought this deliberation to her life in general, and that was lost on no one. Her religion—the conversion to Christianity exerted no hold, you see, beyond a social usefulness—left her with no belief in accident. Everything had a reason, an explanation. Nothing ever simply happened. Blame, or perhaps, to be fair, explanation, could always be apportioned—and this gave her great strength. She could rarely be anticipated. I remember my brother-in-law Cyril saying that it was at mealtimes that his mother plotted her life, which prompted my husband to remark that it was at mealtimes that she plotted other people's lives.

I'm not certain that she actually tried to shape other people's lives. I think she worried about her family in her own way, and tried to spare them heartache by perceiving, reflecting, understanding, nudging. I once said this to my husband, and his response was, You didn't grow up with her. Cyril, who never felt he had his mother's support for his law studies in England, believed it was because she didn't want to let him out of her grasp, but I wonder whether there wasn't some other reason, a reason a mother could see, considering how things turned out for him, I mean...

We mothers are rather curious creatures at times, don't you think, Mrs. Livingston? We gauge the risks we would have our children take by the intuitive understanding we have of them—and so we can never fully explain why we advise against a particular action. Here you are weak, we would have to say, or, Your interest in this field is unmatched by your talent—and how wounding that would be, how brutal. So we wound them instead with our silence. Damned if you do, damned if you don't. I have attempted to avoid doing this with Yasmin—not always successfully, I might add—but on the whole I have not withheld my blessing even when I knew that, because of the world or because of her, I would one day have to soothe the hurt. So my mother-in-law was not a neglectful mother—and let me add right here and now that she treated her daughter no differently from Cyril and my husband, although I daresay Penny would probably see things differently. I suppose everyone was battleaxed in his or her own way...

Yes, my dear, that goes for yours truly, too. Now shush! You know me by now. I'll get there yet in my marshalling-yard sort of way.

You see, for my mother-in-law, everything and everyone had its proper place in the world, and she was never quite sure that my place was in marriage to her elder son. Be that as it may, we established from early on a cordial and safely reticent relationship. We said our good-mornings and our thank-yous. I fulfilled my duties, such as they were. Bought the birthday and Christmas gifts. Helped with the deyas at Divali. Spent my meals admiring my mother-in-law's manner, my afternoons talking and reading with Penny or Celia, my evenings with my husband and the rest of the family. All in all a rather leisurely life, come to think of it.

And then one day, for reasons of her own, my mother-in-law decided to change all that.

[18]

Cyril leans forward in his chair, fingers interlacing. "So we hear you're a famous lady up there in Canada."

"That's overstating the case a bit," Yasmin laughs. "I get recognized sometimes, but that's incidental, really. All I do is read well."

"No," Cyril says with dissatisfaction. "What you doin' is important. You helping people find out what happened in their world. You helping them remember—and forgetting is a terrible thing."

"No," Yasmin insists. "All I do is read well."

Her secret for reading the news is simple: She reads not in her own voice but in her mother's. When she mouths the words that roll at steady pace up the teleprompter screen, she hears her mother's tones shaping them, coating them in appropriate drama: tones leavened by instinctive notions of human reaction. Her success is not hers alone.

Occasionally, Yasmin has been asked to conduct an on-air interview, and her mother has always advised her to use moderation with the confrontational ones. "Weave the rope," she once said. "Present them with the noose. You can even help them put it on. But let them tighten it themselves. Let them commit suicide, if you see what I mean—otherwise you'll be seen as an executioner. And Yasmin, dear, very important: remember—yours is not the outrage. Outrage belongs to the viewer."

The technique exasperates Jim. "Why didn't you move in for the kill?" he would ask. "Why didn't you crush him?" Her reply—"Listen to what he says. He hangs himself"—arouses a snort of derision. She has learnt not to allow Jim's reactions to influence her, although she wishes he would take the time to understand the subtleties of her craft: to see how she plays with the lights of her profession.

Cyril sips his juice, sloshes it around, makes a face, swallows.

Penny, reaching for a sweet, says, "Yasmin, Shakti ever tell you about the time Ma throw her out o' the house?"

She has, Yasmin realizes, been forgiven. "No." Her mother's stories were few, and distinctly undramatic. Of Yasmin's grandmother she had said little, had offered an impression of imperious remoteness, which is what Yasmin sees in the face of the young woman in the photograph

Penny has fetched from the living room: a smooth-faced blankness; dark, serious eyes staring into the camera, unexpectant of the life still to be lived.

Penny glances at Cyril, who says, "I remember. But to tell you the truth, Penny, I don't know if I remember the thing itself—or if I just remember the story. I saw bits, I heard bits. I have pictures in my head—"

"Same difference, then."

"No. If I remember, is my memory. If I remember the story, is somebody else memory. I mean, you think you can remember something that never happen to you?"

But Penny shows no interest; such simple nuance, Yasmin sees, can only be exasperating to her essential practicality, or an unwelcome challenge to her version of events.

Penny looks away, her gaze reeling out towards the horizon. "Shakti always thought she was too good for us, you know. Too good for Vernon. It was clear from the beginning—she din't marry him for himself but for his prospects. This thing with Ma, for instance. If Shakti did only do what Ma wanted—"

"Look, Penny, Ma was being unreasonable."

"So why you din't say so at the time?'

Cyril shuffles uneasily.

"You told Celia not to get involved, not so?"

"I told her this had to do with Ma and Shakti."

"Meanin'?"

"Meanin', if it was anybody's place to get involved, it was Ram's."

"He had other things on his mind."

"Other things." Cyril's face brightens slightly. "Fact is, Penny, Ram was scared o' Ma just like everybody else."

"Nobody was ever scared o' Ma, Manager. Only you."

She gets to her feet, the abruptness of the movement bely-ing the calm she maintains in face and voice. "So don't try to blame him for your failure." Announcing she must see to lunch, her back already turned, she leaves the porch.

Cyril retreats for a brief moment into himself. Then he constructs a smile. "Is an old quarrel," he says. "And point-less. But we can' seem to let it go, you know?" He peers at the glass in his hand and with a sudden movement tosses the juice over the porch railing. "I wish we could, sometimes."

[19]

Yes, well. Who would have thought daisies and daffodils would taste so—

Oh, all right. So I'm exaggerating a little. We aren't drinking daisies and daffodils. But still, who would have thought flowers would have such flavour? Thank you, my dear. Such a lovely gift. So...unanticipated.

Now, to get back to my mother-in-law, the truth is, I understood her game from the very beginning. And because I understood it, I knew it had to be played out.

Simply put, before I had moved into her house, my mother-in-law had made all the preparations for the perfect cup of tea. The water was boiled, and kept a-bubbling. The teapot was warmed, and kept warm. The tea leaves were measured and sprinkled into the teapot. Then she bided her time.

When she judged the moment to be right, she filled the teapot with boiling water. The leaves lashed up and about in a tempestuous swirl. The water darkened. Steam rose like spray. Eventually, of course, the leaves would settle back down to where they had begun, at the bottom of the teapot—but only when my mother-in-law ceased stirring things up.

Think of me, my dear, as the tea leaves...

Uhh! Oh, dear me, I've scalded my tongue. You see what thinking of my mother-in-law still does to me? Even though I tried—I still try—to be understanding. Still, down through the years and even today, I have been unable to forgive her for involving Celia in what amounted to our personal affair. In so doing, you see, she changed forever the nature of my friendship with Celia. I do not for a moment believe that was her intention, nor do I believe that once it was done she regretted it even for a moment. Of the two messages she sent, the only one that mattered was the one aimed—and I use the word in its most brutal sense—directly at me.

I remember when she called me—*Beti! Beti!*—because it was so unusual, that she would call me, I mean. It was early morning still, wash day. My husband had just left the house, calling out good morning to Myra the washerwoman. She lived just down the street, in an old wooden house weathered grey and surrounded by an exuberance of banana trees and mango trees and pomerac trees and orange trees and God knows what else. She would come once a week to wash the clothes, handwashing each piece on a scrubbing board at a concrete sink out back and hanging them out to dry on clotheslines. She used to sing quietly to herself as she worked. By the time all the wash was done, around midday, the first batches would be dry. She would have a quick lunch and then begin the ironing. Everything had to be ironed, including bedsheets and pillowcases, and by the time she was done the evening would always be well advanced. She was not a young woman, Myra, perhaps in her late fifties, and by the time she was done she always appeared to me to have aged by a good ten years. She had wrinkles on her face that she hadn't had that morning; and her hands had endured so much—hours of immersion in soapy water; the endless rubbing and scrubbing; hours of gripping the hot and heavy iron—that they appeared mummified.

But I may have been the only one to notice her exhaustion. Or perhaps to the others, none of this was particularly striking. One evening, as we were all sitting in the porch after dinner, ships' lights sailing through the darkness, the men burping from time to time like miniature foghorns, I spoke of Myra's hardships. I was, I admit, rather pleased with myself, touched by my own observation of her suffering. Showing my sympathy for Myra to the family that evening was a way of patting myself on the back. I expected that others would share my news, and that plans would be made to ease her lot. Already I could feel myself growing modest before Myra's teary gratitude. All my talk about the wrinkles and the hands and the sweat I had seen running down her neck, the humming with which she, I imagined, comforted herself, met with silence. I remember the squeak of my husband's rocking chair, Cyril's unembarrassed burp. My mother-in-law sitting there, eyes shut, as impassive as Buddha. And finally Celia soothing the silence I had disturbed with a gentle *Quite so, quite so*.

In bed that night, I returned to the topic. Hardly had I mentioned Myra before my husband said curtly that she was his mother's employee. Thus ended my efforts at social reform.

And probably because Myra was her employee, my mother-in-law chose her as the instrument of her strategy.

I can still hear her voice calling me to the dining room that morning. *Beti! Beti!*...

Beti? It means "daughter" in Hindi, I think. That's what I was always told.

In any case, the maid had already sorted the wash into various piles for Myra. My mother-in-law was standing among them. She pointed to one pile and said, "That's yours." A glance told me the clothes weren't mine but before I could react she explained that she had decided to lighten Myra's workload. From now on I was in charge of washing Cyril and Celia's clothes.

No, my dear, Myra would still do my husband's and mine. That was her little twist, you see. She turned my concern for Myra against me—turned it into a humiliation by making me into my sister-in-law's washerwoman.

I said no, I would not do it, and walked away.

Angry? No, that was not her way. Instead, she turned to steel.

[20]

Penny, slightly mollified, says, "It was that Myra's fault."

Cyril puts his glass on the floor beside him. Yasmin balances her coffee mug on her knees.

"She was always complainin', that woman. The work was always too much, the money was always too little. But Ma—you know what Ma was like—Ma wanted to help her out anyway. She was no spring chicken, Myra. So Ma thought Shakti could give her a hand, make things a little easier. But—no offence, dear—" she places her fingertips on Yasmin's forearm "—but we all know what Shakti was like, she wasn' about to take kindly to helpin' out the washlady. Which is kind o' understandable, you know—but you remember what she go an' do, Manager? You remember? I mean, really! Ma had no choice, ehh? She had to put her out the house."

Cyril nods: he remembers. But his acknowledgment goes no further than this.

Penny reaches for a kurma, pauses, reconsiders.

Cyril, leaning forward, helps himself to several.

Yasmin looks away, to the sky growing painful and the sunlit sea. Hold on, she wants to say, that's my mother you're talking about. But she does not know the facts, cannot know the facts. So she chooses to remain silent.

Penny says, "Fact is, if it hadn't been for that Myra—"

[2 1]

The next day the clothes were still there, in the living room. And the day after that, and after that, the pile growing larger with each passing day as more of Cyril and Celia's clothes were added.

She had chosen her moment well, my dear. My husband was away at the time, visiting political people in Trinidad and Guyana. I remember thinking, If only he were here...

Celia avoided me. Cyril told me later that she had gone to our mother-in-law and offered to do the clothes herself. My mother-in-law had said that if she and Cyril were running low on clothes, they should buy themselves some more. She even offered to pay for them—and Celia knew then to keep her distance. I remember those days as among the loneliest of my life, my world somehow reduced to that ever-growing pile of clothes.

And then one afternoon, I went to my bedroom for a nap and found the mountain of clothes sitting in the middle of my bed. Something within me went berserk. I stormed out of the bedroom and straight to my mother-in-law, who was sitting in the porch. I wanted to shout and scream at her, but the words would not come, no matter how hard I tried. It was as if my rage had eaten up speech. So I—and I am not proud of this, my dear—I spat at her. One gob, then another, and a third. Each finding a spot on her face.

At that point I stopped, horrified at the level to which she had reduced me. My vision went blurry with tears. I felt her brush past me, heard the door slam shut. I heard the key rasp in the lock.

Some time later, the maid brought me a message. I would not be allowed back inside until I had complied.

I spent the night in the porch. The maid brought me something to eat, Celia brought me a pillow and blanket. Neither stayed for very long. That night a thunderstorm hit —as if nature itself were conspiring with my mother-in-law.

Nothing awakens the irrational more than a wet night spent alone in a darkness relieved only by lightning creeping closer. I became convinced that my mother-in-law was orchestrating every gust of wind, every roll of thunder.

The following morning, despite having been soaked through, despite sleeplessness, I set to work rubbing and scrubbing and wringing out the clothes. My hands quickly grew tired and sore, but I kept on, the labour fuelled by thoughts of revenge: Wait till he gets back, I kept thinking. Just wait till Ram gets back, he'll be so furious...

But of course, when he got back, he wasn't. He was restless and distracted. There were other things on his mind, grander things. He was not indifferent, mind you, just incapable of... Moreover, of course, it was probably too late. We had already settled into a workable peace. I told him what had happened, and although his lack of indignation disappointed me at the time, later on I was relieved that he had simply let things be. I came to realize that fresh confrontation would have changed nothing. Change would have meant finding our own house to live in, and that was unthinkable, nothing short of a complete breaking up of the family.

So this is what our confrontation was about, Mrs. Livingston. Power and control, respect and distance, about the apportioning of loyalties: the son's to the mother, the husband's to the wife, the wife's to the husband, the daughter-in-law's to the mother-in-law. She won, of course, but only because I knew I could not.

Celia? No, she was never subject to such treatment. Many would suggest it was because she was white, and therefore intimidating to my mother-in-law, or perhaps even an object of secret veneration. I believe the explanation was simpler. I believe that, because she was not of our world, Celia in an important way did not count. My mother-in-law expected nothing from her, whereas from me she expected everything. I was the one who had to acknowledge her power, just as she had had to acknowledge the power of her own mother-in-law and so on—

Cruel? No. In fact, it is likely that, as a young bride, she had had to endure beatings—yes, physical beatings—from her own mother-in-law. Yet she never laid a finger on me. But cruelty is relative, isn't it? After all, she did alter for good my friendship with Celia. Even though I had to wash Celia and Cyril's clothes only a few more times—the point made, my mother-in-law lost interest—the fact was that neither Celia nor I could ever see each other in the same way. I had been obliged—and you must forgive me for being graphic, Mrs. Livingston—to scrub Celia's panties clean of her menstrual discharge. After that we were never able to look each other in the eye with the same frankness as before. You see what I mean...

And what about you, Mrs. Livingston? How did you and your...

Oh, but I keep forgetting. Your husband's mother died before you were married, didn't she. Hmmm... How thoughtful of her...

[2 2]

Penny, seeking to change the subject, says, "Vernon use to think his cheeks were too fat, remember that, Cyril? When he was small, people was always pinching them. And as soon as somebody pointed a camera at him he use to suck them in, to give them a more sculptured look, he use to say."

Cyril says, "And his hair was very, very fine. Not like yours, Yasmin. Use to fall all over the place. So he started using Brylcreem. And not just a little bit either—"

Penny laughs. "He use to buy these big jars, scoop it out

with two fingers and rub it in his hair. We had to tell him not to use so much, his hair was sticking flat-flat to his skull."

"He wasn't able to see himself, you know," Cyril says. "We had to make sure he dressed properly. And as for the hair—"

"One day somebody tell him the way his hair was falling down across his fore'd—"

Her pronunciation briefly startles Yasmin: It is so peculiar—and so familiar.

"—he was looking like Hitler. Is then he got the Brylcreem and began slickin' it back—and end up looking like a match-head instead."

"And for a short time he had a Stalin moustache. Is Shakti who shave that one off herself, not so, Penny?"

"Yeah, right. Remember she said she wasn't goin' to sleep next to no man who had a scrub-brush under his nose?"

Hairstyles, moustaches: glimpses of vanity. Yasmin finds herself smiling.

And yet the feeling persists: that she is among strangers with whom conversation does not come easily; with whom, in the uneasy game of picking from the storehouse of memory, the rules are not defined, the traps not marked. She feels herself defenceless before words whose weight she cannot gauge.

[23]

As she and her mother settled in at the table —unfolding the silk napkins, running approving eyes over the candle-lit dazzle of Jim's place settings—Yasmin examined their reflection in the picture window. Against the darkness broken only by swatches of light from the expressway, she saw a painting as it might have been done by Titian or Rembrandt, a wealth of detail subtly focused by a rare sharpness of line, colours rich but unspectacular in the warm light. She saw serenity luminous against an intimation of mystery.

Jim, having removed the soup bowls, returned from the kitchen and placed a plate before her mother. New potatoes with sprigs of parsley, asparagus lightly bathed in a raspberry coulis, petals of red pepper sautéed in olive oil and garlic, all arranged around a complete lobster steaming from the pot.

Her mother said, "Oh, my, what a beautiful plate, Mr. Summerhayes. You have a talent and I, happily, have no cholesterol problem."

Jim, grinning, winked at Yasmin and lit the burners under their butter bowls. "Yasmin told me you like seafood."

"Crustaceans, yes, but as for fish, only the fresh-water variety."

It had been his idea to invite her mother to dinner. He'd said, "Maybe if she gets to know me better she'll stop calling me Mr. Summerhayes." The notion, as endearing as it was silly, had prompted gentle laughter from Yasmin.

"Does it come naturally?" her mother continued, "or is it the result of your gourmet-cooking course? Don't look so surprised, of course she's told me."

"The course, I'm afraid. Plus eating in too many fancy restaurants."

Her mother raised her wine glass, only half filled at her insistence. "To your talents, Mr. Summerhayes."

The shells had been deftly cracked, the meat sliding out with ease.

Her mother said, "Don't you have a cat, Mr. Summerhayes?"

"Yes, Anubis. She tends to get a little nervous when there are visitors. I slipped a little something into her food. She'll sleep the night away."

They ate in silence for some minutes. When Yasmin complimented Jim on the choice of wine, he said, "It's one of the wines we tried at the wine-tasting, don't you remember?"

"You kidding?" she said with a laugh.

"Tell me, Mr. Summerhayes—"

"Jim."

"—did you boil them alive, the lobsters?"

He nodded. "It's the best way to bring out all the flavour."

"And did they scream?"

"Pardon?"

"Did they cry out for mercy to Jehovah or Allah or some such fellow?"

Jim was amused. "To the best of my knowledge, no. But they'd have been underwater, you see."

"Yes, indeed," her mother said thoughtfully. "I suppose the plea would have been gurgled, wouldn't it."

In the laughter that followed, Yasmin thought she had rarely seen her mother so relaxed. And in the vigour with which Jim broke open a claw, she saw the easing of his tension.

Her mother, dipping her fork into the butter, said, "Would you describe yourself as a religious man, Mr. Summerhayes?"

Yasmin glanced at Jim to gauge his reaction to the question, but his face betrayed nothing.

"Religious? No. I've always felt that was one more thing Marx didn't get right. Religion isn't an opiate. It's a placebo for a chronic condition. Like alcohol or tobacco or recreational drugs. One of the ways we survive our fragile moments.

We need it, don't we? This belief in something larger than ourselves, and eternal."

Her mother thought about this for a moment. Then she said, "Very eloquently put, Mr. Summerhayes, but you haven't really answered my question, have you. What about you? What do you believe in?"

"I believe in light," Jim said without hesitation.

"Light." Her mother repeated the word, considering it, turning it over in her mind. "What in the world do you mean?"

"I mean that, for me, light is a living entity that, in turn, creates life. I enjoy playing with light, discovering its properties, looking for ways to mould it. We would die without light."

"The same is true of air, isn't it?"

"Yes, but imagine finding yourself alive in a world of perpetual darkness. Hardly seems worth it."

"The blind might not agree with you."

"Ah, but the blind can feel the light. Its warmth, even its movement. They know it's there. Even the blind need light."

Yasmin said, "He dreams of designing buildings just for the light, Mom, buildings that would appear to be practically made of light."

Her mother, nodding slowly to herself, turned the concept over in her mind. "Good," she declared finally. "The human belief in divinity—it's a weakness, you know. Merely a way of diminishing the sheer wonder of humanity."

Later, after dessert, when her mother had gone off to "use the facilities," Jim said to Yasmin, "You don't expect that kind of thinking from someone her age. That kind of courage. Or is it arrogance?"

"I'll tell you something about my mother," Yasmin said.

"If she finds out that anything exists beyond this life, any- thing at all, she'll be utterly unconsolable. That's been her strength. There's nothing after this life, so she takes what this one brings her and does her best with it."

Jim shared the last of the wine between himself and Yasmin. "I envy her," he said.

[2 4]

Through double doors thrown open to the balcony, Yasmin confronts a midday sunshine sufficiently harsh to wash sharpness of line and colour from the distant greenery; sufficiently harsh to suggest that it alone has seared the concrete balcony floor clean of the green paint that still fringes the edges like dried spills.

She has been offered the chair at the head of the table, facing those open doors. On her left sits Penny, on her right Cyril. And across from her, at the far end of the lengthy table, sits Ash: silhouetted against the light of the doors, shadowed and silent, only peripherally part of the passing of dishes, the clink of cutlery, the serving of food.

Amie's rubber slippers flop softly on the polished wooden floors as she brings another dish to the table.

Cyril says, "Amie, I have to say—you gone and outdone yourself for our guest."

Yasmin, taking the cue, says, "Thank you so much, Amie. All this food. Must've taken you all morning."

Amie pauses, gazes at her with disquieted eyes.

Oh, God, Yasmin thinks, she's not accustomed to being thanked.

Then Amie gives an almost imperceptible nod, turns away and vanishes into the kitchen.

Cyril says, "So, tell us about this husband of yours. Jimsummerhayes, notso?"

"Jim," Yasmin says, as Amie returns with glasses of ice water. "Well, what can I tell you…"

"Everything," Cyril says mischievously.

She picks up her knife and her fork, steeples them over her plate, tines to knife tip, her hands resting still on the table. Jim: she rapidly sifts and edits memory, wondering where she should start, deciding what she should and should not say. Wondering what her mother has already said.

Amie puts a glass of water beside her plate and as she takes her hand away, her fingers lightly brush the back of Yasmin's hand.

Yasmin is startled: not by the touch itself but by its energy. An energy that is frank and straightforward and pulsing with calculation. Startled—but she contains herself. "Jim," she says finally, "used to be passionate about photography."

Cyril says, "Ahhh."

And as she speaks of Jim's photography, as she attempts, to their polite puzzlement, to explain his obsession with light, other images come to her of an evening when a placid obscurity began to sparkle.

[25]

He told her that he had not been feeling well the evening they met, that he had almost gone straight home from the office instead of to the wine bar.

So why hadn't he?

She looked away through the picture window at the dusk, at the light that evoked for her the scents of fresh-cut grass and earth. The sky, farther up, thickening into night. She looked for stars. There were no stars. But the apartment was high enough that there was no earth either.

He followed her gaze, as if searching the sky for the answer.

Luck, he said finally, with a little smile.

From his table, he had noticed her come in with Charlotte, had seen in her face her wish to leave. Why hadn't she?

Luck, she said. Charlotte. Her persistence was my luck.

She ran a finger down his chest, along the hairless path to his navel, the hair thick and neat to either side, as if combed. Had he intended to call Charlotte, too?

No. Why?

So why had he asked for her number?

Politeness. And besides: "I don't like being too obvious."

"Most men can't help that. Being too obvious." But she was flattered.

"I'm not most men."

"They all say that."

"Would you be here now if I were?"

A dangerous question, she thought, too much so to offer him the comfort of an answer.

He said, "Actually, it was your hands that first attracted me. They were…" Again he searched the sky, and after a moment said, "They move like butterfly wings."

There's something untrustworty about that simile, Yasmin thought.

Night thickened quickly outside the window, its approach as inexorable as a total eclipse of the moon.

"And you?" he said.

"Me?" Then she saw it, a pulse of white light strength-ening by the second. The evening star. How many times had she heard her mother, finger pointing upwards, say: *Always been there, always will be there.* Once she had asked, Why not the sun? Why not the moon? And her mother had said, But they're so obvious, so certain, you can never be quite sure with the evening star.

Finally, Yasmin said, "It was a ribbon. A red and yellow ribbon swirling above you."

He looked quizzically at her.

She saw that her answer made no sense to him. And she saw, too, that he was prepared to accept it without question, this answer that revealed nothing. She took his hand, pressed it to her cheek, smelled the drying musk of her excitement on his fingers.

She had the knowledge now: of his hands, of his flesh. She knew him to be a man of sensitivities and of passion sav-agely edged. This knowledge was, she knew, the stirring of an entire world within her.

[2 6]

Cyril says, "You have a picture of him?"

Yasmin shakes her head.

"Not even in your wallet?"

"No room," Yasmin says. "Technology. Too many pieces of plastic." But the joke is not taken up, is greeted with hes-itant nods.

Penny says, "You like the food? It different, eh? From the Indian food up in Canada?"

"Delicious." Yasmin resumes chewing.

"This food we eating," Cyril says, "is not really Indian food. Is *West-Indian* Indian food. So far from India, the people couldn' always get the same spices, they had to make do. Is history, is change, this food."

Across the table, Ash, who till now has concentrated silently on his food, lets his cutlery clatter onto his plate. With only partial vision because of the dazzle behind him, Yasmin sees his young face sculpted tight by slivers of light, and she wonders what it is that has prompted his anger.

"Careful, Manager," Ash says. "You comin' close to sayin' we not really Indian."

"I'm talking about the food. Racially, yes—"

"So what else matter?"

"Everything?"

Ash's eyes glitter at her. "And what about you?" he says. "You and this photographer husband of yours—"

"He's an architect."

"Whatever. You have chil'ren?"

"Ash," Penny says, her eyes staring him into silence. Then, unexpectedly, she places her hand on Yasmin's. "Sorry, dear, he don't—"

"It's all right." She takes a sip of water. "We had a daughter, Ash. She died."

"Recently?"

He is unperturbed. And although she doesn't know whether his equanimity arises from coldheartedness or youthful curiosity, she finds it refreshing: no one ever asks about her dead child; it is as if she never lived.

"About eight years ago. She'd have been just a little younger than you now."

"And you ain't have any more?"

"All right, Ash, that's enough," Penny says. "Can we talk about something more pleasant, please."

Without missing a beat, Ash says, "So you're a journalist." His tone is one of challenge.

She doesn't bother to explain that she's a news anchor. "You don't like journalists," she says instead.

"Not particularly."

"Well, that's all right," she says, smiling. "Neither do I. Particularly."

[27]

Her mother never failed to pass along comments from Mrs. Livingston and the other neighbours. Yasmin was good yesterday. She reads the news so well. That was a lovely dress she was wearing. Green's her colour. Or red. Or black. Tell her to smile more. Tell her to smile less.

Their view of her was somehow proprietorial, as if in knowing her mother they all had a stake in what they saw as her success. She could hear pride and anxiety in her mother's voice, and for this reason kept her own dissatisfactions to herself.

She used to believe that the dissemination of news was an honourable undertaking in a world that made sense. The packaging of detail, the wrapping in context, the attempt to suggest design: it was a way of making the world safe while contemplating its horrors. Like a roller-coaster ride:

hanging out over the edge of extinction, surging at the sky and flirting with the earth, tossed for a thrill secure in the knowledge that, ultimately, the danger was an illusion.

And yet she came over time to view the world as capricious. Accidental violence and terror were indiscriminate. And although political terror chose carefully where and when to strike, and even telephoned warnings, the obstinacy of flying metal made a farce of its scruples.

The damage, which she viewed at an intimate remove, engendered a gentle insecurity, hardly more virulent than distaste: a hunger for friends, family, home. She acquired the knowledge that certain parts of the world—often lands of great beauty crackling with tensions explicit but unknowable—were best avoided.

Only later did she see as a turning point the day a magazine asked her to travel to Sri Lanka, to experience its sectarian brutalities and report back on them. She knew nothing of the place save from news reports of the civil war. She had no special expertise. Her sole qualifications were her race and—in one of those twists that convince editors of their own cleverness—possibly her gender. Charlotte was aghast at her refusal of the assignment—it was a chance to work "in the field"; the magazine was of a stature that made reputations—but Yasmin was not hungry enough to offer her flesh to the capriciousness of terrorism, nor desperate enough to accept gain from suspect editorial views. She suggested Charlotte for the assignment. She never heard back from the magazine.

And so when the opportunity was offered, she opted for the chair, the teleprompter, the certainties of local celebrity.

The newscast was devoted in the main to local cautionary tales—fires and accidents, rapes, murders and robberies

—stories, she often thought, that offered viewers the relief of having themselves survived another day unscathed. She could take little comfort from Charlotte's admonition that she stop looking for significance in everything. As a story producer, Charlotte saw her job as simply telling the tale well, with brevity and accuracy. Yasmin's job in introducing the stories, she said, was to seduce viewers into watching—which had once prompted Jim to comment: "So you're like her pimp."

Rare was the broadcast that did not end with a light-hearted moment. Only a tragedy of profound emotional dimension could exert sufficient solemnity beyond its two or three minutes to merit a sober ending. The laugh she was required to muster for the end of every show provided Yasmin with her greatest challenge. Often the best she could manage was a wry smile, leaving it to the jocularities of the weatherman and the sportscaster to provide the guffaws. Leave 'em laughing, so they'll be back tomorrow for more tastefully leavened tragedy.

When the all-clear was called and the lights snapped off; when the laughter died at the cut to commercial, she would remove her earphone, gather up her script and—feeling a little saddened, a little untrue to herself—go to remove her make-up. The task absorbed her enough that she could distance the thought that despite the sincerity that ruled in the newsroom, despite the intense labour of getting the story and making the deadline, it was not news of the world they offered but simple sketches of it. Notes. Momentary shivers.

The adrenalin rush and the tension that braided her insides while she was on camera would be hours dissipating. But by the time she said goodnight and walked to her car, her longing for complexity would have been put away until tomorrow.

[28]

Cyril says, "Ram always had lots o' journalist friends. They were useful—and not too choosy about the facts in those days, either."

"So what change since?" Ash interjects.

Cyril ignores him. "I mean, we had some fellas—you hand them a story line, anything you want to make up, and by the next morning they have the full story written up as if they gone out and spent the whole night investigating. They quotin' people left, right and centre. They see this, they see that. And the only time they leave their typewriter is to get a drink or go to the bathroom, you know." He cocks an eye at Yasmin, and quickly his expression changes from mischievousness to concern. "You all right?" he says.

Yasmin puts down her knife and fork. She is uncomfortably hot. Perspiration trickles down behind her ear, between her breasts. "Yes, I think so. Just need some fresh air."

Penny says, "Ash, put on the fan."

Ash goes over to large floor fan standing in a corner. Its blades whine into a blur, stir heated air at Yasmin.

Penny offers her water glass. "Have a sip," she says. "It'll cool you down."

But the water too is warm, and thick on the tongue. Yasmin's stomach grows heavy.

Ash says, "Imagine grandpa used to cut sugarcane in this heat? The years makin' us softer and softer."

Cyril says, "I'd like to see you in the middle o' winter, mister. With icicles hangin' off every danglin' part."

Penny leans in close to Yasmin. "You want to take a little lie-down?"

"Yes, thank you," Yasmin says, pushing back her chair.

Already she can feel the darkness of a deep fatigue crowding her, blossoming in a silence so inert that Penny, Cyril and Ash hardly seem real.

[29]

You baffle me sometimes, my dear. Are you saying that the numerous Sunday afternoons we have spent watching from my apartment window, you have understood nothing of what you were seeing?

Baseball? Oh no, my dear, that comparison of baseball to cricket is far too simplistic. It's a bad habit, you know. I had to break my son-in-law of it. Cricket is a highly complex game in a way that baseball is not. One might as well compare plum puddings to hot dogs.

But why in the world would you want me to explain cricket to you?

Oh, you do, do you? A better understanding of *me*? A curious notion. But then, come to think of it, I've always suspected that this country's outlandish love of hockey reveals a sinister side hidden beneath our placidity...

Well, since you insist. To begin with, there are eleven men per team and two umpires, and when the game belonged to gentlemen everyone dressed in white. Even rolling up the sleeves was frowned upon. From what I see, international teams now dress in the most outlandish of colours, greens and yellows—

But that was not a problem. You knew who your players were, you see. One didn't need team colours or numbers. In any case, while one team fields, the other bats two at a time, a batsman at either end of the pitch, which is that strip of denuded ground you've seen from the window of my apartment. The object is to defend your wicket—three sticks called stumps, on top of which are balanced two smaller sticks called bails—and to score runs by hitting the ball in such a way that the batsmen have the time to exchange ends. Runs are also scored by hitting the ball along the grass past the fielders so that it rolls beyond the boundary of the field—that counts for four runs—or by hitting what in baseball would be a home run, for six runs. And the batsmen go on hitting the ball and making their runs, all of which are added to the total—

Are you following this, my dear? You look somewhat—

Yes, there are various ways to strike out, only we don't use that word. A batsman gets out by failing to hit the ball and allowing it to break his stumps. By hitting it into the air and having it caught by a fielder. By using his pads to prevent a ball that would have hit the stumps from doing so—that's an illegal move called an l.b.w, for leg-before-wicket. Or by failing to reach the opposing wicket before a fielder breaks the stumps. When a batsman is out, the umpire signals by raising a finger at him—

No, not the middle, dear. The index.

So the basic principle, you see, is quite simple. The bowler bowls the ball, the batsman hits it and, if he has the time, exhanges ends of the pitch with the other batsman by running—

No, the other batsman does not hit the ball. He just runs until it is his turn to face—

I-do-not-know-why. The game calls for two batsmen at a time, do you understand? That's the way it is.

And this—the batting and the scoring and the getting

out—goes on until until ten of the eleven batsmen are out. It's really quite simple, you see—

Unfair? What do you mean unfair? To the *eleventh* batsman? My dear, all I can say is, life is unfair, and so, despite all its rules, is cricket… My, my, what a curious thought—

Yes, there are equivalents, I imagine. Baseball's fast ball becomes fast-bowling, curve balls and the like become slow-bowling, following the same principle of making the ball move in unexpected ways. Then there are variations such as googlies and yorkers. And of course, it has its dangers. The ball is very hard, you see, and should it hit a batsman in that most tender of spots—Shall we just say, dear, that I suspect many a future family has been prematurely aborted on the playing fields of England…

Naughty of me? My dear, I have witnessed the contortions of players hit in the roots of the family tree. It is not a pretty sight, I assure you.

Yes, it is a complicated game, highly structured, with complex rules and arcane terminology. And yes, I agree, it is a game best understood by those who grew up with it. But insular?

I see what you mean. A world unto itself, in a way that baseball or hockey is not. I will not argue the point. But you think this tells you something about *me*?

Rules? Rules are boundaries. They shape games and life.

Yes, my dear, my husband did indeed have a powerful personality and it would have been easy to be swallowed up. But, you know, at a reception one evening in London, I was introduced to a man as the wife of Vernon Ramessar. The fellow said, "I am not interested in the-wife-of," and walked away. Rude, yes—and I was deeply offended. Until I realized that I myself wasn't interested in the-wife-of. I don't know who the man was, but I've always been grateful to him for that.

[30]

Waiters came and went in the manner of visitant shades, movements governed by a discretion that subdued their presence in the muted light. In a far corner, a middle-aged couple—she in shimmering evening gown, he in black tie—shared a bottle of champagne, their table sufficiently distant that their conversation, animated and happy, came to Yasmin as a pleasant murmur.

Jim held his wine glass up to a wall lamp, twirled it slowly, watched the light leap and shimmy from crenellated crystal to ruby wine and back again.

"Sometimes I dream of orchestrating the stars."

The glass cool and smooth at her lips: she let a little wine flow into her mouth, felt its liveliness on her tongue.

In a voice softened by wonder, he said, "See how the light moves on the glass? How it surges around the rim, down the stem? See how it shatters and yet remains whole?"

Yasmin watched his fingers caress the glass stem: as if they were seeking to engage the fleeting intimacy of the light.

"Imagine, Yas! A building with that kind of life in it! Light so integral, so innate, that it can't be separated from the ceiling and the walls. Light that practically inhabits its structure…"

"A pregnancy of light."

"Exactly."

Their salads arrived.

Jim's voice lost its wonder. "We should have had oysters."

"You feeling weak?"

"Some oysters contain pearls."

"Not in restaurants, they don't."

He fished suspiciously around his plate, fork poking at the shredded lettuce, diced red pepper, slivers of kiwi and artichoke heart.

"See any pearls?"

"Just looking."

She smiled at his earnestness, at the deliberation with which he explored the salad.

He said, "There's a tribe in Borneo or somewhere that believes you can see your future in your food. You try to spot shapes, they're supposed to mean something."

"What do you see?"

He poked around more, forking lettuce aside. "Only greenery. And too much dressing." He gestured helplessly with his fork. "You?"

She shook her head. "I don't even bother with the fortune cookies in Chinese restaurants." She picked up her fork. "Do those Borneo tribesmen ever see lottery numbers in their pots?"

"I don't think they have lotteries in Borneo. They've been spared that scam, at least."

Yasmin turned the salad over with her fork. "I see—well, maybe that's a car there. A big car. Or, hell, maybe it's just a piece of artichoke. And there, that's a—" Her fork fished through lettuce, eased aside a disc of kiwi. And then the tines rose from the bottom of the bowl, and she saw on them a ring of gold, olive oil gistening on its diamond cluster. She held it suspended between them, uncomprehending. Let it slide from the fork onto her linen napkin. Watched the oil flare into the cloth.

Then she saw Jim's face, more serious than she had ever seen it.

"Hold it up to the light, Yas. Watch it sparkle."

A mingling of scents in a phosphorescent darkness. Salts, musk: the essential variables.

His heart throbs at her cheek, his fingertips reading, fearful, from her pulse.

Her tongue circles his nipple, heartbeat reverberating into her, through her: a wave of echoes given substance.

Her senses—taste, smell—snake down, across his slow undulation, a crackling expansion of flesh and bone, racing blood. His navel, moist and salty, a nest of startling sensitivities. And lower still, to his erection nodding warm at her cheek.

Her lips brush silk, sighs—his, hers—echoing around her skull as her mouth closes around the rhythms of his passion made flesh.

Stillness. His fingers running through her hair.

And then, limbs in pantomime, rearranging themselves. He hovers above her like a man momentarily bewildered before a feast.

He lowers his face to her back, tongue meandering down her spine, sketching pathways of passion with a rugged reverence.

Querying, cherishing, stirring storms in every pore.

Her body seems no longer her own, captured now by him as his has been by her. Teeth nibble at her skin, warm breath billowing onto her greatest privacy, tongue reaching out and under to her own passion made flesh, liquefying.

A long night skating along a Saturnian ring of ever-flaring intensity: as if this energy could know neither limit nor diminishment.

A night as long as a harbinger of forever, exploring the codes and places of intimacy until exhaustion claims them in the febrile light of dawn.

[31]

A light the yellow of old daffodils seeps through her eyelids, flickers uncertain across her sight.

She wades through senses unanchored in the larger darkness. Odours unfamiliar: dust not her own, a moistness of musty earth.

When the light grows steady, she lets her eyes open to a prickle of alarm.

"M'um send me, miss. The ele'tricity gone. She din' want you to wakin' up in the dark."

"Amie."

In her hand is a candle planted crooked in a brass candlestick.

Yasmin sits up in the bed. "How long have I been asleep?"

"A long time, miss. Is evenin' a'ready."

She tries to read her watch, but the light is insufficient.

"You feelin' like drinkin' something? Tea maybe?"

"Tea. Yes, that sounds good."

Amie places the candle on a dresser, turns to go.

"But Amie, the hydro's gone, how are you going to boil the water?"

"Gas stove, miss. We use to this."

Yasmin leans back on the headboard of the bed, draws her knees up. How long, she wonders uneasily, was Amie there before she woke up—just standing there watching her sleep?

[32]

Charlotte glanced at the receipt, smiled at Yasmin, folded it into her purse. Then she slipped a large tip under the ashtray and waved at the waiters standing in a white-shirted, black bow-tied frieze at the bar.

Outside, the street slumbered through a mid-afternoon lull. Perhaps it was the sunshine thickened in the muggy air, or perhaps the third glass of wine the waiter, appreciative of Charlotte's flirtations, had offered free of charge: to Yasmin, even the streetcars rumbled by on velvet.

Charlotte said, "I've been meaning to ask you—you notice how Jim walks?"

"You mean the forty-five-degree-angle feet?"

"Exactly. As if he's trying to walk off to the left and right at the same time."

"I know."

"And?"

Yasmin shrugged. Jim's feet, the manner in which they fell, were to her his engaging flaw, suggesting to Yasmin aspects of his past and his personality that would always be unknowable.

Charlotte, forehead furrowed above her sunglasses, gave

her a glance of exaggerated concern. "So, Yas. You're really going to do this, eh? Join in holy matrimony? Tie the knot?"

Yasmin eased her gaze away: to tables of knitted hats, jewellery of stone and plastic, suns and stars tie-dyed onto T-shirts: the leisurely aspirations of sidewalk commerce. She made Charlotte wait for her response—herself waiting for Charlotte's response to her silence, for the expected quip that this time was so slow in coming.

Finally Charlotte said, "Guess we won't be closing any more bars."

"Guess not," Yasmin shrugged.

"So why, Yas? Why are you marrying him?"

"I love him, Charlotte."

"Yas, those feet…"

"Exactly. Those feet. And those hands, and those arms that seem to gather me up. And these dreams he has of playing with light, of all things. He's like a kid who wants to make whole worlds out of play dough. I've never met anyone like him, Charlotte, yet I feel I've known him all my life." Yasmin paused, breathless before the mystery.

Charlotte said, "Should I warn Jim?"

"About?"

"You and men. And that little fridge you've got somewhere around your left ventricle that switches on when they start not measuring up."

"Aren't you laying it on a little thick?"

"Am I?"

"I expect a lot. So what? Besides, Jim's up to it."

"What makes you so sure?"

"I just am."

"It's not the first time I've heard that."

"That's why I know I'm right this time."

Charlotte took her arm, faced her squarely. "All right, Yas, I'm with you. Just promise me—keep an eye on the little fridge, okay?"

Yasmin pressed a finger to her nose. "Click," she said.

Charlotte, smiling thinly, gave a sad little twist of her head. A minute later, she said plaintively: "Who's going to play with me now?"

Irritated by the question, Yasmin said, "Charlotte, that tip—it was too much."

Charlotte paused, jabbed her sunglasses higher onto her nose. "You've never been very good at being single."

Yasmin stopped, turned to face her. In a voice composed enough to ease the hurt, she said, "You're right."

[33]

Had Charlotte served her this cake...

But, then, Charlotte would never have dared.

Had her mother served her the cake, a reaction of theatrical horror would have been acceptable.

But unfamiliarity, she thinks, imposes obligation: her mother's view now become her own.

Under Amie's unsettling gaze, she forks a notch of the cake—yellow fringed in pink—into her mouth. Her tongue goes limp at its dissolution into oil and sugar and a desiccated mealiness. She follows quickly, too quickly, perhaps, with a sip of the tea.

Amie says, "It good, eh, miss?"

"Yes," Yasmin replies. "It is." She keeps to herself that

she is speaking of the tea and not of the cake. She resists the temptation to ask who is responsible.

"Is Mr. Cyril who make it," Amie volunteers. "Don't forget to tell him, okay? He tryin' hard."

Yasmin smiles. "D'you think we should be encouraging him, Amie?"

Amie purses her lips, shakes her head slowly, like a mother too tickled to be disapproving of her child's mis-chievousness. "Mr. Cyril that way, miss. He like doin' things with his hands, nuh. He always out in the backyard diggin' and hoein', tryin' to grow cabbage and lettuce and tomato. Now he spendin' time in the kitchen. But you know—"

The lights flash back on, and in the sudden illumination Amie falls silent. She retreats visibly into herself, her hand reaching back, as if in blind search of the open door. She tells Yasmin that Mr. Cyril says he will drive her back to the hotel when she is ready. She leaves the room without a further word.

On the dresser, the candle continues burning a steady flame.

[34]

Even though sunlight flooded the apart-ment, Jim insisted on lighting candles. Then he signalled for the music, and the opening notes banished the rumble of conversation.

To marry to the sounds of Vivaldi's *Four Seasons* was his decision—more befitting the occasion, they had both thought, than Charlotte's suggestion of the *1812 Overture*.

The judge who would marry them, an old friend of Jim's family, stood beaming before the picture window, aware, Yasmin thought, of his dramatic effect against the sunlit greenery of the valley. As they waited for the sedative to take effect on Anubis, Yasmin saw a small red car emerge from behind the judge's left shoulder as if fleeing the folds of black silk; saw it scamper along the Parkway and vanish once more behind the trees. And in a moment of lightheadedness, she wished herself in that car, the music electrifying, Charlotte at the wheel, riding the knife-edge of abandon.

Presently Anubis's mewling quieted down, the scratching at the door stopped, and the judge, voice weaving above Vivaldi, indulged in memories of Jim—"a young man of promise and drive, potential and ambition"—and of his friendship with Jim's parents, "with us in mind and spirit if not in person."

Jim tightened his fingers around Yasmin's, a moist and yearning clasp. His parents had welcomed the news, his mother quickly hatching plans on the telephone for a wedding in Montreal: the guest list to be drawn up, the caterers to be hired, the church to be booked.

A week later she had called back to express concern over the cultural differences between her son and his fiancée.

Jim said: What cultural differences?

You know, she replied. Stop being obtuse. And besides, think of the children, *half-breeds*—Jim was staggered by the word—society would never accept them.

Jim said: Mother… And then he used the word *racist*. Yasmin watched him hang up on his mother's indignation, her hands reaching for the pieces as he crumbled.

"…a sensitive boy who knew his own mind. I remember one day…"

He mailed his parents an invitation anyway. The judge, attempting to mediate, assured Jim they would attend. A week before the ceremony, his father telephoned to say his mother was not well. Nothing serious, he said, but the trip would be too much for her. They both sent their best wishes. No, his mother could not come to the phone, she was taking a nap. And, by the way, the gift was in the mail.

This notion of cultural differences: Jim, unnerved, wondered about Yasmin's mother. He suggested that Yasmin see her, alone. He felt her mother to be what he termed spiritual —delicately so—not in terms of religion but of traditions. He was uncertain, though, how thoroughly she separated the two; was uncertain how she imagined her daughter's wedding.

Her mother heard her out in silence. Religious belief, she said finally, had been granted to neither of them. Religious theatre unsupported by belief left them both cold. Ritual for the sake of ritual became a parody of itself.

Her mother said, "My brother's daughter, your cousin Indrani whom you once met in Belleville—yes, I know you don't remember her, you were young, there's no reason you should—your cousin Indrani took the unusual step of converting to Roman Catholicism in order to marry the man she loved. Religion today, my dearest, is mostly an inconvenience. Choose your own theatre, my dear Yasmin. I'll be happy to buy a ticket."

The judge cleared his throat. "In my work I see many things that cause me to despair. But today, as I stand here..."

Yasmin wondered what Charlotte, standing close behind her, was thinking. Told of the plans, she had not hidden her disapproval; had said, "Yas, I know it's a life sentence—

but a judge? Are you serious?" She had not, however, been long in admitting that she was disappointed only because she herself, when her own special day came, wanted it to be grand and impressive; she wanted to feel herself breathless in the midst of pageantry.

Suddenly the judge's eyes moistened. He fell silent, leaving the air to Vivaldi. And Yasmin understood with disbelief that his own words—whatever they were—had moved him to speechlessness. And then the sound of sniffling told her, to her greater disbelief, that his words had moved Charlotte, too.

Yasmin wondered what she had missed. A glance at Jim offered no clue. His gaze was lost in the distance, somewhere in the rolling greenery, somewhere—perhaps—in Montreal.

A hand touched her shoulder and her mother whispered, "Never mind, dear. Greeting-card sentiment. Good show, though."

The ceremony moved briskly after that. She was asked for and gave her assent. Jim was asked and gave his. They exchanged rings, a matched pair. At their kiss, their guests— her mother, Charlotte, Mrs. Livingston, Garth, colleagues from the station and the architecture firm—came alive, as if taking a collective breath of relief. They were shepherded to the dining table, where many pairs of eyes peered over their shoulders as they committed themselves to what Gorgeous Garth, with less than impeccable timing, had earlier referred to as "the sinkhole of modern optimism".

A champagne cork popped to scattered applause. Her mother offered a prim kiss. Charlotte passed her a flute of champagne and a heavy silver knife gaily beribboned. Somewhere, Yasmin knew, there was a cake.

[35]

It was very delicate, much more so than these cups you and I use, Mrs. Livingstone. So delicate in fact that the sun seemed to suffuse the white porcelain, turning it luminous. There were circles and squares, and symbols of various kinds drawn on it, and a seven-pointed star radiating out from the centre and up the sides. A very pretty cup, but clearly one not made for drinking from. It was ceremonial, you see, in the manner of the chalice you Roman Catholics use for blood-drinking—

Do you think so? Disrespectful? But my dear, you are the ones who have chosen to sanctify the grotesque. And let me say I do not enjoy your tone of condescension: of course I know what symbolism and ritual are all about. But, you see, what I truly object to is that these people, with their rugged grasp of metaphor, have chosen to look down on others for doing in reality what they do symbolically—and I fail to see how the symbolic consecration of the act is in any way superior to its enactment. For we are talking in the end about the same spirit, aren't we, the same idea: Is the priest who imbibes Christ's spirit through drinking his symbolic blood and eating his metaphoric flesh any different from the Aztec warrior who imbibed the strength of Cortes's men by making a meal of their arms and legs?

You don't. Well. Yes—but is it that you don't see it, or that you won't see it, Mrs. Livingston? Is it your inability or your refusal? My, my, we don't like the question, do we. Careful, my dear: Clench your jaws any harder and your dentures will shatter.

In any case, be that as it may—it's all beside the track, isn't it? The drinking of the tea, like the drinking of the wine or the symbolic cannibalism, was not the point. The point was the meaning that flowed from them, and I suppose that Victorian tasseomancer's cup held special significance for Celia, since it had come to her from her brother. She brought it back from her only trip to England, where she had gone to see her parents after her brother lost his life in a motorcycle accident.

When she returned to us, I asked after her parents. She said they were bearing up. Then I asked if she had been able to comfort them: what had they done together? Were they religious people? No, she said, they were not religious beyond the conventions, so they had all sat together. For two months. And when my curiosity prompted me to prompt her with a single "And?" she said that was it really, just a lot of sitting together. There was not much to say. I understood then that she was of a family, perhaps of a country, that knew no gnashing of teeth, no tearing of hair: that viewed grief as an internal matter. And this was astonishing to me.

That cup, once her brother's and in some way consecrated by his death, became her tea-leaf reading cup. And, intrigued by the cup, my husband for the first time allowed his leaves to be read. I remember his amusement when she saw his leaves shape themselves into a torch. It was one of the shapes they were considering for the symbol of his political party, you see, although Celia and I didn't know it at the time. He insisted that she do the leaves a second time, and again she saw the torch.

I have always felt that Celia confirmed my husband's belief in his destiny, and for that I have always harboured a certain resentment towards her. But then, I suppose we all look to apportion blame to others, don't we, Mrs. Livingston? Everybody has a little role to play when things don't go right. Even innocent Celia, who found comfort and a little specialness by seeing visions in her dead brother's cup.

[36]

Cyril says, "If we live long enough, almost everyt'ing'll betray us."

Penny sucks at her teeth in impatience. "Oh, hush up, Manager, you does get so depressing when you go all philosophical."

"I just not afraid to say what you always thinking, Miss Rise-an'-Shine. I mean, take a look." His gaze invites Yasmin, too, to follow the chop of his hand down from the dimly lit porch to the front yard: to an impermeable darkness rent only by the headlight beams of the two vehicles waiting below. "You remember all those quiet nights? The stars, the insects chirping, a cool evening drive into town to have a coconut or a ice cream cone at the botanical gardens? Jus' jump in the car and take off?"

Penny shakes her head. "Nostalgia, Manager, jus' nostalgia."

"Yes, perhaps. But you know where nostalgia come from? Is when the present don't live up to the promises of the past. When you can't even do today what you used to do yesterday. When you can't even jus' jump in the car—" again his hand chops towards the great darkness "—and take a little run into town."

Yasmin, uncomprehending, asks if there is a problem. "I could take a taxi back to the hotel," she says.

Cyril snickers, and as he does so, Ash, down below, steps into the car lights and calls up.

Penny says, "All-you better get going. Ash starting to get a little impatient."

Yasmin, uncertain still, hesitates. Cyril takes her by the arm and, escorting her down the stairs, explains that nightfall brings to the island a chaining of gates and a locking of doors and travel in convoy through the brooding anarchy of its darkened streets.

[37]

Jim remembered at the last moment that in Montreal he was not allowed to turn right on a red light. Pressing on the brake, he said, "It was a fine life, you know. Growing up here. Very different from the rest of the country. And we knew it, too. We were *the* big city."

She heard in his voice the regret of arrogance lost— an arrogance that would emerge nostalgic and self-pitying were Jim like those other home-grown refugees who hungered for past glories and the flavour of foods left behind.

But they were no longer in the city. A brief stretch of highway had brought them from the downtown hotel to the suburb where he had grown up. He had given her a brief tour: the park slightly sinister with gatherings of young males; the cinemas burned out and boarded up; the Métro station beside the expansive grounds of a private girls' school. Now as they drove along the main street, he saw only changes: the tavern, once hermetically male, now a bistro; new restaurants of varying ethnicity; a scattering of specialty shops.

Just past an Ethiopian restaurant, Jim turned right onto a street tunnelled through twilight beneath a canopy of braided branches. Houses—dark-red brick, shadowed balconies—huddled together in close discretion.

Yasmin said, "Do you think they'll be unhappy we're staying in a hotel?"

"And not with them, you mean? Not likely. They like their privacy. Besides, there really isn't room. My old bedroom's still there, but it was hardly big enough for me when I was growing up."

"You don't have to make excuses for them, Jim."

"They'll be civilized," he said, drawing the car to the side of the road and stopping. "They are always...exquisitely polite."

In Jim's snapshots, his mother appeared larger than the woman who opened the door. Or perhaps, Yasmin thought, she had just been expecting someone larger than life—larger than the woman who, even though expecting them, peered out with timid eyes and a smile brittle with dentures.

Jim said, "Mom," as if identifying himself.

"Jimmy," she replied, as if in delayed recognition. Eyelids fluttering, she offered her cheek.

Jim appeared to blow on it. "Mom, this is Yasmin."

"Why, yes!" his mother exclaimed, turning to Yasmin as if surprised by her presence.

Yasmin remembered to smile when Mrs. Summerhayes' eyes—pale grey and disconcerted—met hers. "Mrs. Summerhayes," she said, extending her hand.

Mrs. Summerhayes' fingers lightly brushed hers. Then, with an almost comic awkwardness, she led the way into the house.

Yasmin hesitated, stepped forward only when she felt Jim's palm press at her lower back—in encouragement, but with insistence, too.

The foyer was small, crowded with a coat rack and an umbrella stand, a telephone table at which she could picture Mrs. Summerhayes standing during the inconsequential conversations she had had with Jim over the eight months since their marriage. To the left, a carpeted stairway led to the second floor. On the right, through a wide doorway, a living room of composed sobriety: a red-brick fireplace swept clean of ash; armchairs and sofa upholstered in the same soft grey; table lamps shaded blue; a mahogany coffee table sitting on a square of cement-grey carpeting. What brightness came in through the small cut-glass windows was readily absorbed, making it a room—a house, she sensed—without light.

"These are for you," Yasmin said, holding out a cone of flowers to Mrs. Summerhayes. "Jim said you like tiger lilies."

"Why, thank you," she said, flustered. "You really shouldn't have." She put the bouquet into the crook of her arm. "Jimmy, why don't you show Yasmin the garden? Your father's out there. I'll find a vase for these." Then she bustled up the stairs.

Jim led Yasmin farther into the house, down a narrow corridor, through the kitchen—loose planks creaking beneath dulled linoleum, a tiny window sheathed in lace, the stove and refrigerator incongruous with newness—and out the back door to a small porch overlooking the garden: a minuscule square of lawn enclosed by a wooden fence and plunged in shadow by the neighbour's leafy maple.

Jim's father was crouched at a flower bed that ran the length of the far fence. The bed was bare, his father absorbed in turning over the loose, dark soil with a garden-ing trowel.

Jim took Yasmin's hand—his palm moist and nervous—and quietly called to his father.

Mr. Summerhayes looked up without looking back, held up the trowel in greeting. "Jimmy," he said. "Do architects know anything about soil? All the hydrangeas turned brown and died."

"Sorry, Dad. The only things I know how to grow in soil are buildings."

"I've mixed in fertilizer, a bag of bone-meal. Nothing seems to help. I'd almost say there's some kind of poison in the soil."

Jim led Yasmin down the steps to the middle of the lawn. "Dad," he said, "this is Yasmin."

Mr. Summerhayes looked around, his squint accentuat-ing the wrinkles that radiated from his eyes down his cheeks. "Hello," he said. "Do *you* know anything about soil?" His hair was shock white, his eyebrows unblemished black.

"Not a thing, I'm afraid."

"Oh well." He laid the trowel on the grass and slowly got to his feet. Dusting his hands, he stepped towards Yasmin. "How do you do," he said.

"A pleasure to meet you."

Turning to Jim, he said, "Where's your mother?"

"Upstairs getting a vase for some flowers we—"

"Tiger lilies?"

"Yes."

"Jimmy, the vases are in the kitchen cupboard. She went upstairs to take her sinus medication. She reacts."

"Since when?"

"She always has."

"Why didn't she ever tell me? I thought they were her favourites."

"No, they're what you've always given her. She just never had the heart to tell you."

Jim sniffled unhappily and shook his head.

His father patted him on the shoulder. "Never mind, my boy." Then, turning to Yasmin, he said, "Well, shall we go inside and have a chat? Young lady, what can I get you? Tea? Coffee? A bit of sherry, perhaps?"

[38]

Cyril drives at careful and deliberate speed through the quiet night. His eyes flit constantly around, searching less in the flow of the headlights than into the darkness that resists their reach. Ash, driving an old truck, follows them with the imminence of a shadow.

Yasmin, held by the revealed details of a landscape no longer seen, feels sequestered by the darkness. And the knowledge that both Cyril and Ash are armed—a machete at Cyril's feet, an unspecified weapon on Ash's passenger seat—is itself somehow suffocating.

Cyril drives in a silence Yasmin does not feel free to disturb, but as they leave the coast road behind and enter the town he relaxes sufficiently that his breathing eases into inaudibility. Yasmin understands then that his tension is unsummoned, that he is not merely being dramatic.

Slowing his speed, he gives a burst of nervous laughter. "I suppose Penny right, you know. Nostalgia. Maybe is ol' age. But these days is as if everything bothering me." Another burst of nervous laughter. "I guess I becoming a crotchety ol' man."

Yasmin, with a sudden desire to comfort him, says, "Looks like you've got a lot to be crotchety about, though."

"Yeah, but—"

He slows, but does not stop, at an intersection.

"—I can hardly even watch cricket any more." For the first time during the drive, he lets his eyes flicker from the road to her. "You know cricket?"

"Kind of. Mom used to watch it from her apartment. I know the basic rules."

"From her apartment? Where'd she live—in a stadium?"

Yasmin explains about her mother's Sunday afternoons, about the binoculars and the view from the window.

"And these cricketers," he says. "Did they wear whites?'

"Always."

"Always," he mumbles, and for a moment appears to reflect on the word. Then he says, "Strange, eh, how some customs survive better in exile. These days, cricket become big business. TV and everything. Now the players wearing colours. Green, yellow. Shows up better on TV, nuh. Some o' them makin' millions."

The regret in his voice prompts Yasmin to ask whether this is not a good thing, but her question goes unheeded.

He says, "You know, my bes' memories of Shakti is at cricket. Her and Celia—Celia was my wife, nuh—drinking tea and eating sandwiches and watching the match day after day."

He slows, but does not stop, at a red light. "Some laws jus' too dangerous to obey," he explains. "You don't want to stop in the nighttime if you can help it."

Assuring himself with a glance in the rearview mirror that Ash is still behind, he says, "Celia use to try to predict the cricket results from tea leaves. She had more than a passing interest in tasseomancy. Shakti never tell you about that?"

"Mom," Yasmin says evenly, "never told me much about anyone."

[39]

No, no, Mrs. Livingston. In your left hand. Now, swirl the cup slowly. Clockwise, please. With gentleness. Once, twice, three times. There we are. The idea, you see, is to allow the leaves to settle into the pattern they wish. Now tip it into the saucer and pass it to me. There now, gently does it.

It was like a parlour game she played, you see, my friend Celia. When the cricket was slow or the afternoon long. She'd read up on it, knew what many of the symbols meant. An anchor meant success, a cat's head peace and contentment—but if she saw a complete cat poised for battle, well, then, it was a sign of conflict. You can imagine what a horseshoe or a clover leaf meant, or a dagger for that matter. The most disappointing was when she discerned letters. Those were taken to be the initials of someone you should pay attention to, but for good or ill she could not say. I cannot begin to explain the contortions we would go to, Mrs. Livingston, to apply initials to people we knew. But there are thousands of symbols and signs and what-have-you, so that offered her a kind of freedom, you see. It's the fun of tasseomancy. It's a game of imagination from beginning to end.

But sometimes... No, I'm afraid I'm not seeing... Maybe if I turned it this way. It depends on the light, too, you see. Celia always sought indirect light. Too much brightness and too much darkness tend to obscure the patterns, for the symbols are as much a question of shape as of shadow. Let's see now. Perhaps if you tilted the lamp shade a bit, do be a dear. This way—no, no, that's too much. Back a touch, that's it, yes, that's better.

Truth to tell, Celia never had anything of great interest to say. I don't know whether my leaves were uninteresting or whether she simply wasn't very good at it—rather like myself, might I add. She attempted to be encouraging, I suppose.

But there was this one day, when we were at the cricket. India or Pakistan must have been visiting, for I remember only dark-skinned men at play. It was early afternoon, the players had just taken the field after lunch and play was still sluggish in the afternoon heat. Celia took my saucer as I have just taken yours, bent over it and peered with her habitual concentration at the array of wet leaves.

I remember looking up from the field of play, above the bleachers on the far side, to the heat haze that dulled the colours of the hills beyond. For some reason, a comment my husband had made the night before about the weather we were having came to me. Hot and muggy weather, the sun like open flame on the skin. He'd called it heart-attack weather, and my brother-in-law, Cyril, had responded that, with the multitude of fires that were breaking out almost uncontrollably all over the island, and with the drought we were experiencing, heart-attacks seemed the least of our worries. It was then that I heard Celia say, "Oh, my."

I turned to her as she pronounced her reading unsuccessful and poured my leaves back into the cup. Just at that
moment, one of my husband's political men appeared. Celia
saw him scanning the crowd and pointed him out to me. I
waved to catch his attention.

He ran up and came along the row to me. He was hurried, rough, he trod on toes. I was about to pull him up for
his lack of consideration when he said "Miss Shakti—" and
a terrible look came over his face.

No, Mrs. Livingston. Not my husband, and not a heart
attack—though this is what I, too, thought.

No. This is how I learnt that my parents had both per-
ished in a fire. A cooking accident. My mother...

And when my father tried to save her he too... In that
weather the flames were voracious.

My husband was at a poliical meeting, forging alliances.
A delicate moment for him, so he sent his man with the news.
You know, I don't remember leaving the cricket grounds
and, indeed, Celia told me later that my husband's man had
had to pick me up insensible halfway to his car. She also told
me that in my leaves she had seen with a clarity that startled
her—that "Oh, my"—a perfect, dense circle. As if the
leaves, she said, had woven themselves into a black sun.

[40]

Stores shuttered and barred: rows of dark
iron vertical and horizontal, crossed into Xs, bound into dia-
monds, mannequins' stares gazing unreciprocated through
protected glass.

They turn a corner. Tree trunks and greenery flitter through the headlights. And then, not far ahead, the flashing blues and reds of emergency: police cars, ambulances.

Cyril says, "But what *junjhut* is this." He pulls quickly to the side, Ash immediately behind, his lights filling their car.

They sit in silence for a moment, trying to read the pantomime in the coloured lights. But movement is minimal, and half hidden by vehicles.

A rear door opens and Ash slips into the car. He says, "Is right in front o' the hotel."

Cyril says, "You have another news flash for us? We have eyes, you know."

His tone tells Yasmin that he is unnerved. She places her hand on his, to calm him. He takes a deep breath, crosses his palms on the steering wheel in a gesture of indecision.

[4 1]

The tiger lilies sat in a simple vase on the coffee table, an embarrassment on display, a rebuke that would not go away. Jim, eyeing them unhappily, mumbled, "What was the fucking point anyway?"

Yasmin caressed his arm, but he would not be consoled.

When his mother brought in a bowl of potato chips, Jim said, "Mom, maybe we should put the flowers somewhere else?"

"But why, dear?" she said, taken aback. "They're beautiful."

Quickly, Yasmin said, "It's Jim, Mrs. Summerhayes. He reacts."

"Oh, does he? But Jimmy, why didn't you tell me?

I'll… Why don't we put them in the dining room. Yes, the dining room."

Jim sat there on the sofa beside Yasmin, and said nothing; merely watched with an ironic detachment Yasmin found painful and unattractive as his mother scooped up the vase and bustled off with it.

Jim said, "Don't try mediating, Yas. See? Even there she couldn't tell me she's allergic."

"Has she always scurried around like that, or is it me?"

"Mom's always been a scurrier. That's how she's always operated. At the supermarket, in church, preparing dinner."

"I wish you'd told me that before."

"Why? What difference does it make?"

"Me. You and me. Our wedding. Scurriers don't like surprises. I must have been a big one, bigger than she could ever have imagined."

"That's no excuse—"

"No, but at least I'd have—"

"Here we go then," Mr. Summerhayes called as he came in holding two glasses of sherry. He had washed, changed his shirt. "One for you and one for you. I'll be back with mine in just a minute."

"At least," Yasmin said quickly, "I wouldn't have got the idea she was just simple and hateful."

"But she was—then, on the phone."

"Nobody's just one moment, Jim."

"But I've had a whole lifetime of her moments. And I don't think I'm any further along than you are."

Only Mr. Summerhayes, ensconced in the embrace of his armchair, retained the comfort and presence of mind to give flow to the conversation.

He talked about his efforts to master the flowerbed, about the labour of digging, about the stones and shards of glass he had sifted out, and the nutrients he had kneaded in. He had been to the university library, had consulted periodicals, and had learned to marvel at how much could be done with so little. He had made several trips to the botanical gardens, had consulted a gardener at the local nursery. He had done everything right, and had been careful not to allow his desire to exceed his grasp. Hence the decision to begin with the simplicity of hydrangeas, six full-grown, healthy plants purchased at the nursery.

"But they failed to thrive," he said, draining the last of the sherry from his glass. "So they had to go." He sighed, turned the glass around in his palm. "However, it's a recent enthusiasm that's proving to be—how shall I put it?—a recalcitrant mistress."

At the metaphor—pronounced with careful relish—Yasmin saw his Mrs. Summerhayes' eyes flutter, saw her fight a sip of tea past tightened jaws.

"Ah, well," he continued. "I shall push on and—who knows?—one day she may see fit to surrender her virtue."

Mrs. Summerhayes placed her teacup on the coffee table with studied deliberation. She got to her feet. "If you will excuse me, I must see to supper."

Mr. Summerhayes said, "But isn't supper seeing to itself, my dear? Sizzling nicely away in the oven?"

Jim said, "Spoken like a man who knows nothing about cooking."

Mr. Summerhayes cocked an eyebrow at him. "Taking her side, are you, Jimmy? And you know about cooking, do you?"

"I certainly know more than you do."

Mr. Summerhayes snorted in amusement. "Not much of an achievement, if you ask me."

"Did I?"

"Jimmy," Mrs. Summerhayes interjected, "why don't you show—Yasmin?—your old bedroom."

Yasmin took Jim's hand. "Yes, I'd love to see it."

As they headed up the stairs, she wondered about the intonation with which Mrs. Summerhayes had said her name: as if her tongue had had to work its way around the vowels.

As if she had pronounced it for the very first time.

[42]

As they walk towards the lights, Yasmin notices her companions' growing reluctance; senses the vertigo of living in a country where the law and the lawless are equally feared.

Ash whispers, "This ain't Canada, you know, Miss Journalist. You can't just go up to a policeman and start askin' questions. You ain't got no first amendment rights here, you know."

"You're mixing up your countries," Yasmin replies over her shoulder. "We haven't got a first amendment in Canada either."

It is alone that she approaches a policeman; alone that she explains the situation. She gives him her passport, shows him her room key; knows that she is—for Cyril and Ash watching her watching him take her passport to a figure flagrant with authority through wearing casual civilian dress—now part of the pantomime. But even here, on its periphery yet close enough to feel the heat from the idling engines, the scene remains indecipherable.

She senses Cyril and Ash's approach; and to Cyril's "Well?" can only shrug.

Presently, the policeman returns. Giving back her passport, he tells her that the hotel will be closed for some time; that she can retrieve her things—no need to check out, no need to pay. He steps aside to let her through, but his palm flutters up in restraint when Cyril and Ash attempt to follow. "You stayin' in the hotel too?"

"No, no," Cyril says. "We just going to give the lady a hand."

"No can do. You wait here."

Ash says, "We jus' goin' to give the lady a han' with her luggage, man."

Yasmin says, "It's just one suitcase. I can handle it." To end the discussion she turns and follows another booted policeman up the stairs of the hotel, knowing as she strides along behind him that she is, for Cyril and Ash, once more merging with the pantomime.

Yet, even from within, the pantomime retains its enigmatic movement: life slowed to a flipping of frames. Mystery in shards, riddles partially posed.

[43]

Even with the light on, it was a room constructed in strokes of darkness: shadows on white.

"Did you bring a lot of girls up here?"

Small, too, startlingly so, smaller even than the captain's

cabin on the World War II Corvette she had visited in Halifax harbour. The ceiling low, the walls monkishly bare. A small table stood in front of the window; a narrow bed occupied one corner.

"You kidding? Mom was always home. Didn't stop me from dreaming, though." He appeared awkward in its confines, his limbs too long, his energies suddenly rattled and bottled up.

"So this is a virgin room?" she teased.

"In a manner of speaking. As far as I'm concerned."

She shut the door, the brass latch clicking with reassuring authority. "So what did you dream about?"

"You know," he said, fingers interlocking below his belt. "The usual schoolboy fantasies."

"I've never been a schoolboy."

He laughed. "Schoolgirls."

"Was this your bed?"

"Yes. But the table wasn't here. I did my homework at the dining table."

She sat on the bare mattress, her palm testing its firmness. "Where'd they get this? An army-surplus sale?"

"Comfort wasn't a consideration." He sat beside her, his fist thumping twice on the mattress, as if to pound it soft. "I once helped my dad put a sheet of plywood between their mattress and the box-spring. Good for the back, he said."

"Doesn't sound as if you had much fun in this room." But she liked the glimpse of the young man he had been: all that fervour contained.

"Oh… I don't know. I used to smuggle in a *Playboy* or two once in a while."

"So, those fantasies of yours—not just schoogirls, huh?"

He smiled. "You know—one thing leads to another."

"I know." She ran her fingers down his neck, the skin soft and dry, and along the hard ridge of his collarbone. "Want to lie back? See if I can guess some of those schoolboy fantasies?"

"Yas, you're crazy. My parents—"

She pressed at his chest, and he offered no resistance. As he let himself fall back onto the bed, she pressed in close, molding her body to his through the encumbrance of clothing. Her lips to his ear, she whispered, "Call it revenge. Close your eyes and let me make it sweet for you."

But she saw, looking at him, a face etched by an infectious anxiety. Sweet revenge was beyond him.

[44]

Over the shoulder of her escort she sees sombre-faced men and the backs of heads, white helmets and khaki caps. They move together through a sense of crowding, of stifling intimacy: everyone wants to have a look.

She sees fatigue, hears sighs and murmurs.

And as her escort precedes her into the elevator, the corner of her eye pivots backwards: catches a tablecloth fluttering down onto the security guard, prostrate, inert, skull-less.

Above the hum of the elevator she says to the policeman that last night there was a young woman on duty at the desk. Jennifer.

The policeman bites at his lower lip. He confesses to knowing little more than she does. They robbed the safe, he says, and he's heard that the desk-clerk—yes, a young woman, maybe this Jennifer, maybe not—was taken. At gunpoint.

A hostage?

Probably not, ma'am. More likely part o' the booty.

Yasmin shudders. What d'you mean—part of the booty?

The policeman gestures at the opening door. Your floor, ma'am, he says. Hurry it up, please.

[45]

Time softened, minutes as if dissolving at the edges.

The sense of timelessness was seductive. But this time-lessness—issued of lives lived for decades in the same manner, in the same place—was disconcerting, too.

The placemats, of delicate lace, were kept in a plastic bag in a buffet in the dining room; beside them, rolled in a bag, were silk napkins.

When Yasmin admired them, fingering the texture of one and then the other in the sunlight leaking through the lace-curtained window above the buffet, Mrs. Summerhayes said, "They've endured the years well, haven't they? Mr. Summerhayes and I received them as a wedding gift."

"Ahh." Wedding gifts: an area Yasmin thought best left unexplored. She hadn't known what to do with the engraving of the Montreal skyline the mailman had delivered.

And perhaps exercising the same discretion, Mrs. Summerhayes drew her attention to the cutlery, neatly arrayed on blue velvet in an oak box on top of the buffet. "Just knives, forks and dessert spoons will do," she said, setting out plates and wine glasses. "There. Shall we call the men and get on with it?"

"God, yes," Yasmin muttered.

"Pardon me? What's that?"

"I'll call the men," Yasmin said.

Garlic, the tea-leaf odour of rosemary, the meatiness of roasted lamb.

Mr. Summerhayes, leaning forward in his seat at the head of the table, clapped his hands in anticipation. "Ahh! Your mother's specialty. Wreck of lamb."

Mrs. Summerhayes, placing the silver platter in the middle of the table, said, "Actually, it's a *crown* of lamb."

"You must admit, my dear, that the crown appears to have been through a bit of an anti-monarchist rebellion."

"This new butcher, I'm afraid. He's not terribly competent. The string came undone in the oven."

But an effort had been made. Yasmin saw that. The sliced cherry tomatoes lining the serving dish; the paper frills slipped onto the ends of the sprawled bones; the sprigs of parsley that sat like a stand of baby bonsai in the central stuffing. "It looks lovely," she said.

"It is a bit of a mess," Mrs. Summerhayes said, not apologetically, as Yasmin thought at first, but with mock bemusement.

Jim, sitting beside Yasmin, missed the humour. "Oh, it'll be fine, Mom," he said in a tone dismissive with impatience.

Mr. Summerhayes, summoning gallantry, said, "I'm sure it'll be delicious as always. Now come on, my dear, sit yourself down and let's get on with it."

"Yes," Mrs. Summerhayes said, abruptly taking her seat across from Yasmin. "Let's get on with it."

The lamb turned out to be tough, juices expelled, the flavours of the garlic and rosemary flowing off with them.

But the chewing around the table was determined, Mr. Summerhayes' the most vigorous. As he helped himself to a clutch of lettuce and quartered artichoke hearts—wielding the salad spoons with one hand, as if they were chopsticks— he explained that he had learnt long ago to approach meat with caution. At a dinner function one Christmas—what with all the chat and laughter and whatever—a piece of steak had wedged in his throat.

"Do you know what that's like?" he said, his dark eyebrows rising at Yasmin. "I'll tell you what it's like. It's as if someone has suddenly slammed a door shut in your windpipe. You feel the air leaving your lungs—with nothing, absolutely nothing, to replace it. Airtight. You can't even gasp. Everything starts going dark. Your eyes water. And you know, with absolute, undeniable certainty, that you're about to die."

He paused, filled his mouth with lettuce, speared a chunk of artichoke heart.

Mrs. Summerhayes, eyeing her plate, said, "My dear, must you—"

Jim concentrated on his food, slicing dutifully into the lamb.

"I vaguely remember half standing, unable to explain, of course, but as luck would have it my neighbour at the table, a French-Canadian fellow, recognized what was happening. He wasted no time in delivering a powerful uppercut to my solar plexus. The blow sent me flying several feet, but the meat was dislodged—and I've never forgotten what that first breath felt like. It was like sucking in life itself.

"Some people thought a fight had broken out and came running from around the room, making directly for the poor fellow. I'm afraid he absorbed a fist or two before I could explain that I was probably the only anglophone in the province who will be eternally grateful to a French-Canadian for belting him one."

Mrs. Summerhayes, her food barely touched, suddenly rose as abruptly as she had seated herself moments before. Her chair slid silently backwards, and in silence she bustled out of the dining room.

Mr. Summerhayes' eyes froze in her wake. He crossed his cutlery on his plate, dabbed at his lips with the napkin and, mumbling pardons, followed her out, his pace leisurely but measured.

"You have to understand," Jim said after a moment, with a sidelong glance at Yasmin. "It's the most exciting thing that's ever happened to him. He loves that story. But Mom —it's a whole other matter. If that guy hadn't punched him, Mom would've been left with a two-year-old, no job, no insurance, and a new house mortgaged to the sun. So she hates that story. But he tells it anyway. She thinks it's his way of telling her, and me, to be grateful."

He paused, and she followed his gaze out the window above the buffet: through the points of light in the lace, to the slats of fencing that appeared somehow even closer now than they had outside.

"And one other thing. That guy who punched him? The company eliminated his job a couple of years later. Dad had the task of firing him. Couldn't have been easy. I'm sure he lost at least a couple minutes' sleep over it."

Yasmin took a sip of her wine, a nondescript Chilean red purchased at the corner store. "Aren't you being harsh?"

"No harsher than he's ever been. I don't hate him or anything."

"Her?"

"Her either." He shrugged, sipped at his wine, grimaced. After a moment, he said, "They're like this wine. Drinkable, but with an uncertain bouquet. A personality that's ill-defined, hard to grasp. Not unpleasant by any means, but still, not a wine you could ever grow fond of."

An unsettling simile. Yasmin took another sip. The wine slid warm over her tongue, lapped pleasantly at her cheeks; but as she swallowed, an underlying coarseness tightened the skin, imposing a sensation of rapid aridity.

His parents returned, a new quietness to them. They took their places and the meal proceeded in the silence of an assumed tranquillity.

Afterwards, as they lay in bed at the hotel watching the news on television, Jim said, "I have been trying hard, you see, all my life. Trying hard not to be like my parents. But what I don't know, what I'll never know, is whether I'm just kidding myself. You see how they are. What they're like. Were they always like that, or did the years make them so? I can't picture them young, you know. And photos don't help. I still don't really know what my dad did for a living. He spent his life working for CN, in the payroll department. When I was young, before I knew what the payroll department was, I had this fantasy that he was a train engineer, that he stoked fires and drove a powerful locomotive. Then I found out what payroll meant. I know it's not fair, but he never recovered from my disappointment."

He turned in the bed, pulling the blanket higher on his shoulders against the cold of the air-conditioning.

"You know, Yas, I can take as many cooking courses as I like, I can learn everything there is to know about wines, I can daydream about light as much as I want—but I can't shake this feeling that there's something I'm not getting, something insidious, that'll win out in the end."

Yasmin, seeking to lighten the moment, said, "You could have told me this *before* we got married."

"But you mightn't have married me," he said. "And then how would you have saved me?"

"Have I? Saved you?"

"We'll see." He reached over to brush a curl of hair from her forehead. "You might yet."

Moments before they fell asleep, Yasmin said, "I know why your father's hydrangeas won't grow."

"Why?" Jim mumbled.

"Not enough sunlight."

[46]

Light from the table lamp pools around the telephone, the bulb reflecting in the plastic like a distant sun.

"Hi, it's me."

"Yas. Everything okay? You sound…"

"Everything's fine. But you got your wish."

"What wish?"

"I'm at my relatives. I'll be staying here for a couple of nights, until I come home."

"How come?"

"It's a long story. Problems at the hotel. I'll tell you all about it when I get back. Everything okay with you? Anything new?"

"No, just the usual. You?"

"Well..."

"Oh-oh."

"No, no, it's just a little weird, that's all."

"How weird?"

"You tell me."

And she tells him about Penny and the box that now sits across the room from her on the dresser, beside the smaller box that holds the urn that holds her mother's ashes. Tells him how, after offering her the use of the empty dresser—which she will not accept, for it implies an intimacy she finds unsettling—Penny had left her alone; how, after a few minutes, she had returned with the box, of plain cardboard, unlabelled and taped shut. Tells him how Penny had slid the box onto the dresser and said, Here it is, is what you really come for, not so? And, on seeing Yasmin's puzzlement, had said, Is some of his things, is all we have left. Odds and ends. Vern's. Your father's.

Telling the story leaves Yasmin breathless.

After a moment, Jim asks whether she's opened it yet.

Not yet, she replies. In a curious way, she's savouring the moment. "It's the first time in years we've all been together in the same room."

"Don't be macabre," Jim says, and Yasmin pictures the face he is making: a grimace decades old and thousands of miles distant.

"Does it sound macabre?" She knows she does not intend to be macabre. What she does not know is what she does intend. The word "completeness" occurs to her. It is for now just a word, though, weightless but resonant. Because of this, she says, "Sleep well, Jim."

And as if he were lying groggy beside her on the bed, Jim replies, "You too, Yas."

[47]

No, my dear Mrs. Livingston, I fear your leaves refuse to offer any recognizable shape—recognizable, at least, to my eye. After all, shape and form, even more than beauty, for they come first, are in the eye of the beholder. What to me is shapeless may to another be wondrous.

To discern the fine contours of each other, to define each other's shapes and grasp each other's realities, remains the supreme challenge to all human ability. And today at least, my dear, your leaves are of no help to me. They are good—but only for brewing. This is no reason for despair, or scepticism, however. Just the opposite. As my husband once wrote in a note that became famous, dawn follows midnight. So, on we go. Agreed?

My dear Mrs. Livingston, what's that look on your face? If you're tired, we can call it a—

What is that noise? Is it you? Why are you gurgling —
Mrs. Livingston?
Mrs. Livingston!
Can you hear me?

Two

She burrows into the bedsheets seeking the darkness.

Burrows, ageless, away from the light seeping grey through the ill-fitted shutters.

Burrows deeper into the mattress, seeking out the warmth that is her own infused into the fibres.

Deeper into the scents that are unfamiliar and comforting. Detergent. Steam. The absorbed warmth of the sun that suggests the bright outdoors, and wind, and the brush of fresh-cut grass.

Slides into scents that seduce her whole into worlds of image quickened by sensation.

Night. The air cool and taut, becoming whole again after the searing day.

Above, a veiled quarter moon and stars—clustered, strewn—pulsing like pieces of shattered silver with a chill, radioactive beauty.

His touch—fingertips, lips—sure and gentle, urgent: a exploration that aroused her nerves.

And her touch—palms skittish, fingers afire—incorporeal with eloquence: reaching into him, grasping at an essence that could not be held, like seizing at joy itself.

Sounds—his, hers—liquefied and muted, severing her from herself, moulding her into him, him into her: shaping a multiplicity of one, with no beginning, no end, conjoined by a swirling fierceness.

Electricity as subtle as starlight wove webs between their skins, binding them to the blanket, to the rumbling earth beneath: an electricity feeding on itself, cannibalizing, nourishing, enlarging appetite even as it satiated.

The night rustled, whispered, trilled a distant chant.

She could smell the grass, the soil, rogue traces of the lilac bush. She knew herself to be alive in a way, with a depth, she had never known before, flesh and mind fusing, weaving themselves into an intricacy of hysteria and desire.

When he entered her, it was as if the glittering sky itself were gathering its immensity into her.

Her body slipped from her grasp, senses soaring.

In a final flash of lucidity, she thought: *He is a man made for moonlight.*

It grows hot under the sheets, and stale with her own breath. She stretches her neck, letting her head slip out, to air insensate with enclosure.

She reaches for the water glass sitting on the night table, takes a sip. But the water is too warm, too glutinous. It glides thick over her tongue and down her throat. It does not slake her thirst.

In the distance, the sound of an engine. A car, or perhaps a truck.

She offers herself a deep and steady breathing, but does not open her eyes. She is not yet ready to surrender the sweet moulding of the sheets to her body.

The light that invested the city was cruel: a light that rose from the water with an almost excruciating clarity. A biblical light, Jim once said, the kind of light that could hearten or incinerate.

In the newer suburbs, the light splattered a chaotic brilliance over the unsmudged houses, the fresh lawns, the uncultured shrubs. It left nothing unseen, not the machined beauty nor the spare ugliness, not the possibilities among the clutter.

But in their suburb, older, more overgrown with shrubbery, at a remove from the water, the light extended itself with greater discretion, making its way along streets, past hedges and among houses like a timid voyeur, leaving behind a subtle construction of shadow and revelation, an aqueous and elegant chiaroscuro of privilege.

Summer evenings offered shadows, neighbours distanced by a layered darkness and the occasional congestion of barbecuing odours: scents of singed steaks, potato salads, warmed rolls, cold beer. All the surreptitiousness of the good life ritualized to gentle parody. Even the colours of their houses were muted by by-law to what Jim declared a reticence offensive only to style. The approved pastels, he once said, were to houses what ketchup was to food.

The suburb had grown steadily through the years, its initial anonymity acquiring a genteel personality that Charlotte, touring the house after the acceptance of their offer to purchase, had deemed "introversion with a slow pulse." She gave Yasmin a searching look, and Yasmin saw her disappointment.

What? she said.

But Charlotte's hesitations were formless, her unease vague. She said only, "This area. This house. It's all so...safe."

Yes, Yasmin had agreed. This area, this suburb, was safe. And the house too was safe, conventional. But it was spacious, and not without possibilities. Besides, she said, acquiring it had made Jim feel more anchored.

"And you?"

"You know me, Charlotte."

Charlotte had nodded, not in approval but in confirmation. "You've found another slipstream," she said.

And when, one evening, Jim's new security translated itself into a nocturnal adventurousness on the darkened lawn, Yasmin thought of Charlotte and her tendency to underestimate those different from herself.

Charlotte's scepticism she wrote off as jealousy unbecoming a friend.

Warmth and safety. She gathers her fist in under her chin, pulls her thighs in tight against her belly.

She makes herself small. So small she is as if reduced to timelessness.

[2]

Well, my dear Mrs. Livingston, this is quite the place you find yourself in. So...utilitarian. The curtains do lend a nice touch—even if their giant sunflowers are faded almost colourless. Your son tells me that this is among the best of the private facilities. Hmph! That being so, the public ones must be quite the horror. I mean, my dear, do you know—and you won't believe this—do you know that they drink tea here from Styrofoam cups? Can you imagine anything more barbaric?

Oh, all right, you probably can. And I'm quite aware that this is not a hotel. Still, standards, you know. Life can be so shoddy sometimes...

In any case, we must all do whatever we can, mustn't we. So, you know what I've done? I've brought some of my finest china, two cups and two saucers—you know, the ones with the rose pattern you like so much—and some fine Sri Lankan tea, a silver spoon each, a drop of milk, some sugar packets and a sliced lemon. I know that taking tea is out of the question for you at the moment, but I want to have everything here and ready for when you...wake up.

Hearing, I am told, my dear Mrs. Livingston, is the last sense to go. I hope you can hear me, my dear, not for me but for yourself. I hold your hand, I even hear your voice, but I have no way of knowing whether you know me to be here with you.

You know, someone once said to me that growing up means realizing that your parents are not indispensable. I have learnt that about my grandparents and my parents, all of whom have stepped into that formless void that awaits us all. I suppose that, in the natural order of things, I am next. You can never get used to burying your contemporaries, you know, for to bury a contemporary is to bury a little bit of yourself. Perhaps for this reason, I'm not afraid of what will one day come. In some ways, it's like anticipating an injection. You know that the pain, if pain there is, will last only a few seconds, the staggering enormity of the end hardly an eye-blink in eternity—but one dreads those seconds more than anything else. I am convinced, you see, that leaving this life is not so bad. Leaving it alone, though: Now that is the horror.

My dear Mrs. Livingston, *can* you hear me?

[3]

She is aware that she is not fully conscious; is aware of her senses submerged and hovering.

The sheets lie light on her—on her skin that feels dry and powdery—and the temperature beneath the blankets achieves the cool warmth of Indian summer.

Her muscles lose petulance, grow pliant and calm: She pictures them in gentle palpitation beneath her flesh.

Mummy. Mummy! Make room. Let's snuggle.

Yes, baby, here, come on...

She feels the mattress rock, feels her daughter's warmth against her own, feels her daughter's head on her shoulder, her arm around her...

Ariana.

Then she hears herself mumble: No...

Feels revolt rising within herself. She begins to struggle, muscles suddenly taut and trembling.

Her right arm breaks free, tossing the sheets back, slicing a path through illusion. The air turns rugged, rude on her skin, and yet she must put effort into forcing her eyelids open, effort into seeing and feeling the world around her— the sunlight diffused and whitened, the dresser with its boxes and half-burnt candle, the ceiling scored by hairline cracks—and not that other one that hovers within, as seductive and perilous as the sun to Icarus.

Those hairline cracks: She grasps at their strands sway-
ing sensuously just beyond her grasp like the tentacles of
other thoughts.

[4]

You once told me, my dear, of the time your
husband got up to fetch himself another beer and after a
step or two in the direction of the kitchen slumped to his
knees. And even as his heart seized up in his chest, the only
thing he said was your name.

Your name...

You were his first thought in a situation where you were
also the last.

That too, my dear, I have always envied. I never achieved
such priority in my husband's heart...

Very kind of you to say so, my dear, but you're wrong. I
do know, and my husband himself made it clear to me...

Cruel? No, no, he wasn't brutal about it, he wasn't looking to hurt me. Indeed, I'm certain it never occurred to
him that he was hurting me. And once I had understood his
message, there was no point in discussing it with him. The
message itself was a full-stop, you see.

For me, it began, strangely enough, with whispers—and
went, from there, to words offered but unspoken. This was
one of those moments when you remember precisely what
you were doing, no matter how trivial—and I was plucking
my eyebrows. You remember that barbaric beauty ritual, Mrs.
Livingston? Tweezing out every hair and grease-pencilling

back in an arched perfection? In any case, there I was leaning in close to the mirror, when I heard whispering through
the bathroom door. There was a light knock and Celia
called my name. I told her to come in, and the door swung
slowly open. In the mirror I saw Celia, with Cyril just
behind her. They both looked stricken. And then Celia told
me my husband had been shot.

I don't remember releasing the tweezers, but I remember clearly their crystal clattering when they hit the sink.

They didn't know much more—just that he was alive,
and Celia shushed Cyril when he used the word "still."

At the hospital, the doctor in charge—a childhood
friend of my husband's—told us that although he was badly
hurt his life was not in danger. He ascribed it to luck. One
bullet had passed through his neck, but cleanly, doing
miraculously little damage. Another bullet, had it found its
mark, would have destroyed his heart—but it hadn't found
its mark. A gold medallion—a gift he received for his work
in the community—got in its way. The medallion had been
bent concave and my husband's chest was bruised, but there
was no other damage. His speech-making would be cur-
tailed for a while, the doctor said, and he would for some
time appear to give Louis Armstrong impressions, but eventually his voice too would return to normal.

I alone was allowed to see him. An armed policeman
stood at his door, and his room, darkened, full of machines
and glowing monitors, was in electronic twilight. He was
partially sedated, but that part of him that was awake was
lucid. He couldn't manage a smile, but his hand responded
to mine—recognition, comfort. But then, suddenly, it began
to shake. I was startled, I thought something was wrong, and
reached for the call button. But he seized my wrist, calmed

me—and made me see that he was merely making a writing motion, that he wanted a pen.

I gave him one from my purse, and held up a small note-book so that he could scratch out his words. And what he wrote in shaky block letters was this: *Dawn follows midnight.*

Tears came to my eyes. I stroked his hair and whispered to him that yes, indeed, we would have our dawn, he and I, once past all this.

He shook his head, and uttered a growl. I couldn't decipher what he wanted to say. He repeated the growl, with pain—and when his meaning came clear, I thought my heart would explode. What he had said was, *Torch.* Torch, Mrs. Livingston—the symbolic torch of his political life. That was the dawn that would come.

This was the moment, my dear—and you know that I choose my words carefully—this was the moment when I knew my husband to be in some way a monster.

I almost didn't pass the note on, you know. I almost ripped it up. But he had taken the fight out of me, and so I handed it to Cyril, knowing precisely where I stood in my husband's affections.

Knowing too that, in handing over what was to become an icon in my husband's growing legend, I was sealing myself off forever from one kind of life and condemning myself to quite another.

[5]

The morning sunlight leaking in through the edges of the window is shattered and diffuse.

PHOTO: A NIGHT OF SILHOUETTES. HEADS AND SHOULDERS AGAINST AN UNCERTAIN LIGHT. AND A HAND REACHING UP: FINGERS SPLAYED? FACING THE LENS OR AWAY FROM IT? THE MOMENT MYSTIFIED.

She knuckles the sleep from her eyes, thinking this might clear her sight.

But the photograph she has taken from the box Penny has left behind remains what it is: the merest suggestion of people, of place, and of time. She will have to be led into it, will have to depend on others to show her what she cannot see, no matter how hard or how often she wipes her eyes.

She tosses it back into the box, taps the flaps shut: watches them fall together as soundless as shutting eyelids.

She glances at her watch. The morning is well advanced and already, in the compressed air of the room, she feels the promise of a searing day.

[6]

She knew Jim was already up when the hiss and shuffle of the espresso machine nudged her into wakefulness.

Had it been a sunny summer morning—stretching, she allowed herself the little fantasy—he would have set a small table outside: strong coffee, raisin buns, thick newspapers and a fresh-picked flower in a vase. But it was a Saturday morning in the middle of winter, and the warmth awaiting her in the living room would be dryer, crisper, less diffuse, with a hint of smoke absent from her fantasy.

As she wrapped herself in a thick dressing gown, she pictured him preparing the fireplace: crumpling newspaper, arranging kindling, lighting the arrangement, the whole business performed with a precision and pride that made her think of the accomplished woodsman he claimed to have been in his late teens. When he spoke of that time—of hiking alone deep into the woods to the edge of a lake, setting up camp, gutting the fish hooked from the water—he spoke without sentimentality, describing a life once thoroughly enjoyed but with no regret for its loss. He had the ability, she saw, to fully inhabit the world to which he belonged.

She opened the blinds, peered out. It had snowed the night before—the best kind of snow, thick and moist, building itself up along every wire, every branch, every twig, turning the world monochrome and inverting it, so that everything seemed cast in its own negative: inside out.

She stood there, enjoying her sense of well-being, enjoying the weave of her reflection, indistinct in the window panes, fitting itself into the larger world outside.

She pressed herself closer to the window and, instantly, her breath fogged the glass.

In the living room, everything was as she expected: the fireplace brisk with flame, Jim in his easy chair before it, the coffee, the raisin buns, the newspapers neatly arrayed on the coffee table.

Anubis, curled up in front of a heating duct, cast a baleful glance in her direction then turned lazily away.

Jim looked up, offered a kiss, his palm reaching to caress the back of her neck.

She could see that something was on his mind. There was a quietness to him, part of him absent, absorbed elsewhere. "How was he this morning?"

"He's fine." The reply—quickly mumbled, dismissive because unconsidered—denied itself. He leant forward to pour her some coffee. "Fairly lucid, you know. But these days talking to Dad's like talking to someone who's watching television at the same time." He sat back in his chair, peeled open the newspaper and scanned the pages.

Yasmin sat down, sipped at her coffee. She no longer made a point of being closeby for Jim's weekend calls to his father at the retirement home. They were always painful. The old man's decline following Jim's mother's sudden death had been swift, his resistance to the retirement home heart-rending. Yasmin had found there was little she could do to help Jim except hold his hand and try to still the tremors that ran through it. As the old man's faculties diminished, as his coherence grew less certain, the conversations became more difficult and, one day, Jim told Yasmin that he preferred to speak alone with his father. He could not bear being overheard speaking to him as if to a child. Yasmin understood. The embarrassment was less for himself than for the man his father had become.

Jim treasured his self-possession, a quality Yasmin found attractive even though it made him wary of domestic discord, which she found less so. Disagreement at home disconcerted him. Home was the place to which he retreated, to rest, recuperate, nurse his grudges. He never forgot a professional slight and would, over time, seek out weaknesses, seizing the first opportunity, even years later, for retaliation. Forgiveness, she had learnt, did not come easily to him.

Yet he was not a difficult man to live with: his disposition was hardest on himself. At work, his reputation was that of a friendly man with bite. At home, though, he would disarm rift with a quick apology, giving way more easily than Yasmin would have liked.

Disagreement was, for her, an invitation to discussion, less an opportunity for proving herself right than for being shown flaws in her logic, omissions in her information. She was open to convincing. But Jim was not adept at such strategy. He rarely tried, and when he did it was with a barely concealed peevishness that served only to heighten tension.

She wondered at times how much he cared: Did the domestic matter less to him than the professional? Or was it that the domestic mattered so much that he feared engaging a path that could, if followed to its logical conclusion, lead to irreparable schism?—as it so often had in his business dealings. She glimpsed at such times the insecurities he shared with her in carefully apportioned pieces—fears that remained unresolved within him like a hidden paralysis.

His coffee cup sat half empty beside him, the coffee no longer steaming. He turned the newspaper pages briskly, his scanning eyes barely focusing on the words before them.

After leafing through the sports section—he checked the hockey scores almost as a reflex—Jim said, "D'you know —my parents never used to fight. Then the summer before I headed off to university they had a huge one."

"Stormy days in the Summerhayes household? Unimaginable, if you know what I mean." Yasmin let a faint smile shape her lips: It wasn't that he was predictable so much as that she had learned to read his signs.

"Oh, they never raised their voices. It was a fight of silences. You know—whispers and rattling china."

"What was it about?"

"Money. I think. I was never quite sure, to tell you the truth. They felt it wasn't any of my business. One day, out of the blue, my dad left home. He found himself a little apartment downtown. Then a few months later he was back, again out of the blue."

"And your mom?"

"She made him dinner. As if he'd never left."

"And you?"

"Me? I never knew—I mean, you can never tell—"

"What?"

"Where things'll end up. You know."

Over in the corner, Anubis arose, elongating, and with a single bound, leapt curling into Jim's lap.

Jim chuckled, ran a hand along the silky fur.

Yasmin saw sparks fly past his fingers.

[7]

Penny has left word with Amie that she will be back before lunch; has left in her absence a sense of quiescence.

Cyril—out somewhere, Amie says unsmiling, looking after something or looking for something to do—has left no word.

Then Amie returns to the kitchen and begins, with a discreet rustling, the preparation of Yasmin's breakfast.

Yasmin takes her coffee from the dining table, from the same place set for her at lunch and a quick dinner yesterday, and steps out through the open double doors onto the porch.

It is a cloudy morning, the vegetation a rich moist green, stretching off to hills hazy with mist. She hears, from somewhere far off, the sounds of rhythmic chopping.

She realizes with a touch of surprise that she has not dreamt—or at least that she has had no dreams disturbing or pleasurable enough to be memorable. She has, she thinks, slept with her defences up, images restrained, their betrayals surfacing only through the door half opened by drowsiness. No dreams, then, but summoned mirages more potent

"Breakfas' ready, miss," Amie calls from the dining room.

She turns and with a smile says, "You can call me Yasmin."

Amie seems to consider this for a moment. Then she says, "Yes, miss. Breakfas' ready."

Yasmin steps inside, into the greater shadows of the unlit dining room. "Don't you like me, Amie?"

The question surprises Amie, confuses her.

Yasmin decides not to offer relief. She stands still, waiting for an answer. And as she does in difficult interviews, counts silently: a thousand and one, a thousand and two…

Five seconds of silence.

Then, with no papers to shuffle, she takes her seat, wondering, as she never does before the cameras, whether she is being cruel: decides that she is, and puts Amie at ease with another smile, one that suggests that she is merely teasing.

On the plate in front of her are two slices of fried bread, and an egg fried hard swimming in butter.

Yasmin says, "Amie, d'you know what cholesterol is?"

"You use to eat this every mornin' when you was small-small."

Yasmin goes still. A space opens up in her mind. "Did you know me well when I was a kid?"

"Who you think change your nappies? Gave you breakfas', lunch, dinner."

"You were my baby-sitter."

"Baby-sitter. Nurse. I always been the maid, miss." She
turns and glides back into the kitchen.

Baby-sitter. Nurse. Maid. Forty years: Yasmin feels her
head spin with the airlessness of Amie's life.

[8]

At one point in his career—early on, when
this kind of thing had its place—my husband liked to talk
about our people as being crushed, oppressed, humiliated,
that kind of thing. It was a favourite theme and he often
reached for it during speeches—so he once confessed to
me—not so much because he believed in it as because it was
a guaranteed crowd-pleaser. People love being told how
oppressed they are, did you know that, Mrs. Livingston?
It's like expiation, you see. It lifts all responsibility for their
misery from their shoulders: it is his fault, that fellow over
there, the one with the white skin or the black skin or the
hooked nose or the plummy accent, he's the one who's doing it to me. That was one reason people loved him. He
absolved them of everything, by naming others...

Did he know what he was doing? Of course he did. They
all did. They were just playing the game as it was played
back then—and still is. Stirring people's fears, pricking their
sensitivities—and where there were none, creating them.

Yes, you heard what I said: creating them. And why
should that make me cynical, my dear? Perhaps it's less a

question of my cynicism than of your naivety? I don't know the half of it, I assure you. I was hardly his confessor or his sounding-board. He spoke to me only occasionally, you see, late at night in bed, when his brain would not stop.

Little incidents were best, he believed, because they were hard to verify and provided a basis of fact, which was all you needed or wanted, for that matter. He wasn't terribly interested in what you might call literal truth—but political truth, now that was another matter...

Once, I recall, an opportunity came to him to stir things up a bit. There had been a fight at a rumshop between a black man and one of our people over the correct interpretation of a cricket rule. It ended unhappily for the black fellow. There was some blood, some broken bones. The Indian fellow was arrested. My husband was looking for a cause to raise the political temperature a bit—he believed in keeping things at a low boil—and he seriously considered defending this man in what he called the court of public opinion...

What argument could he have made? My dear Mrs. Livingston, any argument he pleased. It was all in the presentation, don't you see? *The fellow was provoked. The fellow was humiliated. And there are those who say the fellow was called the vilest of racist names!* Nothing needed to be substantiated. As it turned out, he made a speech about the incident in which he said that, after having examined the facts, he could not bring himself—as many were urging him—to defend the fellow. He even wished the black fellow well. Hah! A simple artistry, really: he used them both to exonerate himself of the charge of racial politics. Oh, his politics were racial all right, but the perception was unhelpful. Better to deny it.

That was my husband's genius, you see. He could be reasonable and conciliatory, or he could be a rabble-rouser. He could ignite fires or extinguish them at will...

The truth? To people like my husband literal truth is interesting but not often useful. Political truth is far more valuable, the possible truths my husband was playing with, for instance. My husband, you see, Mrs. Livingston, put thought into everything. He took nothing for granted. Except me.

[9]

An inventive man. Adventurous.

And yet.

And yet there came the afternoon when Jim interrupted the sorting of his books to place the blanket, freshly laundered and wrapped in plastic, beside the sliding door.

She pretended not to see. The gesture was so calculated, so uninspired. The sight of the blanket lying there on the carpet, given purpose, no longer an object of spontaneity, left her with a hollow feeling, her body contracted, as if pulling, saddened, into itself.

Night fell. They had dinner and Jim cleaned up quickly, with a dispatch she found enervating. She remained at the table, sipping at the last of her wine and studying her reflection in the window pane, herself and her world spectral against the darkness beyond.

He switched on the dishwasher and then took her hands in his, enfolding them in palms still damp, palms in which the pulse of his excitement was manifest. He pressed his lips to her knuckles, teeth nipping—with passion?—at the loose skin.

She shut her eyes, her hand distanced from herself, her arm as if disembodied.

And amidst the whirring and sloshing of the dishwasher, she found herself taken unawares by his hunger, by her own. Her reluctance softened. She slipped a finger into his mouth. Felt him, and then herself, shudder.

Once more followed him into the garden.

Once more engaged lust under the stars.

Afterwards, when they had crept back into the house from the night growing chilly, the hollow once more carved itself within her. She had opened herself to the pleasure. But this time no soil had found its way under her fingernails, and the sky had seemed a brilliant canopy, distant and cold. And consciousness, too, had intervened: she had been aware all along of his—and her own—efforts at invention. Repetition had deprived them of effortlessness, and effort had moderated passion.

She left Jim to fold the blanket and went to prepare herself a bath. She poured a lengthy stream of bathfoam into the water, tossed in a couple of oil beads, sat watching the water fall and the mirror steam up.

In the vaguely melancholic mood that came to her after lovemaking, she understood that Jim was a man of both passion and method, the one enlisted to the other. It showed in his photographs, in his designs—only, this evening, one part of his nature had been undone by the other. How easily, she reflected, was the extraordinary made pedestrian.

When, days later, Jim had the idea that the blanket could be turned into a throw-cover for the old sofa in the basement, his suggestion came as a relief to her. It shored up her faith that if the extraordinary could be made pedestrian then the opposite, too, was possible. Jim's choice, then, renewed her faith in the possibility of redemption, and the memory of that first time on the lawn—when all her senses seemed suffused with the very energy of creation—still gave her hope.

[10]

Yasmin composes her knife and fork, conjoined exclamation marks on the plate she has cleaned through obligation.

When Amie offers another coffee, Yasmin accepts. And when she brings it, Yasmin says, "Do you have any grandchildren, Amie?"

"Me? No, miss."

"A husband, then."

"No, miss. I never b'en married."

As Yasmin sips at the coffee, she thinks: But you cannot just have been a slave all your life.

The gap between thought and words is unbridgeable, and so all that remains is silence.

[11]

The pregnancy was unexpected and, at first, Yasmin did not know what to do with the news.

She called Jim. He was in a meeting. "Is it urgent? Would you like me to interrupt him?" She chose to be put on hold. After ten minutes of AM radio, she hung up.

She called her mother, but when she heard her voice she knew she had not chosen well: Just calling to see how you were doing, Mom...

She called Charlotte, her joy rising. Charlotte's reaction —"Oh, shit, Yas!"—evoked a sudden fury, forcing her to hang up: Someone at the door...

By the time Jim got home that evening, she was joyous, and jealous of it. They had dinner. They made love. He fell asleep and so, eventually, did she.

The next morning when she went down to the kitchen, he had already brewed a pot of coffee. He offered her a cup.

She waited a beat. Then: "No, thanks. Coffee isn't good for pregnant women."

Another beat, followed by the shattering of Jim's coffee mug on the tiled floor.

Then he floated up to join her.

[12]

London, Mrs. Livingston! London!

I hadn't expected to like it, you know, hadn't expected to like the English or their ways. England was a fantasy for us in the island. We loved it, loved belonging to the majesty of it—and we hated it, because that very majesty was what kept us, in their eyes and ours, childlike. England would always take care of us—but it would also always tell us what to do.

My husband was among those who wished to put an end to this dependence. So I accompanied him to London wary—which may explain why I ended up falling in love with England and its ways.

Oh, my dear, I could run the names past you now—Piccadilly Circus, Trafalgar Square, St. Paul's Cathedral and on and on—but would they sound to you simply like a list of tourist sites or would they cause your pulse to quicken as they do mine? I could talk to you of afternoon tea in the grand style, of dinners and receptions in settings that...

Ambassador? No, no, there was no such thing at the time. He was named special advisor to the island's delegation. Talks on independence were about to get under way, you see, and there was a lot to do—not only meetings with British officials but with diplomats from other newly created nations. He met a lot with the Indians, I recall, while the others spent their time with the Africans. Even there, our racial division persisted...

It was a big change for my husband—from opposing the government to a post in its diplomatic service—and it came about fairly quickly. My husband felt he was doing valuable work but, perhaps understandably, not everyone saw it that way. There were those who said he had sold out to the first minister, that he was just angling for a big job in the new administration. Even I wondered—feeling guilty, feeling disloyal...

No, he didn't speak to me about it. He simply told me one evening, after he had accepted. It wasn't our way, you see, to discuss his... He felt I knew nothing about such things, and I felt he knew everything.

But my doubts could not survive his passion. That is

what I remember best about this period. His passion—a passion, my dear, that I knew to be incompatible with mere self-interest. I will admit it was not far-fetched to suggest that he dreamed of an important post, perhaps even deputy prime minister: my husband was human, after all. But he was also enough of an idealist to flirt with the idea of biracial government, reconciliation, racial harmony. I suspect he'd always wondered what cooperation might bring.

But, whatever the truth may be, this move was not well seen in certain circles back home. Not to put too fine a point on it, my husband was seen as akin to being a traitor for accepting an offer from the first minister—and those who judged him less harshly still viewed him with suspicion—

What do I think the truth was? Between you and me, Mrs. Livingston, I never really understood why he accepted. I'm not sure he did either, although being the kind of man he was he must have believed that there were good reasons for doing so. Reconciliation and all the rest.

But, you see, after he was shot, the first minister ordered a police guard for his room, he visited him, and saw to it that the section of the hospital's parking lot beneath my husband's window was closed off for the duration of his stay, so he wouldn't be disturbed by car noise. All of which, of course, served to increase the people's suspicion of my husband. There are those who claim that this was part of his game—but I am not sure. I prefer to believe that the first minister was shocked by the attempt on my husband's life, that his humanity rose above his politics. If I didn't believe that, I would have to conclude that our island never had a chance—and I choose to believe in that one shining moment, my dear, when everything seemed possible.

And I believe that my husband, too, believed in it. And this was why part of him was grateful for the first minister's consideration. I think my husband was like the rest of us, Mrs. Livingston—a complex of selflessness, self-interest and venality... Human motive being what it is, my dear, we are simply not equipped to judge one another.

No, the attackers were never caught. There were those who suspected the first minister, and others who suspected members of my husband's entourage. Our world was turning Byzantine, but that we recognized only afterwards, when it was too late. When my husband had recovered, the first minister suggested the London posting as a means of being out of harm's way, of letting things cool down—or, as some suggested, of simply getting my husband out of the way. Normally, my husband would not have accepted, but I believe he was touched...

No, he always maintained that the first minister was a bastard, but he wasn't a killer. If my husband had suspicions he kept them to himself. He never removed the dented medallion afterwards, not even to shower. He was struck by his luck. I remember him holding the medallion in the palm of his hand and saying, with awe, *But gold's such a soft metal*...

But there's more, too, you know. I also suspect this was a period where he lost himself—a consequence, I think, of being shot. My husband would sometimes sit up alone late at night, thinking, and caressing the scar on his neck. I would wake up in bed, finding myself alone, and I'd go looking for him. He was invariably in the porch, in the dark, his fingertips massaging at that spot where once there was a hole—rubbing and rubbing as if expecting a genie to arise from it with answers to all the questions he could not articulate. Not once did I disturb him. He left no room to do so. And looking at him wrapped so tight in his invisible cocoon, I came to see that he was waiting—or perhaps searching—for a better self. No one, not even I, could contribute to that search.

And then London came up, and I think he thought he'd found that new self, and he was impassioned by it—sufficiently so that he broke a promise he'd made to me the night before we left.

The electricity had failed, as it often did back then, and we were in our room finishing the packing by the white light of a hurricane lamp when I suddenly found myself sitting on the edge of the bed unable to move—

No, the muscles themselves were not paralysed. It was a question of desire. I had lost all *desire* to move...

No, I was not afraid. I was more startled than anything else.

My husband sat beside me, took my hand—an unusual gesture for him, one he would not have made were we not alone—and made me a solemn promise that he would no longer allow his work to impede our life together. We would go out in London, to theatres, to cinemas, to restaurants. We would walk and visit the sights. We would have people in, and accept invitations to dinner.

My hand moved in his, my blood quickened. I felt that he must mean it, for he had never spoken this way before. The scar on his neck was, for him, a mark of his mortality.

And right there, Mrs. Livingston—and I tell you this so that you will understand the intensity of the moment—right there with the door closed but unlocked, in the glare and hiss of the hurricane lamp, we shed our clothes and shattered the light.

[13]

Jim was starry-eyed even in exhaustion. Yasmin, needing rest, sent him to the hospital entrance to wait for her mother's taxi to arrive. He would then take her directly to the nursery to see her granddaughter.

He had spent the long hours of the night with Yasmin, holding her hand, feeding her crushed ice, doing his best to coach her in the breathing techniques they had practised in the pre-birth classes. From time to time he had gobbled a chocolate bar or munched on nuts and raisins to keep up his energy for, as the night proceeded, as the contractions grew ever more ferocious, she came to depend on his strength, on his subdued encouragement, to keep going. His attention had not lagged for a moment.

And after a final excruciating push—her hand crushing his, the nurses shouting like cheerleaders—her daughter had emerged, large-eyed and silent as if herself stunned by her miraculous arrival in a world of bright light. Jim took the swaddled baby in his large hands and entered a world of marvel drawn in whispers and tenderness. When, seconds later, he placed their daughter in the cradle of Yasmin's arms, they were together dazzled by the beauty of what they had wrought. For an eternity of moments, with the baby blinking contentedly up at them as at intimate strangers, they journeyed into a world of their own, all pain forgotten, all fear drained away. Never had Yasmin felt so light, so unencumbered. She felt she could fly.

When her mother came to the room, she pressed Yasmin's head to her chest and whispered, "Well done, Yasmin, dear. Well done."

Later, without warning, Charlotte bustled in, the head of a large stuffed dog peeking out the top of a beribboned gift bag.

She pulled a chair up to the bedside, unfurled a length of toilet paper from the roll in her bag and blew her nose. "So," she said, "how wad it? Like pushing an elep'ant through your thinuses?"

Yasmin laughed through her exhaustion. "Not the sinuses. Worse."

"Whoopdedoo," Charlotte said, brandishing another length of toilet paper. "The miracle of childbird."

Her sarcasm sobered Yasmin. Her friend's attitude seemed an attempt to diminish. For yes, it was a kind of miracle: to have this growth—alien to the body yet wholly integral to it—emerge sentient and fully formed from within yourself. Miraculous. What other word would do?

So she said nothing, merely constructed a wan smile.

"So where's the little whippersnapper? Why idn't she here with you?"

"Visiting hours. People like you arrive in hordes, sniffling and sneezing and pulling toilet paper from their handbags. It's safer to keep 'em behind glass. Go take a look. Go." She shooed her away.

"How'll I recodnize her?"

"Just look for the most beautiful baby, you silly twit." Charlotte rolled her eyes.

"Jim and my mom are there. They'll show you."

Charlotte, putting the roll of toilet paper back into her bag, paused at the door. She turned to Yasmin, and in a tender voice said, "Yas, how *do* you feel?"

Yasmin was silent for what seemed a very long time. How did she feel? The answer that eventually took shape in

her mind seemed so utterly simple, she hesitated before saying it. "As if my entire body is sheathed in a silken glove,"
she said quietly. "As if no one had ever done this before, or
ever will again. Charlotte, I know this'll sound dumb, but I
feel—"

"What, Yas?" Charlotte's eyes were suddenly wet.

"Blessed," Yasmin whispered.

[14]

When she sees Cyril striding out of the
trees, a long-handled hoe balanced on his shoulder, a
sheathed machete flapping against his thigh, she is immediately struck by the jauntiness that the morning has brought
to him.

As he nears the house, she sees that there is relish in the
way the sleeveless undershirt clings sodden to his skin; relish in the baggy grey trousers tucked into the high tops of
his rubber boots; relish in the mud that clings to the boots.

When he peers up at her and waves—"Mornin'!"—she
sees relish most of all in his deep, steady breathing, and in
the brightness that is new to his eyes: a brightness that
comes from a place and a time within himself.

"You look years younger," she calls out.

He rewards her with a smile breathless in its serenity.

A few minutes later he brings her towels. "I'm afraid," he
says apologetically, "that the water pressure too low for a
shower, and we ain't have a bath tub. But—" she sees his eyes
twinkle. "—you could have a heavy sprinkle if you want."

[15]

Do you know what my biggest disappointment with London was, my dear? It was those tiny backyard gardens. Somehow I had expected to find only grandeur everywhere. But those gardens! As my husband said once, all you have to do to water them is spit from an upper window...

You think them charming? I suppose, but there was a dankness to them, a suggestion of a kind of underlying swampiness that afflicts all England really. Even on the hottest of days—and it did get hot, my dear—the place never truly seemed to dry out. It was a place I felt at home in, but never comfortable. I never learned my way around, you know, not even London. Took taxis everywhere if I was alone—and if my husband was with me, walking around, say, he would lead the way, map in hand. I never had to puzzle my way through the streets.

But this—wandering around with my husband, resting on park benches and watching the swans, stopping in at tearooms for a spot of refreshment—did not last long. It couldn't, you see. He soon was unable to afford the time off —and then he didn't want to. That's the kind of man he was.

I remember the day this became clear: that his promise to me no longer held. One afternoon his meetings were abruptly cancelled—someone on the other side of the negotiations was ill—and he called to tell me to get ready, he'd be by to pick me up for a walk along the Thames and an early dinner.

My dear, I swear—I shed my resentments faster than I did my clothes for a quick shower. In no time at all, I was dressed, made up and waiting for him in the living room of our flat. I was literally breathless. Now, I'm aware that this probably strikes you as pathetic—that I should be so exhilarated at so simple a prospect. But this was more than a walk and dinner, you see. This was the resurrection of the promise through an unexpected crack in his work.

So I sat in the living room and waited.

And waited.

Shadows grew long in the street outside. Others congregated in the living room. Eventually, I kicked off my shoes, slipped off my earrings, and washed my face clean of the makeup of which I had grown ashamed...

Angry? My dear, it is one of my failings to balk at anger —for which I reproach myself, I assure you. A question of trust, you see. It takes me a while to decide whether anger is justified or not—and by then it's usually rather late in the day. There are those, my son-in-law among them, who admire my patience. If only they knew...

So, angry? No. I will however admit to an ache in my chest and some thoughts, my dear, properly characterized as bitter. I had known for a while that, for my husband, political promises were like cotton candy—sweet on the tongue, but fleeting, weightless, hardly worth a memory. Now I felt that his personal promises were the same.

No, he got in late, you see, after midnight. I wasn't about to wait around moping. I watched some television, had a bite to eat. Eventually, as evening came, I got into bed. I was still awake when he came in. He didn't apologize or anything. He took off his shoes and socks and sat on the bed squeezing his toes and massaging his soles—

It was a way of relaxing, it comforted him somehow.

And he said that he'd got into an interesting discussion with some people from the delegation—he didn't tell me what it was about, he assumed such things would not be of interest to me—and before he knew it hours had gone by, everyone was hungry and so they headed out to a restaurant, where the discussion continued. I remember him yawning and saying, by way of apology I think, You know how I like a good ol' talk, Shakti. And that was it. He put on his pyjamas, got into bed and was snoring within seconds—

Me? I was awake for most of the night—

Selfless? Hardly. The way I see it—and it was that night, lying there in the darkness, that I began to see—his political life fed him in a way that he could never allow his personal life to do. It was all-enveloping because he wished it to be. I understood that night that he thought only of himself because that was what his damned sense of mission demanded. The torch, my dear, burned hard and hot within him. It demanded submission.

So I resigned myself to it, and took to spending my time reading and taking taxis to museums—especially to the British Museum, which is a thieves' palace, but a palace all the same.

[16]

On summer weekends, their suburb brought to mind a community in the aftermath of nuclear alert. The desertion was total save for the occasional cat wandering around in search of adventure, its people off at cottages or on sailboats or enjoying a weekend catching up on the New York shows.

Yasmin had come to view the neighbourhood as a place

where people came mainly to sleep—alone, with their spouses, with other people's spouses—and was helplessly alert to its bedroom noises: snoring, snuffling, the stirrings of insomnia, the guttural whimpering of discreet orgasm.

They were downtown, out at dinner, their daughter at home with a sitter, when Jim first offered the observation that she was *somewhat* paranoid.

He had had a late meeting with a client and had met her at the studio after the broadcast. She saw from his skittishness that the meeting had gone well. Failure made him quiet; it absorbed his energies in introspection. But there was a celebratory air to him that evening. He had performed well, and wished to extend the mood. He took her to a restaurant where the brightest lights were directed at the paintings on the walls, the rest of the lighting sufficiently subdued that the food, elegantly displayed, acquired the surreptitious look of the avant-garde.

They began with a drink. Jim asked about the show. She said it had gone well, but his agitation would let him probe no further. He related his meeting as if reading from the minutes. She listened, nodding from time to time, murmuring sober encouragement. She knew him. As he spoke, his movements became less abrupt, his words more considered, the retelling relieving him of his tensions; he was like a cat scratching at its post.

Their food arrived. Jim cast a cursory glance at his plate. He would not eat until he had talked himself out, and then he would eat with appetite.

Yasmin weighed her fork in her hand, waiting for a pause that would allow the tines to explore her salad without giving the impression of abandonment. When it came, she let her eyes fall to the plate—and saw what she thought to be a stirring among the lettuce leaves. She bent low over the plate.

What bothered her was not that some insect might have found refuge in her food—the movement, after all, was probably only a trick of too many shadows in too little light —but that Jim would not take her concern seriously. Seeing her attention diverted from his words, he went silent, watching her probe among the vegetables. At her explanation, he hesitated only slightly before saying, "Call the station. Get a crew over here fast."

Her fork stabbed at the salad, rapping bluntly on the surface of the plate.

"It was a joke, Yas."

"I know," she said, without a smile. She ate—but with caution, wincing ever so slightly whenever her teeth crunched through the spine of a lettuce leaf.

Jim, forking linguine into his mouth between gulps of red wine, quickly concluded his story. The mood was lost, and an edge returned to him. It was at this moment, as he pinched the middle from a chunk of bread, that he made his observation.

Yasmin, watching him plaster butter on his bread, mulled over the word. *Paranoid*. She thought it a curious word for him to use, a word so distant from herself that she could not even take offence. Careful, cautious, prudent, perhaps even suspicious: but she had always thought this one of her better traits.

He said, "You always seem to be looking for the worst in things. But that's journalism for you, I guess." His fork gestured at her plate. "A delicious meal—it is delicious, isn't it? —and you spend ten minutes looking for an insect."

She reminded him that at university she had spent two winters working part-time in a restaurant. "I've seen the kitchens, I've seen the way they handle food." She had never quite lost her distrust of what went on behind the scenes.

"Call it what you want," he said. "You worry too much."

"Can we just say I'm sceptical?"

"It'll do."

She returned to her salad. Although she was no longer hungry, she cleared her plate of the last morsel, a sliver of carrot she swallowed whole.

[17]

Cyril, too, has showered. He has regained his neatness, smells of fresh talcum powder. A light perspiration glints on his forehead, but his eyes still sparkle. He asks how her shower was and when she assures him that it was fine, says, "Good. Is exhausting sometimes, you know. Having to run from drop to drop."

He slides his hands into his pockets and with a certain solemnity asks her to bring Ram's box—as if it had been his possession and not merely his reliquary—to the dining room.

And it is with a suggestion of ceremony—that sense of relish with which people perform ritual they know to be gilded by immemorial repetition—that he places it on the table, invites her to take a seat and seats himself.

Then he takes a breath that he appears to hold and reaches, blind, into the box.

He places the object on her palm. It is of silver, in the shape of a horseshoe, with a flattened middle tapered to rounded ends. A bracelet of some kind, she thinks—but the wrist required to secure it would have to be massive. A charm or a fetish, then.

Cyril, amused, says, "You don't know what that is, eh?" When she shakes her head, he says, "You probably going to find this kind o' disgusting. Is called a tongue-scraper. An' is for doing just that."

"Ah." With hardly a pause she flips her palm and lets the object fall back into the box.

Cyril laughs. "Back then, brushin' your teeth wasn't enough. We had very Indian ideas of cleanliness. But I won't go into the details."

Yasmin's palm stirs above the open box. Her face—and then her open palm held upwards—registers interrogation.

After Ram died, Cyril explains, Penny simply threw in whatever came to hand. "It wasn't a time for siftin'." Then he pauses, leans forward, elbows on thighs, palms flush together. "Then I pass by and toss in the tongue-scraper."

She sees his fingers interlace, sees a tension wrap them tight.

"You know, Yasmin, that tongue-scraper might be the mos' important thing in there, for me. Tell you why. Is because is the last picture I have of him in my head. Nothing heroic, nuh. Nothing…"

He goes still. And then in a voice not of the present, he says, "It was that morning. His last. He was at the sink, the one in the back, nuh. Bending over. I still see him as if it was this morning. Hair wet. Slick back. Head bent low over the sink. Mouth open, tongue hanging out. The scraper. Somehow it seemed more important than all the speeches he ever give. Probably because he always use to say that the one thing politicians must guard against is the unguarded. And I remember him sayin' he never felt clean until he'd scraped his tongue, that it never seemed to work right until…" He pauses, passes a finger across his lips. "So that seemed more real to me than anything else. More important." He gestures towards the box. "So there you have it. The tongue scraper. Scrapin' away all those old words, all the old promises and the threats, makin' room for more."

[18]

She screamed into the night with all the clarity of her young voice—a scream, at eighteen months, mindful of terror.

Yasmin felt the scream lift her from the bed, felt it impel her with irresistible force to her daughter's room. The child screamed again as she gathered her up in her arms: the body trembling, the tiny hands grasping with blind desperation at the folds of her nightgown.

Yasmin held her close, caressing her back, softly calling her name. *Ariana. Ariana.*

She cried out: Ernie ! Bert! Her favourite stuffed toys, but—was she seeking their security, or were they haunting her dreams?

Her eyes opened and Yasmin saw the confusion of an incomplete transition from one world to the other, the world of dreams as real as the world of her mother's arms.

Then, quickly, the eyes shaped a plaintive and puzzled accusation: Why are you punishing me? they asked.

Unexpectedly the child pressed her tear-stained face to Yasmin's, then, with deliberation, her lips to her cheek.

Yasmin was startled—and moved.

The kiss was not affection; it was a plea from the depths of nightmare, a gesture that said, You are punishing me but I love you still.

Yasmin felt herself crack.

She said her daughter's name again, wiped perspiration from the hot forehead, and her touch proved soothing. The trembling stopped. Recognition softened the child's eyes. Mommy, she said, curling herself more tightly into Yasmin's tightening embrace.

[19]

Really, my dear, just what kind of a place *is* this?

They may have no standards beyond the professional—but must they take exception to those of us who understand there is more to life than plastic and Styrofoam?

They insist that I remove the china. I have explained that it is among the finest china in the world, but this has made no impression on them. The barbarian, you see, my dear, is never far from the gates.

You must understand that I tried. I even put up a bit of a fuss. They didn't like that. They prefer their old people obedient and docile. So they threatened to have me evicted. Well, I marched right up to the office of the Head Hun and as luck would have it ran right into him.

I saw him see me, saw his body express the wish I hadn't

seen him, saw him reach for self-control. He drew himself up, smiled. And I saw him assess me. He saw all that I had seen—only, he went a step further. He assumed—from my race, my age, from my manner of dressing—that I was of limited education and, so, of limited intelligence. I saw he believed he was dealing with a simple granny—much, I imagine, like the one he himself has.

And so I seized the initiative. *You, sir*, I said rather loudly but with great control, *are a bounder!* He was taken aback, he didn't know what to make of that, he may not even have known what a bounder was. But one thing was certain: My speech did not fit the image he had made of me—an image that led him to expect meekness or shrill anger. I saw him falter, saw him realize he would have to deal with me. He wasn't as canny as he thought. Besides, as you well know, my dear, age brings a kind of liberation—the right to speak one's mind without fear. It's a freedom we share with crazy people...

In any case, this young chap invited me into his office. I lost no time in explaining the problem. He was understanding, I'll say that for him. His breeding showed. But still he would not allow the china. He explained that should an emergency arise, many people would rush into the room with a great deal of equipment. The danger of breakage would be great. Not only would I lose my china, but his staff would run the risk of being cut. This made sense to me, and I agreed to his request to remove my china.

Then he attempted to engage me in conversation. I soon saw that word of my presence here had reached him. He complimented me on what he called my fidelity to you. His staff, he said, were impressed by my coming every day, by my sitting here and talking to you—*with* you, I corrected him—for hour after hour. And then he said, "But you realize she—"

I cut him off, my dear. His next words were of no interest to me. I thanked him, but refused to discuss you further. He is responsible for ensuring your physical care. He has neither the expertise nor the right to hold opinions beyond that. I stood up and excused myself.

So you see, my dear, when you wake up I shall still serve you tea, just as you like it. Only I fear I have been reduced to Styrofoam.

[20]

It is the clutch of photographs in his hand, she believes, that prompts Cyril's question. Shakti, he says, her last days. Was she happy? How did she spent them?

With a friend, Yasmin says, in a private nursing home. Sitting beside her bed talking to her. "Once I went with her to visit Mrs. Livingston. I say visit, but it was more like paying final respects, you know? She was in a deep coma and as I stood there beside her bed, I was almost overwhelmed by a sense of visiting a funeral home. You know what I mean— the silence, the body on display. There was no sense of life in the room. Or it was more that life had been reduced to an idea. I couldn't stay long, and excused myself.

"Out in the corridor a man approached me. He introduced himself as the director and asked if he could have a word with me. Well, turned out Mom had developed quite the reputation. Seems the nurses had overheard her talking to Mrs. Livingston—"

Cyril says, "I read somewhere that in some places they does play music or TV for people in comas. Just in case, nuh."

"Yes, but apparently the way Mom spoke, it was as if she was having a conversation with Mrs. Livingston. Not a monologue, if you see what I mean, but a dialogue. It was as if Mrs. Livingston were commenting and asking questions. They were kind of worried. The director wanted to know if Mom was all right, if she usually talked to herself.

"I asked whether she was disrupting the routine. He said no. Was she getting in the way? No. Was she disturbing anyone? No. So what was the problem? There was no problem. Just that, seeing I was there, he thought he'd let me know.

"I thanked him. Then he asked for a phone number where I could be reached, in case there was ever a problem. I gave him my home number.

"As it turned out, they called the number only once. You know. That night—When she—When the conversation stopped."

"Ahh yes," Cyril says. "Ahh, yes..." Then: "Shakti wouldn' have gone quiet-quiet in bed, you know. That wasn' her way. She was the leas' predictable person I ever knew."

[2 1]

Defying expectation, being an original, was her mother's way of defeating stereotype, her personal theatre a response to challenge: She would force others to see her image of herself and not their image of her.

Which was why she would sometimes, and for no apparent reason, go to some length to dress a banal thought in
linguistic finery. Procrastination, she once said, was the lazy
man's way of getting nowhere—or at least of ensuring that
it would take him twice the time to get there. And Yasmin
thought: A stitch in time, Mom.

Which was why Yasmin remembered the one cliché her
mother never sought to adorn: "There are no guarantees in
life." The phrase was, to her mother, a truth so primary it
had to be expressed plainly, and so innate—its tones as
familiar to Yasmin as the sound of her own name—that
Yasmin never thought to ask why it should be so.

It was one quiet evening, the lights low, her daughter
asleep on her, chest rising and falling in seamless regularity,
that she realized the extent to which she had absorbed the
phrase. The thought came to her that this closeness was no
harbinger of tomorrow. This bond that now seemed so un-
breakable could with time become a distance unbridgeable.

No guarantees: Yasmin remained seated there for hours
in what felt like a mild paralysis, determined to possess for
now this yearning, this ache, this warmth and trust, this utter
unconditionality which the future might yet expropriate.

[2 2]

For my birthday—
April, my dear, you know that—
Why, yes, the same day—
Surely I must have. Or I may not have, come to think of

it, after all, it's of no great importance, but it did make things easy when she was growing up. Yasmin and I shared a birthday cake, her candles on one side and mine—a symbolic number, of course—on the other. Now, if you don't mind...

For my birthday my husband took me to one of London's fancy restaurants, the name of which escapes me now—not that it matters, you are unlikely to know of it and, besides, it probably no longer exists. In any case, it was one of those places where reservations had to be made weeks in advance, the tablecloth alone probably cost more than my dress, and the waiters seemed to have been spun from silk.

I couldn't tell you precisely what I ate, but I do remember we all agreed the food was delicious. My husband had invited along some people from the delegation—it really couldn't be helped—so the conversation was lively, if not terribly intimate.

A highlight of the evening came, however, when it was time to pay the bill. You see, this restaurant had the tradition of presenting foreigners with their bill accompanied by a miniature flag of what they assumed to be the guests' country. Our bill arrived under the flag of India. My husband raised his eyebrows in amusement but said nothing, and interrupted a member of our party as he was about to protest. When the waiter left, my husband explained that if we were to tell them where we were from, it would just confuse the poor people. Then we'd have to explain not only where our island was, but also how we—evidently Indians— had ended up there. The history and geography lesson would hardly be worth the trouble. Besides, our flag wasn't official yet, the restaurant could hardly be expected to have one on hand. So he took out his wallet, counted out the bills and placed them under the Indian flag.

As we left the restaurant in a driving rain, my husband remarked that the gesture wasn't so inappropriate—which prompted a chorus of protests from the others. And that, Mrs. Livingston, was the first time I saw schism between my husband and those who thought the way he did.

[23]

She stepped on the ant, then gingerly inspected the sole of her shoe. The ant was splayed, flattened. "Mommy," she called exultantly. "I can kill! I can kill!"

Yasmin took a deep breath. So this is growing up, she thought, this celebration of newly realized power. How had her daughter acquired such knowledge, and why so young? But did it really matter? She would have acquired it anyway; it was, after all, part of growing up human.

"Mommy! I can kill!"

"Yes, dear."

[24]

PHOTOGRAPH: NEWSPAPER PHOTO, EIGHT-BY-TEN. HER FATHER APPEARS TO BE DEEP IN CONVERSATION WITH ANOTHER MAN. HE IS LISTENING. THE MAN IS TALKING. HE IS SHORT, THIS OTHER MAN, AND BALDING, AND ALTHOUGH IT IS NIGHT HE SPORTS SUN-GLASSES. THERE IS GREAT TENSION IN HER FATHER'S BODY. HE DOES

NOT WANT TO BE STANDING HERE BESIDE THIS MAN, DOES NOT WANT TO BE LISTENING TO HIM. HIS HAND IS WRAPPED AROUND THE BOWL OF A COFFEE CUP, THE TENSION IN HIS FIST REVEALING HIS STRUGGLE TO CONTAIN HIMSELF. HERE AGAIN, A DIVISION OF ENERGY: THE EFFORT AT RESTRAINT AND WHAT SHE THINKS TO BE A MASCULINE DESIRE TO CRUSH—MASCULINE NOT IN ITS ORIGIN BUT IN ITS MANIFESTATION. IN NO OTHER PHOTOGRAPH SHE HAS SO FAR SEEN ARE HIS EMOTIONS SO EVIDENT AND SO RAW.

She smiles to herself in satisfaction: She has perceived in the photograph a grain of authenticity: what he reveals despite himself.

But then she wonders whether she is reading too much into the image. Jim has often accused the newscast of breathing life into stories that would otherwise expire after a few laboured gasps. She knows he is right: They show videotape of a twister lifting a barn but would not bother to mention it if they didn't have the tape. You people, Jim says justly, see more in pictures than is there. He had tapped a fingernail at his photo of the Swiss mountain-side: the triangle of darkness, the triangle of brilliance. "It's not a statement," he said. "It's just a moment. Hardly news-worthy."

So she wonders: Might her father's reluctance to be there come from merely a headache or hunger—just a moment? Might the tension she detects arise from irrita-tion with photographers or responsibilities awaiting him elsewhere?

She can never know the answers, must draw her own conclusions, must hope there is some truth in them. It is, she consoles herself, like writing a novel or researching a biog-raphy. She can enjoy no certainty greater than conjecture.

Cyril tells her this other man went on to be prime minister. He was her father's great rival. He held Ram in great esteem, Cyril says, but esteem born of the fear and hatred one has for an equal who may yet spoil one's own dreams. A clever man. He sent Ram to London to join the team negotiating for independence. Ram thought there was hope they could work together. What he didn't understand, Cyril believes, was that this man's greatest wish was that Ram would disappear—and, of course, he did.

The sunglasses? A medical condition, says Cyril, although precisely what remains unknown to this day, years after the man's death. It was said that light—all light—was painful to him, that it prevented him from seeing. And then there was, of course, the mystique sunglasses conferred: the sense that they were to protect not his vision but his thoughts.

[25]

"What is she doing?" Ariana was scandalized. Yasmin followed the pointing finger to a swimsuited woman stretched out on a towel on the grass, a straw hat covering her face.

"She's sunbathing, dear."

"That's silly."

"Why?"

"She needs water to get clean."

"She doesn't want to get clean, dear. She wants to get brown."

"Like me?"

"Like you."

Her daughter pondered this for some moments. Then she said, "Mummy, if I do that, will I get white?"

"It doesn't work that way, dear. You'd get browner."

Her daughter thought about that, too, and then said, "I'd like to be white some day."

Yasmin caught her breath. Her daughter had reached into the tree of forbidden wishes and plucked poison. Yasmin, driven by a prickling shame, wanted to protest. Wait a minute, she wanted to say, Hold on, what's wrong with...? Where did you get...? But she stopped herself. Her daughter had spoken innnocently: the shame was not hers. The shame, she understood, arose from her own fear of the reaction of others: What in the world, they would wonder, had Yasmin been teaching her daughter?

And seeing her daughter safe from the peril, she began to see things as her daughter did—and understood that at the heart of her own reaction lay a grand hypocrisy: Why was it acceptable for that woman to dream of being brown, but not so for her daughter to dream of being white? And she wondered which was more dangerous: for her daughter to speculate on the impossible or for that woman to expose herself to the ravages of the sun? And yet it was, she knew, the mere beginning of a moral thread her daughter would be unravelling for the rest of her life.

Yasmin said, "Would you want daddy to be brown?"

"No."

"Would you like me to be white, like him?"

"Daddy's not white, silly!"

"He's not?"

"No. He's kind of...peach."

[26]

Why is it, do you imagine, Mrs. Livingston, that so many young people are given to bemoaning the loss of olden days they see as good? Is it simply, do you think, that time is the biggest fence, and so offers a vision of the greenest grass? It's such poppycock!

Take my son-in-law, for instance. Once, at tea, Mr. Summerhayes was mourning the loss of the art of letter-writing. Letter-writing, of all things—in an age when communication has become instantaneous. He had an idea that the old way—hours spent composing a letter by hand, a mail system that took weeks to deliver that letter—was somehow superior. Like so many young people, and a few older ones seeking to take advantage of their gullibility, he has varnished the past. I think he felt he was demonstrating his sense of history, the poor fellow.

May I confess something to you about Mr. Summerhayes, my dear? I do not totally trust his passions. He has them, he has passion for Yasmin, none of it is simulated—but I do not believe he trusts them himself. I do not believe that he believes in them. You see what I mean...

In any case, my dear, Mr. Summerhayes seemed to feel that not only were people in the good old days—that's us, my dear—more articulate, but we proved it in lengthy missives to one another. Some did, I suppose. I've never forgotten that lovely story you told me about your husband's love letters. Even that thrill eventually turned to unease, though, didn't it? I'm still not certain that your son would have been startled by those glimpses of the naughtiness of his father's mind, you know. Children aren't *that* naïve.

Understand, my dear, I'm not saying you were wrong.

We all have the right to prune our worlds, and those aspects of our lives that will survive us. And, yes, it *was* a lovely gesture, burying them with him. But still, I did detect a hint in your voice of a certain sense of loss, didn't I?

I've written few letters in my life, you know. At home there was no reason to. And in the year we spent in England my husband took care of the correspondence. I wrote no letters home—at least not on paper. I did compose letters in my head, elaborate descriptions of what I was seeing, reflections on the life we, or rather I, was living. But I wrote none of it down. You see—and not even Yasmin knows this—writing for me is a laborious process from which I derive no pleasure. I know many words, my dear, and they come to my tongue with a certain ease, but the moment I try to order them on paper—putting the letters and then the words themselves into systematic and harmonious form—now, that is another matter altogether...

There was, I will tell you, one letter I composed that I do wish I had written down. It was neither long nor elaborate, but it spoke from the heart, and it was addressed to the one person instinct told me would understand what I was trying to say.

[27]

          She squatted on Jim's lap, facing him, her little fingers—their shade and shape irrefutable proof that she was her parents' daughter—tenderly exploring the contours of his face. She looked to Yasmin like someone sightless moulding a mental image: she ran her fingertips up his temples and along his hairline, down across his forehead to his eyes and nose and smiling lips. She tickled him under the chin and made him laugh. Then she leaned in close and cupped her palms around his ear.

Jim listened. Then he said, "Well, uh, I don't know. Maybe."

She whispered again.

Jim's eyes flashed with amusement at Yasmin. He said, "I'm not sure. Why don't we see what your mom thinks?"

She grew shy, clambered off his lap and ran off to her room.

Yasmin looked expectantly at Jim.

He leaned towards her and spoke in a quiet voice: "First, she wanted to know if—when she grows up—if she'll have big breasts just like Mom's."

"Oh, God."

"Then she wanted to know if they'll go flippy-flop too, just like yours." He let his smile show.

"Flippy-flop."

"Flippy-flop. Can you believe it? I could hardly contain myself—"

"You should've just answered her question, Jim, instead of bringing me into it. You embarrassed her. Why do you think she asked you and not me?"

"Yas, the whole thing was funny, I thought—"

"Jim, the next time she wants to talk to you, talk to her."

"It *was* funny, Yas."

"Yeah. Until you embarrassed her. She's your daughter, Jim. Start taking her seriously."

"Look, I do take her ser—"

"Mummy, I want a drink of water."

"I do take her seriously, Yas, but—"

"Mummy! I'm thirsty!"

Yasmin stood up. "Watch that tone, young lady." Then she went off to the kitchen to get her daughter some water.

[28]

Dear Celia:

It will come as no surprise to you that it is raining as I write these words. You are always the most homesick during our rainy season, as if yours were a land of perpetual wetness. Do you remember how the sound of water dripping, from the roof, from trees, would mesmerize you and turn your eyes red and moist? I remember that about you—that, and the silence that came to you. You were inaccessible at those moments, your soul in flight.

We are spending a weekend in the country, in a little town that is all honey-coloured stone. Nearby is a quiet river lined with rushes and weeping willows. The innkeeper tells us that, in fine weather, the water is crowded with rowboats—but the weather, as I've said, is not fine, and there'll be no rowing for us.

Right now we are sitting at a window table in the local pub. We are alone, save for the barman polishing mugs. Through the rain-streaked window panes I can see the drops exploding onto the cobblestones, and the dampness causes me to pull my coat more tightly around my shoulders. Ram sits across from me, a mug of beer in front of him. He is absorbed, probably thinking about his work, the papers he has brought along, but which he has left behind at the inn. I sip my tea. Watch him. Watch the rain.

Unexpectedly, he reaches for my hand, enfolds it lightly in his. We do not speak. His touch alone tells me of his awareness.

It is enough. And for those long minutes of rain, my dear, here in
your land, my pores gasp, my nerves unfold, my soul takes flight.
    I have been shown, Celia, what it is to shatter deliciously.
        Love,
        Shakti

[29]

        For lunch, Amie brings sandwiches, egg
salad, chicken salad, in white bread trimmed of its crust.

    She places the platter on a space Cyril clears of the scat-
tered photographs, dozens in black-and-white and faded
colour—but so few take her beyond their stilled moments.

    As she eats, Yasmin shuffles through them: her parents
at the Coliseum; her father sitting, weary, at the Acropolis;
her mother wrapped in coat and shawl beside a river;
Buckingham Palace; the Alhambra; her mother in that same
coat and shawl—the same day, perhaps, rainy—smiling at
the door of a pub, the Beggar's Alms.

    Yasmin has been to many of these places, seen many of
these monuments. She too has snapshots of similar decom-
position—Jim's word—that reveal as little as do these, too
hasty, too shorn of personal context to be repositories of
memory. They have remained unviewed for years in the
albums to which they have been consigned. She looks again
at the photo of her mother at the pub door, thinks *Where we*
had a drink.

    Amie returns with bowls of strawberry ice cream.

    Penny says, "I love straw-breeze. Can' get them here any
more, though. Only frozen, and is not the same thing, eh?"

For the first time since her return just before lunch, Penny speaks without an edge. She had come in, looked unhappily at Cyril and Yasmin sitting at the table, at the box and the revealed photographs. Her frown had spoken of betrayal: all that they had done and said untrimmed, unembroidered.

Cyril had said, "Din't know when you were coming back, Penny. Thought we'd start without you."

Now, though, after long moments of uncomfortable silence: *straw-breeze*. The regret in her voice unfeigned. The hurt—distrust?—has been swallowed.

The power, Yasmin thinks, of the unsaid.

Her parents grin before the Eiffel Tower and, perhaps moments later, offer obligatory smiles to a busker's camera as they enter a bateau-mouche.

Cyril says, "You know why they call it a bateau-mouche? Is not fly-boat as you might think if you studied French in school. Is because they make them in a town called Mouche. Is Shakti who tell me that, you know. Her head was full o' that stuff."

Yasmin nods. "I grew up with her, remember? Mom liked to impress people."

"And make them feel a little foolish too, I think," Penny says.

Cyril purses his lips. "Yes. Maybe. But not in a bad way, eh? Just in fun."

"Yes," Penny says, unconvinced. "Perhaps jus' in fun."

"Or," Yasmin says, "maybe not."

Amie collects the bowls and returns immediately with tea.

Yasmin, insisting that she has already eaten far too much, refuses to join Cyril in a slice of his cake. She seeks to placate him with a smile but he chooses not to reciprocate. And neither, she sees, does Amie.

[30]

They compromised on the Christmas cards. She would write to her friends, he would write to his, and they would divide equally those they had in common.

Hers were done quickly in characteristic scrawl, envelopes addressed, stamps affixed. Greeting cards were not communications she lingered over. Then she sat back and watched Jim. He sat upright at the dining table, working assiduously at the task, fountain pen shaping his cursive script. And it was peering at that script, watching the lustrous black ink dry quickly on the card, that she saw he had written his name first, hers second, their daughter's last. She told herself it was a minor matter, but she knew there had been a time when, writing both their names, he'd instinctively written hers before his.

She turned away, picked up her stack, squared and patted them into a neat pile. She told herself she was being over-sensitive, *paranoid*, but she could not forget the importance of little things which, together, lent significance to the inconsequential.

Jim looked up. "Done already?"

She shrugged.

"Got any stamps?"

She pushed them over to him. "But you'll have to lick them yourself."

[31]

Cyril excuses himself: a quick errand. Penny, preoccupied, goes to freshen up.

Yasmin steps out onto the porch, the sun burning down rugged and unhindered with a heat that causes her to shiver.

Ash is standing at the railing awash in sunlight. In his hand he balances a pellet gun. At her approach, his index finger stiffens at his lips, sustaining a silence already established, then swiftly directs her attention to a tree down below.

She sees branches and midday shadows between the leaves. He alone sees prey. "What are you hunting?" she whispers.

"Blackbirds," he whispers back. "The blacker the better."

He raises the stock of the pellet gun to his shoulder, levels the barrel into the support of his left hand. Holds his breath, willing himself to stillness, index finger curling around the trigger. Then the gun cracks like a door snapping shut. From the trees a crow flaps unhappily away.

"Are they pests?"

"They all over the place. Some o' the ugliest birds you ever see." He breaks the barrel, inserts another pellet.

"But are they pests?"

"They does steal, yeah. It in their nature, nuh."

"But killing them—a little extreme, wouldn't you say?"

"You might. I wouldn't. You ain't have to live with them."

"You sound as if they scare you."

"Them? The little black boys? No way."

"I thought we were talking about blackbirds."

"Black whatever. And I tellin' you now—no fockin' way."

His gaze falls to the ground below, eyes flicking through the grass in search of further prey. Swiftly he brings the gun to his shoulder, aims at the ground, fires.

Down below the grass is disturbed by a sudden frenzied whipping: a lizard, head bloodied, tossing around on itself.

"Another pest?" she says, voice hardened.

Reloading the gun, he sucks dismissively at his teeth. Then he takes aim and fires again.

[32]

Some newscasts clawed their way into her stomach, raking at her until she could feel herself beginning to shred. Today's, she consoled herself, could not get any worse.

She steeled her stomach through the ads and the promos, and as she saw the opening graphics on the monitor, gave herself permission to simply read the text as it presented itself on the teleprompter. The lead item was the kind that left no emotional room for ad-libbing a personal touch into the text; it offered no scope for editing in a conversational tone even as she read.

She cleared her mind, and when the red light lit on camera one, when the floor director's palm chopped her cue, she began to read:

TRAGEDY STRUCK A BELVEDERE FAMILY THIS MORNING WHEN
FOUR-YEAR-OLD MELISSA EDWARDS WAS ABDUCTED WHILE PLAY-
ING IN THE FAMILY'S BACKYARD. HER BODY WAS FOUND FOUR

HOURS LATER IN A GARBAGE CAN TWO BLOCKS FROM HER HOME.
POLICE SAY SHE HAD BEEN SEXUALLY ASSAULTED. GARTH ROBERTS
HAS THE STORY.

It was in this yard that four-year-old Melissa Edwards...

The monitor showed a small backyard crowded with a swing set and sandbox; then the camera panned to the rear of the house—small, detached, a disorder of things that suggested haste rather than poverty—and zoomed in on a window.

...keeping an eye on her daughter from the kitchen window...

The window that hung closed and empty now. Yasmin shuffled the pages of her script, trying to keep busy, trying to keep an ear on the report without absorbing its details.

...turned away just for minute, but long enough for...

Her daughter had brought to her an almost manic clarity, the ability to see every possibility of peril small and large, from fingers disintegrating under rocking-chair skids to voices raised in panic from the midst of flaming houses. She had gained a renewed sense of the precariousness of life, the phrase that reporters so often applied to the American vice-president—*just a heartbeat away*—acquiring an acuteness that went beyond cliché.

...beaten and sodo...

The utter helplessness of an infant, and the terrifying trust of a toddler, made the sanctioned execution of those who would harm them no longer seem so repugnant. Her daughter's vulnerability, she acknowledged, had evoked in her the most primitive of reactions. Holding Ariana, confronting that vulnerability, she knew herself capable, in the child's defence, of actions otherwise unimaginable.

Police have arrested a thirty-three-year-old drifter...

Her view had narrowed; it had simplified. She no longer cared to debate the morality of an eye for an eye, could no longer accept absolution of perpetrators in the larger social picture. "So the guy's a drifter," she said sourly to Charlotte standing beside camera one. "Context is no excuse."

"Revenge, then, Yas?" Charlotte asked.

No, not even that. She found herself nagged by a more complex notion: that the brutality of certain acts removed the humanity from the human who had committed them. Execution would not solve the larger problem, she admitted, but it would solve the smaller one: this little cancer, at least, would not kill again.

...mother is under a doctor's care. This is Garth Roberts for Newsline in Belvedere Township.

At the cut to commercial, Charlotte approached the anchor desk. "What's happening to you, Yas?"

"I've had a child," Yasmin replied, shuffling her papers, and that child had brought her awareness of aspects of herself she'd never before known existed. What Yasmin did not say was that even as she heard herself expressing these thoughts, she could not believe that she was saying them.

It was later, well after the newscast was done, after the studio had gone dark, the crew had dispersed and the make-up had been cleaned off, that she could allow her jaws to clench and her hands to shake.

Charlotte said, "So what is it you want, Yas?"

Yasmin thought long and hard. "I want my daughter, on awakening to darkness in the middle of the night, to know beyond all doubt that she is safe."

When her hands no longer shook, she drove home.

[33]

That's not me!

The images were over two years old, and her daughter's reaction to seeing this other self for the first time on videotape was the same as Yasmin's had been on hearing her own voice from a tape recorder: the known self seemed absent.

"That *is* you, honey."

Ariana laughed, her joke rewarded by the concern that clouded Yasmin's face.

"I know, Mummy."

Yasmin saw that she had been teased. Snarling in mock displeasure, she grabbed her daughter and began to tickle her, the laughter shrill and manic in delight. Soon her daughter fought free and ran off, leaving Yasmin with the answer she would have given had the girl been older, the answer she had grown accustomed to over the years in response to the moment of fright—*It's not me!*—that had come to her in childhood.

Yasmin crossed her hands on her lap and let her mind summon the tinny sound: *Hello, my name is Yasmin. Mary had a little lamb...* It was without source, sound without context, but the tone recollected in all its strangeness still caused her heart to quicken.

No, honey, she would have said, that isn't you. That's you as you were the moment those images were made. You've changed in countless ways, you're changing every minute—so that person there, that stranger you pretend not to recognize, is not you. She is the You that used to be because every you is momentary, you are an act of ongoing creation.

And for reasons she could not identify, Yasmin thought of her mother.

[34]

PHOTO: THE DAY MAY HAVE BEEN CLOUDY, OR PERHAPS THE YEARS HAVE EFFACED THE CLARITY OF SUNSHINE BY IMPOSING ON THE BLACKS AND GREYS A POWDERY FILM THAT HAS TURNED THE IMAGES TENTATIVE. THEY ARE LINED UP ONE BESIDE THE OTHER IN FRONT OF A LOW WALL, A CONCRETE FENCE PERHAPS, ABOVE WHICH IS A SKY SO BLEACHED THAT IT SUGGESTS NEITHER COLOUR NOR CONTEXT. THEY STAND IN DESCENDING ORDER OF HEIGHT AND AGE, THREE CHILDREN UNDER TEN, ALL SKINNY, ALL BARE-FOOT. THE BOY WHO WAS TO BE HER FATHER, THE ELDEST, OFFERS A HALF-SMILE TO THE CAMERA, AND A SQUINT THAT APPEARS TO BE TRYING TO SEE THROUGH THE LENS TO THE PHOTOGRAPHER'S EYE; THERE IS ABOUT HIM A LACK OF SELF-CONSCIOUSNESS, HIS SHIRT UNBUTTONED, HIS LEFT FOOT RAISED AND PROPPED ON, OR PER-HAPS SCRATCHING AT, HIS RIGHT CALF. BESIDE HIM STANDS PENNY IN T-SHIRT AND SHORTS, FACE INEXPRESSIVE, EYES GAZING NOT AT THE CAMERA BUT JUST PAST IT; SHE IS SLIGHTLY PIGEON-TOED, BUT THE CURVATURE OF HER SHOULDERS AND THE WAY HER ARMS HANG DOWN HER FRONT TO HER INTERLACED FINGERS REFLECT A CERTAIN UNEASE: PENNY SEEMS NOT TO KNOW WHAT TO DO WITH HER BODY. TO HER LEFT CYRIL STANDS AT STIFF-ARMED ATTENTION, HIS SHIRT TUCKED NEATLY INTO HIS SHORTS, HIS FEET PERFECTLY ALIGNED. A TOOTHY GRIN SCREWS HIS FACE INTO A GUILELESS DELIGHT, EYES GAZING WITH FRANKNESS INTO THE CAMERA.

Penny says, "You know, when he was small, Manager here use to eat dirt?"

Cyril's eyes narrow unhappily into a sidelong glance at his sister.

"Yes, dirt. Imagine!"

"Ringworm," Cyril says defensively. "I had ringworm."

"Yes, but Manager, man," Penny says with rising merriment, "you eat enough dirt to feed the worm and plant a garden in your belly to boot."

"And who use to feed me the dirt, spoonful after spoonful?"

"Don' go blaming me again."

"Ey, look, I don' remember none o' this, but Ram always swear that it was my loving sister—"

He falls silent, defence severed by Penny's laughter.

Penny says, "When we were chil'ren, we ran around barefoot. We threw stones, we played sword-fight with sticks. We climbed trees and fell off walls. We took our scrapes and our parents din't go crazy. They were too busy, they din't have time to worry 'bout us every minute. That was the life we lived."

Cyril says, "But we went to school, too. And when we din't do our homework, we got strapped and caned. And they hardly knew about it. That was the life we lived too."

"You making them sound negligent. They weren't negligent, they were busy. Is why they changed so much at the beach, always shouting after us. They had more time to see the dangers."

"No, no, don't misunderstand me. I not saying they were negligent. Is our memory I talkin' about. 'That was the life we lived.' *We* din't live a life, Penny. You did, I did, Ram did. If I get your drift, you remembering freedom."

"Yes, in a way."

"Is not exactly how it stay with me. That was the life *you* lived. Or the life you remember. I remember climbing the mango tree, and I remember the day Ranjit fell off and shattered his right arm. I remember the months he spent teaching himself to write with his left."

"And Ranjit ambidextrous to this day."

"Yes, but is jus' a party trick, Penny. He shattered his arm and it leave him with a lifelong party-trick."

"So what you have against party tricks?"

"Nothing. If is a clown doing them."

"Is always been your problem, Manager. You always thought anybody who liked a good time was a clown. Remember—Vernon use to say you were born old?"

"But he din't really mean old. He meant boring."

"Well, anyway, you can't help it if it in your nature, eh?"

Cyril acknowledges her words with a grunt and a weave of his head. "Guess not," he says.

As Penny, victorious, tugs the box closer and rummages through its depths, Cyril says, "And Shakti, Yasmin—what kind o' mother was she?"

[35]

It was only after she had retrieved all the hidden chocolate Easter eggs that her daughter, satisfied with the total, ventured the opinion that there was no Easter bunny.

"Why not, honey?"

"There's no Easter bunny town, so the Easter bunny has no place to live. So there's no Easter bunny."

Yasmin glanced at Charlotte. "At least it's logical."

Charlotte gritted her teeth. "Little fascist," she mumbled. Then she turned to the little girl. "So where'd all those Easter eggs come from?"

"The store, silly."

In her daughter's realism, Yasmin saw her mother.

Easter Sunday had never been the occasion of egg hunts in their apartment. From her earliest memory until she was in her late teens, it was a morning marked only by a box placed by her mother beside the cereal bowl on the dining table; in it would be a single large Belgian chocolate egg, inside of which would be a variety of smaller fine chocolates.

In the late morning, having returned from church, Mrs. Livingston would come by with a small box of what her mother sometimes referred to, with dissatisfaction bordering on disdain, as drugstore Easter eggs, colourfully wrapped chocolates the size and shape of hens' eggs stuffed with a sweet yellow-and-white concoction the consistency of stiffening glue. Yasmin would accept the gift with what she later understood to be a baffling pantomime of loyalty: with a show of gratitude to Mrs. Livingston, with a covert glance of disgust to her mother, with a haste in her room to unwrap and consume one or two of the eggs.

Her mother's gift would have cost five times Mrs. Livingston's, but to Yasmin Mrs. Livingston's—meant to be devoured rather than savoured—was by far the more appealing. Her mother always assumed that if large sections of the Belgian egg remained weeks later it was because Yasmin wished to relish it for as long as possible. The thought gave her pleasure, and Yasmin never enlightened her as to the true reason. They were lessons—the infantile appeal of a certain crudeness, the keeping of secrets for reasons other than egotism—that Yasmin, on having her own child, did not forget.

Nor did she forget the nature of her relationship with

her mother. She had no memory of hugs and caresses, or of kisses beyond the obligatory. When she was ill, her mother would administer medicines and rub her back and chest with ointment, but there was no sense of companionship, of maternal vigil: her mother would say goodnight with a pat on the head and not look back.

Later on, they recommended books to each other, told each other of movies to be seen or avoided. An intellectual relationship, Yasmin thought, when she was of an age to flirt with such evaluation—and yet, the closest they had ever come to a theological discussion was the Easter Sunday her mother, seeking to provoke a reaction from Mrs. Livingston, happened to mention that she found the entire idea of Easter—the crucifixion, the burial, the resurrection—rather grotesque.

Yasmin paused on her way to her room: "Gee, Mom, the idea of eternal life kind of appeals to me considering the alternative." Often her mother appeared to be bullying Mrs. Livingston, but this was the only time Yasmin came to her defence.

She knew her mother to be what others called a charming woman—Charlotte was always dazzled by her—but charm, she had concluded, required distance in the way that stagecraft did; there was a vital element of wilful illusion to it. To sit too close to the stage was to see the frayed edges of the costumes, the sweaty armpits, the effort behind the illusion. But a certain measure of personal theatre was important to her mother, a woman of affectation but not of pretence. Her airs were meant not for others but for herself. She practised the idea of her life in a way that avoided sham and hypocrisy, happy behind the façades that made her real to herself.

And yet it was those façades, to which they both played, that denied Yasmin the physical affection whose absence she noticed only when, a mother herself, she felt the hunger to hold her daughter, to feel her warmth and the pulsing of her blood. When she kissed her daughter, she offered more than affection. There was something holy about it. A communion. It was, each time, like conferring a blessing.

Yasmin was not resentful that her mother had apparently felt none of these emotions. Nor was she angered by their absence. She was simply puzzled by it.

[36]

Our departure from England was rather precipitate. One day my husband called me with the news that we had to return home. Within a week we were gone. We had expected to be there for another year or two. There was so much we hadn't done or seen. But it couldn't be helped. His political enemies, you see, had found a way of getting at him even there, thousands of miles away from our island.

Perhaps it was my displeasure at being forced to leave a land to which I was finding myself more and more attached —precisely, I think because of its strangeness, because of my lack of natural attachment to it. Nothing was expected of me, you see, and so I could make it all up as I went along. I suppose it was inevitable, wasn't it—that I would fall in love with a land that gave me such freedom. So you see, my dear, that it was England was immaterial. I might have developed a similar passion for France or Spain or Italy. But the passion was there, and it led to a displeasure which—at least at first—caused me to lay the blame squarely at my husband's door.

It all began with a cable—a simple, silly cable of greetings to his people back home. A political anniversary of some sort. But that cable, which was of course made public, reminded his political enemies about him. And it gave them an opening. Once they had that opening, that point of vulnerabilty—well, my husband in their position would have done the same. He too would have found a way to profit from the situation.

First came the accusations of betrayal. As a member of our delegation in London, he was expected to represent all our people and not just his people. This cable of fraternal greetings—just what was his game? his enemies asked.

Then came the more serious allegations. I have never fully understood what happened. My husband, as I've said, did not share the details of his work with me—but there were accusations of bribery. Evil tongues wagged that he had received pay-offs from certain British sugar interests—a way of ensuring continued special access to the plantations after independence. Now my dear, my husband was many things, not all of them laudable, but he was not a thief. I did not for a minute believe these accusations, but the truth was immaterial. He could never completely clear his name—all politicians were assumed to be corrupt, you see—but that would not be a hindrance. What mattered was that he return to the island and take up the cudgels. As my husband well knew, ours was a world in which courage was valued over probity.

He never found out who was the source of the accusations. It was always *They say* or *I hear* or *Apparently*. But my husband suspected someone on the British side of the independence negotiations. It's all rather Byzantine, but my husband believed that the British and his political enemies back home stood to gain by ensuring he had no political career to return to in the island—so they had conspired to smear him. Nothing from his enemies back home could surprise him, but the British! He had expected better. And yet there was an entire history too, full of ugliness. So the abstract encountered the personal, and this was the beginning of his hatred for the British—a hatred, it must be said, he would cultivate. It was too politically useful to pass up, you see. An easy way to whip up the troops, if you see what I mean. But I'm getting ahead of myself, aren't I?

I recall a particularly bitter tirade one evening, once he appreciated how well the net of rumours had been woven. England! he said. What a country! Their children roast cats alive for pleasure, you know—part of their brutish side. They've lived for so long pretending to be refined and mannered, but they can't prevent the primitive from breaking through the masquerade from time to time. That's when you see what they're really like. English reserve? Afternoon tea? Theatre, my dear! Masquerade! And he added in our island dialect, Ol' Mas! Not'ing more than Ol' Mas to muffle the anguish of the sizzling cat. But at times like this the agonized meows intrude upon the discreet clink of cups on saucers.

And when I pointed out, my dear Mrs. Livingston, that they were giving us our independence, he said, Independence? That's just their way of getting rid of us, don't you see?

Then he calmed down, sat alone in the darkness, and began to think.

He was a clever man, my husband, and had the luck to

have enemies who constantly underestimated him. Within a day of our return to the island, he had turned things around...

My...

Is it me, my dear, or has it grown hot in here? I'm parched, and even a little light-headed. I think I should fetch myself a sip of water. Perhaps take a little toodle around the block. Yes, a walk. Just the thing.

Never you fear, my dear. I shall return.

[37]

When she found herself offended by others' condescension to her gender, her race, or her background, her mother would say, "It's the garlic soup incident all over again." And she would tell the story that Yasmin had heard so often she could summon it only in her mother's voice.

"She asked me, you see, what my favourite food was—as people tend to do when you first meet. Where are you from? What do you do? What movies do you like? Oh, she was genuinely interested, as they usually are, wanting you to feel welcome and comfortable and all the rest. She had a big smile—American teeth: you know, large and white and shield-like, filling the mouth to overflowing. And she had that way people have of leaning toward you when they want to make sure you notice their interest—the kind of interest that seems to be begging for your blessing. It makes you uneasy and unforgiving.

"In any case, I explained that I was quite partial to garlic soup. Oh, the smile wavered slightly, this was a touch too exotic for the lady, but I explained—you know, a cold soup, with garlic and ground almonds, quite delicious. She thought about this for a moment, nodding, her eyes glazing distantly. Then a sparkle appeared in them, and she leaned in closer. 'And is there,' she said, 'curry in the soup?'

"I paused briefly, to deal with my surprise. Then I said, sharply, I'm afraid, 'It's a *Spanish* soup.' Only with difficulty did I refrain from adding 'you twit.' Sincerity is no excuse for stupidity, I'm afraid.

"It's a pressure they put on you, you see—to recognize how open and accepting they are. They mean well, of course, but what really matters to them is what you think of them, and they have no idea how blinded they are by their good intentions. They don't see they are melting you down into stereotype. She didn't know what to make of me, this lady, and she couldn't handle me on my own terms, so we managed to lose each other rather quickly after that."

[38]

PHOTO: SHAKTI AND VERNON SIDE BY SIDE ON AN AIRPORT TARMAC, BEHIND THEM AN AIRCRAFT MARKED "BOAC." THEY STAND TOGETHER, YET THERE IS NO CLOSENESS BETWEEN THEM. SHAKTI'S ARMS ARE FOLDED. VERNON'S LEFT HAND HOLDS HIS HAT BY THE BRIM, HIS RIGHT GRASPS THE HANDLE OF A BRIEFCASE. THEY HAVE BOTH LOST WEIGHT, LOOK FIT AND RELAXED. SHAKTI WEARS AN INDIAN VEIL—AN OHRNI, PENNY SAYS—AND A FORM-FITTING DRESS AND PUMPS: A BLEND OF TRADITIONAL MODESTY AND

MODERN DARING. VERNON WEARS A LIGHTWEIGHT SUIT, THE
JACKET UNBUTTONED, AND—A BRIEF AFFECTATION THIS, CYRIL
SAYS—A BOW TIE. HIS SMILE IS GENUINE; IT PROCEEDS FROM THE
EYES. TO HERS, THOUGH, THERE IS MORE OF A SQUINT; IT IS AT
LEAST PARTIALLY SUMMONED. HE APPEARS HAPPY, SHE, FATIGUED.

Penny clicks her tongue. "Shakti wasn' happy that day. The day they came back home. I can't say I was surprise. She never wrote. At leas' Vernon sent a little note now and then. They didn' live away all that long but, you know, by the time they got back Shakti was a'ready like a little English-woman."

Yasmin asks what she means.

She considers for a moment. "Airs," she says. "Full o' airs." She sits back in satisfaction, as if the answer contains a self-evident explanation. Then she says, "As for Vernon, what you must never forget is that he was sincere. Politics wasn' a game for him. It wasn' a end in itself. His goals were high—and because they were high he didn't mind sacrific-ing himself."

Had she heard this from a politician, Yasmin would have thought it self-serving. Hearing it from Penny, she does not know what to think, feels trapped between what she knows to be usually true and what she wishes to be true.

Cyril says, with a laugh, "You know, funny thing. He liked rhetorical questions. To make people think, nuh. And he'd get vicious if anybody tried to answer. At the end of every meeting he'd ask, 'Any questions?' but before anybody could say anything he was up an' out. 'Any questions?' For him, that was a rhetorical question, too. He jus' expected everybody to understan'."

Yasmin constructs a smile. She knows this trait, knows it

in Jim, knows it in herself—and she also knows there is nothing amusing about it.

When Penny says this was a sign of his magnanimity—that he held everyone to be his intellectual equal—Yasmin wonders how it is that she has managed through the years to retain such a level of naivety. Or is it, she wonders, of more recent vintage? Is she hearing from Penny the betrayal of the years, the gilding of memories that would make them precious—the past, then, turning brittle and untrustworthy?

[39]

You must forgive me, my dear. It must be the dryness of the air in here, I simply couldn't bring myself to return yesterday. They recirculate the air, don't they? They must, with windows that cannot open. The air feels so artificial. However, here I am. I slept well, and now feel refreshed and fit as a fiddle—an expression that makes sense only because of alliteration.

I have spent the morning thinking about my husband. Remembering. He towered beside me, you know, have I mentioned that? It was not so much that he was a tall man as that I was—am—the height that you see. Short enough, as Celia used to tease me, to seek shelter under a mushroom.

And he had this peculiarity—have I mentioned it?—of putting his hand on my shoulder. It was a small gesture, unremarkable, but it was his way of showing me affection, particularly when we were in public. He never hugged me or put his arm around my shoulders—he wasn't that kind of man—but when we were outside, on the way to a function perhaps, or during our walks in England—when he wasn't performing, you see—he liked to rest his right palm on my left shoulder. Always that palm, always that shoulder. As if I were a kind of support.

I loved that gesture, you know. It let me know he knew I was there. And there are still moments today—unexpected moments—when I seem to feel the press and warmth of his hand, a kind of phantom touch...

What do you suppose that means, my dear?

[40]

"A doctor," her daughter said. "I want to be a doctor when I grow up."

Yasmin was disappointed. She had hoped for a child with greater imagination. She comforted herself with the thought that at this young age everything was the product of a phase; that this too would pass, like the colic or the piercing of a new tooth.

"You can be anything you want to be, honey," she said. "You can be a dancer or a painter or a writer. You can be a pilot or a lawyer or an architect like daddy."

"I can be anything I want to be?"

"Anything."

"I want to be a man."

"Well, maybe not quite anything, dear."

"Oh, okay."

Yasmin glanced over at Jim. He had taken refuge behind his open newspaper, and she saw the pages tremble from his silent laughter. Biting at the insides of her cheeks, she mumbled, "Can I borrow the sports section?"

[41]

Penny says, "Ah, the beach."

PHOTO: VARIOUS TONES OF GREY DISTINGUISH SEA, SAND AND SKY. VERNON, SHAKTI AND PENNY POSE IN SWIMSUITS FOR THE CAMERA. VERNON IS CLOWNING, FACE DISTORTED IN A SCOWL, FINGERS CLAWING AT THE AIR. SHAKTI APPEARS THOUGHTFUL AND PENNY SLIGHTLY REMOVED, AS IF SHE HAS JUST REMEMBERED SOMETHING THAT SHE NEEDS TO ATTEND TO. IN THE FAR BACKGROUND, SITTING ON THE SAND AND STARING OFF TO THE HORIZON IS AMIE, YOUNG. SHE IS INCIDENTAL, NOT A MEMBER OF THE PARTY. SHE IS WEARING A LONG DRESS. A THICK BRAID HANGS DOWN TO HER LOWER BACK.

Penny pauses—and then, bizarrely, giggles. Her fingertips brush the sleeve of Yasmin's blouse. "Girl, you wouldn' believe how Amie use to snore. You wouldn' believe how air going in an' out o' that little body could roar so much, like water tumblin' over Niagara Falls. She drown out the sea, she make the walls tremble, nobody could sleep."

That little body: legs drawn up, arms reaching around the knees in a clasp of self-comfort: a gaze that couldn't be read, that couldn't see through the decades—or could it?—to the immutability of the moment. The dress has a pattern, now just a suggestion of grey, but the braid is intricate.

And there's Vernon, Penny continues: playing the fool, acting up. As usual. One evening at the dinner table, she says, as Amie cleared away the dishes, Vernon's mischievousness led him to imitate her snoring: a monstrous gurgling sizzle, a liquid hacking, the squelching slap of wet tongue.

"It was the funniest thing, girl. We laugh! We laugh so hard. Even Amie. She laugh so hard she break two-three plates if I not mistaken." She wipes at her eyes. "Remember that, Manager?"

"I remember."

Her laughter subsides. "If it have one thing nobody can take away from Vernon, is his sense of humour. He was wild!"

[42]

The sounds from downstairs—muffled music, the occasional clank of heavy iron—cushion the silence in the living room.

The shuffling of photos, Penny and Cyril each clutching a handful, acquires a dry edge. Together the sounds suggest isolation, as if no world exists beyond them.

Suddenly there is a shout. Then an exchange of shouts. Amie, high-pitched and angry. Ash, at a lower register, suggestive of greater control.

A door bangs, a stream of chattering laughter emerging from its brief echo.

Penny, tossing the photographs back onto the pile in front of her, says, "But what biting Amie so these days? She going around looking as if she working in a funeral home—and listen to her now, shouting like a fishwife."

"What you blaming Amie for?" Cyril says without

looking up. "You know the boy always up to some *jhunjut*. He always provoking her, man, Penny."

Penny sucks her teeth and shuffles through the photos with the tips of her fingers, making a mess of them.

A PLAYFUL PHOTOGRAPH, SLIGHTLY ILL-FOCUSED BECAUSE THE LENS IS TOO NEAR THE SUBJECT. A CLOSE-UP OF HER FATHER IN A HAT, BRIM PULLED LOW OVER HIS RIGHT EYE, THE LEFT SQUINTING FROM THE SMOKE RISING FROM A CIGARETTE PLANTED BETWEEN PURSED LIPS. BOGEY.

Penny says with excitement, "Remember the hat, Cyril? He pull it off one of the journalist fellas and start joking around? Remember that day?"

Cyril nods: If he shares Penny's memory of the day it is with tempered excitement.

Penny says, "What a joker. Always teasing people. And the more he loved you, the worse he tease you." She pats Cyril on the knee. "Remember the day he make you shine his shoes? That was so funny."

Cyril does not reveal whether he found it funny or not —but Yasmin sees his jaws shudder and lock. Quickly she says, "He smoked. I didn't know that."

"Smoking was still all right back then," Penny says, her tone defensive. "Everybody did it. Even the old ladies."

"Take it easy, Penny," Cyril says. "Yasmin was just—"

"He start smoking when he was young. Like everybody, nuh. Drinking, that came later. In fact, there's a story—"

"You not going to tell that old tale, ehh, Penny?"

Penny pointedly ignores him. "Vernon was in high school and one lunchtime he was puffing on a cigarette when a teacher see him. But Vernon see the teacher at the same time and in two-twos the cigarette was gone. You know what he do? He suck it into his mouth, chew it up and swallow it. Jus' like that. Teacher couldn' do nothing. No proof, no punishment. He went around telling the story, though, thinking to make Vernon look foolish. Instead, he turn him into a hero for the other boys. He was so popular, the next year the school make him head prefect. I always believe that is eating the cigarette that turn Vernon into a politician."

Cyril claps his palms on his thighs, turns a wistful gaze on Yasmin. "Is as good an explanation as any, I suppose."

Shoes clattering on the floor, Ash comes in. He is sweaty, and emits a strident energy.

Penny says, "What that was all about, Ash?'

He gives her a look of defensive ignorance.

"With Amie. The shouting."

"Oh, that." He smiles mischievously, scratches at his temple. "She treatin' me like a child again. I liftin' some iron, with the radio on, nuh. Out of the blue she come and tell me to turn it down. It too loud. It hurting her ears. Well, I tell her no—" his voice rises, as if his reaction was self-evident "—and just like that she start to shout at me. So I shout back. Is just music, Amie, you acting like a wet blanket. And you know what she say? Wet blanket? What wet blanket? Who wet the blanket? Who goin' to wash it now? I have enough work, you know!" He breaks into a roar of laughter.

Penny clamps her teeth together, but a laugh breaks in Cyril's throat. Penny's determination falters.

Yasmin, restraining herself by biting at the insides of her cheeks, feels her lower lip begin to tremble.

Penny glances at Cyril. His eyes are closed, his cheeks jiggling.

Penny's eyes focus on the betrayal of Yasmin's lower lip and as her body begins to rock in silent laughter, in the seconds before she must bury her face in her hands, she manages to tell Ash that he must apologize to Amie.

Yasmin, suddenly moved, thinks: Dear Amie. Dear, dear lady...

[43]

The afternoon sun slanted into the garden. Sam the yardman had mowed the lawn that morning and the fragrance of fresh-cut grass still hung faintly in the warm air, the silence given gentle rhythm by the sputtering of a neighbour's sprinkler.

They sat across from each other, Yasmin and Ariana, glasses of lemonade on the metal table between them. Each held a book, her daughter's concentration intense on the page. Yasmin pretended to read in order not to break the spell.

At six years of age she was not a precocious child, but she was bright. She had inherited her grandmother's eyes, ink-black and intelligent, jealous of their intimacies. Yasmin could see a reassuring strength, a self-sufficiency, glinting hard and brilliant between the ever-diminishing layers of helplessness and dependence. She had an interest in music, was reasonably athletic, and had adjusted well to the rigours of school. Yasmin took pride in her daughter's every accomplishment, as did, she knew, all parents in their children, at least those children who were loved.

After a while, her daughter shut her book and said, "Mummy, when can we go see the ponies?"

"Which ponies, dear?"

"The ponies in the park."

"I don't think there are any ponies in the park, honey."

"Yes, there are. They live in the woods in the park. It's their home."

"And who told you that? Somebody at school?"

"No. A man."

"What man?"

"Just a man. He was in a car."

The world fell away from Yasmin's perception: the sunlight dimmed, the sprinkler fell silent, the smell of grass gave way to a sudden airlessness. "Where?"

"At school."

"I thought you said he was in a car."

"Yes, in a car, just outside the playground."

"And what did he say?"

"He told me about the ponies."

"Did he want to take you to see them?"

"Yes, but I told him I can't go, I have to go back to class."

"And what did he do?"

"He said it won't take long in the car, but I wanted to play with my friends some more so I said no thank you." Her daughter's voice had fallen to a whisper.

"When did you talk to him?"

"I don't know. Maybe...two days ago?"

Two days—but her daughter had not yet developed a sense of time. It might have been a week.

"Had you ever seen him before?"

"No."

"Has he been back?"

"No."

Yasmin put her book down, reached across the table and

took her daughter's hands in hers. "I want you to promise me something."

Her daughter waited, her eyes disquieted.

"Promise me that you will never, ever, speak to strangers, men or women."

And Yasmin was saddened to see fear crowding her daughter's eyes, the indispensable fear, the fear that only men could safely discard with the years. She felt she was doing her daughter violence, crushing her innocence with the weight of centuries: male weight, female centuries.

Her daughter slid off the chair, came to her, sat on her lap. "Mom," she whispered, sliding her arms around Yasmin's neck. "Can we go see the ponies sometime?"

Yasmin hugged her close. "There aren't any, honey. There aren't any ponies." Young or old, she thought, it was painful knowledge.

Her daughter said nothing. She burrowed her head into her embrace.

Yasmin closed her eyes, felt the world simplify into warmth and softness and the brush of her daughter's breath.

This love of her daughter: it was immeasurable. It was, she knew, her only knowledge of the infinite.

[44]

Many a time, my dear, you have remarked on the peculiarity of my speech, as has Yasmin, as has, I am certain, my son-in-law. I am enamoured of linguistic precision. Do you know that my husband is the one responsible for making language precious to me? All those years of living with a man to whom words were weightless have made me picky. This is why I grow impatient whenever you say absurdities such as "It's raining out," as if it could ever rain elsewhere. Or "I thought to myself"—who else would you think to, unless you're psychic?

My husband, you see, believed firmly that nothing said in the heat of an election campaign should be taken seriously. And so he felt free to promise the world—independence, he said once, would be like a magic potion, it would solve all our problems—and he was genuinely surprised and offended when he saw that people expected him to deliver the world. He was astounded that there were those who truly expected independence to provide perfection, astounded even though he was the first to say it. It was as if part of him believed that people should be swayed by politicians, but without taking them seriously.

So, my dear, I have grown picky over the years. One learns, as you well know, how to survive.

There was a kind of genius, you know, in the way he managed through language and theatre to reverse his fortunes after we returned to the island. It was simple, but daring. He broke with the government on what he claimed to be a point of principle. Dramatically, of course—a press conference, a show of suppressed outrage. Anything else would have been useless. The first minister, he said, was manoeuvring to marginalize our people in the post-independence world. Realizing this had made it impossible for him to continue at the London delegation. It was a matter of conscience.

The hacks latched on to this. The next morning every headline read "A Matter of Conscience." And within twenty-four hours my husband was a hero among our people. The cable was forgotten, the bribery accusation was forgotten, and my husband assumed, with relish, the mantle of protector of his people.

The other side called him a traitor, of course. They said he had betrayed the first minister—

What do you expect me to say, my dear? That my husband was a crook? I cannot say that. I will say this. He managed his money prudently, and it is undeniable that we returned to the island with a great deal more money than when we left. But he had mentioned his investments to me, you see, so I was hardly surprised. He was a shrewd man. I have never seen any reason to doubt his word.

It is how I live today, you know. His investments continue to ensure I want for nothing. There are people, you see, professionals, who look after things. Every month a substantial amount of money is credited to my account. I am occasionally asked to sign documents, which I am happy to do. They may be robbing me blind for all I know, these gentlemen in their well-tailored suits, but at least they aren't robbing me into the poor house.

My husband was a clever man, you know, he was shrewd, and he was prudent. A man of vision, as they used to say. God alone knows where I would be today were it not for his vision.

But it was that vision, too, that took us back to the island, and to the games and intrigues that would eventually lead to the events that brought Yasmin and me to this country.

[45]

Ash, a tall glass of ice water in his hand, pulls up a chair and slouches into it in a manner that suggests

utter self-possession. The tendons in his neck stir and palpi-
tate as he takes a long draught from the glass. Yasmin thinks
him a young man absorbed by physicality.

"Holdin' on to yourself must be hard up there," he says,
his conversational tone belying the sharpness of the gaze he
levels at her.

"Pardon?"

He rubs at his eyes. "I mean, you don't find it a little bit
unnatural?"

"What are you talking about?" Yasmin makes no
attempt to hide her irritation. She wishes now for silence:
Penny and Cyril have presented her with so many images
to sort through, so many visions to sift. Neither of them,
though, appears to mind the interruption, reminding her of
something her mother had once said: that back there, on the
island, silence belonged to no one; it was communal property, to be sliced into at will.

"I ain't know if I could do it."

"What?'

"You know. Livin' in a white man's country."

She weighs his words, wondering from which vision
they have issued. "From the sound of it, you aren't exactly
thrilled about living in a black man's country either."

Penny laughs, but the nature of her laugh—which side
she comes down on—remains enigmatic.

Yasmin watches his features freeze, his eyes deaden; sees
him struggle with her remark.

"Look here, Ash, I belong to where I live—"

"Yeah, yeah, I know. Citizen o' Canada, the world, the
whole fockin' universe."

Cyril says, "Ash, watch the adjectives."

His vehemence startles her—and she understands that

what she perceives to be the narrowness of his world is to him the core of his essence: the core that comforts him and makes him radical in its definition and its defence, the core that would suffocate her with its airlessness. She feels like patting him on the head.

"You foolin' youself, you know," he continues. "Nobody makin' place for you, maybe they let you sit at the table a little bit, maybe they smile sugary-sugary and toss you a few scraps. But you better behave. You act up, and is strap to your ass and out the door."

"You've been to Canada?"

"No. But almos' every plane that land here bringing back somebody they deport. Besides, is not the point. Point is, I know where I belong, I know my people, I know my history. Our history. All the years of oppression."

"The oppression. You feel oppressed, Ash."

She has merely reflected his words back at him—an old trick—but he takes the reflection for understanding. His features hint at a softening.

"By..." Her palms flutter open in interrogation.

"You know who by. They always tryin', you know." His lips hint at a smile. "But is not jus' today. Is yesterday, too. All that humiliatin' history. We have to get rid of it, you know. We still in chains"—His fingers jab at his chest—"even if we ain't know it. Even if we think we made it big somehow. Here"—his gaze sharpens at her—"or in other people land."

"But as I understand it Indians were never slaves." She glances at Cyril—her knowledge is patchy and superficial—and he nods in confirmation.

"Slaves. Indentured labourers. Is jus' a name, man. Our people had contracts, eh, but that contract was jus' a form o' ball an' chain, to take us away from the homeland and keep us there. That contract make all of us weaker. It steal the lifeblood from Mother India, and it turn us into little people." His vehemence thins his voice into that of an angry boy. "Little people."

Cyril says, "Cool your blood, Ash. You not going to convert nobody here."

"No, go on," Yasmin says. "I want to understand what you're saying."

"I sayin' that you ain't know it, but you ain't as special as you think. Maybe you're some kind o' TV star up there in Canada but it really have no big difference between you, me and all them people breakin' their back in the cane fields jus' like our great-great-grandparents did."

"No, Ash," she says after a moment. "Listen to yourself. What you're really saying is, if I'm not with you, I'm against you."

"Exactly," he replies, pouring a little of the cold water into his palm and spreading it on his face. "Is a battle for survival. Is black, is white, there ain't no room for grey."

If he is lucky, she thinks, the look in his eyes—that sparkle of youthful aggression—will turn baleful with age. If he is unlucky, this manner that appears only partially cultivated will remain untempered, and he will risk being consumed by his anger. Which is all right, she reflects, except that anger aflame is unselfish, and indiscriminate in its hunger. "That's simplistic," she says. And sad, too, she wants to add, but does not. She senses him to be a young man who will easily dismiss being dismissed—he will fall back on his dreams of an ultimate revenge—but who will not take kindly to pity, against which she suspects he has no defence.

His gaze moves away from her to the glass in his hand:

back into the trees and the shadows. "Suit yourself. This ain't your home anyway."

"Is it yours?"

When he leaves a few minutes later, his presence remains behind, a force felt but unseen, and it seems a very long time before Cyril, speaking into the chaotic silence, says, "Is best to let him go on. Let him have his say. Sometimes is the only way to deal with lonely people."

[46]

"Mummy, what am I?" The question was posed with great seriousness.

"What do you mean, honey?"

"I mean, where am I from?"

"You mean what place?"

"Well, Gino's Italian, and Eduardo's from South America, and Nadia's from Egypt."

"Who are Gino and Eduardo and Nadia?"

"They're friends in my class."

"I see. Well, you were born in Canada, so you're from Canada."

"Mo-om, they were born here too. That's not what I mean."

"Okay. What do you mean?"

"I mean, what am I *really*?"

Yasmin gathered her daughter's hair into her palm. It was long and thick, as lustrous as a clear midnight sky. And the words that came to her as she pondered her daughter's question were the inadequate words of a mother: You are yourself, she wanted to say, a child unique to this world, born to parents united by history and geography and myriad migrations. You are a child whose existence could not be predicted, a child whose future waits to be discovered. Let no one limit you with imposed notions of the self.

But all this, she knew, was too grand. Its complexity would defeat the directness of the question. Gino was Italian, Nadia was Egyptian: such were the simplicities her daughter was seeking. But she could not bring herself to offer the comfort of a facile answer. And yet when the response come to her it sounded plaintive and evasive: "Isn't it enough to be Canadian?" she said.

Her daughter shrugged. "I guess."

Yasmin released the spray of hair, watched it fan across her daughter's slender back—watched the light shimmer as if alive through its darkness.

[47]

Penny excuses herself. Cyril, seizing on her absence, says, "You know that story about when Ram imitate Amie's snoring? Well, is Amie's eyes I remember. Tired eyes that turn hard-hard when he put on his little performance. And I don't remember her laughing, not for a second. Oh, she break two-three plates, all right, but not from an excess of joy, I'll tell you."

"Are you saying he was a cruel man, Cyril?"

"No, no. Cruelty wasn' part of his make-up. Not what you might call intestinal cruelty, nuh. He had to work at it.

And sometimes this did make it hard to distinguish between his kindness and his—well, cruelty, harshness, call it what you want. On top o' that, as Penny rightly say, he had a wild sense o' humour. Like all of us, nuh."

And he tells of a young man, an admirer of her father's, who used to hang around the campaign, helping out, doing whatever needed to be done.

"One evenin' out o' the blue Ram start teasin' the fella. Jus' blowing off steam, but mercilessly. You see, the fella was all skin an' bones—in fact, more bones than skin. Ram start saying things like, every time the fella jump, you does hear him rattle. Or, when he needed pants, all he had to do was boil a couple pieces o' macaroni and slip them on. And soon everybody join in. Lots o' jokes about boners—not having one but being one. And before you know it, the fella burst into tears an' run out. Never came back. Couple of us felt bad, went looking for him, couldn' find him. But Ram—Ram said, No big deal, he have to learn how to take a joke or he'll never do anything in life. An' in a way he was right. That's the way we were. You had to learn to take the fatigue."

"Fatigue?"

"Teasing, nuh. Is how we say it."

Yasmin says, "It's the same everywhere. I had to put up with teasing at school."

Cyril leans forward, palms rubbing dry against each other. "I know what you sayin'. And you right. To a point. But there was, to my mind, something shameless in the way we…"

She notices the sudden narrowing of his eyes.

"You see we din't believe that people like that fella, or like Amie—people who work for us, people who below us—

we din't believe they had feelings. Or at leas', they did, but their feelings din't count."

His right eyeball wanders as his gaze drifts sightless past her.

"For some of us, they still don't."

[48]

The thing about my husband is this: he believed in the torch Celia saw in his tea leaves. He believed that in holding up that torch for his people—our people— he was also holding up a torch for us, his family. He believed that in loving them, he was also loving us. It was part of his self-delusion.

And I thought that his dreams, which went well beyond the possibilities we had been brought up to expect, could accommodate the big We and the little we. What I didn't realize was that the big We would prove to be a demanding mistress. She fed his appetite and in so doing made it larger, to the point where he could never be satiated. He would spend long days at his desk, keeping himself sharp with coffee, whisky, almonds and sugar cubes.

Yes, my dear. Almonds and sugar cubes. He kept a jar of each on his desk. He'd crack the almonds open with a judge's gavel and pop the nut into his mouth along with a sugar cube.

His quiet moments at home—and they were not many —were spent dreaming of his next encounter with her. He began hungering after her.

Jealous, Mrs. Livingston? Is that how I sound? But I

suppose... Yes, of course I was. Your word is appropriate. Wouldn't you have been? It was the hardest thing, you see—understanding that my husband's attentions had been seduced away from me so totally, and in a manner that left me no room for manoeuvre. I am still surprised, you know, when successful politicians willingly surrender their power. To lose in the polls is one thing, but to retire, to give it up for no compelling reason, is quite another. It still strikes me as extraordinary.

I remember the first political rally I attended. I remember it because it was also my last. There was a stage with chairs on it and flaming torches—flambeaux, as we called them—at each corner. There was a microphone and crackling speakers. Somewhere off to the side a tassa band was drumming out its rhythms...

Ah yes, it's an *East* Indian drum band. Its rhythms can be quite infectious. I've seen many fellows—fuelled too, it must be said, by the island rum—surrender to its joyous demons. Why, I too have felt —

No, no, Mrs. Livingston, not in the least like voodoo. Oh my, the very thought!

Anyway, I was asked to sit in the front row beside my husband, but I chose to take a seat in the second row behind him. From there I could see everything, you see, without self-implication. Tongues of flame from oil drums defining the perimeter of the square, hundreds of faces shimmering up towards us in the flickering darkness. Not ironical or cynical, but rapt with anticipation.

Sometimes there were hecklers, too, and they were the voices that stayed with my husband afterwards, the ones he brought home with him. He would vent anger at them for hours, while Cyril—dear, foolish Cyril who liked to call

himself my husband's campaign manager—poured him tor-
rents of whisky and tried to calm him. It often took hours.
Cyril once confided to me that he thought my husband
expected to be loved by everyone, even his political enemies.
He thought he had gained an insight into his brother. Poor
deluded Cyril. He took himself so seriously. No one else
did, you know.

Then the speeches began, but I remember not a word,
not a promise, not an idea. What I do remember is this:
those faces animated by the words, solemn one moment and
ecstatic the next. And when it was my husband's turn several
warm-up speakers later, the sweat that broke out on the
back of his neck, and the way his spine—it was a deep spine,
like a crevasse down the middle of his back—the way his
spine defined itself through the soaked fabric of his shirt. I
remember the stiffness of his left arm—it was with that hand
that he gripped the stem of the microphone—and the gesticulations of his right. Gesticulations of caution and exhor-
tation, the pumping fists of the passion that is, let me be
blunt, a kind of masturbation...

Mrs. Livingston: Are you all right?

My language? Scarlet? My dear, what in the world do
you mean?

Masturbation? It's a perfectly good word. It describes
a physical action, like spitting or vomiting—only masturbation is surely more pleasurable. Besides, I thought I
was being rather poetic—the pumping fists of passion and
all that.

No, I'll grant you, it's not Wordsworth—but that's a
recommendation, isn't it...

The point is that all of that effort, some of it natural,
some of it contrived to simulate naturalness, had its effect.

My husband conducted the crowd and I saw what Cyril meant when he said he had the touch of a master. It was quite unsettling, actually. This quality, which others admired in him, had quite the opposite effect on me. How could the little we compete with the adulation of crowds? I left that rally deflated, and promised myself I would never attend another. It was a promise that I kept.

[49]

          Cyril says, "He wasn' what you'd call a delicate man."

Penny frowns but says nothing.

His words cause Yasmin to reflect that delicate is an adjective that would do justice to Cyril himself, to his gentle fragility—his fault lines concealed, but barely.

"Give him a san'wich or a roti and he'd take it in the palm of his hand, really *hold* it. No dainty-dainty tea-an'-crumpets little-finger-in-the-air for him."

She imagines large hands, thick-fingered, with broad nails trimmed close. She senses a physical strength rarely employed—but when called upon, displayed with ferocity.

"Once I saw him take an orange in his hand an' squeeze an' squeeze until the thing just kind o' exploded."

Cyril spreads his palm, then snaps the fingers into a clench. She sees a small hand, plump-fingered, with nails of painful transparence. Senses the possibility of a vexed impotence. Imagines, yet, the orange collapsing into a pulpy mass.

"And when he *et*, he *et*. Big bites. In fact, when he et, he always brought to mind a teacher I had in primary school. I remember a class when he was teachin' us how to eat. 'Masticate properly. Masticate every mouthful thirty-two times.' Not chew. *Masticate*. That's what Ram did."

She imagines the working of his jaws, his wet lips, his relish.

Penny says, "Masticate thirty-two times?"

"Thirty-two."

"You supposed to count or what?"

Cyril nods. "He asked who masticated thirty-two times and guess which fool put up his hand. He said I was lying. And he was right."

"Why'd you do it?" Yasmin asks.

Before he can answer, Penny says, "Habit."

[50]

It was hard on me, you know, Mrs. Livingston, harder on me than on my husband. A brutal experience, watching him get bloodied in battle. I felt his pain more acutely than he himself did—or perhaps more than he could afford to let himself do. I remember thinking that my fears for him appeared greater than his fears for himself. He was certain he would prevail, after all.

One of the hacks—and there was a quick gathering of hacks around my husband—one of them said, admiringly, that he had the skin of an elephant. And then he added that these attacks—which to me appeared so vicious, for they went after the man and not after his ideas—that these attacks were like blunt arrows, glancing off my husband's hide. I remember his words: It would take an elephant gun to bring down a man like that. The admiration was palpable in the words, and I knew I should take pride and comfort in them but I could not, for it seemed to me that even blunt arrows must hurt—even though my husband never winced, not once, not even to me in private.

I remember overhearing a conversation he had with Cyril not long after our return. They were having breakfast together—fried bread with scrambled eggs swimming in melted butter, strong coffee—not the instant powder but beans freshly roasted, ground and boiled and sweetened with streams of condensed milk.

You know, this was the one thing my husband pined over during our time in England: this breakfast. I tried making it for him two or three times. Now, cooking was never my forte, nor one of my ambitions—it fulfilled nothing in me—but I tried hard, for him. Not once did I succeed. He complained each and every time. His tongue, he said, recognized nothing: The bread was too light, the butter wasn't salty enough, even the eggs made him grimace—he dubbed them too English, by which he meant wan and flavourless. So after we got back, he indulged himself—and continued doing so until renewed familiarity dulled the appetite...

As for me, there was one thing. You won't know it, though. It was a fruit. We called it pomerac. It had the shape and consistency of a firm pear, was red as an apple on the outside and as white as cotton on the inside. Of course, I would occasionally hunger for the taste of a mango or sour plums or—another fruit you wouldn't know—chennet. But those were tastes fairly easily satisfied, what with all the coming and going delegation members did between the island and London. Pomerac, though, was the one thing no one ever managed, possibly because it was not widely available...

No, it was not difficult! My dear, you underestimate me. Pomerac was most easily obtained from a tree in one's own backyard, you see, and I was quite aware I had exchanged backyards—as I did a second time years later, when I moved to this country. One must be realistic, mustn't one? This obsession with one's own appetite that has become part of the modern age—I don't think it's a terribly healthy thing. Metaphorically speaking, too many people exchange backyards and seem to think it perfectly acceptable that they spend their time pining for pomeracs, if you see what I mean.

But how in the world have I ended up talking about an obscure fruit? Ah, yes. My husband's breakfast, with Cyril.

That morning, I overheard my husband say to his brother that he was quite aware some people accused him of opportunism—working for one side, then the other, then back again. And he acknowledged that they were right.

Cyril, being Cyril, demurred.

Don't try to hide from it, my husband said, let's figure out how we can use it.

I understood my husband enough at this point to see what he meant. His goal, you see—his goal beyond the personal—was the betterment of our people...

Our people? Hah! That, my dear, is one of those mischievous questions. We—those of us who belong by birth—have always instinctively known who our people were, we have never had to define...

Unlettered, I would say, by the tens of thousands. And physically wasted, by all that badly compensated labour in the sugar-cane fields and rice paddies. Bound together by alienness and religion—and defined, yes, by race and a shared if false notion of a larger belonging, for we believed ourselves to be still of India—unlike those with whom we shared the island, those whom slavery had severed from their homeland. A grand illusion on our part, but it was what shaped this idea of Us and of our people. It was what gave power to my husband and those who worked with him. It was this sense of our people—a people bereft—that gave my husband his dream, and his sense of mission. Political power. Economic power. Social status. These were not empty words to my husband, nor were they vague concepts. He used to say that cane-cutters had to give birth to doctors, and that we had to go from milking cows to milking the economy.

So you see, he would have worked with anyone who would help him achieve his ends. He *was* an opportunist. Political ideology, party loyalty and such things motivated him very little. The kind of success he dreamed of could have come to him only with the success of our people…

What kind of success did he dream of? I'm not sure he could have put it into words—but, as I understand it, he dreamed of exercising an immense personal power, despite which our people would one day wish to erect statues of him. He wanted to be able to hurl thunderbolts—and still be loved.

What Cyril failed to appreciate was that my husband had the ability to see himself through his enemies' eyes. And he was at ease, though a man of ego, accepting even a poisoned view of himself with a kind of dispassion—that elephant hide of his. It gave him great strength, you know—for he knew not only his enemy but also, in this game at least, himself too.

How often, though, those arrows ricocheted off him and found me.

[51]

"Hi, how was your day?"

"Fine. Yours?"

"Did you watch?"

"You were fine, as usual. Eyeshadow a little on the heavy side, though."

Or: "*Sh*edule. *Sk*edule's American. But on the whole, fine. Just fine."

Fine: the word set her teeth on edge. Like *nice*, a nonsense word, emptied of all weight but the dismissive.

[52]

My husband's rehabilitation was his own creation, and the hacks were his handmaidens. Material was spun everywhere for them, even within the family. There was this particular story—the way they told it, my dear, they made it sound as if he could fly.

They said: When he was just a little boy he fell out of a mango tree.

They said: He should have broken his arm or his leg or even his neck.

But he fell softly, they said. He came down light and easy, like a leaf or a bird, or a cat expending a life.

Sometimes they said he had fallen from the top of a coconut tree. But always there was height, and lightness, and a miracle of invulnerability. No one ever explained how a little boy could have managed to climb to the top of a coconut tree—but hagiography makes no concession to practicality.

My husband had no memory of this event, and knew it might be apocryphal. But he liked it, appreciated its usefulness. Once he said, with a kind of wonder, "How much we lose of our own lives…" Convincing himself, you see, that it could have been so, making it part of himself the way some actors absorb the details of their characters.

Do you know that I actually got to the point where I decided I would ask my mother-in-law about the incident. Had anything remotely like it occurred? But my mother-in-law had a way of frustrating my plans.

A month to the day after our return from England, my husband and I were awoken before dawn by a tapping at our bedroom door. My husband got up while I turned in the bed and tried to fall back asleep. I was certain this was about yet another of his political matters—little fires that had to be extinguished at the most inconvenient hours. But the quality of the knock at the door had alerted something in my subconscious and, contrary to my habit, I found myself listening—with greater alertness when in the whispered exchange I recognized the maid's voice.

My husband said to me, Go wake Cyril, then he hurried out wearing only his pyjama pants and undershirt.

A few minutes later, Cyril, Celia and I found my husband and the maid in my mother-in-law's room. They were standing beside her bed, looking down at her. A single glance told me what had happened. Her face was more serene than I had ever seen.

[53]

She threw herself backwards onto the snow-bank and swept her arms up until her mittens met above her head. Then she leapt to her feet and, ignoring the snow that clung to the back of her head, her coat, her legs, examined the result with a critical eye. "Look, Mom," she said. "An angel in the snow."

"Yes, you are," Yasmin said.

"Not me, Mom." Her daughter was peeved. "Look. In the snow. I made an angel."

One of millions, but to her daughter an achievement. Yasmin made a show of admiring it.

"Make one, Mom."

"Now? Here?"

"Pleeease, Mom?"

Yasmin could not tell her daughter that she had never made an angel in the snow. She did not wish to tell her that public displays of exuberance had been offensive to her mother's sense of propriety, and that her age of rebellion, such as it was, had come too late. She had by then grown into the reserve that would temper outburst. *Such an obedient girl*, her mother would sometimes remark with a wounding satisfaction. Yasmin had always been careful not to damage that pride in her reserve—the reserve some would take for gentleness.

"Mummy! Make one!" Her daughter was becoming impatient.

"But you already have, honey. And such a beautiful one, too." But as she heard herself speak, as she detected the deceit in her voice, Yasmin knew that her daughter, had she been old enough to be familiar with the expression, could justly have accused her of making excuses—excuses for an acquired inadequacy.

"Mo-om…"

And suddenly the plea—its tone curious with elements of request and of permission—was irresistible. Yasmin spun around, let herself fall back onto the snowbank.

Ariana squealed in delight.

She drew her arms upwards as her daughter had done and then rolled forward, getting to her feet with a futile effort at elegance.

Her daughter was thrilled.

They stood together for several minutes gazing at the figures they had made, the large angel beside the small: a fresco, Yasmin saw, of protectiveness, the one keeping watch over the other.

[54]

She seizes a handful of his photos, lays them out on the table before her, shuffling them into a picture gallery of the passing years.

The eyes: almond-shaped in youth, frankness leavened only by the shadow of a deeper wariness; in later years, the outer edges foundering, as if burdened by gravity, the shadow having risen overwhelmingly.

The mouth, shaped in the early photos into an un-prompted smile, later on follows the line of the eyes, as if weighted down at the corners by despondency or disap-pointment—or merely the sadness of a man who under-stands too much.

His hair is always full and neatly combed, parted on the left side and brushed back from the forehead. But as its early blackness acquires thin streaks of grey, the mass loses body, appears to sit more heavily on his head.

She sees then how his flesh thickened, skin darkening, acquiring the texture of old, soft leather.

These changes: the years made manifest. She feels suddenly that she is seeing the wordless minutiae of him, peering at a road map to shapeless darknesses within his soul.

Her hands grow moist. Her heart pounds. These changes: They are more graphic than she can stand. They offer a closeness of encounter she is unprepared for.

With a sweep of a hand she banishes them from sight.

Cyril blinks at her, puzzled. Then he knuckles his eyes. Penny yawns.

"Let's take a break," Cyril says. "Is hard on the eyesight, looking so much into the past."

[55]

She resisted placing blame on her daughter. What blame there was surely belonged only to her and Jim.

How many little exchanges, the inconsequentia of daily life, had gone half-spoken or unshared during those years of interruption? How many threads left unspun? Was that when the silences began settling in, like little holes appearing in the web that bound them—with all the conversations that began *Guess what I read* or *heard* or *saw today* only to peter out into *Tell you later*—a later that never came?

From the soothing silences of nothing to be said to

the sullen silences of words left unsaid: When had they exchanged one kind of silence for the other?

He did not call her. Instead he drove home, ashen, from the hospital.

And at home, he told in a voice gone insensible how he had driven up to the schoolyard, parked across the street.

How the teachers hadn't seen her.

How he hadn't seen her.

But how she had seen him. He told of the blur of her clothes catching his eye, and the sudden fear that came to him. That caused, perhaps, the seat belt to jam, his fingers beating useless at its mechanism.

How his attention was diverted by the seat belt. How he heard the squeal of brakes.

And looked up.

And up.

To see: "She was flying, Yas. Her coat open. Like wings. Flying, like a bird. Her face—startled. No more than that. Startled. As if in wonder at this sudden flight."

She drove as if crazed. She was not stopped. Had she been stopped, she did not know if she would have been able to make the policeman understand: that her daughter was at the hospital; that she had flown like a bird from the bumper of a car; that she had come down on her head, remaining miraculously unmarked except for a bruise where the neck had snapped.

That she had to cradle Ariana in her arms.

To comfort her for the last time.

For ever.

As her husband had not done.

[56]

Cyril, who was far better at such things than my husband, arranged the funeral. He did have a certain managerial ability, you know, but for the smaller things; politics was too large a sphere for him, he found it unmanageable. Two days later, under the direction of a pundit, they both performed the cremation ceremony.

I wish I could say that it had all the dignity befitting the circumstance. But I cannot. Someone—not Cyril or my husband, I am sure; most likely one of the hacks or hangers-on—arranged to get some political mileage out of it. Reporters and photographers clustered around the pyre like flies around excrement. Even family members were elbowed out of the way.

And afterwards, at a reception back at the house, the flashbulbs kept on popping as my husband—and only my husband—received condolences. Poor Cyril, who had arranged all of this, was off in the kitchen being consoled by Celia. I caught him at one point, you know—peering out at my husband standing there like a one-man receiving line. And watching him—watching the mixture of disbelief and resentment that marked his face—was for me, as strange as it may seem, the saddest moment of those sad days. That, I think, was when I learnt to be careful about underestimating Cyril.

When the newspapers ran photos in the coming days, you'd swear that it was only my husband who had lost his mother, and that everything—all the sadness, all the mourning, all the arrangements—had fallen on his shoulders alone.

Also, an almost imperceptible change came to my husband—near impossible to describe, in fact. Many words come to mind, none of them accurate in itself. But if one were to take a pinch of one, a smidgen of the other, and a whiff of the next... You see what I mean? A new dignity, a new strength, a heightened remoteness. An imperiousness you saw only swiftly, when his gaze shifted right or left. A sense of a heavy stillness that had lodged at the very centre of his being. My husband was never impetuous in action, and something—perhaps just an immeasurable lengthening of the pause before he spoke—told me that he was now no longer impetuous in thought either.

A few days later he put his hand on my shoulder and said with great seriousness, "I'm not afraid of death any more."

And you know, my dear, I wished he hadn't told me that. His words depressed me. For death, it seems to me, is something that should be feared. Not to fear it is to diminish life itself.

[57]

Yasmin remembers looking at her daughter run.

Remembers the jaunty, stiff-legged run of the toddler. The heedless abandon, the ragged sense of self.

Remembers thinking that one day her daughter would be graceful.

It was the sight of her mother that added another level of horror and grief.

Trembling in her embrace, cheek palpitated by the

rugged beating of her mother's heart, Yasmin felt from behind a wind coursing through the hole ripped in time.

Its chill settled on the nape of her neck, a frigid blade vibrating a whistle of emptiness.

And for the second time in her life she was given knowledge of the infinite.

[58]

Your son loves you, does he not, Mrs. Livingston?

Ah, yes, my dear, it is plain to see—as plain as the pleasure that the thought gives you.

But do you have any inkling what he thinks of you as a mother? Would he hold you up as a paragon of motherhood, or would subtle resentments overwhelm his esteem...?

You would say no, wouldn't you. Hmm, extraordinary...

As for Yasmin's view of me—a certain measure of self-awareness is among my acknowledged faults, as you well know. While I do not pretend to read all the shadows that inhabit Yasmin's heart, there is one that...that we share.

One that is of my own creation.

That is beyond my understanding.

Inexplicable.

It began the moment Yasmin held out to me her newborn baby—

Yes. My...my granddaughter.

The moment my fingers touched the swaddling blanket, there, in the hospital room. With the pink curtain drawn against the despair of the woman in the next bed and the nebula of bouquets that mocked her baby born premature and incomplete. With the bassinet at the foot of Yasmin's bed like a formation of rock crystal with a pillowed hollow. With my son-in-law on the other side of the bed, still in the grip of time arrested. There, as I took the baby in my arms, it came to me, this...

This...indifference.

You know, my dear, I am not generally given to regret. I regret in my life only those things before which I have found myself powerless. They are not many, but they remain open wounds, not suppurating but raw.

That indifference towards my granddaughter, you see, was to remain with me for the rest of her short life. Why it should have come to me I cannot say, and all those details of the moment remain with me in a way that suggests I am looking to them, and not to myself, for an explanation. I am looking, in other words, to place the blame on them because my muted feeling has always perplexed me so.

I played the role of grandmother to the best of my ability. I baby-sat her occasionally. Or rather, I watched her and she watched me—we kept an eye on each other. I might help her complete a jigsaw puzzle or sharpen a crayon now and then. I made sure she never went hungry or thirsty. And at times when she was a toddler she would climb onto my lap and fall asleep—but this was always at her request, never at my bidding. I was not averse to it, just not enthusiastic. I gave gifts, of course, at the appropriate occasions. When I went visiting, it never occurred to me to bring along a treat —which upset Yasmin enough that, one day as we drove up to their house, she slipped me a bag of candy with which to surprise the girl. She was puzzled, Yasmin, and probably hurt, although we never spoke of it.

How does one explain it, my dear? How does one justify such detachment from one's own grandchild?

The girl was a charmer, you know. She fairly radiated happiness in her slightest movements. Rare was the time she would simply walk across a room. She skipped or she danced, and she cartwheeled across lawns, as if the energy of her happiness could barely be contained. It was the kind of childhood happiness that one envies, that one wishes would never be lost. And because of this, it was also the kind of energy that prompted more sober moments, for one could not help reflecting that life itself, circumstance, would cause it to diminish. Life, after all, is not a dance across a field.

But what perhaps imposed on those moments an even greater soberness was my realization that she reminded me of Yasmin before she lost her father, before she and I came alone to this land. That change—the suddenness of it, I assume—had heightened Yasmin's natural watchfulness. It had made her quieter—

Level-headed, you say? Yes, she has always been a thoughtful child. But that change, from exuberance to pensiveness, was marked. And one day I saw the promise of it in her daughter.

It was a little thing, really. She had not long been in school when she picked up that dreadful habit of nail-biting, which had plagued Yasmin well into her teens. I had finally succeeded in breaking Yasmin of the habit, and when I saw her daughter ripping at her nails with her teeth, I said to her with some exasperation: Am I going to have to break *you* of that habit too?

The little girl said nothing. She folded her hands on her lap and and gave me a lengthy, saddened gaze that emerged from deep within, a gaze that was neither challenging nor rude but which yet managed to suggest that I had over-stepped my bounds. I saw Yasmin so powerfully in her eyes —in her reflected understanding of the limits to our rela-tionship—that I let things be. When I saw her again some weeks later her nails had grown back and her fingertips were no longer mangled, and I understood that the child, like Yasmin, married a capacity for joy to a capacity for sorrow to—most important of all—a capacity for moving on.

This was knowledge that would serve me well. When my son-in-law called with the dreadful news, my insides felt seared, my brain as if set afire by the setting sun. But all that conflagration of feeling was for Yasmin. For my grand-daughter, beyond the painful knowledge of life severed too early, there was still this diffidence—strengthened, if any-thing, by the the nature of the personality I had glimpsed.

I cannot tell you, my dear Mrs. Livingston, how deeply I continue to regret that strange lack of grandmotherly feel-ing, how deeply I hate that part of myself over which I have no influence.

[59]

The bookcase is of dark walnut, the books behind its glass doors hard-covered and jacketless, and so neatly arranged their value appears contained in display rather than in usefulness. Yasmin presses in close, trying to see beyond her own reflection. The titles printed on the spines have faded, and the imposed twilight of the living room reduces them to a hieroglyphic illegibility.

Her concentration is such that the first she knows of

Amie's presence is her soft "Here, miss." She feels the press of a palm on her lower back, sees Amie's reflection stretching up, on the tips of her toes, her other arm reaching to the top of the bookcase for the key.

The lock opens soundlessly, the doors swinging out under their own weight. Amie steps back as Yasmin edges into the release of settled dust and musty paper. Without the barrier of her reflection, the titles assume shape in flecks of silver and gold. Greek philosophers—Sophocles, Plato, Epictetus—familiar to her only through a university course in the humanities two decades ago. *The Iliad* unaccompanied by *The Odyssey*. She eases out *Utopia* and on the inside of the cover—the spine cracking—reads her father's name scrawled in faded blue ink. "Were they all his?" she asks, replacing it.

Amie nods.

Beside *Utopia* is a three-volume set of *War and Peace*, an Everyman's Library edition bound in cloth of dusty red. A blemish on the spine of Volume II—a streak of dry white paint—arrests her eye. And unexpectedly the paint turns liquid in her mind; falls through darkness with the swiftness of a shooting star, splatters onto the spine, streaks briefly, coagulates, hardens...

[6 o]

Books to my husband, my dear Mrs. Livingston, were not merely bound pages with words printed on them. They weren't like magazines, which were disposable, or newspapers which could be used for wrapping parcels in stores. No. Books were icons! My husband valued learning, you see, not for its own sake but for its useful-ness: the more you understood, the more finely you could plan.

He read very few modern books, because of his belief that the world contained nothing new, that new wisdom was merely old wisdom draped in finery. And as for fiction— well, my dear, I need hardly tell you! He was always dismis-sive of the books Celia and I read on our lazy afternoons or at the beach. Pearl S. Buck. Anya Seton. Marie Corelli. Part of me resented it at the time. In dismissing the books he was somehow dismissing us, but I see now that he had little space in his life for romantic reverie. He couldn't afford it, you see. His ambitions required that he harden his emo-tions. He never knew that I knew what a great effort of will that took—and it was through Celia, Cyril and Count Leo Tolstoy that I found out.

His birthday was coming up, I don't remember which one, but it hardly matters. I know you disagree with me, Mrs. Livingston, but I do believe you are being excessive when you claim that each and every one of your husband's many birthdays is clearly demarcated in your mind. What a lot of clutter your mind must contain, my dear...

In any case, his birthday was approaching and I had lit-tle idea of what to get him. Clothes were of little interest to him. He dressed well, if unimaginatively—that was political, you see. He had to dress impeccably—not expensively, or visibly better than his followers—but his clothes had to be just so. What else was there? A bottle of good whisky, per-haps, but that was the sort of thing his political people got him. It was Celia who suggested Count Tolstoy, not the work about that foolish woman, which was her favourite, but *War and Peace*, which she said was a man's book. I thought it an intriguing idea.

We found a lovely edition at a bookshop in town, three volumes, if my memory does not betray me, with red dust jackets on which was a photograph of the author as a young man—sideburns, moustache—and not the elderly sage with the beard one usually sees.

I gave him the gift the morning of his birthday, before he set off, and he seemed delighted. He thanked me, gave me a brief peck on the cheek, and then proceeded to do an extraordinary thing. He removed the dust jackets and shredded them. I was appalled, but Celia found her voice before I did. What in the world he was doing? He explained that, to his eye, dust jackets cheapened the appearance of books, as did paper covers. Neither of us knew quite what to make of this, but then something intervened—the telephone rang, perhaps, or he was called away—and there was no opportunity to pursue it.

I remember Cyril picking up the books, weighing them in his hand and saying to me, "He won't read them, you know." He was certain about this, but I gave him no chance to explain. It was not something I wished to hear, and so I cut him off by insisting that he would.

And he did. With surprising speed. Volume one. Volume two. And then out of the blue, some way into volume three, he slammed the book shut. I remember the moment, a Sunday morning, sitting on the back porch after breakfast. A sudden, violent *thwack* that startled everyone. He put the book down on the floor and stood up in great agitation. And looking at me but speaking to us all, he said, "He thinks people like me are useless."

I was upset, naturally, and wished to be alone with him,

to calm him. But Cyril stepped over to me and advised that I let him be. I thought him impertinent. This was my husband, he was unhappy, it was my duty to comfort him. But Cyril was insistent. He asked me to come inside with him, there was something he wished to show me.

The moment we were out of earshot, Cyril chose to remind me that he knew his brother better than I did.

I pointed out that he'd been wrong about his not reading the books.

That, he replied, only proved my husband's loyalty to me. Such a gift from anyone else would have been relegated to the bookcase in the living room. "Fiction, you see," he said. "It's a problem for him."

But he doesn't take fiction seriously, I pointed out. Why should that be a problem?

"But that's where you're wrong," he said. "He takes fiction very seriously. Too seriously."

And he told me a little story that has always struck me as both far-fetched and comforting. I will tell you that story with the warning that part of me suspects it of being a publicity man's confection.

He handed me a large book he had taken from the bottom shelf of the bookcase. It was *Oliver Twist*, beautifully bound, with a leather spine and corners, and covers that resembled wood grain marbled in gold. It was from a special edition of Dickens' works, as I recall, and had been given to the island's libraries as a gift by a shipping line, I believe. They came into my husband's possession in the usual way—a friend of a friend who worked for the library...

Cyril let me examine the book for a moment—it was a fat volume, with some weight to it—and then told me how, some years before, when he was a much younger man, my husband had spent days and nights devouring the books. He used the word "obsession" to describe the intensity my husband brought to the enterprise, and confessed that he himself had found Dickens' thicket of words too demanding to be pleasurable.

One evening he was sent by their mother to call his brother to dinner, and to his great surprise found him face in hands, weeping. Yes, weeping! Real tears! he said. And it was that book, *Oliver Twist*, that had caused it. On seeing Cyril, my husband grew furious. He threw the book at him, seized him by the shirt and made him swear he would tell no one about what he'd seen. Cyril promised—and he kept that promise for years, until the day my husband exploded at Tolstoy and so, in a way, at me. "Fiction speaks to both his head and heart," Cyril said in conclusion. "But he accepts only the first."

Do you know, Mrs. Livingston, my husband later threw out the Dickens with no explanation, but he did not have to explain his action to me. I understood, you see, that he did so not because they were not precious to him but because the books were too precious.

You say that is not possible, Mrs. Livingston? It is not logical, I will grant you that, but possible—I am here, my dear, to tell you that it is. It was the only way, in our context, in the context of the times and of his ambitions, that he could survive.

As for the Tolstoy, he kept them, among his other books. But I understood he'd done so only out of consideration for me, not for *War and Peace*. During the fever of one of his campaigns, his people were preparing placards by pasting election posters onto cardboard. The paste was homemade—flour and water—and not very good. They needed heavy objects to hold the posters in place until they dried. I remember spotting among the bricks and stones and tools several books, including the three volumes I had given him. So in a way, you see, my gift turned out to be useful after all.

Now, if you will forgive me, my dear, I really must visit the conveniences. All this tea, you know.

[61]

"Do you think he read all these books, Amie?"

"Sure, miss. He was readin' all the time, you know, when he wasn' workin'."

Yasmin quickly surveys the other titles. "He didn't read much fiction, did he?"

"Pardon, miss?"

"This. *War and Peace*. It's the only novel."

"Is a special book, miss. A birt'day present. I remember him unwrappin' it—"

"Who from?"

"From Miss Penny, I think, miss."

"Oh. Penny…" She is vaguely disappointed, the drop of dried paint losing its magic, becoming just a spill with no sparkle to it.

Amie says, with concern, "Everything okay, miss?"

Yasmin slips the book back into its slot, closes the doors on the bookcase. "Everything's just fine." But she lets Amie turn the key.

[62]

The week before, Ariana had got it into her head to change the part in her hair from the centre to the side. The change was small, yet sufficient to alter the fundamental balance of her face—this face now puffy and powdered and shaded in a way that looked lifelike only to morticians.

Yasmin stared endlessly at that face now barely recognizable, searching for familiarity. When someone—she did not know who—hugged her and whispered how beautiful her daughter looked, she had barely been able to restrain herself. No, her daughter did not look beautiful, she was ugly in a way she had never been...

Yasmin reached out to touch the face: her fingers fled immediately, singed by its unnatural coldness.

As she pulled her hand back her mother, sitting by her, took it and warmed it in hers.

She sat, staring, seeking true recognition: an acknowledgement that went beyond words of this new reality.

Hours passed.

Jim had seen to the arrangements: the pastor, the church, casket, candles, flowers. It was in this way that he was beginning to piece himself back together.

Grief led to exhaustion, exhaustion to numbness, and out of that numbness rose anger at the mortician's attempt to give the corpse an appearance of vitality—an anger which in a distant part of herself she knew to be irrational but which another part of her recognized as the beginning of her own reconstruction. This cosmetic dressing was, she thought with bitterness, an attempt to transcend that succeeded only in making the ugly look uglier, the next logical step being to prop the corpse up in a chair. And Jim, in selecting a burial outfit, had chosen a dress recently bought and never worn—she remembered with a mind suddenly seething the day she chose it, the moment she paid for it: remembered with stabbing pain the joy she knew it would give her daughter.

So that everything conspired to make Ariana unrecognizable. Yasmin did not know whether to be grateful or outraged, and so let herself be tossed back and forth between the two along a continuum of numbness.

Time collapsed.

Comings, goings.

Garth, Charlotte: hand in hand, a couple now. There had been no fanfare, merely the hiring of moving vans. Charlotte hugs her, says she must call when she is up to it. Lunch, just the two of them. Like in the old days.

Producers, reporters, people from Jim's firm.

Words whispered and meaningless, embraces of helplessness.

And then, a trick of the light: her attention drawn to her daughter's hands resting one on the other, the fingers small and plump and still full of the promise of grace. It was with a shock that Yasmin recognized those fingers: knew them with a wrenching intimacy. She felt her blood engorge her veins: those fingers wrapping themselves around hers, exploring her neck, her arm, pressing in gentle curiosity at her vaccination scar.

She saw those fingers moving, felt the warmth they gave and the warmth they took.

Then she heard her daughter's voice.

She heard herself cry out: *Ariana!*

And then she shattered.

[63]

My daughter?

Yasmin. Yes. She is a calm child, isn't she? "A ship becalmed in a storm." That's what her uncle Cyril used to say about her. When things were bad, he had only to look at her, to observe her playing or sleeping, and he would feel better.

She was born during a storm, you know, in a house at the beach. The contractions had begun the night before, and by early afternoon of the following day had grown ferocious. Clouds began piling up above the horizon, as they often did—or do—at that time of day, layer upon layer billowing out of nowhere, white at first but quickly growing darker, grey at the edges with centres ripped from a starless midnight...

Dramatic, my dear? Of course it was dramatic. A child being born, a storm building. What more could you want? And of course I stared out at the sky. There was a window, there were people all around, and life was about to change forever. Of course I stared out that window, at that sky, at those clouds! What else was I to do?

Now, where was...? Ah, yes. Those clouds, and the steely sea ending suddenly at a rigid horizon. All this greyed immensity, holding its breath. You could see it coming to life, you know, far off in the middle distance. Lightning crackling from cloud to water, a distant, attractive spectacle, all action and no sound, like a silent movie...

You enjoy storms, Mrs. Livingston? So do I, you know. Quite apart from their sheer beauty—lightning is the most strident of natural phenomena, don't you think?—I enjoy the helplessness they impose. All one can do with a storm is wait it out. It lifts all responsibility from you, doesn't it—

temporarily, of course, which is why it's enjoyable. Rather like getting into an airplane. For this brief time, you have no choice but to abandon yourself to your fate—a very Hindu experience. Or perhaps, if you will, a brief glimpse back at the helplessness of childhood. And then once it has passed, one's arrogance of taking responsibility and seeking control must return—this is what makes us human, I know, but it can be so tiring at times, don't you agree?

In any case, you could see the storm gathering force, whipping itself into life. Then, quite unexpectedly, the wind fell off. The whitecaps diminished, the breakers were gentled. You could see far off the rain falling into the sea, a grey chimera obliterating depth and focus, ripples of light preceding its passage towards land—towards us. And in the sudden silence, the rain whispered in. It was faint at first, a fine machined sound, but as it reached the beach it gathered the ferocity of a roar. You could see the drops pockmarking the sand. And as they pounded a din on the iron roof Yasmin was born, emerging whole and perfect and as silent as a carp...

Yes, my dear, a carp. And that has been her strength all her life.

[64]

The light outside has progressed in a steady metamorphosis towards evening: from rugged afternoon yellow to thinned whiteness to a golden wash enriched by the midnight blue materializing behind it.

Penny warns that she should not wander too far from the house. "It does get dark-dark fast-fast," she says. "And you never know."

Cyril, stretching, sucks his teeth. "Don' worry, girl," he says. "Go take your walk. Nothing going to happen. And if you get los', just follow the stars."

At the bottom of the stairs, a dim light beneath the porch catches her eye. Cautioned, she pauses in the shadows.

In the light circumspect in its feebleness, Ash sits shirtless astride his exercise bench, a dumbbell grasped in each hand. His skin, deep brown and flawless, appears plasticized with perspiration, the muscles finely sculpted, as if by a classical hand.

Suddenly he looks up, directly at her. "Help you?"

She steps into the light. "Just taking a little stroll before dinner. I didn't mean to disturb you."

"Is all right, no problem." Then, in the conversational tone he affects when issuing a challenge, he says, "You know India have the nuclear bomb, eh?"

"Pardon?" The incongruity of his question causes Yasmin to doubt she has heard him accurately.

"I said, you know that India have the nuclear bomb."

"Yes," she replies, with a tentative curiosity.

"And you know that Canada ain't even have a nuclear hatpin."

She nods, amused now.

"So if India and Canada come to blows, you know who going to win?"

"I don't think too many Canadians lie awake at night worrying about that, Ash," she says with a smile.

He releases the dumbbells. They thud to the ground

with a metallic clatter. "Tell me, nuh, all journalists as literal as you? Or as stuck-up?"

"Stuck-up?"

"Look at you." His open palm slices diagonally at her. "You standin' there thinkin', The stupid boy actually think India and Canada might go to war one day. Not so? Is what you thinkin', eh?"

"I can't say I thought of the word 'stupid.'"

"Whatever. But you standin' there feeling all high and mighty in front o' this ridiculous idea. Is not that I think India and Canada going to go to war, I not stupid, you know. Is the idea of power. One have the nuclear bomb, the other one don't. One does twitch, and the neighbours take notice. The other one does twitch and, who cares?"

"And you want people to notice when you twitch."

He smiles at her, eyes narrowing. His thumb presses to his chin, his index finger crosses his lips.

A pose, Yasmin thinks, the gesture of an older, more calculating man: But his theatre is convincing only to himself. He appears at this moment so very, very young. She turns to go.

"You know," he drawls, "you have no idea what I talkin' about."

"Don't be too sure, Ash." She begins a slow walk away across the moist, hardened earth.

"I know who my people are. Do you?"

She stops, peers over her shoulder at him. "Just who *are* your people, Ash?"

"I belong to the diaspora," he says. "We are millions." He bends down, picks up the dumbbells and curls them to his shoulders, biceps labouring. Veins swell on his arms, sinew tightens and seethes across his chest. "And we understand now that all power flows from the centre."

The centre. But he speaks easily of places of which he has no real knowledge. "Have you been to India?"

"Have you?"

"It wasn't a challenge, Ash. Just a question."

"Never been to the sun either, but I know is hot."

"But do you know why it's hot?"

"Don't need to, and if I did, the library full of books and magazines."

"But if you're going to worship the sun, wouldn't you want to know everything about it?"

"You believe in God?"

"I suppose."

"You know everything about him? To believe, all you need to know is enough. Is like Auntie Penny and your father. She always telling that story about him, you know, about how he fall off a garage roof when he was a baby and hardly get a scratch. She never explain how a baby manage to get up on a garage roof in the first place but it hardly matter. Vernon the perfect. Vernon the god. They ain't shoot him, they crucify him. As far as Auntie Penny concerned, he was never just a man. And it ain't have nothing wrong with that. Is like me and India. Is not just a country, is a soul. And I have it inside of me, in my flesh, in the blood running through my veins. I ain't know the details o' the chemistry but it there, true and alive, and more important than any so-called facts."

His words chill Yasmin. They are so contrary to everything she believes in. They strike her as a denial of the mind, a return to the belief of illogic. Ash is vehement in seizing a world made wholly of magic and mystery—and even though she knows it to be often necessary, the only people she fears are those with no wish to know how little they know. She knows now that she fears Ash, and that she fears for him.

She steps out of the light, glances up at the sky. There are no stars to be seen, there is nothing more to be said. So she turns away and, to the clanking of metal, returns up the stairs, to the dining room and its world rampant with shadow and image.

Silence reigns at the dinner table, cutlery clattering muted on china.

It is, Yasmin reflects, as if each of them has retreated into unvoiced thoughts after all the talk. And yet she finds that she herself has no thoughts worthy of the name: that her mind is too congested with shards of image and incomplete sensation to shape coherence.

Cyril, when he is done, pushes his chair away from the table, presses a fist to his lips, and belches gently. He says, "You should see the posters the boy have up in his room. All these fellas dress up in saffron robes, jumping up in the streets with forks and swords. Is not so much different from the Carnival, nuh, excep' that these fellas taking themselves very seriously."

Penny says, "The boy always goin' on about being oppressed. How? Look around at this land! So we not as rich as before—who is? Ash could do anything he want to, study anything he want. Lawyer, doctor. But this *jhunjut* is his choice. Is not easy, that's for sure. And I not sure that he's wrong. Still, he can talk oppression all he want, but if he turn out to be a not'ing in this life is his own decision."

"His karma, you mean," Cyril laughs. Then he turns, sober-faced, to Yasmin. "All it really mean as far as Ash concerned is that the boy don't know what to do with his life and these people he involved with giving him some easy answers. They giving him something to be passionate about. Is why I give up arguing with him. He have his colours, nuh, and he holding on to them tight-tight."

Penny says, "Oppressed, eh? Sometimes I think somebody should o' oppress his ass a long time ago."

"But Penny," Cyril says, "who—if not you?"

[65]

You know, Mrs. Livingston, it is every parent's melancholy thought that, God willing, there is a good part of a child's life one will never know. It is only right, it is part of the natural progression of things, almost a law.

Yet… Yet, it can be painful, for one would give anything to be able to watch over the child, do anything to ensure the child's happiness. And to die with so much unrevealed feels like a kind of abandonment…

You would go further, my dear? Yes, you are right of course. Indubitably. The only thing worse would be to live knowing it all. To have seen the end of the child's life story, as Yasmin has. What horrid knowledge it is to have. I felt a part of her freeze solid when her daughter died—I felt it happening even as I held her in my arms, do you see what I mean?—and it has never unfrozen. I expect it will be so for ever. It is a way of surviving, you see: freezing within ourselves things that would otherwise kill us.

[66]

It was weeks later, as her mind worked at reconstituting itself, that she first wondered whether her daughter was now privy to a knowledge that lay beyond human possibility. Did she have an answer to the question Yasmin had never truly asked herself, that she had only idly speculated on? Had little Ariana gone beyond her parents, journeying alone into an unseizable light—or had she merely vanished into a void so total there was room for neither questions nor answers?

Yasmin resisted the void, wanted to believe in the light: was tempted by its hope but fearful of it. And as she wrestled with herself, tossed from one to the other with metronomic regularity, Icarus came to her, arms awash in feathers, flying towards the sun, bathed in a brilliance she could see but not embrace.

[67]

A silence had settled on the house.

A silence that was porous and layered, and as if clotted onto the walls.

The silence absorbed sounds and noises. It absorbed speech, all those words sincerely offered and gratefully received—draining them of weight, sucking them into itself and threatening, at times, to pull her in too.

It was into this silence, and because of it, that her mother, sitting beside her on the sofa, clasped Yasmin's hands in hers and said, "I am, as you well know, dear Yasmin, no philosopher. And no matter how much I wish I did, I do not have the means to lessen your pain. But I do have something to say that might... Well, make of it what you will.

"This is something your father's brother Cyril said to me many years ago, minutes before you and I boarded the aircraft to come to this country. Although he had been at moments almost incoherent with grief for your father, Cyril was extremely lucid when it came to looking after our welfare. I remember that there, at the airport, he suddenly spoke to me about what he called partings, about how life was shaped by the inevitability of partings. He said that birth and death were the most momentous, for they changed everything, but that there was between them a host of other partings, grand and small, that exerted influence on the direction of our lives.

"I remember he took a long look at you and said that, while parting was always painful, fighting it was useless, it was an unavoidable force in human life and so we had to seek ways to embrace it. He was speaking of your father, of course, and how we all had to come to terms with his loss.

"Yasmin, dear, his words have stayed with me through the years, often coming to me in my idle moments. And I believe that they have influenced my life, and through me, yours. Make of them what you will, my dear, now and later."

Yasmin sighed, the silence, held at bay as her mother spoke, surging back when she fell silent.

"It doesn't offer much solace," her mother continued. "I know that. It may be that no solace is possible. But at least looking at things this way might help you put order in what seems like chaos. I have lived through many partings in my life and I've survived them all. As, my dear Yasmin, will you."

Then she raised Yasmin's hands and pressed them to her lips.

[68]

Cyril shuffles through a handful of photographs, peering at each before tossing it aside. He seizes another handful and repeats the process.

Yasmin asks what he is looking for.

"There was this mark," he says vaguely. "His lucky charm." He examines another photograph. "You see it anywhere, Penny?"

"You wasting your time," she says. "I mean, you could hardly see it on him, after all. It was long—" She turns to Yasmin, index fingers drawing vertically away from each other in an imaginary six-inch line. "—but it was so thin. People knew it was there only if Vernon pointed it out. He was conscious of it, you know?"

Yasmin says, "What's this about its being his lucky charm?"

Cyril sits back, crossing his legs, relaxing. A smile comes to him. "It wasn' funny at the time. A brawl broke out at a political gathering one evening. I couldn' begin to tell you what it was all about. All I know is, suddenly everybody was fighting and we were trapped up at the front. Eventually the melee reach us and somebody take a swipe at Ram with a razor. He was lucky-lucky-lucky. It din't go very deep, he ain't even bleed much. Din't take long to heal up either, but it left this fine-fine line. For months he kept looking at it in the mirror, hoping it'd go away, nuh. And finally one morning, he run his finger down it, give it a fond slap, break out into wild laughter and announce that it had to be his lucky charm because if the razor'd come any closer it'd have cut his face off like a mask. He thought it was really funny."

"Well," Penny says. "At leas', sometimes."

Yasmin cannot share the humour. Her mind has already gone beyond the story. She thinks: So no photograph shows the mark. Had Cyril not thought of it, it would have been lost forever. What else is there? she wonders with a certain sadness. How much more remains unrecollected, unearthed, untold? Her stomach tightens at the thought, but she knows she will reconcile herself to this, too, as she has to so much.

PHOTOGRAPH: A NEWSPAPER PHOTO, EIGHT BY TEN, LOOKING UPWARDS FROM THE GROUND TO A DAIS WHERE HE IS IN FULL RHETORICAL FLIGHT, EYES NARROWING OUT TOWARDS AN UNSEEN CROWD, THE REACH OF THE GAZE AND THE ANGLE OF THE HEAD SUGGESTIVE OF LARGE NUMBERS. HE IS PLAYING TO HIS AUDI-ENCE—THAT IS OBVIOUS—BUT ALSO TO THE CAMERAS, ENERGY DIVIDED BETWEEN THE HEATED EXPECTATION OF LISTENERS AND THE COOLER EYE OF THE LENS. HIS POSE APPEARS CADENCED FOR POSTERITY, A FLUTTER OF VANITY LIFTING HIS CHIN AND LENDING ELEGANCE TO HIS GESTURING HAND—A HAND SHARPLY DETAILED IN THE BLAST OF LIGHT. THE WRIST THICK AND ENCIRCLED BY A NAME-BRACELET OF HEAVY SILVER, THE SPLAYED FINGERS PLUMP, THE NAILS BROAD AND TRIMMED SHORT. A HAND SOMEHOW SUG-GESTIVE OF A CERTAIN EASE, A SELF-SATISFACTION. THE KIND OF HAND, SHE THINKS, THAT WOULD ENGAGE WORK WITH ENTHUSI-ASM BEFORE CONFERRING ITS COMPLETION ON OTHERS. BUT A

HAND OF RELISH, TOO: EASY TO IMAGINE THE FINGERS PINCHING A
SCRAP OF BREAD INTO A PLATE OF FOOD, SCOOPING UP RICE AND
CURRY SAUCE WITH THE DEXTERITY OF A MAGICIAN.

She thinks: Eyes may be the mirrors of the soul, but hands are its agents.

She searches for herself in his hands.

In vain.

[69]

Ariana lies propped up on pillows in a bed. She is flicking slowly through a book, waiting patiently—as she knows, as Yasmin knows—to die.

Evening comes. Yasmin and Jim—at least possibly Jim, she is not sure, is merely aware of a presence beside her —enter a hospital operating room. Her daughter lies on the operating table, propped up still on pillows, eyeing with serene curiosity the actions of the operating team gathered in white around her. The doctors, Yasmin sees, have removed both of her daughter's knees and are sewing her calves to her thighs. When they are done, her daughter stands up and walks stiffly around the bed.

Yasmin feels a surge of hope: She's going to live!

But quickly the hope recedes. She cannot deny what she knows: This evening Ariana will die.

She awoke to a tightness of breath, her daughter still briefly with her: that innocent serenity in the face of horrific knowledge. A sob broke from her chest: a full, liquid emptying.

Jim stirred, switched on the bedside lamp.

She told him, with difficulty, of her dream.

Jim was silent for a moment. Then he said, "Yas, when you look at me, I cease to exist."

Yasmin made no reply, for she knew it to be true.

[70]

Penny holds up a small book, hard-covered. A child's book. "But what this doing here?" she says.

Yasmin's heart skips a beat. A child's book among her father's things.

Cyril looks, shrugs.

Yasmin reaches out for it.

"I wouldn' go jumping to any conclusions," Cyril says, raising a cautionary hand.

The book slips easily from Penny's grasp into Yasmin's. The top part of the cover is ripped away, only the letter T left of the title. What remains shows a faded painting, of sky and sun and a solitary feather drifting away, and when she opens it, even with the greatest of care, the spine cracks with the reluctance of age. The first page is blank, but on the second, she sees in the upper right-hand corner a name.

Her name.

Written in an adult hand.

Cyril leans over, says with compassion, "Is not Ram's handwriting."

But it will be a few moments before she can tell him that it doesn't matter. That the book is the first thing since her arrival in the island with which she has felt intimacy. This old book, this old legend.

Icarus.

Cyril and Penny say goodnight. Yasmin gets into bed. The house settles into darkness.

She pulls the sheet up to her neck, the mattress beneath her accommodating itself slowly to her shape.

Already, she thinks, odours have become sufficiently familiar to pass unremarked.

Then, Icarus light on her chest, Yasmin slides easily into sleep.

Three

Morning brings an uncertain sky, distant blue hardening behind slabs of grey-bellied cloud luminous at the edges.

Cyril, squinting upwards, says, "At leas' they have silver linings."

Penny grimaces into her coffee cup. "God, if he not depressin', he embarrassin', you don' find so, Yasmin?"

She is halfway through her second cup of coffee, the flavour of the fried bread from breakfast still on her tongue. The coffee is dense and sweet, its steam whitened by the condensed milk. It tastes of a foreignness that would not be delicious elsewhere. Only in this landscape of alien greenery lit by an alien light could it give her pleasure. Like an espresso with two lumps of sugar and no milk in a little cafe near the Louvre. Like an early afternoon beer on the Ramblas.

This coffee, and her enjoyment of it, belong here. She knows they cannot accompany her.

Yasmin asks about her father's date of birth.

On the year, there is no disagreement—although Penny and Cyril have to work it out between them and settle on a must-have-been.

The month, too, they agree on, after some toing and froing between May and June.

The day, however, cannot be conjured. Cyril remembers seeing several, in articles, in election pamphlets. He once asked his brother which was the correct one. Ram had smiled—that teasing way that he had—and said that if he could identify the right one he would buy him a bottle of the finest Scotch. But Cyril never got the chance to engage the challenge. On the evening after the funeral— a large and boisterous affair, anger wrestling grief to the edge of rampage, "that anger that we still see today, in Ash"—Cyril bought himself a bottle of the Scotch and finished it alone, although he has no memory of having finished it, only of being alone. He turns a baleful gaze on Yasmin.

What, she wonders still, about his hands, his fingers, the lines on his palms? She has always known her hands and feet to be unlike her mother's, longer and less slender. So are they, then, feminine versions of his? Did he, like Cyril, have long, fine hairs that haloed in sunlight from the edges of his ears?

But there is no point in asking. Neither Penny nor Cyril, she sees, can grasp the weight of such things above the deafening din of the deeds: the shape of a fingernail above the nobility of the act. She thinks: Veneration blinds.

Cyril says, "Maybe we should take care of Shakti today."

Penny, swallowing, gives a little wave. "Not today, Manager. Remember what the pundit say."

Yasmin says, "My plane leaves tomorrow afternoon."

"Tomorrow morning, then," Penny says with finality.

[2]

It was dark in the study. Through the window the night sky pulsed with the lights of distant worlds.

Jim sat behind his desk, Yasmin before it. Neither could say how long they had been sitting like this. The house around them had gone inert. Lamps recessed into the shelves of his bookcases glowed without reach from behind books and bookends.

A stack of bound reports leaned against a trophy won in a recent office tennis tournament. Silver and gold columns separated by strips of red and blue plastic on top of which a little gold figure waved a tennis racket. In the enervation that followed their daughter's death, he had been reluctant to participate but he had dug deep within himself, past the darkness, and he had done well. He had, one of his colleagues said, beaten the hell out of the ball.

He acknowledged that the trophy was not a thing of beauty, it was garish, but still he had wanted it in the living room. Yasmin, resentful of the object yet jealous of it, refused. She knew that her refusal had hurt him. But she saw it as a trade: a little hurt for a little hurt. And she wondered how it was that they had come to be here: from passion in the dawn to late-night accountings of displeasure.

"There's a reason for everything, Yas. Even this. You have to believe that."

"*I* have to, Jim? Or *you* have to?"

It had been months. Jim had carried on, his cheekbones growing more prominent, ribs more sharply etched against his skin. And Yasmin too had continued to function, colleagues remarking on her strength, calling her an inspiration.

Every week, though, there were new greyed hairs to tuck behind the black.

After two months, her mother had said it was time to deal with Ariana's room. Yasmin had not entered it since the morning she last sent her daughter off to school.

Slowly she was getting used to the idea of loss: the loss of warmth, the loss of presence, the loss of knowing the life her daughter might have lived. But she could not accommodate her sense of a life unrealized. There were moments when she thought the pain would rip her apart from inside. She felt damaged, a mass imploding. To enter her daughter's room was, she feared, more than she could endure: to see the hair tangled in her hairbrush; to be reminded of the smell of her; to envision her gestures in the things that she had used.

[3]

Cyril, right eyeball wandering askew, says, "She was always like that, you know. From the first time I met her in the library. Great, great ambition. Curious, curious mind. Nothing fazed her. Business, politics, you name it..."

PHOTO: CELIA APPEARS TO HAVE JUST BEEN TOLD A JOKE. HER MOUTH IS OPEN WIDE IN MID-LAUGH, THE TEETH SMALL AND EVEN, HER LEFT EYE OBSCURED BY A SPRAY OF FLYING HAIR. YET—IT MAY NOT BE LAUGHTER. SHE MAY HAVE BEEN STARTLED. IS THAT HUMOUR IN HER RIGHT IRIS, OR AN UNLEASHED PANIC? THE PHOTO-GRAPH HIDES AS MUCH AS IT REVEALS. OR PERHAPS IT IS CELIA HER-SELF WHO DOES SO.

He looks away, remembering.

"Then after we got involved we settled into a quiet life, reading, studying, a little dinner in a restaurant from time to time. She was good for me, you know. Calmed me down. We planned to stay on in England after I was called to the bar. I'd join a firm—a small one, nuh, nothing grand—and we'd continue living that quiet life.

"But then one evenin' some fellas decided they didn't like my colour, and let me know it with their fists. From that evenin' on nothing was the same. I couldn't get my mind to concentrate. I mean, here I was readin' law and those fellas were still out there runnin' around free and there was nothing the law could do. All those nice principles, those fancy words: all empty, meaningless. I jus' couldn't go on.

"And Celia decided she couldn't go on in England either. So we came here. But, you know, there was nothing for her here. She tried. She tried hard. But what to do with all that ambition? All that curiosity? She became good friends with Shakti, they use to spend hours together, talkin' I suppose, nuh. But still…

"Swimming became her outlet. She was a brave lady, you know. She use to go far out past the breakers to where the sea was still and deep, like a huge swimming pool, nuh. And she would swim and swim and swim—she was proud like hell of her strength.

"I use to get kind o' frighten. She was out so far. What if she hit a bad current? Or got a cramp? But she had a thing about going farther and farther out, challenging herself, nuh. Ram use to joke with her, tellin' her to watch out for the cruise ships.

"And then one Sunday morning she swam out and didn't come back—"

Penny, listening quietly, says, "It was a Saturday."

Cyril shrugs. "I remember it as a Sunday. Don't matter anyhow. Fact is, she didn't come back. Who knows why? Current, cramp, shark. Only thing we know is, she didn't come back."

Penny says, "Remember what Shakti—"

"Yes, but she was in shock. It didn't make no sense."

"Shakti said Celia was tryin' to swim back to England. She was the last one to see her, you know, far, far out, swimmin' strong towards the horizon."

Cyril rubs his eyes. "Oh, God…"

Penny says, "You know what I think? I think is ambition that kill her. Reckless ambition. She jus' din't know when to stop."

Cyril clasps the photo to his chest, his gaze rushing over Yasmin's shoulder.

In the dining room frantic with voiceless phantoms, she sees a young man's eyes in an old man's face. Eyes perplexed and disquieted—manic with the unanswerable question, How is it that I have come to this?

[4]

The most wrenching thing in bringing up children, do you not agree, my dear Mrs. Livingston, is to oblige them to do all those unpleasant things that life offers —the things we really cannot escape…

Yes, yes. Absolutely. Cleaning up their room. Doing their homework. But I had in mind more substantial things. Accepting defeat with grace, for instance. Responsibility for a pet. Dealing with death. It was a difficult thing, for me, you know. Death, I mean. I grew up in a rural area, you see…

No, no, not the countryside. Our island was too small to accommodate the concept. We were not far from a town of some substance. But where my parents lived was, at that time, attainable only on foot. The house stood some way into a cocoa estate, and to get there you had to follow a narrow path from the main road through the plantation. Even on the brightest day little sunlight penetrated to the ground—it was always twilight, you see—and the night was impenetrable. We used torches but the darkness seemed to absorb the light of the flames. And there was no electricity, of course, the house was lit by kerosene lamps. We had to invent our own entertainment, and in this environment it is hardly surprising that the telling of ghost stories was a favorite pastime.

I was young. I had no stories to tell. But I listened. And from the stories I learned that the world was as populated with ghosts as with people. They roamed everywhere, malevolent souls who had been improperly dispatched after death, so that they were condemned to wander aimlessly, terrorizing the living. It was said that the cocoa estate was the kingdom of the dead. We children were warned not to venture into it, for we would not return. We were told that only dogs could see them, that dogs could sense the presence of death, and that they would howl when they did. We had dogs, of course, and they howled every night. I was so terrified I would not peek out the window as some of the older children did in hopes of seeing a ghost for themselves. Is it any wonder that I developed a fear of death as paralysing as the fear some people have of cats or airplanes?

I remember, vaguely, the death of some relative. A man who had been run over while bicycling home from work.

We were all obliged to attend the funeral. I remember the stifling heaviness of the atmosphere, men standing around smoking and talking in hushed tones, women sniffling and dabbing at their eyes. And I remember when the body was brought to the house. How the men lifted the coffin with gentle, holy effort. How the women began to wail and sob. How the man's wife, or perhaps his daughter, I am not clear on this, how she lunged for the casket and attempted to throw herself on it. Oh, my dear Mrs. Livingston, my heart speeds up even now, as I tell you of these things, the fear I felt as a child returns to me like hot and cold rivulets shuddering through my body...

Yes, yes, some tea. My mouth has gone dry, as it did that day so many decades ago...

It was at this point that I buried my face in my mother's dress and would not be budged. I wanted to see no more, hear no more. I would not be calmed, and so was taken away to a quieter place. Shielded.

I acquired the reputation of being a nervous child, and so was shielded further from anything that might upset me. No one told ghost stories any more.

And yet I wonder...

I wonder whether it might not have been better for my parents to shield me a little less. To help me, you see, get used to the idea of death. But this was not the way of parents at that time, and the urge to shield remains part of the parental condition. I do not blame them. I eventually outgrew the outrageousness of my fear. I learnt how to deal with death through dealing with it in life.

Then my granddaughter died and this question returned to me. The child's room had to be emptied, you see. I was fearful that it would become a shrine of sorts, her things undisturbed, a home for a ghost. And so, two months later, I insisted the room be emptied. I insisted it be Yasmin's job, and I agreed to be there to help her. My son-in-law could not remain in the house. He went to his office where, I suspect, he did nothing.

Yasmin's knees buckled when we entered the room, and she leaned on me for support. I opened up the windows, ripped the sheets from the bed. I forced myself to be vigorous. Yasmin made the effort, bundling the sheets, readying garbage bags. Then she opened the child's closet. Her dresses were still hanging there. Yasmin gave a little moan, and fell to the floor. I helped her up, led her to the living room and brought her something to drink.

Then...

Well, to be brief, Mrs. Livingston, I finished the job. I emptied the room. I put the clothes and toys and books into garbage bags for donation to a charity. Her more personal effects —her drawings, her play jewellery, the modelling clay which I imagined would still bear her fingerprints—I threw out.

And I wonder still, my dear Mrs. Livingston, did I do the right thing? Might I, in sparing Yasmin, have left a wound unhealed that might have closed more successfully through the execution of the painful duty? Or, to put it another way, have I left ghosts in my daughter's head?

[5]

Ash thrusts the tabloid before her without warning and she accepts it automatically, noticing as she does so that his fingers are dark with ink, as if he has recently had his fingerprints taken. The paper is cheap, fibres fat and so damp Yasmin feels that, if she squeezes, it will drip.

Her eyes find the words just ahead of his pointing finger:

ASHES RETURN

The cremated ashes of Mrs. Shakti Ramessar have been returned to her birth place. Ramessar, wife of one-time local politico Vernon "Ram" Ramessar, moved to Canada after her husband was killed under mysterious circumstances by

Yasmin turns the page, looking for the rest of the text.

Ash says, "Don't bother looking. It end there."

Cyril, sitting across the tale from her, studying her, says, "Page five. Imagine."

Yes. Page five. Interposed between a story of rural incest and another of urban decapitation. Her father's place in history?

Cyril says, "The hacks moved on a long time ago. And we have no historians."

Ash says, "We like the tree falling in the forest. If nobody hear it falling…"

Yasmin frowns through the quickening of her heart. She folds the paper in two, hands it back to Ash.

Cyril rises, hands flattening on the tabletop, pressing himself up—as if he is tired or drained, somehow enfeebled. He wavers briefly, then steadies himself. "Come, Yasmin," he says with a sudden decisiveness. "Let's go for a drive."

[6]

The cynics were the ones who said of Celia, Couldn't she see it coming? And the critics were the ones who asked, Did her own leaves hide truths from her? The cynics were the ones with the smirk, and it was from the critics that one sensed a measure of anguish. Critics are optimists, don't you think? As for the cynics, I've always believed them to be people who have given up. There is something airless about them.

It was a way of laughing at her, you see, of mocking her. I hold it to be disrespectful. Yes, I admit she may have brought it on herself to a certain extent. This reading of the leaves was a parlour game, but its unspoken arrogance aroused resentment. What, after all, is more arrogant than purporting to see into the future of others?

People liked Celia, they had no wish to wound her. But she had another arrogance, you see, my dear Mrs. Livingston, although she did not see it as such. I may have mentioned before that she was extraordinarily proud of her swimming. She was not a large woman, but her shoulders were wide and muscular, her arms long. She once told me that when her strokes had found their rhythm, there was no effort and no pain. She felt she could go on for ever. Her strokes were powerful enough that both my husband and Cyril, after repeated failures, declined to race her anymore. And she was courageous too, going far out, beyond the breakers. I remember Cyril standing at the shore following her progress through binoculars, her arms like white wings flashing, creating hardly a splash as they cut through the green water.

Many thought that she was showing off, but the truth is

that Celia believed she was being like us—being an islander, that is. Islanders, she assumed, were swimmers, we had to be, you see. She somehow, or perhaps conveniently, forgot that England too was an island, and that swimming has never been among the qualities for which Englishmen were admired.

And this was why people chose to belittle her afterwards, I've always believed. It was not so much because of the leaves. It was, rather, because of her inability to see...

Excuse me for a moment, my dear, I seem to have something in my eye. Now where have I put my purse? Ahh, here it is...

Yes, Yasmin says the same thing. She too thinks me old-fashioned, but I do prefer my hanky. You cannot perfume a paper napkin, after all. Now if you'll excuse me for just a moment...

[7]

The route takes them along the coast for a while, the road rising and dipping—glimpses of cliff walls, the sea mottled in a zebra pattern of blue and bottle-green —until it bends inland and begins a steady rise into the hills.

In the silence, Yasmin becomes aware of the sounds of movement: the wind whispering in through the open windows; the murmuring engine, the tires searing along the asphalt. Since entering the car Cyril has said nothing beyond, "We going to the north coast."

Knowing this, though, is of no help to Yasmin. Her

sense of direction, usually dependable, is scrambled. Every corner, every twist and turn serves only to confuse her more. She has no idea where they are going—but she is with Cyril, and so she knows she is safe.

Presently the road narrows, no longer following the contour of the land, but cutting its way through walls of rocky, reddish earth that enclose it on either side.

Soon the banks of earth give way to vegetation that is thicker, less delicate, with eruptions of dense bamboo and formidable trees, thick-leaved and braided with lianas. The forest floor is an unkempt embroidery of twigs, trunks and branches, the earth dark and wet—and, beyond a few feet, mysterious with darkness. Yasmin sees giant ferns, and shades of green defiant in their subtlety.

Cyril points out a poinsettia, a splash of red in the emerald gloom. The flower changes colour every six months, he says. Then, with a light laugh: "Women says it's got the character of a man. Inconstant, nuh."

Branches overhead reach across the road, blocking out the sun. The air turns cool, and a rain so fine it is like thick mist forces them to turn the windows up.

A tropical land—but Yasmin shivers.

Cyril turns on the windshield wipers, and Yasmin's heart begins to pound when she sees, in the gloom not far ahead, that the road comes to an end—not petering out, but an abrupt termination. She sees a rigidity of blackened tree trunks, and a shower of heart-shaped leaves as large as broadsheets. "What is this?" she says, her throat tight with tension.

"We almost out," Cyril says. "This is the summit. Not much of a view, I know, but that going to improve. We'll be heading down to the coast in a minute or so."

Her tension swiftly recedes. The road does not end—it was an illusion of the forest and the light. She regrets her fear and the rush of distrust—wants to apologize, but restrains herself. Cyril has apparently not noticed. An apology would require an explanation—and that would cause him unnecessary pain.

She is still making an effort to force her body to relax when, as they round the unseen corner that has betrayed her to herself, the forest falls away and she is momentarily blinded by the sunlight.

The descent to the coast is swift, the road less winding, the vegetation less thick.

It must have something to do with the breeze off the sea, Cyril says—a breeze which, with the windows rolled down again, is constant and warm and thick with salt.

And with the sun too, he adds. The sun which scorches the earth, drying it out and turning the forest friendly.

Yasmin says, "It's like a different world."

Cyril nods. "We're a small place, but the land reaches very high. And you never know what you going to find around any corner."

The slope grows shallow, the air heated as the sea breeze falls off. A wide bay comes into view, the water whitish in the distance. It is defined by a flat green peninsula on the left, and a loaf of rugged cliffs much farther off to the right.

The road flattens out, the view is lost, and there is the sense now of a narrow coast: grassy fields ending in foothills on one side, on the other palm trees, sand, and the endless water, now an iridescent blue.

Yasmin says, "What's the real colour of water? Sometimes

it's white, sometimes green, sometimes blue, sometimes all three."

"The water?" Cyril says. "Water has no colour. You know that, Yasmin."

[8]

If she squints, she could be witnessing the lumbering of giants, light scattering among their tall and slender shapes.

Cyril says, unexpectedly, "He said to me once, You realize Lenin's real name was Ulyanov, Stalin was Dzugashvili, even Molotov was really Skryabin. Aliases belong to revolutionaries, movie stars, writers and criminals. Nobody can ever really know them.

"And I was puzzle at the time to see that he seemed to envy them. Strange, eh? Puzzle me still.

"But you know, he felt that politicians should cultivate what he use to call humorous vagueness. On one level, say nothing but make them laugh. On another, reveal nothing but be hail-fellow-well-met. Humorous vagueness. You getting my drift? Of course some people criticize him for taking it to extremes, but you know, Yasmin, dear—how he couldn't?"

Yasmin thinks: This is all practised, these are things he has said to himself, and probably to others, many times. She says, "I thought palm trees grew wild. They all seem to be in rows."

"They are. They were planted. Long time ago. All this

is a coconut-tree plantation. Is only from a distance they look as if they growing every which way."

She decides she prefers the distant view, focuses on the light between the rows. She sees surf, rolling and tumbling, and beyond it the oily wavering of a horizon growing choppy.

He says, "Nobody ever understood Ram, you know."

Yasmin relents. "Did you, Cyril?"

He doesn't take his eyes from the road. "I said, nobody."

[9]

You once asked me, my dear Mrs. Livingston, if I intended ever to return to my island. Do you remember that? One is often asked that question here, particularly by those like yourself, who were born and raised in this country. As if you cannot quite believe that this country is worthy of a greater loyalty from those born elsewhere. Or perhaps, as if you cannot quite believe in the reality of the country and, so, of yourself. Does that sound harsh? I suppose it does, doesn't it...

I was rather short with you, as I recall. No, I said, with no further explanation. I saw that I had hurt you, but that the moment had passed for pursuing the matter. I resolved to find an opportunity to explain myself more fully. That opportunity never came, and so I will create it now.

I have told you about my brother-in-law, Cyril, and his wife, Celia. I have told you about my close yet somewhat problematic relationship with Celia, and I have told you about the difficult situation in which Cyril found himself

having returned to the island from England with no achievement to his name.

What I have not told you is that through everything,
Celia and Cyril continued to love each other. A love that was
far more tactile than that between my husband and myself.
He would take her hand, she would rub his back and shoulders. They were, I think, a happy couple—happy to be in
each other's company. I could not begin to tell you what
they spoke about in the intimacy of their room, but one had
the impression that they spoke, and of much besides politics. In company, they paid attention to each other, approved
each other's words and ideas.

But I know that Celia feared for their future. Cyril was
drifting, so different, she once told me, from the eager law
student she had met. He had dreamt of qualifying and
returning to the island to work with his brother, to realize
the dreams they shared. Then he had changed his mind and
dreamt of a quiet practice in England. And now here he was,
working for his brother, a hop-to-it man with no dreams of
his own. And that was putting it kindly, for among my husband's people Cyril was known as the useless man.

She was galled when they began referring to him as the
Manager. She knew what he did, knew the title was empty.
She knew that, in their eyes, his thoughtfulness, his gentleness, counted for nothing. And the attention he paid to
Celia earned him, in that world of ambitious men, an
unshakable derision. It was not lost on Celia that any future
they might have was entirely dependent on my husband.

As time went along, as Cyril's status remained on the
shelf, as it were, it all began to take its toll on Celia. I saw the
effects. You saw that there was no tension to her hand in his,
that there was a listlessness in her fingers. The back rubs she

gave him he now had to ask for, and she would peform them with an abstracted expression that revealed the great distance between her thoughts and her touch.

And there came a day when I realized they no longer touched each other. The same day that Celia said to me, with great seriousness, that her brother was calling her home.

[1 0]

They cross a small bridge, of iron painted silver and floored with wooden slats that clack under the tyres.

Just beyond the end of the bridge, Cyril pulls off the road and parks on the narrow verge. They get out and he leads her back to the middle, through a silence absolute save for the distant buzz of a cricket. The water appears unmoving, as still as a lake.

Cyril says that the river, channelled in a valley between two low hills, begins in the mountains—he once saw it many years ago, raging down along a bed of stones—and that it ends here, wide and placid.

Yasmin thinks: the colour of rust. But then, she reminds herself, water has no colour.

He points out that the tide is low. Off in the distance, the river dwindles to a narrow stream that cuts through the beach sand to the sea.

"It looking quiet and harmless now," he says. "But come high tide, is a different story. The sea overflows the beach, opening up the channel. So you have sea water rushing in and river water rushing out. You can imagine. A different story."

He leads her back to the car. "This is where Columbus never came ashore," he says. "So they named it Columbus Landing. Ram always thought there should be a question mark at the end of the name. But, you know, we in this place never let the facts get in the way."

He stands for a moment, looking around, sniffing the air. "Hasn't changed much over the years," he says with some surprise. "We use to come here all the time when we were young. We use to fish from the bridge. Ram took his fishing very seriously—did you know that? Anybody even so much as whisper, he'd say, Shhh! The fish have ears." He motions her into the car. "Let's see if the path's still there."

He drives slowly ahead, eyes peering at the trees and vegetation lining the road. After a few minues he says, "It wasn't this far. We must've missed it." He turns the car around, and not a minute later give a little exclamation of triumph. "There it is!" he says, pointing.

Yasmin is sceptical. She sees nothing more than a thinning of the vegetation between two large trees.

But Cyril presses ahead, easing the car between the trees, and at last, in the twilight, she discerns the beaten earth of a very old passage. It is overgrown, no vehicle has passed here in a long time. But the car moves easily ahead, clearing the brush before it.

[11]

These things happen very quickly, don't they, my dear Mrs. Livingston? Fundamental change in people close to us—and what's insidious is that change of this nature occurs so deep within the person, we're unaware of its presence until it's taken hold.

Seemingly from one day to the next, Celia withdrew into herself. She rose late, taking breakfast—usually just tea and fried bread—all by herself on the porch. I tried talking with her—small talk, nothing grand—but she remained unresponsive, and I remember standing in the doorway, looking at her, and being struck by the thought that she seemed somehow to have shrunk—into herself, I mean. Physically.

She became irritable, particularly with Cyril. He himself, it must be said, had begun retreating into a smaller world, whether from a full understanding of his situation or in reaction to Celia's own retreat I cannot say. But now, when they spoke even of the simplest things, their conversation was riddled with disagreement, misunderstanding and, worst of all, disapproval.

One morning she looked at him and said, "You aren't going to wear that tie, are you?" But of course he was standing there, arms full of my husband's papers, *that* tie knotted around his neck. More than making him look foolish, she made him feel foolish, which I suppose was the point. And he replied like a foolish man. He said, "I guess not," and immediately put my husband's things down to go change the tie. But Celia pursued him. "So why did you put it on, Cyril? You know how ugly it is." He had no real explanation. He said he had put it on without thinking, which confirmed her suspicion he had put it on merely to annoy her.

It was horrible to watch—and watch we all did, for they exercised no discretion. Just as they had made no secret of their affection, so they made no secret of their disaffection.

When Cyril was not there, Celia would sit by herself in

the porch or under a tree out back, engrossed in a world far from the one she inhabited. A distance difficult to gauge for she now kept silent about the travels of her mind.

I tried talking to her once, hoping for the kind of confidence we once shared. Foolishly perhaps, I remarked that she seemed unhappy. Only people in search of companionship enjoy having their unhappiness noticed. Those, like Celia, who want solitude resent it.

A quick coldness came to her. She said, "Yes, well..." and turned away.

In the coming days, Cyril began to see that she could not be mollified. I watched as he gave up on excusing or explaining himself. Any word beyond a simple acceptance of what she said would infuriate her. She saw it as talking back to her, and that was a right—I am speculating here, you understand, my dear—a right she felt he had forfeited.

She had often spoken, before, of how much she had given up in marrying him, in leaving England, in accepting a life so utterly alien. But she had spoken with no rancour: as if it were an adventure she had embraced. I admired that about her. I felt it took great courage. The same courage which had forbidden her to see her husband as the useless man. The courage which, I began to see, had deserted her for reasons withheld from me. I felt that she was now left with only the dissatisfactions of the life she had chosen.

Understand, my dear. This was a change that occurred over a period of two or three weeks, no more. Celia had told me that they had fallen in love very quickly, and they seemed to be falling out of love just as quickly—a sign, I think, of the passion they shared.

The tensions in the house became palpable, and it was my husband, I think, who suggested we all go off to the beach house for the weekend. Cyril was unsure, but when he saw the brightening that came to Celia—the brightening we all saw—he seized on the idea.

Oh, hello. You again. Time to turn her?

Mrs. Livingston, my dear, I must leave for a few minutes. This is a sight I cannot bear. This rolling of your body. This physical helplessness. I shall return, my dear, never you fear.

[12]

Through the darkness Jim said, "All these years, Yas. The years of long days, the evenings, the countless weekends. And now this."

His breath was raucous, the rattle of ice in his glass a startling counterpoint.

She said, "At least you got a shot. There'll be another."

He sniffled. "This was it, Yas. *The* building. A construction of light."

His shudder vibrated in the night, a disturbance of the air that separated them.

"It's over, you realize," he said.

"There'll be other projects, Jim. You may have to dim some of the light next time around. Didn't anyone at the office—"

"Yes, but no one else understood what I was trying to do. This design was my baby."

My baby: Her heart pinched. Yes, perhaps he had found a baby to replace, or displace, the other. She knew the thought to be harsh, unkind, but she knew, too, that it was true. Even as she resented him for it, she ached at his failure. Success would have brought him a new strength, and perhaps that strength would have fed them both.

"I insisted. I didn't want any obstructions to the flow of natural light, I pictured a flood—"

"But you're always so careful."

"There's a margin, Yas, between being careful and being creative. And sometimes the more creative you are, the narrower the margin becomes. Perhaps I let the margin become too narrow."

"You've been over the calculations?"

"It would have held up." His glass clattered on his desk. "It would have held up."

In the silence she could hear his brain racing: skittering over calculations, speculating on stresses.

"I've been undone," he said, "by clients without courage. Colleagues without vision. You should have been there, Yas. When it came to the crunch, no one'd back me up. When the client said no, he couldn't take the chance, there was utter silence. Then someone turned off the light."

[13]

Yasmin thinks: Yet another world.

As they approach the beach, the quality of the earth changes from a packed brown clay to a sandy white. The brush grows sparse, the vegetation thins out.

They park in the shade of the trees, not palms—there are none in sight—but leafy giants with gnarled trunks.

They are widely dispersed, their branches high above creating a canopy that mottles the sand with shadow.

They walk barefoot and in silence to the beach—wide and flat, painfully bright in the sunlight.

A caution, Yasmin notices, has come to Cyril. There is something watchful about him. She asks what is wrong.

After a moment, he says, "I wish the place had changed, even a little."

He turns around and begins walking along the beach away from the river channel.

Yasmin follows, the sand hot on her soles, a fine dust powdering her toes white. She sees the beach curving beyond his shoulders; sees it ending not far ahead in boulders and rock and plants reaching rope-like tendrils out towards the sea.

Cyril calls, "There used to be a—Look, it still there."

She follows his raised arm to a spot beneath the trees—more numerous here, clustered. And at first she sees only shadows and trunks. Then, behind them, a hill of rock and boulders. And finally, nestled in the greatest darkness amidst the trunks, the regular but crooked lines of a house.

Cyril cuts across the sand towards it, his pace quickened. The house, he says, has always been here. A fisherman's shack. There used to be a family: a man, his wife, and innumerable children. "I use to envy them, you know. I thought they had an idyllic life. No school, growing whatever vegetables they needed. The father and the eldest son heading out in their pirogue every morning before dawn to set their seines."

"Seines?"

"Fishin' nets, nuh."

The house, when they get to it, is small: hardly enough

for a couple, unimaginable for a family. Of simple construction—wooden planks nailed to posts—it has not withstood
the years. Many of the planks are black with rot, some have
fallen askew, the door is gone and the roof has caved in,
forming an almost elegant frieze of poles and dried palm
branches.

Yasmin says, "It couldn't have been a comfortable life,
though."

Cyril nods. "I know. I see that now. But back then… It
was a fantasy I had, and fantasy does only grow in ignorance.
You know, we use to come here often, but we never spoke to
them. Never even really went close. This was their part o'
the beach, and over by the river was our part. They never
went over there, either, at least not while we were here."

"What d'you think's happened to them?"

"Who knows? He steps closer to the ruin, thinking, but
jealous of his thoughts. Then he shakes his head, turns and
strides away back towards the beach.

Yasmin catches up to him just as he enters the sunlight.
"Actually," he says without breaking stride. "There was one
time when Ram spoke to the father. He had to, you see. He
needed to borrow one of his seines."

[14]

There. Back.

You do appear to be more comfortable now. Does that
feel better? Even your breathing seems easier, there's a
touch of colour to your cheeks. I would like to think that's a

good sign, but I have grown fearful of looking for signs, as you know.

Now, where was I? Ah, yes. That morning.

A Saturday. Glorious weather. A detail I remember for several reasons, but particularly because the day before, Friday, had been full of cloud and rain. The drive to the beach that evening was unnerving. The road was narrow, you see, and unlit, and even if there had been a moon—which there was not—the coconut tree plantations to either side would have obscured it thoroughly. The car's headlights seemed to be without reach, not so much illuminating the road as creating shadows around it, and many of the stories from my childhood came back to me. Stories of *douens* who kidnapped people and of *soucouyans* which drank human blood—and particularly the tale of a mysterious white woman dressed in a flowing white gown standing beside the road with a lantern. She had been known to lead the unsuspecting into the depths of the forest and abandon them there. My fear must have been obvious, for Celia, sitting in the back seat beside me, took my hand and squeezed it in reassurance.

So when I awoke late the following morning to a clear and sunny day, I was delighted. I took my tea out to the porch. How the sun sparkled off the water, my dear! How it dazzled! And the horizon—the horizon was as sharp as a stencil. As real as a destination.

My husband and Cyril were already down on the beach, sitting side by side. My husband was scooping up sand and letting it run slowly from his fist, a sign of restlessness. This sitting about did not come easily to him. He had had to cancel several weekend engagements but he had felt it imperative that Cyril and Celia get away, and he knew they would not come by themselves.

You might think this was simple thoughtfulness on my husband's part—and you would not be wrong. But there was more. Although he never told him so, my husband depended a great deal on Cyril, not only as a hop-to-it man but also as a sounding board. Cyril, he had said to me, never offered a single original thought—but he had an ability to reflect your own ideas back at you in such a way that their merits and faults came clear. But the problems with Celia—whatever they were, Cyril had given no hint—were distracting him. They had made him careless and absent-minded, and had to be solved before he caused serious damage. He planned to send them off for a walk together later that evening, to give them a chance to talk things out.

Then something caught my eye on the floor of the porch. A shard of china. Then several. Patterns: a horseshoe, a heart, the crescent moon.

And with no effort my mind reconstituted the tasseomancy cup. I thought: Oh, dear...

Alarm, you see, came slowly to me—but it came steadily. I scanned the beach for signs of her.

And then far out in the water, distant, distant beyond the breakers, a head and two arms flashing like wings, urging her on, pulling her farther and farther away, towards the line that could never be reached.

I don't remember realizing what was happening. I don't remember my teacup crashing to the floor. But later, after the hysteria had calmed to grief, my husband told me that I had wailed a banshee scream.

That day, my dear, Cyril lost the only anchor he had left. He became, in my husband's word, irretrievable.

Yes. Precisely.

Irretrievable: it is the only word.

[15]

"We were young. I must've been eight or nine. Ram would have been sixteen or seventeen. We were out here for the weekend. Fishing, nuh. A little swimming. Me, Ram and a bunch o' his friends. They brought me along because Ma said they had to. The plan was to spend the night right here, sleeping on the beach—not that Ram and his friends planned to sleep, mind you, they brought along enough beer to last the night—and go home the next day. Not something you want to do these days, by the way. In those days there weren't people running around wanting to cut off your head for no reason.

"Anyway, towards evening I was sitting with my fishing rod just up there, on the other bank, this side o' the bridge. Ram and his friends were a little bit upriver. The water was deeper, and they were diving off some rocks. They weren't far, I could hear them shouting and laughing.

"Then suddenly the laughing and shouting stop. Dead silence. Then: Splash-splash-splash! As if all of them diving in at the same time. I knew something was wrong. I drop the rod and run through the bush, and when I got there they were all going crazy diving and diving under the water. Real frantic, nuh. One o' them, a fella named Kamal, a longtime friend, had dived in and didn' come back up. At first they thought it was a joke he was playing, he was that kind o' fella—but this was no joke.

"I don't know how long it went on, their diving and diving, looking. And then it got dark. Ram wanted to keep on diving and the others had to hold him back. I mean, they even had to throw him on the ground and hold him down.

"Then he saw me standing there, scared out o'my mind—and that calmed him down. I remember he started to howl. Fear. Grief. They let him up and he hug me tight-tight, so tight I could hardly breathe—and, I'll tell you, Yasmin, is as if I can still feel that hug. His arms wrapped around me, his whole body shaking. Is the only time he ever hug me like that—but is enough for a lifetime, you know?

"After a while, he let me go. He'd regained his composure, nuh—and it was something to see, I'll tell you. He was calm, in control. As if he'd taken all the shock and the grief and packed it away somewhere, and his brain was in charge again.

"That was when he went to talk to the fisherman. The tide was rising, you see. He figured that Kamal had dived head first into a stand o' broken bamboo underwater. The bamboo must've pierced him somewhere—his skull or his neck or his chest—and he was stuck down at the bottom. But the rising tide was going to stir things up, and Ram figured the currents might dislodge the body. And since the incoming water widened the channel—this channel right here—he needed a seine to spread across, so the body wouldn' float out to sea.

"He came back with his seine. The others had already lit a fire, so they could see what they were doing. They buried two poles deep in the sand on either side of the channel and tied the net between them. Then we sat waiting, everybody around the fire—just over there, nuh—excep' Ram, who waited at the water's edge with a torchlight, looking for his friend's body.

"I fell asleep—fear still does that to me, you know —only to wake up some time later, probably close to midnight, to see all the others standing beside the river. I remember I'd gone from one bad dream to another —I couldn' tell you what they were, not even then—and when I woke up and remembered what had happened I thought I was still dreaming. But there they were, standing right there, kind o' huddling together. I knew right away that I wasn' dreaming—and I knew too what they were doing there.

"The fire was blazing—they'd kept feeding it, nuh, nobody wanted it to be dark—and I remember watching from where I was as Ram emerged from the water with Kamal's body in his arms. Both o' them glistening wet in the firelight. Kamal's arms and legs limp, his head hanging back and rocking, like... Like I don't know what. A wet rag? But a rag was never alive. I just remember a kind o' horror. He had no tension in his body. His mouth was open and I could see plain-plain a big piece of wood sticking from his head. Turned out Ram was right about the bamboo.

"Believe it or not there was a discussion about what to do. A discussion Ram put an end to with some choice words, I tell you. You see, some of the fellas wanted to put him into the trunk. That way we could all leave together. They were afraid, they didn't want to wait while... In the end, they put him into the car and Ram and one of the others drove him to the police station. There was no hospital here then, you see.

"A week or so later, Ram drove back here to see the fisherman. He brought him a new seine. He felt that the old one was spoiled. So he gave the fella the new seine and asked if he could have the old one. No problem. He took the seine, brought it right here to the riverside, doused it in kerosene and set it on fire."

[16]

Tell me, my dear Mrs. Livingston, are you certain, and I mean absolutely certain, with no tincture of a doubt, that your husband loved you?

You are, aren't you. Then you, my dear, are either unnaturally lucky or perilously trusting, and it is not for me to venture a guess as to which. My, the very thought! To live loved and without doubt: It has a touch of the miraculous, wouldn't you say?

And—now that I think of it—were you as certain of this when he was alive, still a man of flesh and blood, strength and weakness? A man with whom you had to mesh your life day after day?

Yes, of course, I should have known. You are a veritable fountain of certainty, aren't you, my dear? I will admit, though, that I wish I had had a few drops from that fountain when I was younger. There are a few things worse, it seems to me, than living with doubts you can express to no one— hardly even to yourself.

What it comes down to is this: I always knew that my husband held me in a certain esteem, but it was an esteem that had little to do with me. He would have offered it to any woman he had married: the traditional esteem of a man for his wife—for her role, as it were, for the part she played in the fabric of his life. I doubt that his sentiment for me ever went beyond that—he touched me with warmth, but I saw him offer this same warmth to others—yet I have no doubt that this was what protected me from the single-minded cruelty he would occasionally inflict on others...

No, no. Not just for incompetence or failure. Sometimes for no reason at all. It was his way of keeping people in line. Some, the less important ones, he would slip money to, twenty dollars here, twenty dollars there, go off and have a drink, boys. But the others...

I remember one evening a group of them came back to the house after a day running around the island doing whatever it was they did. My husband, Cyril, several of the usual hangers-on. They were tired and sweaty, they had clearly gone deep into the rural areas, probably visiting the cane farmers. They settled in the porch—in chairs, on the floor —and my husband called to the maid to bring whisky and ice. He carefully removed his shoes—they were filthy with mud and God knows what else—and so I went over to get them...

Of course, I could have left them for Amina. But—I'll be frank with you, my dear—this was a little strategic move of my own. I always made sure my mother-in-law saw me cleaning and polishing my husband's shoes. It brought me a little measure of domestic peace, you see. And even after her death, I carried it on. Simple habit, nothing more.

So I went to collect his shoes from him—but he stopped me. He said Cyril would do it.

Cyril laughed—uneasily.

My husband held the shoes out to him: Cyril?

Cyril laughed again—a forced laugh. He was aware of the sudden silence, knew he had become the centre of an unexpected drama. He said, rather lamely, that he didn't wish to take the pleasure from me.

My husband said he had stepped in cow dung that afternoon, and he had no intention of having his wife deal with that: Cyril?

He sat there for several long seconds, my husband persisting until I thought Cyril would cry. Finally, Cyril took the shoes and went off into the house to do as bid...

Celia wasn't around. She would not have tolerated it, to be sure, but this happened afterwards, you see. After she had...

Well, in any case, later I asked my husband why he'd done it. He said he thought Cyril was becoming a little lazy, he needed sharpening up, he was taking this manager post of his both too seriously and not seriously enough—by which he meant that Cyril was more in love with the title than with the duties. But I sensed this was just an excuse. I sensed that there was no reason. The truth was, my husband had humiliated his brother because he felt like it.

Imagine, if you can, Mrs. Livingston, living with a man like that—a man respectful of you, or at least of your status, but who would spare no one else, not even his brother. And if he would not spare his brother, what guarantee was there that he would always spare me?

So I envy you, my dear, the certainty you claim to have had in your husband's love. I envy you—and, at the same time, I cannot bring myself to believe you...

But that, undoubtedly, is my problem.

[17]

They drive on.

Light succeeds shadow succeeds light. A mirage of coolness and dry sand.

Yasmin thinks: There, I could burrow deep.

At a bend in the road, he slows down. She does not see the track through the palm trees until he has turned onto it

—a road of sorts, leading away from the sea. Unpaved, uneven, but he drives with confidence. He knows the way well.

Presently, the trees fall back and they are at a large clearing of moist, beaten earth. At the far end stands a house, raised several feet off the ground on thick wooden poles. The house is old, of wood weathered a rich brown. Many of the planks have warped; the window shutters all hang off plumb. But its state does not suggest disrepair. Quite the opposite: merely age, and the normal ravages of climate.

Cyril parks at the edge of the clearing and asks her to wait in the car for him. He promises not to be long. She watches him walk towards the house, and she finds confirmation in his manner that he is at ease here: his feet know the ground.

When he is halfway there, the front door opens—she glimpses an interior of contained shadow—and a man emerges. He hurries down the stairs with an awkward, stiffened gait. He is tall and rangy—not young, but vigorous in the economical way of those accustomed to a life of hard labour. His attire—hat, soiled khaki shirt and trousers, black rubber boots—conceals him, makes his age difficult to assess.

Cyril is the first to offer his hand, and the man responds shyly with his own. He is not accustomed to such gestures. They speak briefly, then the man turns and lopes back into the house.

Cyril slides his hands into his trouser pockets, his lips pursed in a whistle she suspects is tuneless. He glances back at the car, but does not wave.

The man returns, a sheet of paper in his hand. He shows it to Cyril, who examines it with interest. He makes a comment. The man replies, then points to something written on the paper.

Yasmin decides Cyril is checking on some business: accounts of some kind. Her eyes wander to the forest at the far end of the clearing, to the density of its darkness and its promise—threat?—of the inexorable barely contained.

Cyril folds the paper and hands it back. They part company, the man returning to the house, Cyril heading back to the car.

The man stands in the open doorway, framed by shadow. Watching.

Cyril, businesslike, gets into the car, turns the key and drives back through the coconut trees with the same confidence he showed when driving in.

[18]

The road ahead narrows, asphalt crumbling at the edges, trees rising now as if from beneath the paving.

Cyril says, "Hope it don't hurt too much."

To Yasmin's quizzical glance he says "Your tongue, I mean. Don't bite it too hard, nuh."

She offers a gentle laugh, unable to decide whether or not this is an invitation to inquire.

"His name is Caleb. Built that house with his own hands —no plans, nothing. Just an idea that he manage to expand over the years. He's a good man, hard worker."

"A friend?"

"Not really. I help him out a little."

I help him out a little: yet an unlikely pair.

"We were young when we met. Both had wives and futures we couldn' see. I was out here with your father, doing some work, nuh. Caleb helped us, he knew the area. Anyway, whenever I was up here I'd stop by, just to say hello. In politics, a little hello once in a while does go a long way."

And on one of those visits he found that Caleb's wife had fled, leaving him with two teenaged sons and a young daughter. The boys had already established their own futures with their father, working vegetable plots, rearing chickens, hunting wild game, catching and selling crabs during the season, trapping *cascadoo*—an armoured fish, he explains, fine-boned and delicious curried—in the swamps.

But Caleb wanted his daughter to have a different life. Cyril remembers asking what he meant by that, remembers the silence that came to him, the way he had scratched at his head in embarrassment: he could not put into words what to him was only the vaguest of concepts. A life away from here, away from the trees and the swamps, a life where she would not be ground down by physical labour as her mother had been. She was only seven, there was time yet to shape a new life.

Cyril had discussed the girl with Penny. Penny suggested waiting a few years, until the girl was ten or so. Then they might be able to find her a position as a maid.

Cyril sighs. "At leas' she help me understan' something important," he says.

So he made arrangements on his own. The girl was boarded with a family in a town some distance away—a town with a school where she could be educated. The expenses were all assumed by Cyril. "It was no big deal, you know. Couple o' uniforms, books, room an' board. Penny does spend more on Christmas presents."

That was twelve years ago and she was now on the verge of graduating from high school. If she did well at the

A-Levels—and the school report Caleb had just shown him indicated that she would do very well indeed—then she could, if she wished, go on to study nursing. Through contacts he had maintained from his days in politics with Ram, he had already taken steps towards a modest scholarship for her.

"You've seen the house," he says. "You know how they get water? From the rain, runnin' down a pipe from the roof to a barrel outside. Look, I can't pretend to tell you what Caleb life is like. I ain' know. Or at leas', I only know what I see. And what I see is things like that barrel full o' rain water."

A sensation of sand comes to Yasmin: the grains fine and warm, molding themselves to her, a cast for eternity. Ahead, a cocoon of shadow and light.

"You see the distance that girl has travelled?" Cyril says. "You see the distance she can still go?"

And what does Penny think of all this?

"She doesn' know. Nobody knows. Is nobody's business. You have to understand. People would jus' bad-talk me. Is blackmail, or is my love-chil', or something else nasty. Is bes' kept quiet."

Are there others?

A few. Only a few. "People think I'm a useless man, Yasmin. I know they laugh at me, and not always behind my back." A grimness shapes his face. "But maybe the useless man not so useless after all, eh?"

And for the first time in years, Yasmin feels herself awed.

Yasmin asks, "Did he know my father?"

"They must've met a couple o' times. But—"

But: the word hangs there in the warm air of the car, a

gentle pulse echoing back onto itself. Yasmin reaches for it, swallows it. Feels it float, fluttering, into her head.

"You see"—and his tone is thoughtful, pleading—"you see, if Ram had a fault it was that he had little sympathy for people who wanted just to make a living. He couldn't understand them: couldn't understand how they could be happy with what he saw as a small life, small pleasures: 'Daily livin', bringin' up the chil'ren.' It was hard on him, pretending to care—because only by promising to make these things possible could he build the larger life he wanted for himself. When Ram didn't have to pretend, he didn't. He let others barter the enthusiasm in his place.

"So they must've met a couple o' times. But they wouldn' remember each other. He wasn' memorable enough for Ram, and Ram wouldn've made himself memorable enough for him."

[1 9]

The firm's assessment was completed two weeks later. The five double-spaced pages were lying on the dining table when she returned home after the newscast. Jim, fixing himself a whisky and soda at the counter, nodded at it. "It's unsparing," he said. "As it should be."

"What does it say?"

"See for yourself."

She ran through the pages quickly, not bothering to sit, absent-mindedly accepting a sip of his drink.

On the first page, the client's requirements were reviewed. On the second, Jim's design was described. On the third, in brutally passive language, all of the design's shortcomings were highlighted: corners were too tight, pillars too few, margins too narrow.

He said, "If they'd given me a chance, I could've saved her."

"Her?"

"It."

[2 0]

"This was his favourite spot."

The coastal road has brought them here, to a promontory high on the cliffs she saw earlier. She finds it an unsettling coastline—flat and straight one moment, winding and rising the next; from palm trees and beach to jungle vegetation and cliffs; and everywhere paths hidden from her eye. It occurs to her that, despite her moment of panic in the mountains, she trusts Cyril. But she knows too that she trusts him, in part, because she must. The blind wandering in an alien landscape have no choice but to trust.

It is windy here, the water down below at the base of the rocky cliff choppy and violent, flaying itself against the boulders.

"I don' know how he ever found it. Hardly anybody else knows about it. This was where he came when he wanted to do some serious fishing."

"Do you fish?"

"Not since Kamal. But you know what they say about fishing. Is not really about catching fish. Is about being by yourself, letting the mind wander. Thinking, nuh."

He clasps his hand behind his back and wanders over to

the trees lining the far edge of the promontory. "Actually, I only came here once with him. I been back many times since his death. You're the first person… Even Penny's never been here." He walks up to a tree and slaps the trunk. "See this tree?" He turns around point to another about twenty feet away. "And that one?"

"This happened when we were older." Ram was probably in his early twenties and a couple of his friends were moving away, to the States. So he invited a bunch of us up here for a night of camping and fishing.

"We didn't have much in the way of equipment, jus' a big tarpaulin that we used to make a tent. He ran a rope from this tree over to that one, threw the tarpaulin over it and tied the edges down. Makeshift but workable. Then we lit a fire and settled down for some ol' talk. Had a few beers. Jus' joking around, nuh. Relaxing. Eating.

"Everybody knew that things were about to change. Once people start moving away, it doesn' stop there.

"A little later that evening, after the sun set—and it was no big deal, it set on the other side—Ram and some o' the fellas get out the fishing equipment and set off down the cliff with a torchlight. There's this rock about halfway down where he used to fish from. It was starting to get cold—the breeze, nuh—so I went into the tent and cozy up with a torchlight and some comic books.

"They came back some hours later, without a single fish —but, as I say, is not the point. They stayed up for a while, talking, having a last beer. And eventually they came into the tent and stretched out too. It was starting to get pretty cold, the wind was picking up, and the tarpaulin was starting to flap in places. Ram had to tighten it down.

"Anyway, some time later that night, I don't know what time exactly but it was damn late, this loud, booming, cracking sound woke me up. And I don' mean gently. I remember opening my eyes and wondering what the hell was going on. The wind was whipping, I could hear thunder —and just as some lightning crack, one end o' the tarpaulin rip right out and fly up into the air like a sail unfurling. Everything started to blow everywhere. Blankets here. Comic books there. You name it. And then, boom!—rain start to pelt down. And I mean buckets and buckets and buckets. In a second we were drenched. Us, tent, food, everything.

"We scramble like devils, running around in the dark picking up this, picking up that. Finally, we jus' drop everything and headed for the cars. And that's where we end up camping—in the cars. Wet to the skin. Along with every mosquito in the neighbourhood. For the rest o' the night all you hearing is slap-slap-slap.

"By next morning, storm was gone, sky was blue, sun was glorious—and all of us looked as if we had chicken pox. Everything was wet, no way to get the fire going, so forget coffee or tea. The bread you had to wring out if you wanted to eat it. I had peanuts for breakfast.

"You know what Ram do? He strip down to his underpants, hang his clothes on the rope to dry, picked up his fishing equipment and headed down to the rock. The rest of us weren't too happy, I'll tell you, we wanted to head back. But he won the day. We were here. The weather was nice. Everything would dry out. Jus' keep on going. So we did.

"You know, Yasmin, years later when he got into politics those fellas were still there. Through t'ick an' t'in. And when things got rough, I bet you anything that just about everybody thought about that night right here—that dark and stormy night, as they say—and jus' keep on going."

There is no path—or at least, once more, a path discernible only to Cyril.

The way down is precipitous: hard earth studded with stones and chipped rock. She follows quite literally in his footsteps, placing her feet where he places his.

He offers his hand, but she refuses: Should he tumble with her hand gripped in his, he would pull her down too.

Although the waves are far below—their movement an audible suck and splash against the rocks: a liquid rustling—she can feel their power, and the power of the sun above, in the fine spray that lights on her skin and evaporates immediately.

The descent is slow but steady, her eye so fast on the placement of Cyril's shoes that she is almost surprised when he says, "Here we are."

Here we are: his fishing rock. She looks at it, sees that it is just that—a rock—and she wonders at her vague disappointment. She asks herself what she expected, and finds she has no answer. It is what Cyril has all along said that it was, she tells herself: the rock from which he fished.

Slate-grey and smooth, smaller than she expected but in all likelihood just the lip of a much larger boulder buried within the face of the cliff, it provides adequate room for four people, five at a pinch. But, beginning to feel beyond its geology, she sees that it is a place for one, the world reduced to immodest sky and water. She senses, then, the eloquence of its seduction. Senses herself strangely disarmed, and yet, standing here unsheltered, not exposed.

Cyril, behind her, says, "Look at this." He is crouched in the far corner, his fingers reaching down to the surface of the rock.

She looks. She sees nothing.

Cyril snatches a handful of earth from the cliff wall, rubs it onto the rock, then brushes it away with delicate sweeps of his palm.

Now she sees it. Or them. Two letters, each about three inches high. Brown on grey. Not letters, she corrects herself. Initials: VR.

Cyril says, "He broke his favourite knife doing this."

Yasmin goes weak at the knees. A sudden vertigo: She lowers herself to the ground.

Cyril says, "This is as close to him as I can bring you, Yasmin."

She touches the rock: traces the letters with her knuckles; brushes the earth from them, exposing them.

She reads the gouges with her fingertips.

Her ears detect the bite of steel on rock—and for a moment the letters come as clear to her as the day they were cut.

Only when she feels herself overwhelmed by the need to clasp them, to make them material in her palm, do they dissolve.

Only then, in her sight suddenly misty, does she lose them.

And only then does she let herself heave in Cyril's arms.

[2 1]

The sea is held back by a braid of boulders, large, grey rocks intricately veined in white. Cyril has drawn her attention to them with the remark that, were they to return to this spot in a hundred years, they would find the boulders reduced to pebbles. "That," he says, "is history."

Their precarious solidity is, however, fitting, for here—
a narrow strip of gravelled earth poured and battened down
between the boulders and the roadway—seems a precarious
perch for a village. If the island were to shrug, Yasmin
thinks, it would all tumble into the sea.

They have stopped at what Cyril refers to as a "parlour",
a roadside convenience store. It is no more than a small
wooden room with large, open front doors, the planks
painted pink; the window shutters, propped open with
sticks, green; and the galvanized-iron roof its natural zinc.
Despite the bright sunlight, a bare bulb hangs burning from
a long cord.

"Mornin', mammy," Cyril says heartily to the aged
woman seated behind the counter.

She nods in response, too preoccupied with her own
thoughts to respond to Cyril's friendly greeting.

He claps his hands as if in anticipation of a feast and
orders lunch. "Two aloo roti, please, mammy. One hot-hot
and one—" he glances at Yasmin, a look that is partly in
assessment, partly in challenge "—and one medium."

Yasmin accepts the challenge. "Make it hot-hot," she
says, the words strange on her tongue, like an expression
from an unfamiliar language.

Cyril frowns. "You know what you doing?"

"I've never met a pepper I couldn't eat, Cyril"

"Must run in the family. You sure?"

Yasmin shakes her head. "I can't exactly back out now,
eh? And by the way, since you're probably wondering—yes,
I know what aloo-roti is. Curried potato rolled in a kind of
pita bread."

"Now look, Yasmin." He places his palm on his heart.
"If you going to tell me that Shakti used to make it, you

going to give me a heart attack. Some things just not in the realm of possibility, you know?"

"No, no. It's just that back home you can get everything, just about every kind of food imaginable. Including aloo-roti. Nothing's really exotic any more."

The old woman places their meal on the counter, the sandwiches wrapped in wax paper. As Cyril pays, Yasmin finds two words echoing in her mind: *back home*. She hears the words shaped by her mother's voice, she hears them shaped by her own, and she is struck for the first time at the difference in implication: the same words signifying different worlds.

[2 2]

Do you know, my dear Mrs. Livingston, how some faces suggest the past?

From the photographs she has sent to me over the years, I see that my sister-in-law Penny has grown into a handsome woman, with that edge of severity so many handsome women seem to acquire. And yet, in her face you still see the essential features of the child I never knew and of the young woman who became a close friend. I believe, Mrs. Livingston, that no matter what experience life brings us, the person we were meant to be never disappears. The essential personality, I mean. I believe it has been so with Penny. She is a woman who has endured, despite everything.

No, her life has not been particularly harsh. She has always lived in a certain comfort. But one aspect has always been—how shall I put this? *Problematic* should just about cover it. You see, Penny was treated by men with a level of deference not accorded the other single women in our circles. I mean, they were always polite, but with the other unmarried women there was often an undertone of flirtation, a suggestion of naughtiness, if you will. With Penny, however, this was never, ever, in evidence, and was the cause of some pain to her. She was not an unattractive young woman, with all of the normal yearnings of her age, but men, I imagine, found the proximity to my husband intimidating. Smacks of cowardice, doesn't it? Harsh, I know, but I remember too well Penny's frustrations, her bitterness even, to understand and forgive. Simply put, I do not *wish* to understand and forgive.

What I remember with great sadness was the regularity, and a certain indiscrimination, with which Penny would develop crushes. She would convince herself of the attractiveness of one available man after another, often men with whom she had little in common. These crushes never led anywhere, of course, and I was the one she would come to, once the failure was clear, to conduct a cleansing postmortem. All the virtues she had perceived would be turned around, remade into flaws. The men would suddenly be sickly or untrustworthy. The dazzling smile a leer, a shy helpfulness, effeminacy.

I listened, I agreed, I helped her move on. I believed, you see, that the right one would come along in his own good time. That the virtues would remain virtues and Penny would find happiness.

Then one day, it happened.

She and I were walking in the yard after lunch, watching the clouds build up at the horizon, when she suddenly blurted out that she had met a man.

[23]

Even in the great heat of early afternoon, the rocks are cool to the touch, the white veins as if embossed on the grey stone.

They sit beside each other, Cyril facing the sea, Yasmin facing the coast along which they have driven. The boulders closer to the water, she sees, are cracked and worn, littered with pebbles torn from themselves.

Cyril says, "He probably caused you a lot o' tears over the years, eh?"

Yasmin fills her mouth with a bite of the roti. In this way she is better able to treat his question as rhetorical. The truth, she knows, would hurt him: She has no memory of ever having cried for, or because of, her father.

"Well, never mind," Cyril continues. "Ram never worried much about causing anybody tears. He had a ferocious temper when he was young, you know. Is only when he got old enough to realize his tantrums weren't impressing anybody that he learn how to control it—and to turn it to his advantage. He din' lose his temper too often when he grew up, but it was there and he let it explode when he thought it would help. Kind o' like a volcano with a control button, nuh."

Behind him, a young man steps gingerly across the rocks to the edge, where he sits, legs dangling above the gently-lapping water.

Cyril says, "The roti not too hot?"

Yasmin shakes her head. "Told you."

The young man she estimates to be in his early twenties. He is tall and thin, and views the world through a continuous squint. The tail of his shirt is untucked, the long sleeves

rolled past the elbow; the hem of his trousers are slightly
flared, and he is barefoot. He sits there on the boulder as if
in contemplation, bony shoulders hunched towards the sea.

"Although, knowing Ram the way I did," Cyril continues, "I pretty sure things would've been different with you."

Yasmin resists the temptation to ask why this should have
been so. She knows Cyril's message is of intention; it is meant
to be comforting—but intention projected into a future that
never came to be is to her futile, a feather too loosely
anchored to provide lift. She no longer allows herself to
dream of the shape her daughter's life might have acquired.

"I remember once he used you to weed out a sycophant.
Now, he din't mind sycophants, but the mindless ones he
couldn' stomach. He knew this fella'd just had a baby, so he
showed you to him and said, You ever see a prettier baby
than this one? I bet even yours not as pretty. And the fella
said, I have to admit, Mr. Ramessar, your baby prettier than
mine. That was the end o' him."

"Glad to know I was useful," Yasmin says, tearing an end
of the wax paper back from the bread.

"With you he'd've been different," Cyril repeats.

Yasmin sees that Cyril has not taken his story beyond its
details—to him it is just a tale to tell, one of her father's
quirks—and a sadness comes to her.

But Cyril does not notice. "You were his daughter," he
says. "His 'daughts'. The apple of his eye. I can't say he
spent hours playing with you, he din't have time for that
kind o' thing. But he gave you a special attention. If you
were around, he always knew where you were and what you
were doing. Even if he had a meeting—"

"I distracted him?" And even though she does not
intend it to be so, the question emerges with a bitter edge.

The young man behind Cyril reaches absent-mindedly for a pebble, tosses it into the sea. Then another and another. He is, Yasmin thinks, like a man fondling worry beads, the action automatic, divorced from his consciousness.

"Yes. In a good way. We used to have a swing hanging from a mango tree. One day, you were out there with Amie, I think, swinging away—"

White on blue up and down spinning around and around and around faster and faster

White on blue glimpses of green white on blue up and down faster and faster white white white

"—and somehow you slip off the seat—"

Hold on tight!
Faster and faster green white blue
Don't let go! Don't —

"—practically flew through the air—"

A cascade of green brown blue white
Umpg!
Green. And brown. And white on blue

"—and landed hard on your head. I think it almost knock you out."

And darkness crowding in at the edges
A gathering up in hands
The shadow of a face against the blue

"Man, Ram was out there in a flash making sure you were all right. I never seen him so scared. He start shouting at Amie as if... I mean, I was afraid he was going to hit her."

"Hit her?" But her attention is divided, engaged still in wrapping the context newly revealed around images that have drifted forever in her mind.

"In a manner o' speaking. He wasn' that type o' fella. Truth is, Ram wasn' easy on the people he loved, but you wouldn' believe how far he was ready to go for them."

[24]

His name was Zebulon Crooks and he was what used to be known as a preacher-man. He travelled around the island holding rowdy revival meetings in a canvas tent he erected on local sports fields. In the remoter areas, entire villages would flock to him. He was known to offer a good show. A heady sermon, rousing music, and quantities of his special holy water—tap water, it was rumoured, leavened with cheap whisky—to quench the thirst.

In town, however, his appeal was less impressive. There were other entertainments, you see—rum shops, cinemas—and this forced him to go out into the streets in search of an audience. That was how Penny met him. She was in town to do some shopping and, hurrying along to catch a taxi back home, she suddenly found her way blocked by this tall, handsome man holding a leaflet out to her. She took it, and he engaged her in conversation all the way to the taxi stand.

By the time she told me about Zebulon that sultry afternoon, they had seen each other twice, each time taking tea at a café in town. Penny was clearly quite taken with him and, from her account, he with her.

Attractive? The word does him no justice, my dear, none at all.

Zebulon was a striking man, with eyes that seemed afire one moment, gentle the next, and lips that gave the impression of a constant struggle to restrain a smile. For a man selling God, there was something unmistakably devilish about him. Add to this his great and unfeigned charm, and it was no wonder that Penny was infatutated with him.

Penny's problem was what to do next—

No, no, his beliefs were hardly an impediment. Remember that my husband's family had adopted Christianity, and that religion was for us mostly a flag of convenience. Zebulon's fervour and its peculiar manifestation might have been somewhat—shall we say, embarrassing?—but, still, he was not unsuccessful at what he did and, as Penny pointed out, his religious act bore some resemblance to my husband's political one.

No, my dear, the problem was far more intractable than that. The problem, you see—as I knew immediately it would be, as Penny knew—was Zebulon's race. Neither his charm nor his looks nor his success could save him from being black.

A war council of family and hangers-on was called. Penny and I were not invited. I was not surprised. Penny, furious, stamped off and locked herself in her bedroom.

After some time, my husband emerged and asked to speak to Penny alone.

Penny, beside me on the sofa, reached for my hand and grasped it tight.

My husband sat on the other side and took her free hand. And he spoke in a voice, and said things, that made me immensely proud of him, all the while detesting him for the position he was putting his sister in. What he said was: *Penny*—or he may have said *My dear Penny*, I don't remember—*you know that I am not fond of our African compatriots, and I will not insult you by pretending that I am not personally aggrieved by the feelings you have developed for this man. But let me make one thing clear: My feelings are immaterial. If you decide, on reflection, that you wish to marry this Zebulon Crooks, I will throw you the biggest, fanciest, splashiest wedding this island has ever seen. And I would extend a hand of welcome*—and here he squeezed her palm with such vigour she winced—*a hand of welcome to your husband as I would to any other brother-in-law. I would wish you both all the happiness of this world.* Then he paused, shutting his eyes as if from an excess of emotion. *But, Penny*, he continued, *there is something else for you to consider. Understand as you go rightfully after your happiness that your marriage to this man would effectively end any hope I have of political success. You know my constituency, Penny, you know the loyalties on which my support is based. Your marriage to a black man would make me a laughing stock.*

That night, without seeking counsel, not even mine, Penny decided that she would no longer see Zebulon Crooks. She quietly announced the news the following morning at breakfast. She was composed and clear-eyed—she had slept well—and ended by saying that her decision was final and she did not wish to speak of it ever again, nor to defend, justify or explain it. Her gaze elicited a silent promise from each of us.

I kept that promise, even though I firmly believe to this day that Zebulon Crooks would have made Penny a warm and caring husband. I believe—perhaps I wish to believe—that he was Penny's one true chance for happiness.

The tragedy is that Penny, too, believed this and has lived her life in consequence.

[25]

Yasmin's eyes follow the arc of the young man's pebbles as they tumble through the air in a slow spin.

Cyril says, "We don' get too many tourists up here in this part o' the island. They go to the other beaches, down south, nuh. That means we have to groom those beaches. But we don' need to do that here, we not trying to impress anybody. Besides, all this heat and humidity don't exactly encourage movement, if you see what I mean. Why bother picking up the garbage when there just going to be more of it next Sunday?

"You know, Yasmin, it have people who trying to take all those things my generation saw as vices and turn them into virtues. We don' speak the Queen's English here—but is the Queen's English we use when we write. Except now, it have people who want us to write the way we speak. Is not broken English, they say. Is *our* English, we must take pride. Just like it have other people who say, all this garbage remain here not because of laziness but because a kind of indolence is part o' the island life-style.

"Now, you and I know that indolence is just a nice word for laziness, but we trying hard not to be too judgemental down here, at least not with ourselves. We go with the flow, we roll with the punches.

"But Ram wasn' like that. He believed in doing things,

not just pretending. That was the problem, you see. In the years leading up to independence—a happy, optimistic time —he thought everything was possible for us. Even when he said, Let's do X, and people did Y, he didn't want to give up.

"But everything change when he came back from England. That first evening, he said to me, I was a damn fool, Cyril. And before you could blink twice, he reinvent himself. He became less talkative, but sharper, brisker, more calculating. Nobody ever knew what he was thinking. So he became more difficult and lonelier, too. Sometimes he would just humiliate people for no reason—something he'd never've done before. He had a sense of shame, you see. But that sense became simple knowledge, so that he was able to overcome it. He forced it not to be a burden.

"He could've wash his hands o' the whole thing and just walked away, you know. Your life would've been very different. But he couldn' do that, wasn' even tempted. He was too hurt, too bitter. And for somebody like Ram, vengeance was the best antidote. His dream, my dear Yasmin, became his weapon.

"There were darker days personally, but politically, I knew that a kind of curtain had come down. Not even Ram believed any more. And so enemies began to multiply."

Yasmin feels lost in the profusion of possibilities, feels dazzled by the consequences of choices made and not made. She raises her face to the warm breeze riffling the surface of the water, to the sunshine sparking electricity from its immensity of ridges.

Cyril asks if she is thirsty, and offers a soft drink. He gets to his feet, dusts the seat of his pants and totters off across the boulders back to the parlour.

The young man tosses another pebble.

Yasmin leans forward, following the pebble through the air. She sees it land on the water with no splash; sees it go under with no ripple.

The young man, sensing her movement, turns towards her, his face—fine-featured, skin tightened on the skull—remaining mask-like.

She smiles, and when his mask remains indifferent she sees that, beneath the hooded lids, his eyes are dense, his pupils milky. The smile freezes on her lips—and a shudder arrests itself only at the sound of Cyril calling to her, asking whether she wants a strawberry soft-drink or banana.

[26]

She sat for a long time, watching the silhouette of Jim's profile against the shadows.

In the months since the company's review, the empty lot on the edge of the city, destined to filled by a design other than his, had come to haunt him. She sensed that with his urgency depleted, he would be left with only dread.

Finally, she said, "Where are you, Jim?"

His profile twitched in irritation. "I'm right here." He slapped the arm of the chair, as if the mere physicality of the act would underscore his reply, lend it sufficiency. Anubis, curled at his feet, looked up, looked around: eyes glowing malevolent in the dark.

"Yes. But I've been sitting here alone. Where were you?"

His face shifted towards her, but she sensed he was looking with unseeing eyes: unwilling—or perhaps unable, she could not tell—to emerge from a world to which he afforded her no access. A world, she suspected, in which a great deal more had been shattered than a dream of steel and glass and fields of light.

She said, "Are you searching for the light, Jim?"

"No. No. That arrogance is gone. I'm just looking for a way to carry on, I guess."

"But you're working. You *are* carrying on."

He leaned forward in the chair, a burdened silhouette. "You don't understand, Yas—"

"How can I? You sit there all wrapped up in yourself, saying nothing."

He remained a while in silence before beginning, tentatively, to speak. He spoke, then, of the long years of long days, the labour of countless evenings, of having endured the effort comforted by a sense of decades yet to come. But he felt now that he had lived the greater part of his life, that the decades had diminished, that the chance to create the building of his dreams had come and gone, and he was left with nothing beyond warehouses and strip malls to fill the years to come.

"It's like when I found out what the payroll department was. Only it's not my dad, this time it's me. Maybe that's all I'm suited for. Payroll, not the locomotive."

"If you really believe that, Jim, then hurry up and get used to it."

"Get used to it? I'm not talking about a few more grey hairs here, Yas—"

"You think I don't know that? I *am* on your side, you know. So you don't drive the locomotive. So what? You do good work, everybody knows that. Perseverance is an underrated quality, Jim. I wouldn't be here now if my mom hadn't persevered after my dad died. And as for your dad—"

"What about him?"

"Maybe he wanted to be a train engineer, you ever thought of that? But he got a good, boring job and he stuck with it because he had to. There's something admirable in that, isn't there?"

After a moment he said, "You don't believe that for a moment."

"And you don't want to. Isn't that what it all comes down to, Jim? What we want to believe?"

He said nothing for a long while, the silence deepening between them.

Finally he straightened up, the chair sighing. "This belief of yours in redemption, Yas. Are you being optimistic? Or just delusional?"

She stiffened. "I fell in love with you, I married you. So which of your two words should I pick?"

[27]

Cyril, steering with his left hand, says, "Do you still believe in Santa Claus?" His right elbow is propped on the sill of his open window, hand gripping his soft drink —a clear yellow liquid, crystalline and pretty in the sunshine.

"Santa Claus?" Her soft drink, which is sweet, red, and as reminiscent of strawberry as grape juice is of wine, has left her mouth sticky, her thirst unslaked. She holds the bottle, half-filled and warm, on her lap.

"Ram and Shakti's first big fight, believe it or not. You must've been two or three. She wanted to teach you about

Santa Claus. Magic. The mystery in life. He was dead set against it. He thought that Santa was bad for the morale. Taught things like getting something for nothing and encouraged chil'ren to believe in fairytales. Besides, Hindus don' believe in Christmas—"

"She won, eh?"

"Natch. After all, even we had Santa Claus—Father Christmas, nuh—when we were growing up. One orange, one apple and a box o' soda biscuits. Ram could'n say much when I remind him o' that."

Yasmin thinks: *She won. Natch*.

Cyril says, "You must still believe."

"How so?"

"You wouldn' be here otherwise, would you?"

[28]

That the restaurant had not changed through the years was, as Jim remarked, a singular achievement in a city where permanence was finite.

It was here, in this large room rendered intimate by a phrasing of shadow and light, that she had agreed to marry Jim; here, in this room where elegant waiters moved with spectral judiciousness, that they had celebrated her pregnancy; here, where discretion marshalled sound, that they had marked her accession to the anchor desk.

The champagne that Jim had ordered was uncorked and approved with nonchalant formality. As they clinked their glasss, Yasmin thought of the middle-aged couple who, on the evening that Jim asked her to marry him, had sat at the corner table conversing amiably. Her mind distanced itself, turning back to observe them. She saw that they had become that couple, but without amiability, and what at the time would have been a comforting thought now proved an unconsoling one. It awoke the dread—for that was not too strong a word—that she had been feeling for some months.

There was no identifiable reason for it. Her forty years they were here to celebrate had taken no unusual physical toll: a few wrinkles, the silver strands that had come to her following Ariana's death dissimulated among the dark mass of her hair. Her one unusual Pap test had turned out, upon further examination, to be innocuous. Her breasts had remained lump-free.

And yet a certain uneasiness had come to her somewhere between her thirty-seventh and thirty-eighth birthdays. Before then, age had not mattered except as a way of marking the milestones of her life. But thirty-seven, following on years informed by a knot of ineradicable heartache, came quickly, and it tugged in its wake the looming certainty of forty.

Forty. A large number—an age she could associate with herself only in gentle disbelief. Her mind was sharp, her limbs strong, her enjoyment of life—as she thought of it —undiminished, within reason: How could she be forty? Middle-aged. Life half lived, if she was lucky. It cast a shadow.

Jim had wanted to have a party for her: invite everybody. But his idea had struck her as inappropriate. She wanted something smaller, more intimate. Secret. A restaurant, then—and not one of those places where tone-deaf waiters belted out "Happy Birthday" around a cupcake. New restaurants, each offering new concepts in food and decor, opened every day in the city, but Jim opted for the known and dependable. She was not surprised.

The waiter came for their order. She chose the rack of lamb. She usually had salmon. Jim raised an eyebrow in surprise, then ordered his usual filet mignon, "as red as a sailor's sunset." He conferred in knowledgeable murmur with the waiter over the choice of wine.

When the waiter had gone, Yasmin said, "Do you still think about the light?"

Jim cocked his head, his eyes narrowing. "The what?"

"Never mind. Nothing."

He reached into his pocket, placed a small box in black velvet on her plate.

As she opened the box and lifted with a show of delight the strand of imperfect pearls, she couldn't help wondering what had happened to the arrogance and originality of his years gone by.

She has thought about it, of course.

The possibility of dismantling the life that has outlived its beauty.

This is how she has imagined it: the wrapping of the silverware and the vases and the lamps; the boxing of the books; the bundling of linen; the removal of furniture; and the suitcases maniacally stuffed: a methodical undoing of the life, the house, stripped of personality, returned to a shell of brick and echo.

This division of the spoils appears to her to be a mere formality. She covets nothing beyond the photographs of her daughter. Take it all, her mind says to Jim. What is important is to begin again—and the avoidance of rubble.

And yet this is what stops her: this thorough dismantling

which would be like ripping out sections of gut; the inevitability of rubble; and the vagueness of what would come next.

For, despite everything, she cannot imagine herself happy.

There is fear, there is suspension of breath, but there is no rapture.

Later, as they got ready for bed, Jim said, "It really isn't so bad, you know."

"What?"

"Age. You get used to it."

But it was not a matter of adjustment. It was not a matter of age itself. The problem, she suspected, was the possibility never broached, and now beyond reach: the possibility of another child.

Yet, after a moment, she said, "That's the problem, isn't it."

But he didn't hear her over the rush of water from the tap, and when he climbed into bed, the moment had passed.

Lying beside her, forearm thrown over his eyes, Jim said, "There's a coldness at your centre, Yas. A ball of ice that survives beneath all those layers of warmth." He turned, pressed himself to her side, his head on her shoulder, his thigh crossing hers.

He had aroused her despite herself, and in the enlivened darkness she had rediscovered a youthful energy, an energy without age. Now, with just a few words, he had returned to her the anxiety he had caused her to forget.

His palm, lying moist on her belly, crept up her side, touch lightening as he found her breast, skimming slowly across the nipple—she winced: it was sensitive still—and settling on it, grasping lightly at her flesh and at the pearls she had not removed. It was an artless gesture and, following on his words, grotesque.

She reached for his hand, removed it.

He hesitated. Then he turned onto his back and mumbled goodnight.

She rolled onto her side, away from him, and stared wakeful into the darkness. For beyond everything—beyond the pleasure she had received and given; beyond the anxiety in her belly and the mindlessness of his touch—was the certainty that, in identifying that deeper coldness within her, Jim was right.

[29]

Cyril says, "They stopped here that day. He needed to pee."

Yasmin leans on the car and looks around. Sand. Palm trees widely dispersed. A beach that is broad and flat in low tide, the waves unfurling themselves with whispering grace.

"They say that if he—"

"Who says?"

"Actually—there were two people with him that day. A driver and a political advisor. Whatever we know we got from the driver before he died. And—I warning you now—is not much."

"Did you talk to him yourself?"

"No, no chance o' that. The fella manage to talk to the ambulance attendant on the way to the hospital, and he's the one who told the police."

"Who told you."

"Right. So you see, all this is fourth-hand information."

"Was there an investigation?"

"The police looked into it, yes. But you know, nobody was ever—"

"I know. An immaculate killing. But Cyril, this is a small place. Surely there were rumours."

"Sure. And there was a rumour for everybody. Maybe it have an answer somewhere on a piece o' paper, but I don' believe it. The only thing we know for sure is that Ram and his two people were killed, shot, a little bit up the road, after they stopped here so he could relieve his bladder."

Yasmin walks from the car, out from beneath the trees to the beach. The sunlight is bright, reflective, an oblique afternoon light, and the breeze coming off the sea is steady and cool, tangy with brine and fresh fish. She says, "What is this place?"

"Just a beach. A pretty popular one. Crowded on week-ends, nuh." He gestures at a line of garbage—discarded cans and paper cups, empty containers of every kind—pushed neatly far up the beach by the high tide.

"Was it crowded when he—"

"No, no, it was during the week. Afternoon. It was probably pretty much like this."

They stand together in the silence, listening to the waves and the breeze, to their echoes among the lengthen-ing shadows.

And finally Yasmin says, with a frustration that surprises even her, "What was he about, Cyril? I don't—"

Cyril takes her elbow and says quietly, "If you ask me, Ram was a man who spend his life looking for vengeance—and I mean big vengeance, vengeance on history, nuh—and in the end is what kill him. We don' know who pull the trigger, and at this point it hardly matter. You see, I come to believe that what really kill him was the beast within."

Her gaze reaches out over the water and she wonders whether her father, too, in what he did not know to be the final moments of his life, had looked out and shivered at its endlessness.

[30]

The road swings gently inland, rising once more. The friendly vegetation of the seashore gives way to a denser growth that occasionally suggests impenetrability.

After a sudden steep rise the road levels off and Cyril slows down. He says, "It was around here... Yes, just about there." He pulls to the side and turns off the car. "They were waiting just up the road. Waiting for his car. They pulled in front of them, forcing them to stop. Apparently Ram got out. Then he saw the guns and started running, there, into that field."

She sees no field, just a stretch of tall grass distinguishable from the surrounding growth only by its lack of trees.

"It was a vegetable garden back then, some local farmer, nuh. Ram probably thought he could disappear into the forest but they followed him. The two other fellas were shot in the car. As for Ram, they count twenty bullets in the autopsy, he din't have a chance."

He turns off the car engine, and in the silence Yasmin's mind begins to struggle with the story. The cars. The roadblock. The flurry of panic and movement. The explosion of gunshots and the sounds of crashing glass.

Had there been moments of clarity—when fate came clear and inevitabilty invaded the soul? Had there been time for final thoughts—or just a blind and wrenching panic?

But no answers come to her, and even the scene shapes itself in her head as something out of a gangster movie: fancy hats and double-breasted suits, submachine guns spitting fire.

Cyril opens his door and puts out a foot.

Yasmin thinks: No, God, no…

But she follows, muscles taut with unwillingness, as he pushes his way through the grassy field.

Cyril's eyeball swerves off-centre. He says, "This is where they found him."

Hidden among the grass, camouflaged by moss as thick as knitted wool, is a small plinth. He pushes the grass away, stamping on the blades so that they will not spring back.

"We put this up a year later, a kind of commemoration. Some people had an idea for some kind o' park but, as you can see, it din't get very far." He scratches some of the moss away, revealing a patch of wet and darkened stone. "Is only concrete. We were going to add a brass plaque later, with his name and dates, nuh, but somehow we never get around to it. Life goes on, people get busy."

And a life, Yasmin thinks, is reduced to a lost relic. She touches the plinth. The concrete, cold and damp, turning friable, leaves a sandy residue on her fingertips. She thinks of the boulders beside the sea, of the water steadily reducing them to rubble, of the blind man and his pebbles that left no ripples—and her throat constricts with a sudden surge of emotion that rises from her stomach and erupts, bitter, in her mouth.

Cyril stands back from the plinth. He slides his hands into his pants pockets and after a moment says, "Oh, well." He asks if she wants some time alone, and when she shakes her head he gestures towards the car. "Shall we, then?"

She leads the way back, in a hurry to leave this place.

In a hurry now to care for her mother.

[31]

On the way back Yasmin stops seeing. She has a sense of time stopped on an urgency, her mind occupied by the plinth, and by the box that sits in her room at the house.

A bit farther on, Cyril turns sharply right, following another road into the mountains, and she knows that they are taking another route back, completing the journey by completing a circle.

The vegetation thickens and arches; darkness falls. The headlights of the car hug the grey asphalt ahead. In the mirror outside her window Yasmin sees a black tunnel, its centre a circle of pale light retreating steadily.

Cyril says, "You think you might come back one day? For a visit, I mean. Maybe with your husband?"

"I can't think that far ahead."

"But you must. This trip—is not really a visit, if you know what I mean. You must come back. After all, you're one of us."

His words send a chill through Yasmin. This world— the world of her mother and father—is undeniably part of her. But his words force her to acknowledge a greater truth.

"I don't even know," she says, "what it means to be one of you."

"Is—" He sighs, and in the darkness she sees that he is exhausted. "Is to share flesh and blood. And to understand things without all the words. Is to know that you're home."

"Cyril…" She is grateful he does not see the shake of her head, for she would rather not tell him that by most of his definition, she is not one of them.

They emerge high up into a soft evening light, the world opening up: the sea and sky a rich, dark blue, the sun an orange glow behind the far arm of the mountains. Just above the horizon, as if waiting in the wings, a crust of icy moon hangs in fragile suspension.

Yasmin feels a sweet unravelling within herself, as if her ribs are unlocking themselves one by one.

The road, here wide and well paved, begins a steady descent down the mountainside. As it curves and bends, they drive through a flickering transience of darkness and light. On the plain below, the town emits a dull glow that will harden and brighten as the greater darkness takes hold.

Yasmin feels a stirring of gratitude towards Cyril. This drive, offered as improvisation but clearly calculated, has not had the effect she suspects he intended. He has opened her eyes to the limits of the worlds within her.

The road curves into darkness, headlights flickering on the cut mountain wall on one side and, on the other, drawing the low metal barrier that marks the edge of the cliff.

Suddenly the car wobbles violently, tires rumbling on the narrow verge between pavement and mountain wall —the wall no longer parallel, dead ahead now, filling the vision in a rush.

Cyril says "Shit!" and wrenches at the wheel.

Tires squeal.

Orange. Blue. The cold, cold moon.

The metal barrier, hard and narrow, a band of silver approaching rapidly.

Yasmin's mind races with thoughts of flight, of falling through soundless air.

Cyril wrenches at the wheel again and the car tilts crazily, the headlights marking its path away from the barrier, back onto the roadway. With a jolt and a hiccup, they come to a stop.

Thoughts of Jim flood Yasmin's mind as her lungs— inert, collapsed—balloon with air. Her hands cover her face, palms hot with her gasping breath.

Cyril says, "Well." He touches her forearm. "You all right?"

She nods.

"Sorry 'bout that. I don't know what—" And suddenly his voice breaks. He sniffles, and with an emotion that startles her he says, "You know, I mean well, Yasmin. I'm not a bad man."

His words puzzle and move her. "Of course you're not," she says.

He sighs, sniffles again. Then, putting the car into gear, he says, "Hellofanepitaph, eh?"

The last of the light blends earth and sky with the colour of mercury.

The road takes them through a silvered world.

Past the town, buildings smothered in pewter.

Past the port, anchored tugs and fishing boats like monuments in stainless steel.

Past trees and parks plated in chrome.

It is, Yasmin thinks, like a world perfectly, beautifully preserved. And in the seconds that the light persists, she imagines it a world metalled into time.

[32]

Jim said, "There's no such thing as coincidence, Yas. Accidents don't just happen. They have a logic to them—a logic too cosmic for us to grasp."

Yasmin heard in his voice the sound of a man trying to convince himself. It was not a game she could play: her struggle was to accept senselessness.

"The problem, Jim," she said, "is that I find no comfort in that. None at all."

The effort of speech, more difficult with each word, lent a formality to her sentences. She sounded, she thought, like an actress on stage; sounded like her mother. The words were not filling her void; they were instead falling into it.

Jim rolled his chair backwards, stood up slowly. He paused, a silhouette against the window, as if listening for sounds in the night.

"Neither do I," he whispered.

He made his way around the desk, features emerging from shadow. He placed himself behind her, laid his hands on her shoulders.

She knew that he had heard the echo of the falling words.

Knew that the trick for them would be to catch the words as they fell.

[33]

She eats little at dinner and the conversation, such as it is, is desultory.

Cyril speaks of the day, but Penny is not receptive.

Ash is absent, and no explanation is offered. But Yasmin notices that Penny glances occasionally at his empty chair with a a look that is an indecipherable blend of helplessness, anger, and wistfulness.

Amie, serving, moves with the litheness of a phantom, her feet gliding across the floor as if cushioned by a membrane of air.

It is as if she has woven the filaments of her life into a cloak around herself, Yasmin thinks.

As if a life of servitude has brought to her layers of silence that resemble insubstantiality.

As if hers has become a life distanced to speculation: *as* always followed by *if*...

Does she, Yasmin wonders, hear her own echoes? Does she hear her own heart?

[34]

PHOTO: ONLY HER EYES ARE TURNED TOWARDS THE CAMERA, THE PUPILS DISTENDED AND UNFOCUSED, THE LIPS PURSED THIN AS IF APPREHENDED AT A MOMENT OF INDECISION. SHE HAS BEEN CAUGHT UNAWARES, IS UNHAPPY ABOUT IT. SOMETHING IN HER— THE NEATNESS WITH WHICH HER HAIR IS PULLED BACK PERHAPS, OR THE CARE WITH WHICH HER EYEBROWS HAVE BEEN PLUCKED

*AND GREASE-PENCILLED IN—TELLS OF A WOMAN WHO LEAVES AS
LITTLE AS POSSIBLE TO CHANCE, WHICH ITSELF HINTS AT A FEAR OF
CHANCE AND THE UNKNOWNS IT ENTAILS. THE SET OF HER JAW
SUGGESTS THAT IN THE SECONDS FOLLOWING THE FLASH—THE
LIGHT GLARING OFF HER SKIN, CHAFING AWAY WHATEVER TAN SHE
MIGHT HAVE ACQUIRED—SHE UTTERS A PROTEST.*

"Actually," Cyril says, "she gave me the finger. In the nices' possible way of course."

Penny laughs. "I don't remember Celia ever sayin' a bad word. Not once." The cruel clarity of the fluorescent lighting gives an odd cast to her features—they appear thickened, less refined—so that her words, of fondness, of gentle praise, seem unmatched to her expression. "Of course, back then, we din't. We use to say things like *shite* and *shoot* and *jeezuwebs*."

"But Celia—Celia use to use sign language."

Penny grows sombre. "That was Celia, all right. Signs. Givin' them and lookin' for them."

Yasmin glances again at the photograph: at its preserved hysteria. "Did she enjoy living here?" Yasmin asks.

"It was her home," Cyril replies. "We were her family."

Penny says, "She wanted to be one of us."

Cyril says, "She *was* one of us."

Yasmin sees Penny's lips part, then close; sees her body rock backwards ever so slightly. *She was one of us.* She knows that her question has not been answered; knows that there is no answer. The silence quickly fills with the shrill of the insect chorus from the darkness outside.

Cyril's eyes glitter. He turns away, shuts them. Yasmin sees his Adam's apple twitching through the stiffened muscles of his throat.

Penny reaches out and grasps his forearm. After a moment she says, "You mus' understand, Yasmin. Is only yesterday we were chil'ren."

Yasmin lets the photograph slip from her fingers, watches it tumble soundlessly back into the box.

Not long after, Cyril excuses himself.

Penny gives a thoughtful sigh. "You know, Yasmin, I don' want you goin' away thinking your father was like Manager. Vernon was so different, is as if they were hardly brothers.

"When Vernon was young, two or three years old, he was bouncing on the bed in his bedroom and somehow he fly out the window, fall two stories to the ground, pick himself up and run back in the house laughin'. That is how he was throughout his life. Strong and hardy, always bouncin' back. He did feel things strong-strong. Once he tell me that when he thought of our people, this warmth flooded into his chest. He felt responsible for them, nuh, for all the little people. People like Amie, nuh.

"As for Manager, he always been the kind o' man who sits down to pee. And if it only have a urinal, he'll hold it."

Yasmin holds back her grimace: There is nothing she can do with this image.

"Vernon, on the other hand, would use any tree if he had to go. There you have the whole difference between them. Is why Cyril live a life with nothing to show for it. Always holdin' it in, nuh."

Yes, Yasmin thinks, but Vernon died young, and as for Cyril—he holds in more than you can possibly imagine…

It is only with effort that she respects Cyril's wish to keep in confidence the other world in which he has involved himself, in which he seeks to shape redemption, for others and for himself.

[35]

Do you dream, dear? Are you dreaming now, or are you listening to me with greater forbearance than you have ever shown?

I don't dream very much, you know. At least, I don't remember my dreams. But there was one, many years ago, that has remained with me with startling vividness. Shall I tell you about it?

Yasmin was very young at the time and I had taken her into bed with me for an afternoon nap. I quickly fell into a deep sleep, which was quite uncharacteristic, and found myself in a world best described as the physical manifestation of what is called white noise—by which I mean a world without sky, without ground, without horizon. There were no trees, no grass, no flowers and no sounds. It was like standing in the middle of a large and immobile cloud. And then I wasn't alone. My husband was standing in front of me—only he had aged. He was haggard and white-haired and bent over, supporting himself with a walking stick. I became aware that Celia was standing beside me, and I said to her, You *will* take care of him, won't you. And she replied that of course she would. The curious thing is that through all of this, I felt nothing—no surprise, no fear, no sadness, just a kind of relief when I knew he would be looked after.

Then I awoke, Yasmin in a deep sleep beside me. And from outside, through the open window, the sounds of commotion came to me.

[36]

Penny says, "Appendicitis. It came on fast. They had to take it out. And afterwards they gave it to him in a small bottle, pickled, nuh, in formaldehyde.

"You ever seen an appendix, Yasmin? Looks like a baby's little finger. And sitting in a fridge, is one of the most ghoulish things you can imagine.

"But he was proud of it, your father. Don't ask me to explain. Although I suppose I should be grateful—every time I opened the fridge, my appetite disappeared. Helped me keep my weight down, nuh.

"Funny thing—later. A few days after we cremated him, he came to me in a dream. And it was like that, you understand—I din't dream him, he came to me. And he said, in a clear-clear voice, 'Pen, you forget something. I need all of me. And my appendix still sitting in the fridge. I missing it, Pen, send it to me.'

"I tell you, I wake up in a col' sweat. My first thought was, Is too late. He was already cremated, the ashes were long cleared away and washed out to sea. I couldn' exactly go and toss the thing into just any burning pyre. So I picked up the phone then and there and called the pundit. He wasn' too-too happy to hear from me. It was three o'clock in the mornin' after all, so I can't say I blame him—and I could practically hear his hangover over the phone line. But still, Vernon sounded kind o' desperate—

"He hear me out and said he'd call back in the morning. Which he did. And that afternoon he came over, lit a little fire in the back yard, did a little puja, and tossed the appendix into the middle o' the flames. He said, Just let it burn out and in the morning pick up the ashes and toss them into the river where the rest of the ashes went. It going to find the rest of him, and your brother going to be content. Then he hurry off the way pundits like to do if they not staying to eat—to make you think they busy-busy when everybody knows they headin' straight for the racetrack or the rumshop.

"Anyway, the next morning me and Cyril went down with bucket and shovel to pick up the ashes—only to find that some animal, most likely a stray dog, had got there before us. Everything was scatter around, as if the animal had paw through to see what he could find—and I'll tell you now I don't even want to think about what he might o' found, if you see what I mean. What to do? We pick up what was left—between you and me it wasn' much—and drove it up to the river. At least Vernon never came back to me, so maybe, you know, the dog din't... I mean, maybe it was there after all."

Yasmin does not—cannot—react. She doesn't know how. She gets up and leaves the room. She does not excuse herself.

And it is only a few minutes later, as she stands on the porch filling her lungs with the moist night air, fingertips pressed to the rusted railing, that she realizes she has abandoned Penny.

And then all at once she sees that this is the point—and

the goal—of Penny's story. It is, she understands at last, a tale of loneliness.

[37]

Death breeds mythology. Success breeds contempt. My husband died. I was left to contend with what remained of the success.

You know that there are people who laugh at me, Mrs. Livingston? They find me contemptible. They are people who fail to realize just how clearly I see myself. How clearly I see this persona I have built—everything from the hair so perfectly moulded to the words that I use to the cadences of my speech: They do not realize that I know how unlikely all this makes me, how absurd. The Englishwoman, they call me behind my back. Nor do they realize that this shaping of the self was the only one available to people of my generation rising out of that backward colonial society. Some of us, it is true, surrendered our selves whole, but every struggle has its casualties. I have struggled not to be a casualty.

Those who have followed me, though, have redefined themselves. They are proud of their sing-song accents, their imperfect English, their idioms that are meaningless elsewhere. Their music has travelled the world. They have developed a tribal sense and so have become a new people.

I glimpse these new people, Mrs. Livingston, and part of me envies them. This pride they have acquired in themselves just as they are! Even if it too is absurd—but then, all pride in the self can appear absurd from outside, can it not?

And if they have gone beyond the absurdity they see in me to something new, it is because I existed, because I and my husband and our contemporaries made a way out when there was none. It is no fault of our own that the world has outstripped us.

My husband and his people built schools, you see. Dozens of schools throughout the rural areas to educate the children of the cane workers and the field labourers and the rice farmers. This was the way out: sitting at those desks, writing on those chalk slates, rhyming out the multiplication tables until they became part of you. Education, especially in the large sense, teaches us to ask questions. And questions confirm that we exist. This was my husband's gift to our people. He made us aware of ourselves.

He was honoured for that. He was given a gold medallion on a chain—and ironically it was the only time his words failed him. He could not make a speech, but managed to promise that he would always wear it around his neck, a promise he kept. And that medallion, as I've told you, saved his life. My husband knew who he was, Mrs. Livingston, and he felt that these schools—no longer Presbyterian schools teaching Christian principles but Hindu schools teaching Hindu ideals—would help these children to discover who they were.

We inhabit a world that has made a fetish of identity, Mrs. Livingston. We are who we are, individualized creatures of history, society and family. To listen to your heart, to accept its complexity, is to know yourself. It is to recognize your identity in all its glorious absurdity.

And this in the end, my dear, is my husband's legacy, but one few are willing to see—one, I daresay, that he himself would not have recognized. It is also my husband's monument, and a monument, as we both know, casts a shadow. Half the story is in that shadow, but who ever pays any attention to it?

[38]

She stands alone on the porch engulfed in darkness.

It is late, well past eleven. The sky, cleared, is swollen with stars, the air still and fragrant with earth and flourishing vegetation. All around, insects raise a collective night whistle.

Sleep will not come, her mind too full of Jim, but in the unfocused way of image without thought, as if the shards of this world are summoning shredded memories of the other, whole yet so distant.

He comes to her as a name and, rapidly, as a series of domestic gestures.

Pouring pasta into a pot. Spooning coffee into a filter. Smoothing the spine of a newspaper. Cracking the spine of a paperback.

Then, unexpectedly, as gestures of intimacy.

Arms, bare, reaching up. Finger moist with wine caressing her lips. Hand at her breast, tongue at her toes.

Then:

Eyes caught in unguarded moments. Partly lifeless, partly manic: the revelation of fatigue.

Slouched in his armchair, eyes shut, arms folded, as in a gesture of mortality.

The twist of a head, the seizing of a gaze: a smile unexpected and true, a quicksilver flash from beyond the boundaries of wariness.

[39]

She is blended with the darkness.

Her hand held before her eyes remains invisible, and the few steps she takes are ethereal in their unworldliness.

The darkness has made her incorporeal.

She feels herself gliding through the night, each footfall a jolt of surprise, evidence of a substantiality beyond the reach of her other senses. All that remains to her are the jarring solidity of the earth, the constancy of the stars, and from somewhere off in the distance the sharp, rhythmic report of many drums.

The sound had startled her. It had emerged without warning from a distant darkness so profound it could only be sensed, cutting off the images flooding through her mind.

Drummers, sometimes one, sometimes many, their beats as crisp as the crack of rifle fire, rasping and melodious and so disquieting she is robbed of breath to the point of dizziness.

And now, down here, away from the house, spectral in the greater darkness, the sound seems to come from everywhere. For a moment she is confused, but she quickly steadies herself: returns in her mind to the porch and the direction from which the sound came to her. She knows she must walk away from the house and to the left, into the thickening trees.

The looming bulk of the house steadies her gaze, helps her pick out varying shades of black.

That tree: she knows it.

She wills herself past it. Wills herself to keep on going, towards that sound that fills the night.

Just past the hazy silhouette of the tree, the ground gives way beneath her—a depression in the earth, she realizes as she tumbles. She catches herself on her hands, the ground damp and mossy, but a little yelp escapes her as a stone bites into her knee.

She sits for a moment, rubbing the knee, resolution wavering. But her fingers find no blood and the pain passes quickly. She rises slowly to her feet and continues on.

At the trees, the sound of the drums grows muffled and ubiquitous. She hesitates, tells herself she will take ten more steps and if she seems no closer will turn back. She proceeds slowly, hands reaching out to tree trunks, feeling her way.

At twelve steps, the drumming louder now, a glimmer of light causes her heart to race. She makes her way with a heightened caution past the tree trunks that begin to acquire body and shape.

Twenty steps later—her mind automatically counting as she walks—the drumming becomes tumultuous and demanding, reverberating with a brutal edge. The tree trunks thin out, a bright and flickering light hardening them to silhouettes.

A few steps later—steps cautioned to surreptitiousness —she discerns a clearing and there, at its centre, the leaping flames of a bonfire.

Shadowed against the flames, circling them to the

rhythmic delirium of the drums, men—only men—writhe and jump in ecstatic abandonment. They are costumed, painted, some shorn, some long-haired. Some brandish tridents, others staves.

And then, among them, she spots Ash. He is draped like the others in a saffron robe, his face patterned with white paint, arms and legs bare and glistening in the firelight. In one hand he holds his pellet gun, in the other an unsheathed sword.

Beyond the fire, five men are beating at drums hung around their necks. Their eyes are closed, chests streaked with sweat, arms flailing.

Yasmin's body begins to tremble. Her mind swirls in incomprehension at the nocturnal frenzy that has no place in any world she knows.

She has made up her mind to turn back, to return to the safety of the house, when a hand seizes her shoulder from behind.

[4 0]

Funny thing about regrets, Mrs. Livingston —we don't always regret having them...

Do you know what I mean?

I have never told Yasmin much about her father. Not much beyond anything she could find in the public record if she wanted to.

And what she knows—what she thinks I have told her— is banal enough. That he always did his best for us. That he fought for his people. That he was killed for it.

She was curious about him for a while, in her early teens. But then she seemed to lose interest—whether because this is what adolescents do or because my portrait of him was sufficient to discourage her I do not know. But her interest waned, and she has never attempted to put flesh on his bones and blood in his veins. To my relief, let me say. It would be futile, after all. He would remain just a construction. I do not want Yasmin to have to live with that disappointment.

Among any parent's greatest regrets is what we have failed to teach our children, the knowledge we have failed to impart. We want such fullness for them! So I regret having given this barest of skeletons to Yasmin. But I do not regret having this regret...

Do you see what I mean?

This ignorance, you understand, my dear—it is also my gift to her.

[41]

The dancing and drumming stop abruptly as she is hauled into the firelight, the back of her neck seized by fingers viperous and unrelenting.

The men gather around, chests heaving, bodies glistening, faces etched with hostility, curiosity, confusion—and she sees that they are as unnerved as she.

Ash pushes his way through to the front. "What you think you doin'? You have no place here."

She is a minute in finding her voice, and when she does it betrays rupture. "Ash. I. All this. I didn't mean—" But speech robs her of breath and, gasping, she realizes—in the new slyness that comes to them, easing their tension—that they must think her afraid.

But she is not. Not now. No longer. Of that she is absolutely certain.

And then she sees that Ash, too, understands this, and that her lack of fear is arousing his anger.

He waves the barrel of the pellet gun before her eyes, lowers the mouth to her lips and presses it against them, the metal hard and warm.

She turns her face away.

He presses it to her temple.

It's only a pellet gun, she tells herself—but she cannot clear her mind of the lizard leaping around in its death throes in the grass.

Then, from deep within, her own anger surges. She reaches up, grasps the barrel and pushes it away.

Ash does not resist. Instead, he leans in close, so close she smells his acrid perspiration, feels his breath warm and moist on her cheek and ear. "Look here," he says in an angry whisper. "What else you expec' me to do? You going back to your nice peaceful country tomorrow—and I stuck here. No way out. You understandin' me? No way out."

Her eyes meet his: desperation dark and glistening inches away. In silence, she watches the darkness swell with moisture, watches tears brim, break and scurry down his cheeks.

And she feels for the first time beyond her fear of him: feels the depth of his despair.

She raises a hand to his cheek, lets his tears dampen her fingertips.

This dipping into tears, this unthinking attempt to soothe. She remembers the last time: a fall from a bicycle, a badly twisted ankle, her daughter writhing in pain.

She begins to caress his cheek. His eyes close, his face relaxes into peacefulness.

Yasmin feels herself melting.

But it does not last. Without warning he pulls back and slaps her hand away. "Go on," he spits. "Get out o' here." And to her captor behind, he says, "Take her back to the house."

Her arm is grasped in a firm hand. As she turns to go, she says quietly, "You can't fool me anymore, Ash."

"You saw them?"

"Yes."

"Hellofasight, eh?"

Cyril, sitting spectral in the darkness of the porch, speaks with discouragement. Through the gloom, Yasmin sees his face sagging as if the flesh has detached itself from his skull.

He notices her limp. "They hurt you?" he says in alarm.

"No, it's all right, I fell. The knee's just stiffening up a bit. It'll be fine."

Cyril leans forward in his chair, elbows on his thighs, fingers interlacing. His chin sinks into his chest. "They does get together like this every month or so," he says. "Whipping themselves up, going crazy. Prancing around like a bunch o' bushmen."

Yasmin takes the chair across from his, stretches out her leg, rubs the knee.

He sniffs contemptuously. "They're Hindu warriors. Going to save us all from Muslims, blacks and anybody else who get in the way of the great Hindu renaissance."

"You take them seriously, but there's hardly a dozen of them, Cyril."

"They're not the only ones. There's a whole movement. You does hear talk about hundreds, thousands, stockpiles of arms."

"I saw tridents and staves. Ash had his pellet gun, for God's sake."

"The talk is money from abroad. From India, nuh, and from some o' the rich businessmen here. And secret shipments of guns. Who knows if any of it true."

"Have you asked Ash?"

"Once. And of course he say they're just a religious group and what I have against people learning more about Hinduism? I let it drop." He raises hooded eyes to her. "He say anything to you about the diaspora?"

"The diaspora, yes."

"And the flying chariots that were really rockets, and the flaming arrows that were really nuclear missiles? They reading the scriptures in their own way, you see. And they finding evidence of a great Hindu civilization way back when. And is not great art and poetry, mind you. No, no. Is advanced technology. Jet planes and space travel, telepathic communication. A race of super beings." His fingers unfold themselves and his hands bunch into fists. "Yasmin, there's a whole other world in that boy's head, a whole other reality."

She has witnessed that other reality, and has stumbled onto yet another which Cyril, in his frustration, is incapable of seeing. "And Penny, what does she think of all this?"

"Penny?" he scoffs. "Sometimes I think she waiting for his parents to come back. And in the meantime, the boy growing up. Penny want him to be something—a doctor, a lawyer—and sometimes she does think what he need is some good, hard licks. But she also think, deep in herself, nuh, that what he doing is important. Worse thing is, Penny think that if Ram were alive today he'd be with them, fighting for our people."

The idea surprises Yasmin. "Would he?"

Cyril looks away into the night. "I think Ram would mourn to see where his dream for his people ending up. He used to say, if we don't make this work, this place going back to the jungle. He was half right. Way I see it, the jungle coming to us."

His words are a relief and a comfort. That her father was a man of realistic vision, sensitive to limits, susceptible to despair, offers Yasmin an unexpected satisfaction. Like the glimpses of vanity, it is something she can take away with her.

Out in the darkness the drumming resumes, a line of rhythmic explosions.

"But, you know," Cyril continues, "one thing I can't get away from—Ash and his friends are like Ram's chil'ren. His spiritual chil'ren, I mean. He gave our generation dreams, but we couldn' make them come true. Not without him." He cocks his head towards the sound of the drums. "You see, Yasmin, that is what does happen to dreams that remain just dreams too long. And is what does happen to frustrated romantics. It ain't have nobody more dangerous. They end up blaming the world for their own foolishness."

Then he sits back, eyes closed, lips pursed, like a man meditating on the unanswerable reeling in at him out of the night.

[42]

The knock at the bedroom door is like a whisper, and she assumes that Cyril, like her, is unable to sleep, that he has seen her light and seeks insomniac companionship. She whispers back her permission to enter.

The door opens slowly and she is slightly taken aback to see Amie standing timidly in the doorway.

"Everything all right, miss?"

"Everything's fine, Amie. I'm just having a little trouble sleeping."

"If is the knee, miss, maybe I could help."

Yasmin sees that her sandalled feet fit together as neatly, as perfectly, as the paws of a cat at ease.

"You know about my knee?"

"Mister Cyril, miss. He's a little worried, nuh, he ask me to check up on you."

"There's really no need, Amie. It'll be fine in the morning."

Amie holds up a bottle. It is filled with a liquid the colour of dull gold. "A little bit o' coconut oil, Miss. It good for making the swelling go down."

"It's not very swollen." But she sees Amie's disappointment, is perplexed by it. Relents. "Okay, then. Can't hurt, I guess."

Amie nods, glides into the room. In the manner, Yasmin thinks, of a nun.

Amie, sitting on the edge of the bed, works in silence at her knee, palms gentle on the tender cap.

The scent of the oil—sweet and rancid, unrefined—thickens the air. Yasmin feels its warmth working its way down into her bone.

Amie works patiently, fingers circling and smoothing, the heel of her palm pressing in on the sides of the kneecap.

Yasmin watches her fingers as they work. Slender, bony fingers, with nails cut so short they appear sunken into the flesh.

And she watches her face, her averted eyes, enigmatic with restraint. At moments her lips assume the vaguest suggestion of surfacing humour, but the moments are brief, their source unshared and indecipherable.

There are parts of her, Yasmin knows, that can never be unearthed, thoughts that can never be divined. She likes Amie, but she would be unable, if asked, to explain why. If pressed, she would have to say: Because she is unknowable.

Still, she would like to smooth the silence with an easy conversation, but the only words that occur to her—a comment about the heat, about the stillness of the night—seem banal and contemptible. What she would really like to ask Amie is whether she is happy; about the life she has led, and the lives she would have liked to lead. Questions made for late at night, when confidentiality is assumed and trust remains unspoken. Questions she could not possibly put to Amie, sitting there rubbing at her knee.

And then a question occurs to her that she can ask. "Amie," she says, searching for her eyes.

"Yes, miss." But Amie does not look up.

"Would you tell me about my parents?"

Amie dribbles more oil into her cupped palm. "They was nice people, miss, especially Miss Shakti."

"Miss Shakti—Mom—used to say the word nice doesn't mean much."

"Is how I remember them, miss. Nice people." She rubs her palm together coating them in oil.

"And what do you remember about me, Amie? Was I nice, too?"

She runs both hands up Yasmin's shins, fingertips pressing into the flesh beside the bone. "You still like the clouds, miss?" And for the first time her eyes rise to meet Yasmin's.

"The clouds?"

Amie takes her hands away, crosses them on her lap. "You forget?" She gives a little laugh, as if at her own foolishness, and her voice changes. A warmth comes to it: a voice bereft of tension, edges rounded.

Yasmin feels enveloped.

"Everything was behind the clouds for you. Bird behind the clouds. Plane behind the clouds. You use to like the sky, always starin' up at it as if you looking for something, or as if it had pictures up there.

"And I remember one day you say, Papa behind the clouds. Because he was always gone, nuh, he did leave early-early, before you wake up, and come back late-late, after you was in bed. Papa behind the clouds. People use to say your head was always in the clouds."

Yasmin smiles. The clouds, the sky. The affinity explained. No, not explained, she thinks after a moment. Given a history—and her father given a title. She says, "I used to call him Papa. I didn't know that"

"And Miss Shakti was Mama."

Mama: Mom, Mummy, Mother. So those other words came later, with the new life.

"You grown up nice, miss. Very nice." Her eyes hold Yasmin's gaze. "But you ain't change, eh? Not deep inside. You was a quiet little girl. Like you had a sadness deep-deep inside you. And it still there. Deep-deep inside you. As if you knowed things you shouldn't know."

Yasmin is at a loss for words. She feels exposed, as if Amie has peeled her open and read her entrails.

Amie turns away, embarrassed. She pours more oil into her palm, reaches for Yasmin's foot and begins squeezing and caressing it.

Yasmin feels herself stiffen. A guardedness comes to her, and a growing acuteness of unease. The mood, the sense of connection, evaporates. Amie's touch now feels alien on her foot, as if the attention that was there before has retreated: as if the mind and the hand are no longer dedicated to the same purpose. She does not protest, though. She does not want Amie to go.

Not yet.

[43]

Yasmin was a solitary child, you know. From the very first, she seemed to prefer her own company. She used to love playing with her fingers and toes, pulling on them, tickling them, making herself laugh. On her face there was amazement—the kind of glazed amazement which, in an older person, would inidicate idiocy. Sometimes she would tug a foot right up to her nose and peer at her toes with all the fascination of discovery. Or she would spend a great deal of time examining her hands, as if trying to puzzle out how they worked.

One day, watching her play, my husband said, "Look at her. It's almost as if she doesn't believe she exists."

And I felt then that he had put his finger on it.

[44]

Amie runs her thumb hard up Yasmin's sole. "Mr. Vernon did have this trick, miss. He take a razor blade and slice through the skin of a orange from eye to eye, five or six times. The cuts was fine-fine, finer than t'read, you couldn't see them. An' he'd hide it till he needed it—then he'd take it out and squeeze it till it crush. Everybody was always amaze. Of course, he did need strength to do it, but he couldn't really do it without cheatin' a little. I ain't never been able to decide if he was dishones' or if he was smart."

"Did Cyril know about this trick?"

"No, but Miss Penny... She always keep his secret."

Even now, Yasmin thinks. She ponders the extraordinary loyalty, and after a moment has a thought that unsettles her: Even now, Penny will let Cyril tell a lie in the name of glory.

"For some people," Amie adds, "the dead more important than the livin'." It is as if she has divined Yasmin's thoughts.

The pressure of her fingers tenses onto Yasmin's arch. The tips press into the flesh and they release a sudden electricity that sizzles along her sole into her ankle and toes.

Yasmin yelps.

The pressure ceases. "Sorry, Beti," Amie says.

[45]

There were—there still are—moments when I would look at Yasmin and think, What does the future hold in store for you? I would try to imagine her at various ages, at ages still to come. To imagine her at my age, and older. To imagine her having lived a life such as we all live: full of joys and pain. I have imagined my daughter an aged woman dying gently...

But this is fantasy, for my question has no answer. Circumstance shapes a possibility every day. Still, I come back to it—I want to be reassured that my daughter will have a happy and fulfilling life—and I ache at the impossibility of knowing.

To me this is the only mystery that resonates, my dear Mrs. Livingston. Not God, not the afterlife. But the unimaginability of tomorrow itself for those I love.

[46]

It comes to her like a sudden anger, chill and irrational. She pulls her feet away from Amie's grasp, tucks them under her.

Amie looks up in surprise, her eyes wrenched back from another world.

Through the thumping of her heart, Yasmin says, "There's more. What aren't you telling me?"

Amie goes still. Her chin trembles, eyes grow watery. Her face acquires years. "How much you want to know, Beti?" she says softly.

"Everything."

Her back stiffens, eyes wandering away to the shuttered window.

Yasmin waits, her sight riveted on Amie's profile. She does not even blink.

"Mister Vernon was a saga-boy. You know what a saga-boy

is? He did like the ladies, nuh. And even after he got married with your mother... Everybody did know it. Miss Shakti included. She use to wait up nights for him, till all hours. I can' tell you how much they use to fight. She was smellin' the other women on him. Even your granmother try talkin' to him but...

"Then one day they stop quarrellin'. Jus' like that. Miss Shakti din' wait up for him no more. Is not that he change. A saga-boy born a saga-boy. She kind o' give up, you know? She swallow everyt'ing.

"Is around' then she start paintin'. Every week, she change the colour o' the room. Pink, then blue, then green. Is a kind o' madness that come over her on the weekends. Monday mornin', out did come the paint brushes, poor Miss Shakti doin' the work sheself, in here all day, not eatin' or drinkin'. The smell o' paint was always heavy-heavy, it did give me a headache sometimes. I ain't know how she stand it. Swallowin', swallowin'.

"As for Mr. Vernon, he continue on as usual. The paint smell did bother him sometimes. A couple o' times, he sleep in the livin' room. But I ain't think he ever really understand how much he t'row at your mother. And Beti, he t'row a lot, and not all of it was *paisa*. It have people like that, eh? Money is everyt'ing, and if they t'row enough at you, everyt'ing all right.

"But he, Mister Vernon, did t'row and t'row and t'row —and not only at Miss Shakti. He hit a lot o' people, Beti."

Yasmin says, "You?"

"Me." And she turns away from the window, away from Yasmin, lowering her head so that when the words come again they come from a woman huddling herself into an ellipse of strange and feminine beauty.

[47]

Funny thing about children, isn't it, Mrs. Livingston?

At first we know everything about them. They hold no secrets because they have none.

Then, as they get older, the less and less we know, the more we must intuit—or, if we are honest with ourselves, guess—based on what we have learnt in the early years.

By the time they've attained adulthood, they have grown distant from us, become strangers in ways difficult to grasp because of their familiarity.

It's almost as if growing up entails, in part at least, the hoarding of secrets—as if the self needs a spot that is accessible to no one else. Ever. I'm not so romantic as to claim that in this place is the true self, but I am realistic enough to know that it may be essential to it, in the way that soil is essential to a plant.

This standing apart. So inevitable. So necessary.

And yet...

And yet, so terribly, terribly sad.

[48]

"I wasn' plannin' on being a servant-girl all my life, you know. When I start this job—I was young, just a girl, nuh—my parents had already fix me up with a fella. We was plannin' on gettin' married in a couple o' years. He was workin' in the cane fields, and wanted the time to save some money. And when this job come along, I decide to take it, to save some money too. Is how I end up here, workin' for your granmother.

"I remember the day Mr. Vernon marry Miss Shakti, I remember the day she come here. And I remember dreamin' that one day soon it goin' to be my turn to put on the red sari and sit in front o' the pundit and become the wife of a good man.

"But after the two years he ask for more time. My father say no, after two years he have enough *paisa*. Then he find out that the fella was gamblin' every evenin', and even if he was a hard worker he was bad-lucky too. And it ain't have nothing to do when somebody bad-lucky, nobody know how to change the stars.

"But he promise to change, he promise no more gambling, and my mother convince my father to give him another chance. So I stay on here, workin' for your granmother, givin' my parents some money, savin' a little. Waitin' and prayin'. Not countin' the days no more.

"When Mr. Cyril and Miss Celia come back from Englan', Mr. Vernon decide they goin' to take my bedroom, so he build a little room downstairs for me, put in a little bed and a old dresser. He did forget about light so I had to use a oil lamp for a few months, until he get somebody to run a wire.

"An' it was in that room one evenin' that Mr. Vernon come to visit me. He did come in late, as usual, I remember hearin' his car drive up. And a few minutes later he come knockin' at my door. I get up, open the door a little bit, thinkin' he was hungry, nuh, wanted something to eat. Amina, he say. Amina. An' in his mouth my name was sof'-sof'. I say, Mister Vernon? Something wrong? An' he say, I tired, Amina, I tired, I need to res'. Then he push the door open and step inside the room.

"I get frighten, I tell him he should go upstairs to sleep, but he shake his head and sit down on the bed. Amina, he say again. Little Amie. Then he hold out his hand to me, as if he did need help. I ain't move a inch, but he reach out quick-quick, grab me and pull me to him.

"He put his arm 'round me. I say, Mister Vernon, no. But he jus' hold me tighter. He was a big man. Strong. Next to him I was a mosquito. I was frighten, yes, I was frighten. For all kind o' reasons. So I stop tryin' to... I let him hol', me.

"And then he... Then he start to touch me, Beti. He start to touch me in places no man ever—

"I say, Stop, Mister Vernon. Stop. But it was jus' my mouth talkin'. I try to push his hands away, but they find their way past mine, past my nightie. Easy-easy.

"And despite everything, for all kind o' reasons, and to my ever-lastin' shame, Beti, I din't want him to stop...

Yasmin's world shudders on its axis. Senses unshackle: a deflation of flesh and bone.

She thinks: I do not wish to hear this. But her tongue cannot—will not—shape the words.

Up near the ceiling of the room suddenly contracted, her consciousness hovers cool and expectant.

Amie's voice comes to her from afar, each word hardened, distilled to its essence.

"And to my ever-lastin' shame, Beti, I start to touch him too.

"I never think about the man I was waitin' for. Never think about how far—

"I let him do...

"Because what he did want was what I did want. There. Then. In the moment.

"Is only when he push me back on the bed, gentle-gentle but pushin' all the same that I...

"But it was too late.

"He was a'ready—

"And when he—

"It feel as if somebody was pushin' a knife—

"It feel as if all the air leave my body—

"I did want to scream, but I couldn' scream. I did want to pray, but I couldn' pray. I shut my eyes.

"He was heavy, so heavy, pushin' an'—

"My legs feel as if they was startin' to break off. An' I had to push my face pas' his shoulder to breathe.

"An' I breathe, Beti. I breathe as if I was eatin' air.

"I breathe an' breathe an' breathe, because it was like the only thing I had lef'.

"Then he choke, he stop movin'—an' he was done. Jus' like that. He stay on top o' me, heavy-heavy, crushin' me.

"In a little while, he get off me, sit on the bed and hide his face in his hands. He say, Amina, Amina. He was cryin'. Then he straighten out his clothes and leave the room.

"I ain't know what happen next. If I fall asleep. If I pass out.

"The nex' mornin' I wash out the sheets. The blood and t'ing, nuh. And I t'row away my panties. I wanted to go back home, to my parents, but my father was sick, they did need the little money I was givin' them. So I make up my min' to stay, and put a lock on my door.

"Two months later I find out he did put a baby in my belly."

Image, she knows, is no more concrete than thought.

Yet it is image her instinct reaches for, imagining *it*—

this horror, this hysteria—as a nest of vipers materializing within her.

And yet, when Amie continues, it is in a voice so composed, a voice of such equanimity, that it is, in its grasp of events, like wisdom.

Unexpectedly, Yasmin finds herself soothed.

[49]

Have you ever played the game truth or consequences, my dear Mrs. Livingston? A religious game in many ways. This need to confess secrets that some religions have tapped into. We all need a confessor, don't we?

I have spoken to you about some of my regrets, but I have never told you, or anyone, the biggest regret of my life. Shall I, my dear confessor?

It's one that has come to me only in later life, you know. A surprise, in many ways. I had thought myself well beyond all that...

Listen to me babbling on, will you. As you have probably guessed, I am reluctant to voice this regret, but I am also so tired of it swirling around within me like some kind of hurricane that cannot find land to wear itself out.

You see, my dear, I regret never having known what it is to have—

To have a child growing and stirring within my womb—

To feel my body house and nurture new life—

To feel that new life fight its way to autonomy—

To have breasts swollen with milk to nourish a hungry body—

All this, my dear, is my regret, and my fantasy...

And what of Yasmin, you ask? Yasmin, dear Yasmin, you see, is my daughter—but she is not my child.

[50]

"My father was a longtime stick-fighter, Beti. Everybody did know about him. Everybody did say he could take off a man head with one swing o' the stick. So when he turn up at the house early one Sunday mornin', stick in hand and cutlass tie to his waist, they did know he mean business.

"They try to blame me. They say is me who set me eye on Mr. Vernon. Is me who bring him to my room, is me who...

"My father just start to swing the stick. Mr. Vernon calm him down and say, Come have a drink, man, how 'bout a shot o' whisky. And the two o' them go off together.

"As I done say, it have people for who money is everyt'ing, and if you t'row enough at them everyt'ing all right. My father catch everyt'ing Mr. Vernon t'row at him. He din't even come back to see me.

"So they keep me here, and when time come, take me off to the beach house to have the chil'. I never see the baby, they ain't even tell me if it was a boy-chil' or a girl-chil'. They jus' say they givin' it to somebody to bring up.

"Beti, all that happen forty years ago and not a day does pass when I don' think 'bout that chil'. I still sleepin' in the same room downstairs. In the same bed. Never get married. What man goin' to want a use-up woman like me, eh?

"But you know, is a strange t'ing. For years afterwards, Mr. Vernon use to come to see me—not in my room, never again in my room. He did want to talk, like a little boy, in a small-small voice. He tell me what he was doin', what was happenin'. And I listen, I let him talk, never say nothing. But all the time thinkin', I want to kill you, I want to kill you. But never doin' it because, well, they does hang women here too, Beti.

"So is here I make my life, as a servant girl, t'rough everyt'ing. I never ask for nothing, and they give me everyt'ing I need. And t'rough everyt'ing they keep me on, because everybody, from your old dead granmother on down, they know what they owe me. They know.

"A whole life.

"An' I suppose you have to say they good people. You have to say they does pay their debts."

[51]

It was a bizarre time, Mrs. Livingston. The family knew, of course, but no one else. The mother was kept out of sight, in comfort, I might add, her silence purchased with a promise that her needs would always be seen to. There was some concern for my husband's reputation, although this was not seen as a problem of great magnitude. Where I come from, you see, many would simply have admired his virility... But still, the problem was best avoided.

The charade took some planning. Word was put out, discreetly, that I was with child. I forced myself to eat more than usual in an attempt to put on weight and, in the later months, took to padding my clothes. I kept mostly to myself, sequestered like the mother. The hacks were told that my condition was delicate, that I required bed-rest, and so this was floated about. Only once was the theatre challenged, some cousin commenting that I hardly looked pregnant. I was flustered but my husband leapt to the rescue. You should see her with no clothes on, he laughed, she looks like she swallowed a little football, nothing more.

And this was how the charade was conducted for seven months, my dear—in silence saved by humour.

Humiliating for me, some might say. But, you understand, don't you, that this served my own purposes admirably. The circumstance in which I found myself was not about to simply disappear. It had to be dealt with. I was in the position of having to weigh humiliations, and the greatest, had word of this got out, would have been mine. The pathetic, betrayed wife. I had no intention of suffering amused pity, my dear.

I stuck it through to the very end. I was even present for the birth, which took place in the seclusion of a beach house. A simple process with no complications, performed with surprising ease. The mother uttered hardly a whimper. When Yasmin emerged, she was passed immediately to me —living proof of my virtue and of my husband's.

Now listen closely, my dear, you must promise me that after you have woken up—if you wake up—you will breathe not a word of what I have told you, for I have offered you the truth about the lie that has seen me through years that would otherwise have been meaningless. Yasmin has given shape and sense to my life, and I fear so terribly the moment when I must—and I know that I must—alter the shape and possibly the sense of her own...

But of course, I *shall* tell her. One day. So, at least, I have always promised myself. I owe her that truth. But time has gone along and the perfect moment has failed to materialize. Now I fear it will not come until I am on my deathbed—and even then…

I lack the courage, you see. For Yasmin is my daughter, and I fear losing her as I fear nothing else.

[52]

Yasmin places her hands on Amie's shoulders, gently turns her around.

Amie's eyes are shut, a single tear glistening a path down her left cheek.

She takes Amie's hands, folds them between hers.

And so they sit together, worlds meeting in a dissolution of time.

Slowly the light of a luminous dawn shapes itself into the cracks and moulding of the window and, with imperceptible force, nudges out the night.

They sit until somewhere in the distance a cock crows.

Until sunshine grows bright on the window.

Until time hardens.

Amie takes her hands away, gets to her feet. She looks long at Yasmin through softened eyes. Then she reaches out a hand and briefly presses her fingertips to her forehead.

Four

[1]

Her sleep, unintended, has been that of exhaustion: deep and uneasy, with a mote of restlessness fluttering at the edges.

When she awakes—the room airless, daylight hard and demanding at the window—it is with the sensation of emerging from some faraway place, a region so remote it defies memory.

It is not long, however, before the heaviness in her head clears to a sense of peacefulness, a serenity she has not known in a very long time.

This is her last morning. Today she will fulfil the obligation that has brought her here, into her mother's world. Then she will take her things and depart, back to the world that is hers.

And it *is* hers. She has opened her eyes with this certainty, with a knowledge that bypasses the details of place and passport, an understanding beyond language, that feels embedded in the flesh itself.

A river takes shape in her mind. A river of countless tributaries with no source and no issue. A river unchannelled by banks, its water limpid, flowing unimpeded. A river that is all movement made manifest, suggestive of secrets submerged and unknowable.

She thinks of her family known and unknown. Of the journey begun so long ago, from a land that yet pulsed in her mother, a stranger to it; a land now gone inert in herself; a land extending still its mythic hold on Ash.

She thinks of movement and migration, of beginnings that are not beginnings and ends that are not ends.

She thinks in her mother's voice: Every destination is unknown, but the journey must carry on.

The urn is oval-shaped, lacquered black, and indented in red and gold with a leafy pattern that is vaguely Chinese. Even in the warmth of the room, it is cool to her touch.

She taps at it with her nail. Plastic. Over Jim's objections, she had paid for wood. But there's nothing to be done about that now.

She tries to open the urn but the lid will not budge. At the joint, nearly invisible, a drop of dried glue reveals that it has been sealed. She takes a nail file from her suitcase and pries at the joint, working the curved point into it. The plastic is hard and smooth, shell-like. Minuscule bits splinter off.

Her hands grow moist. Perspiration trickles down her temple. The urn, she thinks, is made to last for eternity, the plastic, which will not even degrade over time, resisting her attempts to force it open.

She wipes her palms on her thighs and resumes the work with renewed determination.

More plastic chips off, larger pieces now. But still the joint does not give. She presses hard, and the file slips, rasping a lengthy scratch into the surface of the bowl. Her back stiffens in a sudden rage, her fist trembling, teeth clenched so tight the pressure rises to her forehead.

Her face falls into her hands, breath hot and fast against the palms.

After a few minutes she calms herself, fingertips pressing circles into her temples, soothing the throbbing pulse.

Then she picks up the nail file and probes once more at the joint, trying to force the tip of the file past it and into the urn.

And suddenly the urn cracks open.

[2]

Look at that. Look at that...

So stellar from afar, like those photos of distant nebulae one sees in magazines, yet so ambiguous closer up. The buildings, I mean, my dear. So many shapes and sizes. Some so high, some so squat. And these colours. Black. Brown. Cream. The greys of brick and glass. A reddish tinge here, gold there. Fishbowl green and sea-blue. Some reflective, some as matte as velveteen.

A lack of harmony. Not your kind of landscape, is it, my dear? Nor mine. Yet it is here we have chosen to make our lives. It appeals to Yasmin, you know. Where I see a lack of harmony she sees the possibility of the unexpected. She sees a unity in all this glass. It offers, she once said to me, the shock of juxtaposition.

But what do you suppose has happened to the greenery?

I imagine there are still vantage points from which the city appears to have emerged organically from the natural state—a suggestion, or perhaps an illusion, of oneness. This view suggests that the greenery has been overwhelmed...

Pity. Remember how proud we were of that?

Look at that. Look at that...

Even in the sunlight, or perhaps because of it, there are signs of the New World growing old. I remember when so many of these buildings were being built—my son-in-law had a hand in several of them: he had an obsession, you know, with glass and light, transparency—and now, to look at them is to remark on their blemishes. The buildings acquiring streaks of grime as we have acquired wrinkles. Or perhaps, more accurately, like grout darkening on a bathroom wall, suddenly detected one day. We are, do you not think, growing tarnished together?

Do you remember, my dear, the day you and I went down to the water's edge—a grand excursion—and sat on a bench enjoying the sunshine and watching the boats sail by? I felt old that day. Do you remember? We realized that neither of us had the eyesight left to see—not just to know, as if in theory—but to positively *see* that there was another side to the lake? I know there is, but I'm no longer certain whether it can be seen with the unaided eye. I thought I would ask Yasmin, but my anxiety has prevented me. I suppose I have learnt to distrust even what I see. Seeing, after all, is not necessarily believing.

And yet, neither you nor I will be around to see the final gathering of the shadows—so why should I be saddened?

Oh, but listen to me! I am going on, aren't I? Never

mind me, my dear. It's a mood. It will pass. After all, despite everything, despite the coming dusk, it has been a day of brilliant sunshine.

[3]

She does not know what she expects to find within the urn—a vague notion perhaps of ash scooped from a cold fireplace—yet she is mildly surprised to find a bag of transparent, heavy-duty plastic secured with a red band. Carefully, but with more curiosity than reverence, she lifts the bag out and holds it suspended before her eyes—a grey assemblage, powder smoothed against the plastic.

She lowers it into the palm of her other hand, letting it settle, assessing its weight, and she finds she is reminded of picking Anubis up by the belly. The weight is the same, as is the way the mass slides into its own limp equilibrium—only the bag is not warm. And when she places it on the top of the dresser, it reshapes itself once more—into an oval, inert and objective.

The tie, not tightened for posterity, twists off easily. She peels the bag open, folding the top down, and after only a moment's unthinking hesitation dips her index finger into the contents.

Some are as slender as toothpicks, others broader, the width of a pencil. It is these larger slivers of bone—interiors finely textured in a pointillist pattern—that have retained colour, some ivory, some suggestive of henna. They are fragile, and after one turns to dust between her fingertips, she handles them like butterfly wings.

Foraging through the dust for the corporeal remains of her mother leaves a grey residue on her hands. She holds her fingers up to her eyes, and is suddenly overwhelmed with a closeness—a sense of intimacy—never before experienced with the woman whose ways and manners cultivated warmth from a prim distance.

She brings her hand to her lips, licks the tip of the index finger, then places its length against her tongue. The dust is without flavour, but gritty. Then, closing her eyes, she slowly licks the dust from her other fingers, from her palm, from the back of her hand.

In the holiness of the act, she feels the distance between herself and her mother close forever.

For the first time in many years, she cries for her daughter, hot tears not of despair but of release.

She cries for her mother, hot tears not of longing but of farewell.

And she cries for herself, hot tears not of fear but of relief.

Thus she knows that her journey may continue.

[4]

The thing, my dear Mrs. Livingston, is that we all dream of making a neat package of our lives—don't we? Closing the circle, squaring the square. When that final full stop is penned in, we want to be satisfied that all the "i"s have been dotted and all the "t"s crossed.

Curious, isn't it—that I should suddenly be littering my

language with clichés? I, who have for so long avoided such linguistic shorthand...

But to get back, if I may, to this notion of the neat package: have people always felt this way, do you think, or is it a consequence of the art we practise? All that neatness we find in novels, biographies and films, where everything fits into a larger pattern, everything is linked, and anomaly proves to be just the logical outcome of something that has gone before. Has art invaded life, offering us, if you will, a new arrogance—or perhaps merely new despair?

But of course, it may be only me. You, my dear, if I dare say so, have never worried about such things, have you? All this nonsense has left you untroubled, hasn't it? And it may be that you are far better off for it.

Be that as it may, though, this urge to impose order—for that is what it is—on something we know to be messy seems integral to my being. But no one's life truly allows that, does it, my dear? Disorder is the design of the package. Even the quietest, least eventful of lives is a messy affair on one level or another.

After all, one is left with so many unanswered questions at the end of it—not to mention so many unquestioned answers. One feels quite overwhelmed at times. For instance, I will never for the life of me understand...

Never...

Oh, my!

The sunshine, Mrs. Livingston!

Look at the sunshine!

Dawn already? It can't be.

Oh, dear me...

Dear me. I—

Mrs.—

[5]

She is relieved, when she goes to fetch the box with her father's affairs, that the dining room is deserted. No awkward questions will be asked, no awkward explanations given.

Back in her room, she shuts the door and places the box beside the urn. Then she sits on the edge of the bed, in the silence.

So here they are, her mother, her father and herself. All the pasts, all the worlds, that they have created. All the pasts, all the worlds, that have created them. Together for one last time.

She wonders briefly what it all means, if anything. The distilled essence of these two powerful people runs in her veins, a river of thought and emotion. But that, she knows, is not all she is, for she is not a prisoner of their worlds. Hers is, even now, a future still to be made.

And she sees, after a while, what it means: that she will return lightened to her world, to Jim and the marriage that is theirs. She knows she cannot predict the future. Jim, after all, has his own worlds floating around within him. Some will collide, some will attain harmonious orbit. But whatever comes, she returns ready.

A few minutes later, Penny calls to her from the door. It is time to go.

The river awaits.

[6]

Yasmin lay startled under the blankets, the ring of the telephone sharpened and magnified in the darkness.

Jim wrenched himself from the bed with an energy uncommon in his first waking moments. Something clattered and fell in his wake as his bustling shadow glided through the grey rectangle of their bedroom door.

Yasmin's tongue lay dry and heavy in her mouth. The shrill of the telephone late at night, its brutal wrenching from sleep to a disorienting darkness, was so terrifying she would not have a telephone in the bedroom. And yet, the distant ring still held promise of terror—and that terror, funnelled through the wild fluttering of her heartbeat, began to shape a cry she did not wish to voice.

Jim answered the phone halfway through its fourth ring. He spoke in a voice of summoned composure.

Yasmin leapt from the bed, senses abandoned in a lightning shear. She did not feel the carpet beneath her feet, saw the doorway glide by her, saw the corridor doubling in length. Saw Jim planting himself before her, his arms opening. "Yas," he said, his face shadowed, indistinct.

She stopped abruptly, two paces from him: a beat of empty time, her senses scrambling, then rapidly reassembling themselves in an impossible silence.

"Yas, it's your mother."

"What does she want at this ungodly hour?" The tightness in her chest was suddenly released; the intake of air made her giddy. "Is it poor Mrs.—" But even as she spoke she realized her own mistake.

"Yas, your mother's had a heart attack—or something."

Another beat of empty time: mind examining each word, searching for its meaning, finding a multiplicity. "I see." And the two words, the two syllables, began a marking of the empty time: seconds counted down through a readying of the self. "And..."

Jim stepped up to her, his hands grasping her arms. "She didn't... She isn't..." His lips parted as he sucked at air: a gruff inhalation. "It was massive —" He tugged her to his chest. She fell into an embrace that felt captive and airless. "Hold on, Yas," he said. "Hold on tight."

But she could not, she lacked the strength. And in the sudden enfeeblement, in a darkness immediate and crackling, Yasmin felt her body contract, muscles contorting— and heard a voice not her own but issued of her throat wail *Ariana*.

[7]

She takes them for a type of lemon—the shape is similar, the smaller ones green, the larger ripened to a bright yellow—but she sees that the ground is littered with them, and that those which have broken open reveal a red meat and dozens of small white seeds. She says, "A nurse found her."

Penny presses her palm to her chest in a sign of distress. "She was a'ready...?"

Yasmin nods. "At first they thought she was asleep. She'd put her head on Mrs. Livingston's bed and they found her like that, still sitting in her chair."

Cyril shakes his head. "Poor Shakti."

Penny says, "An' her friend? Mrs. Livingstone?"

"Livingston." Yasmin shrugs, feigning indifference to the scene as she imagines it: a still-life too still. "No change. She's still there in her coma. Jim and I went to visit her but, you know, there's not much point."

"What about her son?"

"My mom told me that, as far as he's concerned, she's already dead."

"He does visit her?"

Yasmin shrugs again. "I suppose." She looks up at the tree, laden with its fruit.

"I wonder what Shakti did all that time, sittin' by her friend's bedside," Penny says. "If I know her, she probably just sat there doing nothing, keeping an eye out. You and I both know—eh, Yasmin?—Shakti wasn't the talkative kind."

Cyril and Yasmin share a glance, Cyril sealing their silence by saying, "Want a guava?"

"Guava. So that's what it is."

Cyril reaches up, plucks a large yellow one. He rubs it on his shirt and hands it to her.

The fruit is warm in Yasmin's palm but she barely notices it. She is still thinking about how Cyril has pronounced the word. Not *Gwava* but *Gawva*. His speech seems sown with her mother's voice.

[8]

It was as if the apartment itself knew that the irrevocable had occurred.

Only hours—but already a musty neutrality suffused the air, as if the walls were divesting themselves of her mother's unfathomable residue in preparation for the assumption of the next tenant's personality. The objects with which she had surrounded herself—the chairs, tables, lamps, the things on the walls—all appeared displaced, the possessions now of no one.

Yasmin stood at the window and raised the binoculars to her eyes. Sky, cloud, bits of trees and buildings. She lowered her gaze, and the playing field closed in: the crisp greenery, the long and narrow rectangle of denuded earth: sights her mother had seen countless times, sights she would no longer see. And the realization that next Sunday afternoon men in whites would bowl and bat and run and catch struck her as obscene, disrespectful. She could not prevent her hands from trembling as she replaced the binoculars on the windowsill and took a step backwards, away from the sense of indecency she knew to be absurd but before which she felt helpless.

She wandered slowly through the apartment, footsteps loud in this place where she no longer belonged. The bathroom, small and neat, devoid of clutter. The hall closet in which hung only two coats, one tan for spring and fall, the other a winter grey she had considered too sombre for her mother. She paused at the bedroom door, steeling herself for the silence she feared would be overwhelming in this room of greatest intimacy.

She had always thought the bedroom small, but her mother had found it adequate to her needs. She organized herself better in an insufficiency of space. It sharpened the mind, she felt, it pared sentimentality, so that objects found their contexts and disorder was stemmed. Her mother's idea of luxury was precise and severe: it made no concession to baubles.

One Christmas, Mrs. Livingston had given her an elaborate porcelain ashtray in the form of a female hand cupping a seashell. Her mother neither smoked nor knew anyone who did—the source of her friend's inspiration mystified her—and she could not bring herself to admire it. She suffered its presence on the coffee table for several weeks—and then one day it wasn't there. Yasmin asked where it was and her mother, with all the innocence she could command, said, "An accident, dear. I was dusting it. It slipped. Terribly sad. It broke into a million pieces." And then she smiled.

Yasmin proceeded warily into the room, her shoes stealthy on the shining parquet floor, and sat on the edge of the bed. She saw that it had been made up with her mother's customary neatness, and she was grateful for that: mussed sheets, signs of the last awakening, would have been unbearable. A curious comfort, this—and suddenly she wished she could believe in something: a higher power, a place beyond, an idea of warmth in the aftermath of life.

Her mother's belief had been private, shorn of ostentation. Among the perfumes and powders on the dressing table were two objects which had been in her mother's possession for as long as she could remember and which she vaguely understood to be objects of reverence. There was a *deeah*, a small prayer lamp of unglazed red clay that had never been used and which Yasmin, as a child, had enjoyed caressing with her fingertips, the bowl hard and powdery. Behind it stood the Hindu deity Shiva, a brass figurine of curiously indeterminate gender standing on one foot, the other kicking out, his four arms upheld in an elegant gesture of dance; around him was what appeared to be a ring of fire. Religious implements, then—but Yasmin had never known her mother to pray, and so she had come to think of them as objects of sentiment, icons of another life. Mementos. If they had held a value beyond this, her mother had kept it to herself.

Her mother had once said to Jim that she considered herself a Hindu because she could be nothing else. Hinduism, she said, was less her religion than her way of life. She would not eat beef, but could not subscribe to bovine divinity, either: that was an idea that was sensible only in another time and place; in her context, she had said, the logic would mean conferring divinity on her local supermarket. She had an open mind on reincarnation despite the doubt sown in her mind by a grandfather who warned, when she was young, that failure to improve her behaviour would lead to a future life as a stone. "For a long time," Yasmin remembered her mother saying, "I treated gravel with the utmost reverence. I was worried about treading on some incorrigible ancestor." She had, too, a horror of cemeteries, the idea of interment repellent to her. The manners of the religion, she explained, had shaped her, and she had never felt the need to reach beyond its peculiarities, had never felt herself limited by them.

Yasmin ran her palm along the comforter, feeling the silky keenness of its surface. Listening to her mother, she had come to understand that the simplicity of her mother's spiritual notions had been the votive anchor of her life. They were notions unconcerned with a hereafter, or a godhead; they neither held out promise nor threatened disappointment. Hinduism, her mother had said to Jim, was not a religion of proselytizers. Conversion was not possible. One was simply born to the life—or not.

"And despite Yasmin's being born to that life, events changed everything." Her mother did not even glance in her direction. "This is why I foisted on her none of the strictures I accepted for myself." Those were ways of being, ways of seeing the world, which would have been of use only in other, more alien circumstances. The strengths they offered would have been illusory, their implicit fatalism inhibiting in a society of competition and promise. The tenor of her own life had already been decided, she said, and she had made the best of it. But the world to which she had brought Yasmin was a vastly different place, with new imperatives requiring new responses. She would have to seek out her possibilities unhindered by the limitations of her mother's time and place. "This is the reason, you see, Mr. Summerhayes, that I learnt to make hamburgers and to cook steaks. For her."

This, too, was the reason, she went on, that Westerners who turned east in search of wisdom—like the young men with shaven heads and saffron robes who rhythmically proclaimed the glories of Krishna to passersby on downtown streets—were always a source of great amusement to her. They were, she felt, devotees of self-deception—and India, like everywhere else, was full of people willing to fleece those who wished to be fleeced.

Yasmin had never told her mother that those people she found so amusing were, to her, a source of embarrassment. Walking past their public displays of devotion, she could feel their eyes on her, seeking acknowledgement of a kinship they thought they saw in her race. But she had laughed uneasily the day that Charlotte, eyeing a group clanging and chanting on the street, had said, "Boy, what a bunch of cults!"

The light flooding into the bedroom through the undraped window took on a deeper hue. She watched the dressing table and the wall behind it turn lemony, and she remembered something else—so many words once offered in passing, now precious—that her mother had once said to her. "Be glad that your great-grandparents chose to leave India. Would you want to be born into that mess of humanity?"

The light in the bedroom turned the colour of molten gold. She felt its warmth on her shoulders, a warmth that made her aware of a chill proceeding from deep within herself. So much left unsaid, so much left unknown. And yet she began to see that what her mother had given her was best thought of as a kind of freedom. The only question that remained was, freedom from what?

Jim came in, his footsteps soundless on the floor. "Yas? You okay?"

She nodded, accepted the tissue he offered. The tears bewildered her. She had been unaware of them, but they were sufficient to have trailed down her chin and dotted her lap.

Jim stood before the dressing table. He reached for the brass deity. "Ah," he said. "Shiva. He who destroys to reconstruct. Your mother always was full of surprises." He held it for a moment, thoughtful, then he put it back down. "Come, let's go home."

Yasmin crumpled the tissue in her hand, paused for a moment before the dressing table gilded still by the light: the perfumes, the powders, the dancing god.

She picked up the *deeah* and clasping it to her breast allowed Jim to lead her from the apartment.

[9]

The day is overcast, the sky not so much cloudy as veiled, colours muted in the filtered sunlight.

The cremation ground, a field of packed earth that falls off at the far end at a placid sea, is deserted. As they walk in silence towards the water's edge, she is glad she refused Cyril's offer of a pundit to say a prayer. In the heavy air, the silence will remain holy only if unbroken.

She is touched that Cyril and Penny have both dressed for the occasion; that Cyril has insisted on carrying the urn which he holds before him in both hands; that Penny has brought a garland of roses, which will accompany the ashes into the water.

At the water's edge, she stands looking out: at the painful sky, at the glassy, silvered sea, at the distant horizon where they meet. There is, out there, a faint haze, a suggestion of immense evaporation, and for a brief and terrifying moment she harbours the certainty that she finds herself standing on the last fringe of land before the end of the earth. She goes light-headed, and her body sways. She is grateful when Cyril takes her elbow.

Steadied, she takes the urn from him, removes the bag, passes the container back to him. Opens the bag wide and, without hesitation, hurls the ashes out high into the heavy air. They scatter and spread lazily, expanding and floating, a cloud of showering grey.

Suddenly, Amie's words—*her* words—ring in her mind: *Papa behind the clouds.*

And she finds herself jolted into a new watchfulness as she looks out through the falling ash and beyond it.

Looking for the small thing: a hint of movement, a ripening of shadow, a glint of sun.

Looks out even though there is nothing to be seen.

Looks out because you never know.

The ash settles on the water and merges with it.

Penny hands her the garland. With a swift swing of her arm, she throws it into the air, watches it glide red and elegant against the sky.

It is still in the air, spinning in its descent, when she turns away and begins striding back to the car.

[10]

Yasmin whispers, "I feel like burning the box."

Amie shakes her head slowly. "He himself done burn, Beti. A long time ago. Ain't no point. He done do what he done, no changin' that. Beside, he inside us, you know, all of us. For good or for bad. As for the box and them t'ings—"

She folds her arms, glances away towards the open bedroom window, as if reaching through it for what she wants to say.

"Jus' keep him in his box, Beti. Close the flaps and keep him there."

She goes close to the window, splaying her fingertips on the sill. "He up there too," she says. "Behind those clouds."

Yasmin stands behind her, looks out. The day has cleared, the cloud cover burned off by the sun now brightly shining in early afternoon. "But there aren't any clouds, Amie."

"Yes, Beti, it have clouds. You jus' ain't seein' them."

It is, Yasmin thinks, a notion of ubiquity: her father—and her mother and her daughter, for that matter—everywhere, in everything, as integral to the worlds without as to the worlds within.

It is, she thinks, a notion of survival.

Penny waits for Cyril to begin making his way down the stairs with Yasmin's suitcase before saying, "So."

"So." Yasmin repeats the word, accepting the segue to summation. "I'm a stranger here."

"You're not like us." Penny's agreement is immediate.

"You don't like me, do you, Penny?"

"I don' know you."

"You don't want to know me. Or to like me."

"Well, now," Penny says quietly. "Maybe you gone and put your finger on it."

"So," Yasmin says again, the word conveying now the difficulty of saying goodbye: How is it to be done? She will let it hang for a moment, then she will simply turn and follow Cyril down the stairs.

So she is unprepared when Penny's lips suddenly press themselves to her cheek. She holds herself still as the lips remain there for a mindful moment, then slowly peel themselves away as with the tug of a light adhesive.

Lips, lipstick: She has been branded—but temporarily.

Penny is the first to turn away, stepping towards the living-room doors, past the curtains and into the shadows of the house.

Yasmin digs into her purse for a tissue to wipe the lip-print away. Then she changes her mind. She will leave it, for now. She will let it fade by itself.

As it will.

Naturally.

Epilogue

[1]

As the car trundles along the gravel driveway, she turns in her seat and looks out the rear window at the retreating house. Already it seems of strange provenance to her, its shapes and contours of an unknown architecture. She knows its individual rooms, but is not sure how they fit together. She is not sure she could sketch a plan of it.

She glances ahead: to Ash standing shirtless beside the open gates, the chains hanging heavy in his hand.

Then she turns back again, for a final look. And she sees that Amie is now standing at the foot of the stairs, her arms folded, her gaze on the car. And upstairs, at a bedroom window, a lighter shadow against the greater gloom, Penny, also looking out, also following their progress. She raises a hand, but they are already too far, the sun's reflection off the rear window too dazzling, for them to see the gesture.

They approach the gate, and as they drive through she waves at Ash, but he too does not see—or, perhaps, does not wish to see.

Cyril turns, without slowing, from the driveway onto the road—away from the sea ahead and the house behind—and Yasmin finds herself looking back once more.

But all she sees now, and only for the briefest second, is Ash intent at his task of chaining up the gate.

Once they have left the town behind, she sees what she did not see on the evening of her arrival. She sees why the darkness through the taxi window was so unrestrained.

The road to the airport, raised on a bed of packed gravel, runs through a broad plain sectioned off into fields. Some are cultivated, some are wild.

Rice, Cyril says. Tomatoes, lettuce, green peas.

His answers to her questions are brief, laconic. He is not in a talkative mood today. At lunch, he was as if weighted down: as if Yasmin's sense of lightening—a lightening which grew into a kind of restlessness as they left the cremation ground—has found its opposite in him.

His silence wins the day. Yasmin asks no more questions —she realizes she is attempting to make conversation—and, without the effort, finds herself growing indifferent.

Indifferent to the landscape that remains a mass of undifferentiated vegetation.

To the people speeding by in cars.

To the children labouring in the fields.

To everything but Cyril and the meaning of his silence.

She smells the airport before she sees it, fumes of jet fuel drifting heavily over a mass of sugar cane.

And it is perhaps this reminder of imminent parting that prompts Cyril to say, "So…"

It is all she needs, the words coming to her with no effort.

She has a sense, she says, of things falling into place where she had not known they had fallen apart. Has questions now where before there were none—questions which, she understands, are more precious than their answers. She returns to her world, she says, assured of her place in it.

Cyril hears her out in silence. Then he says, "I hear you talking to yourself right now. Is the way it should be. But let me tell you one thing. It would do a selfish old man a lot o' good if one day, when you good and ready, you decide to come back, even for just a little while. A lot o' good."

Yasmin breathes deeply of the jet fuel, aware that now the silence is hers.

As the airport comes into view, Cyril says, "At least you not saying no."

"Will it do?"

"Oh, yes, dear Yasmin, oh, yes. It'll do."

She holds his glance, and she sees in those eternal seconds that his eyeball does not waver.

Only as she pauses on the tarmac and searches for him among the people waving from the terminal does it occur to her that he is the loneliest man she has ever met.

A loneliness that was there, at the entrance to the departure lounge where they said goodbye: in his stiffened back, his moistened eyes, and—most of all—in the single-minded precision with which he walked away after the brief hug: as if following a line he had prescribed for himself well in advance.

She searches for him, and even though she does not see him, she waves, the gesture genuine and heartfelt. Turning back to the aircraft, watching her shoes cover the oily paving, she finds herself hoping that he has seen the wave, and that he has read it well.

The aircraft is full, the passengers subdued.

Skins have been tanned, bodies unwound, and what awaits at the end of the flight are the jobs and the problems and the tensions reassumed. In a few hours, weeks of anticipation will be fading memories and overlit photographs. There will be no partying on this flight.

The carry-on luggage is voluminous and awkward— woven hats, wall hangings, bottles of rum—and it is some time before all is secured and the cabin settles down.

Her seat companion, a large man with a nose painfully reddened, grunts in response to her greeting, turns away and shuts his eyes.

She sits, takes her book from her bag, straps on her seat belt, and waits. In her mind she replays the drive she has just taken with Cyril, going the other way now, following him back to the house.

And to her surprise, an ache of wistfulness tightens in her chest.

Only some time later, when the plane trundles along the tarmac, when it gathers speed on the runway and eases itself off the earth, does she reach into her bag once more and take from it the one object she has coveted from among her father's things.

She holds it up to the thick sunlight flowing in through the window, runs her fingertips over its silky pages.

Icarus.

The silence is absolute.

He soars through the air, gliding along on unseen currents, the earth far beneath reduced to simplicities of green and blue.

He feels the warmth of the sun on his face, a soothing caress through the cool air.

But soon he grows hungry for more. He stares upwards, into the very core of the fiery disc, and heads straight for it: There, he feels, is where he is meant to be. There is where he belongs.

It is not long before the air loses its coolness and the heat begins to sear. He feels the wax softening on his arms, and he thinks of candles melting onto his fingers in his mother's house.

A feather detaches itself, flutters from his arm.

Then another and another.

He strains to maintain height, to maintain momentum. The effort is useless. He feels himself descending.

But even as he falls, even as his arms grow bare, he utters a long and crackling laugh of pleasure. For he knows that he is flying still—and he knows that for this he does not need the permission of the gods.

He watches the sun descend, watches the moon rise.

On and on he flies, borne up by the silvery light, all the while his laughter thundering down with the riotous delight of a man at peace with himself.

[2]

She sees Jim before he sees her. He is lean-ing against a pillar, hands in the pockets of his jeans. She sees that he is watchful, as if afraid he will miss her. And this is why she sees him first: He is looking away, looking for her.

She does not walk up to him. Instead, she puts her suit-case down and stands some distance away, a distance com-plicated by people and movement and the echoing sounds of airport announcements. She stands there, hand grasping the strap of her shoulder bag, waiting to be discovered.

He does not see her immediately—but when he does it is with eyes of wonderment. He straightens up, sliding his hands from his pockets. Then he wends his way slowly towards her, eyes never wavering.

It is that gaze that she holds as he presses himself to her, as he slides his arms around her shoulders.

His lips graze hers, and she feels herself grow warm.

Feels herself beginning to melt.

Traffic is light, home not far away.

In the distance, beyond the carpet of lights that imposes beauty on industry, the heart of the city glows like a cluster of dark crystal.

Jim says, "So what was the question?"

Yasmin smiles. "The question," she says, "is, what are the questions?"

"Any answers?"

"So many that there aren't any. But that doesn't matter. Just having the questions is enough. They say… They say that we exist."

She knows she sounds cryptic, and is grateful that Jim's glance, caught in the half-light from the dashboard, reveals a puzzlement that is not pressing, reveals that he will be patient so that, in time, they can decipher the puzzle together.

She says, "Jim, do you know how immigration works?"

"Not a clue. Why?"

"There's this young man, a distant cousin. His name's Ash. Remind me to tell you about him."

After a moment, he says, "I've got some good news by the way. Mrs. Livingston's come out of her coma."

"Oh, good. Does she know about Mom?"

"Yes, her son told her. In fact he called this morning. She's asking to see you."

"Me?"

"She's got a message for you. Something about your mother."

"Did he say—?"

"No, but she's pretty frail. There's no telling how long she'll…"

"Will tomorrow be soon enough?"

"Tomorrow will be fine." Then suddenly, in a voice choked with an emotion long unheard, he says, "Yas, I love you."

Yasmin holds out her palm and waits patiently until, with delight, she feels his words, their warmth and their weight, alighting.

[3]

I am not a final product, Mrs. Livingston. I am a process. As are you. As is everyone. It is to me the most unsettling, and most reassuring, truth about what young people today call "identity." My dear, I haven't got *an* identity. None of us does. What a great tragedy that would be, don't you think?